WHISPERS

Debra Walden Davis

Actual places/events in and around Springfield,

Missouri: Bambino's Café
Crane Broiler Festival
Cherokee Firearms
Springfield Brewing Company
T-Bairz Sports Bar & Grill
Blue Room Comedy Club
Billiards of Springfield
Garbo's Pizzeria
Harmony House
Hemingway's Blue Water Café

Printed by Kindle Direct Publishing

Available from: kdp.amazon.com and other retail outlets.

Cover art by BespokeBookCovers.com
peter@bespokebookcovers.com

For information about BKS*:
JB Sherry at *mssBKSllc@gmail.com*

ISBN:13: 978-1-7174-2727-4

Songs Quoted in *Whispers*

Part One:
The Anniversary Killer

"My Love Is", composer Billy Myles

"One of These Nights", composers Don Henley/Glenn Frey

"Older Women", composer Jamie O'Hara

"Dude (Looks Like a Lady), composers Steven Tyler/Desmond
    Child/Joe Perry

Part Two: His and Her Demons

"Must Be Doin' Somethin' Right", composers Marty Dodson/Patrick
    Jason Matthews

"You're A Hard Dog (To Keep Under the Porch)", composers Susanna
    Clark/Harland Howard

"When a Woman Loves a Man", composers, Rafe Van Hoy/Mark Luna

"A Lot of Livin' to Do", composers, Lee Adams/Charles Strouse

"Buy Myself a Chance", composers Randy Rogers/Sean McConnell

"You Don't Know Me", composers Cindy Walker and Eddy Arnold

"How to Handle a Woman", composers Alan Jay Lerner/Frederick
    Loewe

"Romance in the Dark", composer Lillian Green

"Unwound", composers Dean Dillon/Frank Dycus

"A Man This Lonely", composers Ronnie Dunn/Tommy Lee James

"There's Your Trouble", composers Mark Selby/Tia Sillers

"Let That Pony Run", composer Gretchen Peters

"Shut Up and Kiss Me", composer Mary Chapin Carpenter

"I Am That Man", composers Terry McBride/Monty Powell

"Take Me Out to the Ballgame, composers Albert Von Tilzer/Jack
    Norworth

"That's What I Like", composers Bruno Mars/Philip Lawrence/James
    Fauntleroy/Johnathan Yip/Ray Romulus/Jeremy Reeves/Ray
    McCullough II

"I'll Hold Your Head", composer Shelby Lynne

"The Night's Too Long", composer Lucinda Williams

"I Want to Go Back", composer Shelby Lynne

"Again", composers Darrell Brown/Radney Foster

"What Are We Doing Here Tonight", composers Chip Boyd/Radney
    Foster

"Someone to Watch Over Me", composers George Gershwin/Ira
    Gershwin

"House Rules", composers Blair Daly/Christian Kane

"Thinking of You", composers Blair Daly/Christian Kane

"You Can Sleep While Drive", composer Melissa Etheridge

For my mother,
Charlotte Skiles Walden
who asked me once how I did it.
From watching you Mom, from watching you.

In loving memory of
Phillip Walden Talburt and Retha Ann Talburt Cartensen

Whisper like cold winds
Close to the bone
Save heaven for lovers
Leave me alone

From the song, "Whispers"
by
Bernie Taupin and Elton John

PROLOGUE

RICK
September 25, 2018
Springfield, Missouri

His cell rang.

"She's home," was all the caller said before hanging up.

Since last Sunday, he had mentally gone over different scenarios on what he would do when she came back to town. What a luxury that had been; now he actually had to choose one or come up with yet another.

He went to his wardrobe for a fresh shirt. Although there were seven neatly pressed and starched shirts hanging on the rod, they came in only two colors; white and blue. This decision was much easier; blue was her favorite color.

He grabbed the keys, locked the door and descended the stairs. Sitting in his Silverado, he pulled out his phone and brought up a picture taken of them at a ball game last summer. She had a hard time seeing it, but they really were good together. In the past few weeks he had decided he wanted her in his life for the long run, but to get her there, he had to bring her history into the open. For them to have a future, he knew they had to visit her past.

Her past. Most people had given up on her, but he was a new player on the scene and where others saw a drowning woman, he saw a survivor. She had been pushed under over and over, but she always kept coming back to the surface, gulping for air at the last moment. He had to make her see that, where he was concerned, her past didn't matter. He cared for the woman she was today, not the woman she used to be.

He put the key in the ignition and turned on the wipers to clear the windshield of drops that remained from the morning's rain. He noted the time on the dashboard before backing the Chevy out of its parking place; it would take him twenty minutes to get to her.

As he pulled onto Booneville Avenue, he thought about the

events that had brought him to this point. Seven months had passed since he had been sitting in a basement bar in downtown St. Louis with his friend, John Hutsell, when John had received a text from his aunt, Jean Wyatt.

"Elle's in trouble again."

John had gone to the street outside the bar and called his aunt. When John returned, he listened as his friend gave an account of Elle's life.

Twenty-one years earlier, John's cousin, eleven-year-old Elaine Stafford had confessed to her teacher in West Plains, Missouri, that she was being sexually abused by her stepfather. The teacher was a mandated reporter, and the stepfather was hot-lined within the hour. Three days later, violating an ex parte order, the stepfather entered the home where Elaine and her mother were staying and shot them both before killing himself. Elaine survived the attack that took the life of her mother and went to live with her mother's sister and brother-in-law, Jean and Patrick Wyatt, in Springfield, Missouri. A feeling of culpability in the death of her mother, along with survivor's guilt, had put Elaine, now known as Elle, on a path of self-destruction, beginning in her late teens and continuing through her twenties.

John had explained that Elle rarely played by the rules, which meant she often ended up in hot water. The problem was, Elle didn't care what happened to her. And when she got in trouble, she rarely asked for help, yet the few friends and family members who still cared about her would circle the wagons anyway. Now, at the age of thirty-two, after years of therapy, John had hoped Elle had finally come to terms with her past; of what had been done to her and what she had done to herself. She had made progress, but the path she was on was never linear. For Elle, it was always two steps forward followed by one step back, with side trips along the way.

He knew that a percentage of sexual abuse victims often became promiscuous later in life. Elle was one of them. For most of her adult life, she had used sex as a weapon, mostly aiming it at herself. The shame and guilt she felt after each encounter only reinforced her low self-esteem. Then, there was the other side of Elle's coin. There were those who thought a lot of men had taken advantage of Elle; that they'd used her to their own ends. Yet, an argument could be made it was the other way around; that Elle used men. The way John described it, Elle had been powerless to stop her stepfather when she was eleven years old, but as an adult, if she initiated sex with a man and then dismissed him, she created the illusion that she was the one in control.

Six months after he had arrived in Springfield, he and Elle had started casually dating. She had wanted a sexual relationship early on, but he had politely refused. The chemistry was there, but he wasn't out to use her or about to let her use him. He'd never been a player, and he wasn't going to start now.

He stopped at a red light. His cell vibrated bringing him back to the present.

"She's home," read the text. Same message, different messenger.

"I know. On my way," he typed back.

The light turned green, and soon he was turning into the private drive of the Wyatt Estate. He stopped at the entrance and looked at his reflection in the rearview mirror. *Last chance, Hadley. Fight or flee.* He took his foot off the brake and continued up the drive.

PART ONE

THE ANNIVERSARY KILLER

I don't want to do this anymore
Go away
Please, just leave me alone
"They Shoot Horses", don't they Jane?

The BIRDS are attacking
So is NORMAN's mother
ALFRED, somebody
Please yell, "CUT"

Excerpt from
Richard Cory, Revisited
by
Debra Walden Davis, 2003

· 1 ·

It was going on four years. The fourth anniversary was traditionally called the Fruit and Flowers Anniversary. He knew because he had looked it up on the internet just like he had every anniversary before.

Their first anniversary had been paper. He had searched her profile and found the boy who had written her love letters in the sixth grade. Of course the sixth grade Romeo hadn't been a boy in a very long time, but it was the paper connection that was important. Keeping with the theme, a death warrant facsimile had been wadded up and shoved down the man's windpipe. Then a picture had been taken of the body and sent to her, making sure it would arrive on Halloween to coincide with November second, All Soul's Day. He smiled thinking of the name Spanish speaking countries had given to the same day; Day of the Dead. After all, it was a far better label.

Three years and four months. None of the others had lasted this long. Despite how people had questioned his intellect throughout his life he knew he was up for this new challenge and come hell or high water, it was a given; Lydia Janssen was not long for this world.

Lydia Janssen hated going to her mailbox. So much in fact, there were times the door of the box wouldn't close due to the uncollected mail it contained. Two weeks ago the mail lady happened to be driving by the house Lydia rented when she'd caught her in the driveway. She'd informed Lydia if the mailbox continued to overflow, her mail would be taken back to the post office. Lydia'd wished the lady had just left a note instead, like a Do Not Disturb sign hanging on a door knob. Didn't the lady get it? That's exactly what Lydia wanted—not to be disturbed.

She dreaded making the short trip to the mailbox more this day than she would have any other day in February. Today was Valentine's Day. For over three years, regardless of the holiday, he'd always sent her a greeting card and despite the fact today was February fourteenth, she knew the card would not contain images of hearts or cupids because, no matter the occasion, his cards always wished her Happy Halloween.

Lydia had hoped her nightmare would end when she'd moved from Rogers, Arkansas, to St. Louis a little over a month ago. But it hadn't. Just like clockwork, she'd received a card from him on Martin Luther King Day, the first holiday after her move. Lydia wished to God he would just kill her and get it over with, but where would the fun be in that, she reasoned from his point of view. So, after steeling herself, she walked from the one-car garage to the curb.

She withdrew the mail from her box and was confounded when all she held in her hand were several junk circulars. This wasn't like him at all. Dare she hope he'd tired of the game? Even better, maybe something had happened to him. Might he have been in an accident? Or maybe he slipped up and pushed the 'wrong person' too far. She decided not to bank on any of those wishes. The card was probably in her landlord's mailbox. Her mail had ended up there before as the one-bedroom bungalow Lydia rented had been built on the same lot as the owners' small two-story home. Both dwellings had the same address on East Redbud Drive with one small distinction: the mailbox for the main house was designated as 6821-A while Lydia's residence was 6821-B.

As she walked back up the drive, she stopped halfway and remembered how she felt upon seeing the small house she now lived in. It was a light blue, box gable roof clapboard affair with flower boxes adorning the street side windows. It reminded her of Aunt Helen's Hollywood bungalow where she'd spent every summer between the ages of twelve and twenty. The highlight of each trip was when Aunt Helen would take her to the set of whatever movie she happened to be working on at the time. She almost smiled thinking of sitting on a stool watching Aunt Helen style Leonardo DiCaprio's hair on the set of *Titanic*. Her friends were envious of her photo showing DiCaprio planting a big kiss on her cheek.

Friends. They were no longer a part of Lydia's life. She'd had plenty while living in Rogers, but after the second anniversary, Lydia knew she had to cut off all relationships with friends, family and even casual acquaintances. Each one might become next year's anniversary 'gift'. It wasn't as hard as she'd expected. After news of the second anniversary hit, several of her friends distanced themselves from her on their own. And who could blame them? She was lonely, but she had no choice.

She actually did have one choice. However, her faith had kept her from taking the coward's way out. But she'd started losing the will to fight which was what had precipitated the move to St. Louis. It was either die or dig her heels in one last time.

Lydia began walking again. She still grieved for her aunt who had died of breast cancer in 2009. And even though her death was not an easy one and she'd been angry with God for a long time, she realized now it was a blessing. At least he couldn't torture Aunt Helen to death like he had others who'd been central in Lydia's life.

Three others so far. This Halloween would make four. For the past three years, on the last day of October she'd received a greeting card containing a sadistic picture of a dead body—not just any body, but a dead body of someone Lydia had loved. He said he wanted her to have someone special to grieve for during the Days of the Dead: a seventy-two-hour celebration beginning with All Hallow's Eve, followed by All Saint's Day, a holy day in her Catholic religion, and ending a day later with All Soul's Day. It was his gift to her. An anniversary celebration so to speak.

As she approached the garage, Lydia used her key fob to click open the trunk of her tan 2015 Chevy Malibu. After dropping her mail in one of two grocery bags, she slid her arms through their plastic handles and pulled the trunk lid down. She went to the passenger side and retrieved her cross-over style handbag. Once it was in place, she picked up the bags and walked to the side door that led to her home. She hit a button, closing the garage door before she climbed the two steps that led to the bungalow's eat-in kitchen area.

Lydia set the groceries on the counter between the sink and the small refrigerator. She removed her cell phone from her bag, plugging it into the wall adaptor for charging as was her ritual upon arriving home. Working the third shift transcribing physicians' recordings to patient files at Madison University Medical Center was ideal since the hospital was quiet at night. Fewer employees to interact with was a bonus.

Opening the door to the broom closet, she tossed the junk mail in the trash. She heard an uncommon, yet somewhat familiar sound. She moved her head slightly to the left. She could barely see the snake in her peripheral vision. As the rattler was slithering towards her, she realized she was an easy target. If she could get on the table, then to a counter, she might be able to reach her phone to summon help. She tried to estimate how long he was. How far could he lunge? Recalling a documentary she'd seen—was it half or two-thirds its body length?

The rattling stopped. She knew it was no guarantee the snake wouldn't attack. She had to make a move. It was now or never.

Lydia grabbed the broom, placed it between her and the snake and jumped. Her right foot landed on a dining chair just before her left hit the table's surface. The snake lunged. Its fangs missed her by mere centimeters. Before it could strike again, she hurled the snake hard enough that it slammed against the base of the oven.

She reached in the closet for her long-handled grabber tool. She positioned the suction-tipped claws on either side of the snake's head and clamped down. She carried it to the garage, dropped it inside the trash bin and closed the lid. Lydia placed her tool box on the hard-plastic cover, making sure the fit was snug before heading back to the kitchen.

Thinking she was safe, Lydia set out to contact St. Louis Animal

Control to arrange for the snake's removal. She walked across the hall to the small den to look up the department's phone number. On her laptop, she noticed an envelope resting on the keyboard. It wasn't standard in size or shape. Its dimensions were akin to those of a greeting card. And it was orange in color. An address label was fixed to its center. It read, "Lydia".

Oh dear god . . ..

He hadn't died. He hadn't been taken out by a Good Samaritan. He was alive and well and he had been in her home!

Lydia ran to her kitchen, grabbed her purse and keys. Once in the car, she drove to a discount store, the nearest public place. Her hand went for the bag's side pocket. No cell phone! She realized she'd left it on the countertop at home, plugged into the wall.

What to do? There weren't any phone booths in America anymore and the thought of asking a stranger for help tossed her anxiety level into the stratosphere. Lydia dumped her purse in the passenger seat searching for her pill container. She found it but was shaking so badly the contents went flying when she opened it. She spied one of the most important blue tablets on the floorboard. Once she had swallowed it she sat back in the car's seat, closed her eyes and practiced the breathing techniques her therapist had taught her.

Her therapist. The last image Lydia had of the woman caused bile to climb up her throat. She opened the door and heaved her stomach contents onto the pavement. When she was done Lydia immediately went searching for another blue pill.

Lydia's breathing slowed after fifteen minutes, though she knew it would take a half-hour for the medication to do its job. She moved the car forward to avoid stepping in her vomit and walked into the store to purchase a new phone.

"He's made contact again," she said. "But, Jimmy . . . this time it's different."

"Lydia, are you in danger right now?"

"I don't think so . . . but he's been *in* my home."

"Are you home now?"

"No. I'm in a parking lot."

"Good. How do you know he's been in your house?"

"Today is Valentine's Day. I was dreading going to the mail box. I knew there would be another card. But there wasn't one in the box. A greeting card was delivered, but it didn't come in the mail. It's sitting on my computer keyboard, Jimmy. He had to have put it there."

"What about your landlords? Hasn't some of your mail ended up in their box a few times?" he asked.

"It hadn't been sent through the mail. It just had my first name on it—no address. Besides, they always put misdelivered items in my mailbox or they hand deliver them when I'm home. They've never gone in the house unannounced. Never."

"Lydia, I'm going to call a St. Louis cop I've worked with. He used to live in Springfield, Missouri, but has been in St. Louis for three years now. What's the address where you are?"

Lydia provided the information after which Matthews asked, "What part of the parking lot are you in?"

"The south end near the gas station."

"Stay on the line," he instructed. "I'll be right back."

Sheriff Jimmy Matthews of Benton County, Arkansas, was still working on the three unsolved murders connected to Lydia. The problem was there were so few clues and all known leads had been exhausted. For all his efforts, there was nothing to show in terms of names and/or descriptions for suspects for any of the homicides. The killer could be standing right next to her and she wouldn't know it.

She knew Matthews' personal life had also taken a hit because of the investigation. He'd worked on her case day and night for several years and during that time his marriage had disintegrated. Even though Matthews had assured her the reasons for his divorce had precipitated his involvement with her case, Lydia knew her reliance on him had exacerbated the situation. If the shoes had been reversed and Lydia was the one waiting at home, she probably would have resented the woman who had caused so many interrupted evenings, too. It was one of the reasons she had left Rogers. Matthews had a nine-year old son and she'd decided the boy's dad would never miss another baseball game because of her. That unspoken promise hadn't lasted very long. Here she was, involving him again.

"Lydia, you still there?"

"Yes," she answered. "Look Jimmy, I'll get in touch with the police department here. You've got enough to take care of without having problems from St. Louis dumped in your lap."

"Hold it, Lydia. This new incident is connected to three open murders in Benton County. It's imperative my office work in conjunction with the St. Louis Police Department. Our case files will shed light on their investigation and vice versa," Matthews said. "He's changed his MO. That means there's a good chance we can develop new leads."

"Okay, I understand, but I can still make the initial contact up here."

"It's already done," he said. "I just talked to Detective John Hutsell. He's young, but he's smart. He's the one who solved the Cross Timbers Murder Case in Springfield. It was featured on one of those true crime TV channels a while back. Hutsell answered when I called. He and his partner were finishing a case report so are available to pick up yours. They will be there soon. Will you be all right till they arrive?"

"Yes—oh, Jimmy, there's something else. When I came home there was a rattlesnake in my kitchen. I managed to get him safely contained but now I'm wondering if . . .."

Matthews completed her thought. "Yeah, I know . . . he's worked with snakes before. Sit tight, Lydia. Hutsell's on his way."

3

Well, that was fun, he thought as he crossed the Missouri state line. A lot of planning and some chance taking, but it had been worth it. He smiled, imagining her terror, first as she discovered the 'pet' he'd left her and then his greeting card. He'd changed his tactics this go around. Despite what he'd been taught, he no longer believed patience to be a virtue. It was old school.

One thing he did like that was old school was sadly going by the wayside: people having to be responsible for themselves. There was a time everyone had to take care of their own crap. Now, they had technology taking up the slack. Computers and cell phones sending alerts if your social security number was accessed or too much money being charged per day. Still, luckily, the majority of people went about their daily lives in a fog. They were just so damned stupid. So unobservant.

Like the lady at the rental counter when he showed his picture ID. She gave it a cursory look. If she'd actually compared the man in the photo to the one standing in front of her, she would've noticed they weren't one and the same. But she hadn't and here he was sitting in a panel van enjoying the view on his way home. He liked driving. Here, in this vehicle, he was alone. There was nobody looking over his shoulder telling him what to do.

He figured the authorities would go looking for the van but it would take them a while to find it, if they found it at all, since he'd rented it in a state other than Missouri. Of course, if they did, the agency and nearby businesses might have cameras from which investigators could get a brief description of him. But that was an 'if' scenario and odds were in his favor that all the 'ifs' needed to find him would not fall into place.

The 'break-in' at Lydia's had accomplished several things in addition to increasing her blood pressure, he mused. He had actually broken a window to gain entrance. He could've used his bump key set but he didn't want to tip her or the authorities to the possibility he had burglary tools. This way instead of increasing security by installing better locks or cameras, they would assume he was as stupid as they were and just replace the window.

Bump keys. They were easily purchased online, and to make it even sweeter, instruction videos were free to watch. Technology working to *his* advantage. But, along with their use came noise and he needed a silent entry for his next visit. So, he'd gone next door to the landlord's home and 'bump keyed' entrance in search of actual copies of keys to Lydia's residence. It was almost too easy. There by the garage door hung a rack with numerous keys—and they were labeled. He took the one to the deadbolt for Lydia's back door and replaced it with a similar one, making sure the brand name was the same and attaching the label. He repeated the process with the key designated 'garage/kitchen'. Again, the possibility of discovery was slim. Bump keys didn't leave tampering marks and the switch wouldn't be discovered unless the owners actually tried to use the keys.

He set the cruise control to five miles under the speed limit then mentally retraced his steps for the last two days. The first phase had been to obtain Lydia's pet, SSSSSam. (God, but that was a cool name!) The groundwork for this operation had been laid years ago when he'd watched *Snake Salvation* on the *National Geographic Channel* with his dad. He laughed thinking how smart it had been to realize the bite of a cottonmouth snake would create the perfect gift for Lydia's second anniversary present. After all, the second anniversary was the *cotton* anniversary. And it had gone so well he felt it was time to branch out, so today he'd employed a different species as he worked on anniversary four.

Though most states banned congregations that used venomous snakes in worship, he'd found one anyway. It helped that authorities in the area tended to look the other way unless a church member actually died of a snake bite. He'd posed as a free-lance journalist capitalizing on the fanaticism surrounding the art and had 'interviewed' Pastor Lewis Cantrell about his snake-handling church services. He knew the comings and goings of the pastor's family from several years back but needed to see if anything had changed. So, he'd taken a little road trip and learned that Pastor Cantrell still worked at the chicken processing plant in town while Mrs. Cantrell continued home schooling the kids down at the church. In anticipation of his trip, he'd reviewed how to catch and bag a snake on YouTube and purchased a collapsible snake tong in a reptile store west of the Appalachians. He'd traveled to Cantrell's rural home, used his bump key to enter and collected SSSSSam without a hitch—or should he say 'hiss'.

He'd stopped at a home improvement store on his way to the preacher's house and purchased a pest poison sprayer to serve as SSSSSam's carrying case. A few miles from his destination he'd pulled over in a strip mall and donned coveralls in the back of the van. It was the perfect cover.

"If" Lydia had any nosy neighbors they would assume he was just spraying for termites at both residences at 6821 East Redbud Drive. After returning to the van, he'd pulled into a rest stop along I-44, put the coveralls in a bag and dropped the bag in a trash bin. He kept the bogus ID and credit card. He figured they could be used a few more times before being 'retired'.

4

Detective John Hutsell and his partner, Trish Rankin, pulled up next to Lydia Janssen's car forty-five minutes after talking with Sheriff Jimmy Matthews. Janssen had googled Hutsell on her new phone and had his photo in front of her when the two investigators pulled up beside her.

"I'm Lydia Janssen," she said after rolling down her window. "Thank you for coming."

The two detectives exited their car with their shields attached to their belts and in full view. Hutsell rounded the front of the vehicle and stood by his partner in front of Lydia's door. Although Hutsell was known throughout Missouri and TV land for solving the Cross Timbers Murder in Springfield, Rankin was the senior detective. She took the lead.

After making introductions, the female investigator said, "Sheriff Matthews briefly described what you encountered this morning upon arriving home. Would you like to follow us to the station where we can talk while we wait for a crime scene crew to become available?"

"That would be fine," Lydia replied. Her voice was flat, emotionless.

As Rankin turned to re-enter the car, Hutsell caught her eye and facing away from Lydia, slightly nodded to his left. Rankin followed his line of sight and saw a small pool of greenish-yellow liquid with chunks of partially digested food about fifty feet from where they stood.

"Good catch," Rankin said after the investigators were belted in.

"She's thin," observed Hutsell. "Wonder just how often she vomits."

"Or even feels like eating at all," added his partner.

They were a few blocks away when Hutsell picked up the tablet sitting on the seat between them.

"The initial photos have arrived from Arkansas," he told his partner after opening the file. "Damn."

"That bad, huh?"

"If you consider the body of a young man in a rubber container surrounded by a dozen cottonmouth snakes bad, then yeah, it's pretty bad."

Once seated in a precinct conference room, Lydia relayed the entire incident to Rankin and Hutsell. She wrapped up by saying, "Since it is Valentine's Day, I did expect to find a greeting card waiting for me—but in my mailbox, not sitting on my computer."

"And you didn't notice anything out of the ordinary when you arrived home?" asked Hutsell.

"Detective, I'm super vigilant—I don't have any other choice than to be," Janssen contended as she looked him in the eye. "There was nothing to suggest my house had been broken into."

"At least in the kitchen and office, correct?" Hutsell said. "You didn't check other parts of the house before leaving?"

"No," answered Janssen in a flat voice.

Rankin stepped in. "He's never entered your residence before, either here or in Arkansas that you are aware of?" asked Rankin as Hutsell made notes.

A man appeared at the door of the conference room with a folder.

"Here you go, John. Hard copies of the case files from Arkansas you asked for," said duty officer, Gabe Fenske. "Oh sorry, I didn't realize you were conducting an interview."

"Thanks, Gabe," Hutsell said. "Just place them on my desk."

Rankin watched as the young woman before her fixated on the file. She knew from experience her partner had noticed, too. She really had lucked out when Hutsell'd joined the department just when her former partner had received a promotion.

Rankin's phone rang.

"Thanks, Liz. We'll see you there in about thirty minutes," she told the person on the other end. She rose to her feet. "Ms. Janssen, we need to proceed to your home as we now have a crime scene unit available."

"Fine. I live at 6821-B East Redbud Drive. I'll meet you there," Janssen said.

Hutsell and Janssen reached the room's entrance at the same time. The detective stood aside to let Janssen go ahead and brought up his left arm in a supporting motion from behind. Lydia jumped and hit the door so hard the knob punched a hole in the wall.

She looked into Hutsell's eyes and with her lips barely moving said, "I don't like to be touched, Detective."

"Yes, ma'am."

"I had no intention of touching her," Hutsell said after Janssen had left the area.

"I know, John. You were just being your polite self." Rankin slipped on her coat.

"Oh, no," said Joe Kleeman who had just walked into the room. "Hey, Mendoza. Hutsell's being polite again."

"He didn't pull out the 'hanky' did he?" asked Luis Mendoza.

"I've told you guys before, handkerchiefs make the man," said Hutsell.

"Joe, what's your guess?" asked Mendoza. "Think he carries monogrammed or plain white hankies?"

"If his mom, the senator bought them, I'll bet there's a big 'H' on the corner of each one," answered Kleeman.

"Say what you will about my mom, gentlemen," Hutsell said. "But she was right when she told me, 'Just remember handkerchiefs and dancing, son, and you'll never be alone'."

"I've got to agree," chimed in Rankin. "By the way, how long since you've been on a date, Joe?"

Luis Mendoza laughed so hard the coffee in his mouth ended up on the floor instead of his stomach.

· 5 ·

He was happily driving down the road when his back-up cell phone dinged a message had been received. Oh well, it was time for a pit stop, anyway. But let's really make it worth my while, he thought, and get a chocolate dipped cone while taking a break. He was reading the signs informing drivers of upcoming gas stations and restaurants when he spied the logo for a nationally known chain. It brought back memories of when he was a child and his father would take the family on Sunday drives. His dad had always pulled into one of these places at the end of the ride and let him order a foot-long hot dog for dinner and a dip cone for dessert. His mom made sure he covered himself with a throw so he wouldn't get his clothes messy because they would always attend Sunday Evening Services before going home.

He loved his parents. They had told him he was as normal as anyone else when he had come home upset because kids at school had made fun of him. They had reassured him he would grow out of his stammer and that his clumsy stage wouldn't last forever. They'd taught him when things got tough, he was always to remember that what was of utmost importance was God's love and through God's help he would be delivered from his tormentors. When he got old enough to fully comprehend what they meant he realized they had been right. One by one, those persecuting him had gone by the wayside. Well, most of them, anyway . . . .

He pulled into a parking space wishing his dad could be there with him. If he was sitting beside him in the van, it would be the son buying the ice cream treat for the father this time. He closed his eyes trying to conjure up what his dad looked like when he was younger rather than the last time he had seen him at the funeral home. He missed his dad, pure and simple. But at least he had his memories.

His cell dinged again.

"She wants to know if you'll be home for supper," read the message.

"Tell her I won't but to text a grocery list and I will get

everything before I come home. Make it sound like I'm doing her a favor—like I'm saving her a trip and she won't have to get out tomorrow," he typed.

"Got it," was the reply.

Surprisingly, the older guy on the other end had turned out to be someone he could count on. Poet had been fired almost four months ago for smoking pot while on the clock. The old man had just gone with the flow and even offered the manager a drag as he walked away. So when the idea of a stand-in had come to mind, he'd gone looking for Poet.

"You got a new job, yet?" he'd asked.

"Nope."

"How you getting by?"

"Hanging out at my cousin's most of the time," answered Poet. "It's not so bad. He lets me crash if I bring him a little weed."

"How would you like to stay in a nice place every now and then and have a little something to jingle in your pocket?"

"Depends. What have I got to do to get it?"

"Pretend to be me."

"Hey, man, look. I don't mind spending a night or two with the local constabulary but I ain't wanting to set up no permanent residence," Poet had told him.

"It's nothing illegal. You got access to a car?"

"Yeah. My cousin lets me use his ex-wife's old clunker to run 'errands'—if you know what I mean," Poet had said with a grin.

"Okay, so all you have to do is sit at my family's place on the river and answer texts from the old lady while I go and do my thing."

"And what's your thing?"

"I like guys, "he'd told Poet. "If my old lady knew, she'd be online looking for conversion therapy retreats."

"To each his own. Can I smoke while I'm there?"

"Outside, in the back only. And you can't leave any evidence, okay? You have to pick up after yourself."

"Where does the car come in?"

"My car will be in plain sight so it will appear I am there should anyone drive by. I will use your cousin's car to drive to my meetings."

"And that's it?"

"Yes. I will leave my personal cell with you and provide an

additional phone you will use to contact me about any messages received. I will then tell you how to respond."

"I'm in," Poet had said.

6

John Hutsell was reading Janssen's file as his partner drove to the sixty-eighth hundred block of East Redbud Drive

"So, what's the gist?" Rankin asked.

"The 'first anniversary' card and photo appeared on October 31, 2015. The photo was of Rob Prasser, a childhood friend of Janssen's. Death due to obstructed pharynx. Wadded up papers were forced down his throat—one was made to look like a death certificate," replied Hutsell. "Hold on a second."

Rankin slowed down for traffic as Hutsell said into his phone's microphone, "Anniversary gifts by year."

"Here's a summary," came a female voice. "First year, paper. Second year, cotton. Third year, leather."

"Oh hell, John. So the body in the container with snakes was for the second anniversary; cotton? Death by *cotton*mouth? This guy is pretty sick."

"Oh, it gets worse," said Hutsell. "Matthews and company have no clue what caused the death of victim number three."

"It wasn't by leather?"

"No one knows. The body was never found. But along with a card and photo was a 'leather' key fob."

"'Splain, Ricky'."

"'Yes, Lucy'," Hutsell said with a Cuban accent. "The victim was Janssen's psychotherapist, Rhona Temke. Temke had a butterfly tattoo on her ankle . . . the key fob had the same likeness."

"John, he didn't . . .."

"Yeah, Trish, he did," Hutsell said. "The killer excised Temke's tattoo, made a key chain out of it and sent it to Janssen. He's definitely got a feel for the dramatic."

"Sick doesn't cover it," Rankin remarked.

"Not by a long shot," said Hutsell as he continued to study the photo. "You know if Kleeman sees this, being the ornery cuss he is, he's going to ask if an ankle bracelet was attached to the fob."

Rankin just shook her head in response as she pulled along the curb at 6821-B East Redbud Drive. She put the car in park and looked at her partner and said, "Kid gloves, okay?"

"'*Kid* gloves', Trish?" he said, questioning her idiom choice for 'handle with care'. "It's a good thing I'm not Kleeman."

"Six-button or opera length?" Rankin said. "Who needs Kleeman?"

Hutsell gave her a look.

"What?" she asked, eyes wide, feigning innocence. "So mom was a costume designer . . .."

Lydia Janssen was standing by her Malibu as a crime scene van drove up and parked in the driveway. She watched as the two detectives met with the technicians, exchanged a few words and then proceeded inside the garage.

"Ms. Janssen, meet Elizabeth Holt and Ethan Martelli. They've been briefed but they may have some questions for you as they work the scene," said Rankin.

"That's fine," commented Janssen.

"Is this the container housing the snake or has it already been removed by animal control?" asked Martelli pointing at Lydia's trash bin.

"It's still in there," Janssen answered.

"Animal control has been notified and representatives should be here soon," Hutsell informed the group and then added, "Shall we get started?"

"The door's open," Lydia said. "I didn't take time to lock it when I left."

Holt handed gloves and booties to all in attendance. With protective apparel in place Rankin and Hutsell entered first. They soon reappeared and informed the rest of the group the dwelling was clear for processing.

"We found the point of entry," Rankin told Janssen. "There's a broken window in the bedroom. You'll want to inform your landlord as soon as possible to have it replaced."

Lydia walked the investigators through the scene, recounting her observations and actions earlier in the day. They ended up in her office where she nodded at the envelope on her keyboard.

"There it is. I didn't touch it," she said as Martelli moved passed her.

"Ms. Janssen, let's tour the rest of the house while the techs get to work. Point out anything that might be the slightest bit out of place," said Rankin.

After a thorough search, the three returned to the kitchen.

"I didn't see anything else," Janssen said.

There was a knock on the front door.

Hutsell looked out the window and announced Animal Control had arrived.

Rankin had Janssen take a seat in the living room. She then stepped into the garage, motioned the city servants over and pointed to the trash bin.

"It's in there, alive and well as far as we know," she said. "We'll need a full report on this one as soon as possible, gentleman: species, habitat, native regions." She handed them her card.

"Will do," said the taller of the two men.

Hutsell had just finished jotting down the vehicle's city number along with the names on the jackets of the attendants in his notebook when Liz Holt appeared at the door of the garage. She handed each detective a mask and motioned them back inside.

"What do you make of this?" she asked, pointing to a container under the sink.

"Ms. Janssen, did you place a ceramic cup containing a yellow liquid under the sink?" asked Hutsell through the covering over his nose and mouth.

"No."

"How would you describe it, Trish?" asked Hutsell as he began making notes again.

Rankin gently tilted the cup with her gloved hand while holding a mask to her face.

"A yellow liquid. Possibly a teaspoon full. Medium viscosity. No discernable odor—but hey . . .," she said, referencing the mask.

Rankin and Hutsell moved to the living room and sat down with Lydia.

"Our part is done for now, Ms. Janssen, and we can't hazard a guess as to how long until Holt and Martelli finish. It just depends on what they find. Have you spoken to your landlord about the break-in and replacing the window?" Rankin asked.

"I've left a message for them and I'll arrange for the window to be replaced on my own."

"Detective Hutsell and I are going to canvass the neighborhood, then return to the station and review the files Sheriff Matthews sent. What are your plans?"

"After the window is fixed I'm going to a hotel room and take a sleeping pill. I'll go to work as usual at 11:00 P.M."

"We'll touch base with you tomorrow, then," said Hutsell.

"Please do so before 1:00 P.M. as I will be in bed by then."

"I'm sorry we can't offer you more at this time," Rankin said.

"Detective, I know how this works. I'll hear from you when you have something to report."

"Goodbye, then."

Rankin placed her card on the coffee table.

"Call if you have any questions or think of anything else."

"I will," she replied as Hutsell placed his card next to his partner's.

7

The front of the card showed a woman sitting on a settee with a man on either side of her. All were clad in Victorian dress. The caption read, "It's a perfect night for mystery and horror." Inside the card was Frankenstein, the creature and his bride, "The air itself is filled with monsters." Then in a gothic font, "Happy Halloween, my sweet." Below the caption was a hand-written inscription in block letters:

> My dear Lydia, I've had girlfriends before but they always left me after a year or two. But you are still here which makes you my 'special' Valentine. And that is why I am planning something 'special' for you in the near future. Until then my sweet . . ..

"The manufacture's name and copyright date are on the back of the card. It was sold in numerous outlets nationwide. There are no fingerprints and the flap was tucked inside the envelope so there's no saliva. Sorry I can't offer more than that right now," said Elizabeth Holt.

John Hutsell took the clear bag encasing the open card offered by Holt. "Quite the romantic," he said before handing it to his partner.

"Both pictures and quotes are from the movie, The *Bride of Frankenstein*," Rankin said to those in the room. "Let's compare it to photos of previous cards and see what we come up with," she said to Hutsell. "Janssen is sleeping now but we can always call Matthews if need be."

Rankin looked up to see three sets of eyes staring at her.

"What?" she asked.

"Bride of Frankenstein?" said her partner. "Of all the Frankenstein movies you know which one a picture and a quote comes from?"

"The ex's favorite holiday is Halloween. Starting October first

26

he's screening as many horror flicks as he can till the big day. And the rest of the year we watched *Svengoolie*."

"Love *Svengoolie*," said Holt.

Hutsell and Martelli exchanged looks.

"You're detectives. Knock yourselves out," said Holt. "But I've got to warn you, Svengoolie is G-rated, John."

"Okay then . . . moving right along . . .," Hutsell said to a smiling Rankin and Holt. "Do you have anything else before we head out?"

"The window was broken from the outside. The screen was not removed prior. No shoe prints, but the ground under the window appeared to be recently smoothed over. He covered his tracks—'LOL' as they say. There are a few tread marks on some glass shards. Maybe we can determine the shoe's manufacturer and style from them. How about you, Ethan?"

"The intruder set some sort of a container on the carpet near the north wall in the office. I found slivers of glass and some soil. The soil is identical to that found around Janssen's home. I think he might have placed it on the ground at some point before using it to shatter the window. Here's a photo showing an outline of the container's base. It's two half-circles with a furrow-like groove in between, about 7.4 inches in diameter," said Martelli.

"Anything on the liquid from the under the sink?"

"Not yet, John. Still waiting on the high-performance liquid chromatography results. I'll send the report as soon as it's available," Martelli said.

"We do have some information on the snake," Trish told the two techs. "It's a timber rattler found mostly in the eastern United States from as far north as Maine down to northern Florida. Western boundaries extend to Wisconsin, south to parts of eastern Texas."

"So pinpointing where it originally came from is more or less a crap shoot," said Holt.

"Yeah," Hutsell said. "It's illegal to transport these snakes across most state lines, but that wouldn't make a difference to our guy."

"Thanks for your work," Rankin said. She and Hutsell headed for the door.

"Good luck, detectives," said Holt.

The partner's returned to the detective unit's investigation/tactical room, commonly referred to as the bull pen, to take stock before heading home for the day. They placed the new evidence bags and photos on the center table, alongside the files from Arkansas.

"Trish, this is the first one with a handwritten note," Hutsell said as he picked up the plastic bag holding the greeting card. "Handwriting analysis will offer little since it's done in capital print."

"Well, put that John Jay College of Criminal Justice degree to work and give a preliminary guess."

"What little I know about handwriting analysis didn't come from John Jay," he said. "There was a lady teaching a seminar on the subject in Springfield four years ago. She was cute as hell and kind enough to provide private tutoring sessions."

"I assume you passed with flying colors," commented Rankin.

"Let's just say she was pleased with my performance."

Rankin laughed while she shook her head from side to side.

"You asked," Hutsell said as he lifted his eyebrows in innocence. "But, back on subject, few people actually write this way and many criminals do so in order to disguise personal traits associated with handwriting. In this example, the letters are extremely rigid. Some analysts feel it may signal a repression so great the writer is moving towards extreme violence."

Hutsell placed the bag on the table next to photos of previous cards. He moved his eyes back and forth several times.

"Come here, Trish. There's little to compare since he's never written a note before, but look closely at the slant of the letters in this latest card next to the others and tell me what you see."

"The slant isn't uniform in this one."

"Correct. Concerning slant, in today's message, he's all over the place. This could indicate the emergence of an alternating personality—which would fit with the fact he's changed his MO. But we have to use caution here. You asked for a guess and that's what you got."

Rankin nodded her head as she continued to study the handwriting on the card in front of her and photos of others sent by Sheriff Matthews.

"I think the best take away from this new card is his admission there's been former 'girlfriends'," Hutsell said. "Which begs the question, has he done this before and if so, how many victims have there been. What do you think? Is it time to send out a bulletin inquiring about on-going investigations concerning deaths due to paper, cotton and/or leather throughout the country?"

"Go ahead and compose one and run it by Vashon before you hit send. Include the Halloween greeting card and Day of the Dead aspects," she said as she walked to the coat rack.

"I will. You know what the press is going to call this guy if there are other victims out there don't you?"

"The Anniversary Killer comes to mind," Rankin answered on her way to the door. "You might as well go ahead and give him the label, John. It's bound to happen."

"I hate that crap."

"Afraid there's going to be another high-profile case linked to your name?"

"I may get lucky this time," Hutsell said. "It may be your name that gets tagged. After all, you are the 'lead' detective."

"Nah, look in the mirror, cowboy. You're kind of pretty," she said with a smile.

8

John Hutsell carried two cups of coffee into the detective squad room and set one down in front of his partner. Like most mornings, they were the first to arrive. The partners had become friends and often used the time to catch up on their personal lives.

"How was the ball game?" he asked.

"Josh made one basket and one assist," Rankin said about her son.

"And Sophie?"

"She had popcorn so she was a happy camper," Rankin answered. "And how was your evening?"

"Had a couple at the 10–7," Hutsell said referring to a basement cop bar named for the radio code for off-duty officer.

"Meet up with Stacy?" Rankin asked with a smile.

"She was there."

"And . . .?"

"Nothing to tell, Trish."

"Damn, John, you know I live vicariously through you."

"Take Gabe Fenske up on his offer and maybe you won't have to," he said.

"It's hard dating with two young kids at home and a demanding career."

"Gabe knows the dictates of the job and he likes kids. He coaches Little League in the summer."

"I know."

"Is it the age difference?"

"I don't know. I just don't think I'm ready to climb back in the saddle," she said.

"It's a nice saddle, Trish."

"Yeah, it is. Shall we move on?" she said, changing the subject.

Hutsell was powering up his computer when Lieutenant Gail Vashon stepped into the room.

"John, call on line three about the Janssen case," Vashon said.

"Got it." He picked up the phone and hit the speaker tab for his partner's benefit. "Detective John Hutsell."

"Hello, Detective. My name is Rick Hadley, Deputy Sheriff out of Shannon County, Tennessee. I've got a couple of unsolved murders that fit your profile. Photos of victims arrived in greeting cards on October 31, in 2011 and again in 2012."

Rankin typed Rick Hadley's name into the bar of her computer's search engine.

"Were there references to the Catholic celebration of Day, or Days, of the Dead?" asked Hutsell.

"Yes. The sender also claimed Halloween as an anniversary date as fits with your bulletin," Hadley added. "And I understand your victim has received Halloween cards throughout the years, coinciding with traditional holidays, correct?"

"That's right," answered the St. Louis detective. "Too many similarities to be a coincidence, don't you think? Are you willing to send us copies of your files?"

Rankin studied the image of Hadley on the monitor. His face was oval and his brown hair was tapered giving him a modern version of a classic men's cut. There was intelligence and confidence in Hadley's deep-set eyes but there was also a hint of sadness. No, she thought, it's more than that. She stared intently into his blue eyes until she finally found the right word . . . lost. And with that realization came the notion that there were two kinds of women in Rick Hadley's life—those who wanted to mother him and those who were in love with him. Nothing in between. She swiveled her computer screen so Hutsell could see a photo of the Shannon County deputy.

"I'm willing to do more than that," said Hadley. "I'll bring copies to you. If you are agreeable, we can pool our resources, lay out the evidence and get a more complete picture."

Hutsell took his eyes off the screen and looked at his partner. He raised his eyebrows in a questioning manner. Rankin mouthed, "Put him on hold." She began typing again.

"Hang on a minute, deputy," he said into the receiver.

"It will take him about nine hours to get here," said Rankin. "Ask him if he would mind sending some files electronically so we can get a head start."

Hutsell nodded in agreement. "Thanks for holding, Deputy. When can we expect you?" he asked.

"I can leave here within the hour and be in St. Louis about six-thirty this evening—maybe a little later, depending on traffic."

"Would you mind sending the files, also? That way my partner and I will have a chance to become familiar with your case before you arrive. We wouldn't be fully up to speed but it would save time."

"Sure, no problem."

"We'll see you around six-thirty then," Hutsell said. "Let me give you our cell numbers so you can bypass the front desk when calling from here on out."

The men exchanged phone numbers as Rankin continued to garner information on Deputy Rick Hadley. Hutsell placed the phone's receiver in its cradle, picked up his coffee cup and stood.

"Ready for a second cup?"

"Yes. Oh, John, you are gonna love this," Rankin said. "Hadley's a deputy sheriff in Shannon County, Tennessee, right?"

"That's what the man said."

"You're either going question his abilities or identify with him."

"Oh, yeah? 'Splain, Lucy."

"The *sheriff* of Shannon County is named Mike Hadley. *Daddy* Mike Hadley."

"He's either riding dad's coattails *or* he's having a hard time carving out a reputation of his own away from daddy's shadow," Hutsell said.

Gabe Fenske walked in the room. "Trish," he said by way of a greeting.

"Morning, Gabe."

"John, the bulletin you sent out last night is getting results. Here's a message along with a printed report."

"Thanks," Hutsell said. "Oh, Gabe, we should be receiving some files from Tennessee shortly. Would—?"

"I'll forward them to Trish as soon as they arrive," Fenske interrupted, completing Hutsell's sentence. Then he smiled and added, "And because you're a tactile kind of guy, I'll make hard copies for you."

"Appreciate it," Hutsell said, smiling back.

He raised his eyebrows and nodded towards Fenske after the officer turned to walk away. Trish narrowed hers causing furrows to appear in her forehead. She moved her head from side to side and mouthed, "Not now." When Fenske was out of hearing distance,

Hutsell, still smiling said, "I know he's young, Trish, but I have no doubt you can keep up with him."

"I'm thinking about it, okay. Are you happy now?"

"'Bout time," Hutsell replied. He sat his cup down and opened the file Fenske had given him.

"What ya got?" asked Rankin.

"A detective out of Elko, Nevada, has an unsolved from 2014. A Halloween card addressed to Jenny Newkirk arrived on October 31. Inside was the picture of the body of her best friend."

"Dang if you didn't call it, John. We've now got at least two other possible victims besides Janssen," Rankin said. "Death by . . .?"

"Drowning," Hutsell answered.

"Which anniversary?"

"First."

"How do you drown a person in paper?"

"In a bucket full of *liquid* paper."

"Oh, hell . . . ."

Hutsell stood, handed the file to Rankin and picked up their coffee cups. "I'll get refills and meet you in the bull pen."

Rankin was holding a printout of an engagement photo of Lydia Janssen and Nathan Lockner when Hutsell joined her. She passed the photo to her colleague.

"Hardly looks like the same person," he said, referring to the bride-to-be. "Reminds me of Nicole Kidman in her early movies. When was this taken?"

"About two and a half years ago."

"The guy in the rubber storage bin with the cottonmouths, right?"

"Yep. Give Matthews a call. Tell him about Elko and Shannon County, Tennessee. Let him know Hadley will be in town tonight," Rankin told the junior detective. "Have Gabe forward what we've got to Arkansas. I'll call Janssen. We've both got follow-up questions and need to fill her in on the forensics."

"Do we tell her about the possibility of new victims?"

"Your choice of words answers that question. '*Possibility* of new victims.' I've never known you to work on gut instinct when it comes to going public, John. You're today's version of Joe Friday, 'Just the facts, ma'am'."

"Oh damn, that's all I need."

"What's all you need?"

"For Kleeman to start calling me, John Friday. Nah, John Thursday would be more to his liking—just so you'd say 'Huh?' and he'd get to explain how clever he is."

Rankin laughed. "Well then, you better stay on my good side."

Lydia Janssen was working in the attached storage room that ran the width of her garage when her cell rang. She pulled down her particulate filter mask and answered the call.

"Ms. Janssen. Trish Rankin here. We've got some lab reports to go over with you along with a few follow-up questions. Are you able to meet with us this morning?"

"Yes, Detective Rankin. I'm home working on a project. I plan to be here till noon."

"Good. My partner and I will see you in about forty-five minutes."

"That's fine."

Lydia stored her sander and headed inside the bungalow. She took a quick shower then started brewing a pot of coffee. She was loading her washer when the doorbell rang.

"Come in detectives," she said upon opening the door. Rankin and Hutsell followed her to the kitchen.

"Coffee?" she asked.

"Yes, thank you," answered Hutsell, who was carrying a tablet and files.

"That would be nice," followed Rankin.

"Cream and sugar?"

"Black," said Hutsell.

"Both," replied Rankin.

Once the coffee had been served, Detective Hutsell opened a folder and informed Lydia of what they'd learned from evidence gathered by Holt and Martelli.

"In addition, this morning we got a report on the substance under the sink. It's snake venom. He actually milked the snake before he left the premises. One thing we know for sure is that he didn't intend for you to die yesterday," Rankin said.

"Well, that makes sense. He could have killed me a long time ago. I think he gets off by making me wish for death just to stop the torment."

"You may have something there," Hutsell agreed. "The other victims that he alluded to in the card left him—why or how did they leave? Suicide is one way they might have chosen. That may be his goal—to drive you to the point where you take your own life."

"Lord knows I've thought about it—even come close a time or two."

"Ms. Janssen, from the very beginning he's fixated on the Day of the Dead. You're Catholic, correct?" asked Rankin.

Lydia nodded in the affirmative.

"And the hospital you worked at in Northwest Arkansas is a Catholic hospital, right?"

"Yes. Jimmy thought of that connection, too," Lydia said. "I couldn't—and still can't—think of anyone in the Church or at the hospital who would do something like this. We focused on newcomers to both institutions in the beginning but we came up dry. Then we moved on to any and all who might have contact with me, Catholic or not. Still nothing."

"One other thing," Rankin said as she rose to her feet. "Our canvassing of the neighborhood has been fruitless so far. Most residents weren't home yesterday morning and the ones that were had nothing to contribute. We left our cards for others to contact us if they have anything to report."

"I'm not surprised," said Lydia. "This is the University District. Most that live here are employed by the University or are students."

All three were now standing.

"Ms. Janssen, on the phone this morning you said you were working on a project," Hutsell said. "Do you have a special hobby that might have provided an avenue by which the suspect would have come in contact with you?"

"I have a small woodworking shop attached to the garage," Lydia replied. "Mostly I make furniture. The entertainment center in the living area is one of my pieces."

"I noticed the wardrobe in the bedroom yesterday," said Hutsell. "Quite the attention to detail. Did you construct it, also?"

"Yes, detective."

"May we see your shop?" he asked.

"Of course."

Lydia headed for the door that opened to the garage and led the two detectives to an area that had originally been designed for storage. She had converted it to a wood shop, complete with a table saw, work stands, and an air filtration system to handle saw dust. Several smaller tools were hung on a peg-board just inside the door above a tool chest.

"Great set-up you've got here," commented Hutsell.

"My father was a high school shop teacher and he taught me well," Janssen said. "Working with wood is one thing that hasn't been destroyed or taken from me."

Hutsell was puzzled by a tool sitting on a work table. "You use a finishing nail gun for furniture?"

"No, I employ joinery and glue." Janssen followed Hutsell's line of sight. "Oh, I see what you mean," she said. She walked to the end of the table, reached down and brought up a decorated piece of wood. "My dad saw several videos on nail gun art and decided to try it. This is one of his pieces. He called it his tribute to the Beatles."

Janssen held up a wooden board that had a circle outlined in nails. Half the circle contained a heart and the other half, a peace sign. Across the top nails spelled out, "All You Need is Love" with "Give Peace a Chance" along the bottom.

"It hung in his work shop. I haven't had time to put it up here. I've been thinking of just using one of those over the door clothes hangers on the closet door and attaching twine to secure it rather than driving a nail in the wall."

"What is your current project?" asked Rankin.

"A footlocker for Sheriff Matthew's son. He likes Spiderman, so I'm going to place a Spiderman throw and toys in the chest after it's finished."

"Going to be one happy kid in Arkansas when you're finished. My son would do a back flip for one of those. When do expect to have it completed?" asked Rankin.

"If things *were* to go according to plan, in a few weeks. But after hearing what was in the card, it sounds like he's got other plans for me."

"Is there anyone you can stay with?" questioned Rankin as she headed for the door.

"That's the whole point, isn't it? No, there's no one. I have been forced to isolate myself. I won't put anyone else in jeopardy."

Lydia pressed a button and the garage door began its climb. Detective Hutsell was almost in the drive when he turned around.

"Will you be sleeping here this afternoon?" he asked.

"I won't sleep if I stay here—no matter how many sleeping pills I take."

Rankin and Hutsell looked at each other and then back at Janssen.

"Relax, I not planning a permanent sleep, detectives."

"If you would, try and recall people you know associated with wood working—suppliers and other enthusiasts," Rankin said.

"I will."

"Where will you be staying—just in case we can't reach you by phone?" inquired Hutsell.

"The Marriot a few blocks from the hospital."

"We'll be in touch," he said.

Once in the car, Rankin asked, "Finisher nail gun?"

"Grandpa was a contractor. Guess how I spent my summers?"

"Constructing?"

"Yep."

After lunch, the two detectives headed back to the station. With Hutsell in the driver's seat, Rankin checked to see if Deputy Hadley had followed through and sent his files.

"Gabe forwarded Tennessee's files. Hard copies will be in the bull pen when we get there."

"Did you know Gabe before Afghanistan?" Hutsell asked his partner while he waited for a gap in traffic in order to make a left turn.

"Not really. My former partner went to school with Gabe's dad. The two kept in touch and when Gabe showed an interest in law enforcement, Scott advised him. Scott and I'd been partners for only a few weeks when I met Gabe. He stopped by often to visit and for the most part the two men were always laughing and joking around. There were a few times though when Gabe walked in and Scott took one look at him and they immediately headed to an interview room."

"Did you ever find out what they talked about?" Hutsell asked.

"If Scott had wanted me to know, he would have told me and I didn't pry. I had my hands full. I was married then, had just made detective and Sophie was still in diapers."

"Do you know why he enlisted in the army?"

"No. I know he qualified as an army ranger and it was in that capacity he was injured. He was flown to a hospital in Germany where his leg was amputated and eventually ended up at Walter Reed. Gabe's dad had just been diagnosed with an aggressive form of brain cancer and was undergoing treatment so it was Scott who flew to the east coast to be with him."

"A slight limp is the only tell-tale sign," Hutsell said as he pulled into the station parking lot. "He shows up at the 10–7 every now and then. There's a couple of women who have let him know they're interested. He's been polite but has never pursued either one. I think he goes for a more *mature* woman, you know?"

"That would make him a wise man then, wouldn't it?" Rankin smiled and got out of the car.

The two detectives stopped at their desks to check for messages before going to the investigation room.

"You want coffee before we start setting up a timeline?" Hutsell asked.

"I think I'll go with water. Hold on a minute." She looked at her phone. "It's the ex. I'll join you in a few minutes."

Hutsell was laying out photos of murder victims in chronological order when Rankin stuck her head in the door.

"Dan was rear-ended and can't make it to Sophie's preschool in time to pick her up. His SUV is being towed so his girlfriend is taking him to rent a car," she reported. "It's his night with the kids so I need to pick them up and drop them off at his place. I'll be back in time to meet with Hadley."

"Go. I'll get things set up while you're gone."

Lieutenant Vashon was standing next to Hutsell, looking at a board covered with photos of murder victims when Rankin returned to the bull pen carrying two pizza boxes.

"Dinner is about to be served in the break room," Rankin said.

Vashon glanced at Rankin and then turned her eyes back to the dry-erase board.

"Okay, John, so you think all these murders are connected. Then you and Trish make the case. I'll see you both in the morning,"

Vashon said. She nodded at Rankin on the way back to her office.

Trish looked at the display Hutsell had organized in her absence.

"Damn, John. How many victims total?"

"We've got three primary and six secondary victims." Hutsell grabbed the pizza boxes from his partner's hands and called over his shoulder as he walked out of the room, "Thanks for dinner."

"Now just a minute, Hutsell. Only one of those boxes has your name on it."

Hutsell set the boxes holding the pizzas on a table in the break room and started for the vending machines.

"Hey, John. Don't bother."

Hutsell turned around to see his partner smiling. Rankin opened her jacket, placed her hands on two long-necked bottles of beer and drew them out of her pockets like they were six-shooters.

"Now that's what I call pulling out the big guns."

The two detectives were storing leftovers when Lynne Corkren, Fenske's evening counterpart, announced over the intercom they had a visitor. They acknowledged the message and made their way to the front office.

"Deputy Sheriff Rick Hadley from Tennessee is in the lobby, detectives."

"Thanks, Lynne," said Hutsell.

"No, thank you detective," said Corkren, smiling from ear to ear.

Rankin looked through the half-glass door leading to the lobby to see Hadley's back. The Shannon County deputy stood at least six-foot-four. He wore a plain white shirt tucked into his Wrangler jeans. A heavy navy jacket was draped over a nearby chair. Hutsell reached for the door knob just as Hadley bent over to adjust the lid of a cardboard evidence box on the floor. Rankin put her hand out and stopped her partner.

"Yes. Thank you, detective," she said, repeating Corkren's words.

Seeing Hadley in the flesh made Rankin recall her initial thoughts about the Tennessee deputy. She had no intention of mothering him or falling in love, but there was nothing wrong with enjoying the view.

Hutsell shook his head. "Let me know when you're through

drooling."

"Don't know if that day will ever come, John."

Hutsell opened the door. "You made pretty good time, deputy," he said as he extended his right hand. "Would you like to freshen up before we get started?"

"Call me, Rick, and I believe I would."

"I'm detective Trish Rankin. Pleased to make your acquaintance," she said, shaking Hadley's hand. "Would you like bottled water or would you prefer coffee?"

"Water's fine, ma'am."

On the other side of the door, Corkren motioned for dispatcher Kathy Ann James to hurry over. Hutsell watched while the three women gawked at Hadley as he walked down the hall and disappeared into the restroom.

"Did you see how long his legs are?" asked Corkren.

"No, sorry. I was looking a little higher—at how well his jeans fit," replied James.

"Did anyone get the color of his eyes?"

Rankin, still playing along answered, "I believe that's what my mom called Paul Newman Blue . . . now I finally get what she was talking about."

"Mouth breathers, everyone," muttered Hutsell. "I'll get the water, Trish. It seems to have slipped your mind. I'll meet you and Hadley in the investigation room."

The door to the restroom opened, scattering Corkren and James.

"We've got things laid out down the hall. If you would follow me," Rankin said. She turned to lead the way.

"Yes, ma'am." Hadley picked up his coat and the evidence box. He followed her down the hall.

"After we heard from you, we were contacted by a detective in Elko, Nevada," said Hutsell as Hadley deposited his box on the table. "He's got a similar case from 2014."

Rankin watched Hadley as he surveyed the display board. Three pictures of women were posted across the top with names, locations and dates under each. Kerry Donlan, Hadley's contribution, was first in line. Arrows were drawn linking each woman to pictures of corresponding murder victims and related anniversaries.

"How well did you know her?" Rankin asked.

"We went to high school together. She was a year behind me.

Kerry was beautiful—inside and out. She struggled in school and after a semester of junior college she decided not to return and instead went to work at a department store cosmetics counter. In fact all three victims, Kerry, her twin brother, Kelly and Zach Rydell were friends of mine."

"You talk about her in the past tense," observed Rankin.

"Three weeks after the murder of her brother, Kerry received another Halloween card for the Thanksgiving holiday. It was too much—she couldn't stand the thought of another person dying because of her and she took her own life."

Hutsell and Rankin looked at each other.

Hadley noticed the exchange. "What?"

"John suggested earlier today that the perpetrator's objective might be to drive his targets to suicide," Trish said. She handed Hadley the card Janssen had received the day before and pointed to the handwritten note. "He talks about other girlfriends leaving him. We know relocation doesn't stop him—he's continuing to stalk Janssen after her move—so what happened to the others? How did they 'leave' him?"

"What about the woman in Nevada—is she living?" asked Hadley.

"Let's call Elko and find out," said Hutsell. He referred to his notes and made the call.

"Jenny Newkirk died of an overdose two days after St. Patrick's Day in 2015—self-induced," reported Hutsell.

"And later that year, in October, Janssen's childhood friend, Rob Prasser, is murdered," Hadley said, referencing Hutsell's arrangement on the white board. "After Newkirk's death, he needed someone new and he settled on Janssen. It makes since, John."

"Yeah, but what about 2013?" asked Hutsell. "There's a gap between the murder of your schoolmate in 2012 and Newkirk's friend, Victor Arhens in 2014?"

"Standard reasons often suggested for such a hiatus are that the doer might have been incarcerated or out of the country?" said Rankin.

"Or there's another victim we don't know about," proposed Hadley.

"You might very well be right," Rankin said. She checked her watch. "Gentlemen, I suggest we call it a night and start fresh in the morning."

"Rick, have you got a place to stay?" Hutsell asked.

"I've got a room at the Sheraton a few miles west of here. What time do you want to meet tomorrow?"

"Is nine am good for you?" questioned Rankin.

"Yes, ma'am."

"Okay, new rule," Rankin said. "From here on out you're Rick and I'm Trish—that is until I have to pull 'rank'."

"And you expect me not to say 'yes ma'am' to that statement?" Hadley asked with a smile.

"Let's just say, it's implied and move on," she answered, smiling back.

"I'll leave you two to secure the area, then," Hadley told the St. Louis detectives. "Good night."

The Tennessee deputy stopped on his way out to return his visitor's badge. He thanked Corkren for her assistance and inquired about local restaurants.

"What type of fare are you thinking about?" she asked.

"Something fast but not standard fast food."

"You like bar-b-que?"

"Who doesn't?" Hadley smiled.

Corkren pulled a take-out menu from the bottom drawer of her desk. "The number's at the bottom. Call and place your order to go. It'll be ready when you walk through the door. Have a good evening, deputy."

"Thank you," he said. "By the way, you've got some pretty impressive detectives here in St. Louis."

"Detective Rankin's home-grown but Detective Hutsell is an import from Springfield. With his work on the Cross Timbers Murder several years back, he could have gone anywhere. Fortunate for us, he chose the Gateway City."

Hadley tapped the left upper portion of his chest in reference to the duty officer's name tag. "Well, Officer Corkren, here's hoping you have a quiet night."

"Enjoy your dinner, sir."

Corkren watched Hadley on the closed- circuit feed as he put on his coat before walking out the door. Shannon County, Tennessee, Sheriff was emblazoned across the back. *Hmmm . . . no wedding ring. My, my, my, but for a young, single woman, I can see where living in Tennessee would have its advantages . . ..*

9

Rick sat down in front of his laptop in the hotel room. He typed John Hutsell's name into the search bar and watched as the first page of results popped up. He read a couple of articles to get background on the detective from Springfield, Missouri, before streaming "The Cross Timbers Murder" episode of *Murder in the Fifty*. The program featured one murder from each of the fifty states in the order in which the states joined the union. The "Cross Timbers Murder" was number twenty-four in the series.

The episode began with an interview by Reporter Tim Bower with retired Greene County Deputy Harlan Price in his home near Wilson's Creek National Battlefield, just outside Springfield, Missouri.

"I called him the College Kid 'cause he'd gone to a fancy school out east. I admit I didn't put much stock in Hutsell when he started with the sheriff's department. Even though he was a local boy, the guy had several strikes against him before he even walked through the door."

"Would you care to elaborate?" Bower asked.

"Well, the kid had connections," explained Price as he sat at the head of a dining table. "Many of us wondered if he had the ability to be a good investigator or was the main reason he'd landed the job due to the fact his mother is a sitting Missouri state senator. And it didn't help that he'd come from money. His grandfather, Leland Nelson, was a successful contractor in the area, and the old man had really raked in the dough when the music theatre business took off in Branson in the early 1990s."

"So, how did the 'College Kid' gain your respect?"

"For one thing, he didn't complain about doing grunt work," replied the deputy. "And he knew how to gnaw a bone. He kept after it till it turned to dust. Then one day, the two of us were coming out of a restaurant, and there by the door was a missing persons poster from three years earlier. When we got to the cruiser, Hutsell asked about the case of missing Josenda Waters."

A narrator took over telling the story while pictures and video played on the screen. On August 19, 2010, elementary school teacher Josenda Waters didn't report to work. It was to be the young teacher's first day in the classroom. Waters was looking forward to getting to know her twenty-three second graders and had spent the previous two days preparing for their arrival. When school officials couldn't reach Ms. Waters they telephoned her personnel record's emergency contact, Heather Stanley. Ms. Stanley, a massage therapist, was in Colorado taking a neuromuscular massage training course and could not provide investigators with information on Waters' whereabouts. She did supply them with the name of Waters' boyfriend, Kevin Deken.

Deken was the next person to be interviewed on the show.

"I last saw Josie on Wednesday, August 18, 2010, at dinner. We met after work at Bambino's Café, close to the Missouri State University campus. She was so excited about the first day of teaching—she was finally going to have her own classroom. We made an early night of it because she wanted to make sure everything was ready for the next day. You know, laying out her clothes, packing her book bag—those kinds of things. I called her the next morning, but she didn't answer. I just figured she was busy so I left a voice message."

Deken's story was backed up by staff at the restaurant, his roommate, and cell phone records.

Authorities checked with Waters' parents, other family members, and friends. No one had heard from her since early evening on Wednesday, the eighteenth. An all-points bulletin was issued for her car, a silver 2006 Toyota Prius.

Deputy Price came back on the screen.

"One of our deputies found Waters' unlocked car on the side of US Route 65 just before the highway enters Christian County. Her cell phone was on the passenger seat in plain view, but Waters was nowhere around. Techs searched the phone for bits of information that might help locate her. There were several unanswered calls and texts but what gave us hope was a series of pictures taken the night she went missing."

"What clues did the photos provide?" Bower asked.

"Well, the first one was a shot of damage done to her left rear bumper. The next picture showed the right front of another car that had also sustained damage. The next two frames were of a man's driver's license and insurance card. From these clues we were able to ascertain she'd been in an accident."

"Was the man involved a suspect in her disappearance?"

"Not for long," the deputy stated. "Brent Inman was a local business man and well known in the area for his community service work. I interviewed him myself and his story checked out."

"What was his story?"

"Yes, he had rear-ended Ms. Waters' car on his way to his family's cabin on Table Rock Lake on the night in question. He and Waters had pulled off the road—it was still daylight—and the two exchanged insurance information. He reported the accident to his insurance company immediately, and since both cars were still drivable, he and Ms. Waters went their separate ways."

"And the evidence bore out his statement?"

"Yes, it did."

The narrator told of investigators' questions and Mr. Inman's answers concerning activities on the evening of August eighteenth. Inman had stopped at a convenience store just before getting onto Highway 65. He'd purchased an ice cream treat known as a Drumstick along with a diet soda. Video obtained showed Inman exiting the store as Josenda Waters was entering her car after filling it with gas. A few miles down the road, Inman dropped the Drumstick which caused him to swerve, resulting in a collision with Waters' vehicle.

Inman and his wife had argued earlier in the evening, so he'd decided to stay the night in their lake-side cabin. Deputy Price found the receipt and ice cream wrapper from Inman's purchase in the cabin's trash can. Inman had shut down his cell for the night—in essence to stave off calls from his wife. When the phone went back on line the next morning, tower records showed he was in Branson, Missouri, and credit card receipts confirmed he had eaten breakfast in the city.

"Sure, there were several hours we could not definitely pinpoint Inman's whereabouts, but we tested his car. There was ice cream residue on the floor board as well as his shirt and slacks. We went so far as to take pictures of him only in his skivvies to make sure there were no scratches or bruises that might have resulted from a struggle with Waters. If he had tried to abduct her and if she had tried to fight him off, there was nothing to show for it."

"And the question had to be asked," said the reporter. "If he had been responsible for Waters' disappearance, why would he have left her cell phone with his information and picture where it could be found?"

"Exactly," added Price. "The story was big news. If anyone had seen anything suspicious, he or she never came forward. So, three years later when the 'Kid' asked if he could look into the case, I let him have at it."

Rick paused the program to answer a call from his father.

"How's it going, son?"

"I'm settled in for the night, but from what I've seen so far, I'm pretty sure this case is connected to ours. The anniversary greeting card angle is so unique, it almost seals the deal."

"Have you seen any evidence that our guy is involved?" the elder Hadley asked.

"No, not yet. I might find something tomorrow, though."

"By the way, your mother says, 'Hi'."

Rick grinned. "Tell her I said, 'Hey'."

He looked over at his computer's screen.

"You know, Dad, this St. Louis detective, John Hutsell, is two years younger than me and is already kind of a celebrity in Missouri."

"How so?"

"He solved a cold case in a town southwest of here several years back, and there is a TV show about him that aired on The True Crime Investigations Channel. I was steaming it when you called. I'll send a link so you and Mom can watch it. *Homicide Hunter* on Investigation Discovery just might have some competition."

"Not where your mother is concerned," Mike Hadley said with a laugh.

Rick heard his mom ask what was so funny.

"Your son thinks he's working with a young Joe Kenda. He's sending us a link to a video about him."

"Ask our son if the young man in question has any good one-liners?" requested Sylvia Hadley. "Kenda's in reruns, and I need some new witty remarks so I can create more posts for Lieutenant Joe Kenda Memes on Facebook."

"I heard her," answered Rick. "Tell Mom I'll conduct a thorough investigation and let her know. She's not to worry—I *will* take copious notes."

"Okay, check in with me tomorrow evening. Good night."

"Will do. Night to you and Mom."

Rick went to the vending machine down the hall and got a cold bottle of water before resuming the video.

Price was talking as a desk covered with files and photos appeared on the screen.

"Hutsell reviewed the case files in chronological order. He then set about re-interviewing persons connected to the case in hopes of developing new leads. The Kid was very methodical."

The camera focused on one picture in particular—a group shot of Waters, Stanley, and friends attending an outdoors get-together.

"We had previously questioned Ms. Stanley about a man who seemed to be lurking in the background of every photo Waters appeared in at a Memorial Day cookout in Springfield the previous year," Price said as more pictures came into view.

"The guy was Justin Yates, Stanley's half-brother—but she had assured us early on there wasn't a connection between him and Waters. Yates had been reluctant to be interviewed—Stanley said it was because growing up their mother would tell them the police would lock them up if they misbehaved. Stanley did arrange for her half-brother to meet with us; she actually accompanied him to the department. But it turned out Ms. Stanley hadn't been completely honest with us."

"In what way?" Bower asked.

"Well, John looked up Stanley, who by this time was living in Wichita, Kansas. He began by asking routine questions. She reacted by saying he was going over ground that had already been covered and accusing John of wanting to make an arrest—any arrest, just to close the case."

"What was Deputy Hutsell's reaction?"

"John decided he'd just have a conversation with Yates himself—this time without his protective half-sister in tow."

"And how did that go?"

"First of all, let me say this about John Hutsell. He can go for the jugular if he has to, but for the most part, the impression one gets upon meeting him is that he's a nice guy." Price smiled and explained. "He does this thing with his eyebrows, where one goes higher than the other and it's 'endearing', so my wife says. Yeah, it could be considered his attempt at disarming someone, but it's definitely not something one would describe as threatening. Yet, Yates could barely hold it together when John asked to speak with him at the library where he worked, even though witnesses said John was polite and genial in his approach."

"What was Hutsell's next move?"

"He arranged to speak with Yates in a room at the library with the door open. Remember, he's just asking basic, routine questions at this time. Not too far into the interview, Yates yelled, 'I'm sorry! I didn't know! I thought she liked me!'"

Price leaned forward, folded his hands and brought them calmly down on the table.

"A librarian came running and told John to leave Yates alone. So now, Hutsell's got a man more or less confessing to being involved in a missing woman case and at least two women running interference. John doesn't have a choice now. He has no jurisdiction—he has to get local law enforcement involved, so he places the call. A few minutes later, Heather Stanley shows up. The librarian had phoned her soon after John had requested to speak with Yates. Stanley tried to barge her way into the room. John put his hands up indicating she needed to remain outside and informed her police were en route."

"Did Stanley comply?"

"She began crying and told John, "'You don't understand. He has Asperger's.'"

"What can you tell us about Asperger's?" the interviewer asked.

"It's a type of autism. Those with Asperger Syndrome are considered to be high-functioning on the autistic spectrum. Justin Yates was diagnosed with Asperger Syndrome when he was in middle school. It affects Yates social interaction and communication skills," Price explained. "Josenda Waters was nice to Justin Yates. He misinterpreted her kindness and thought she was romantically interested in him. He began showing up at Waters' part-time job several times a week, and she began 'running into him' in a grocery store parking lot more often than casual acquaintances should. Waters became somewhat unnerved and spoke to Ms. Stanley about the situation. Once Yates understood his actions were inappropriate, he discontinued them. Heather Stanley had spent most of her life protecting her younger brother from bullies and those looking to use him as a scapegoat. Yates wasn't involved in the disappearance of Waters. It was unfortunate for all involved that his sister hadn't been forthcoming early on in the investigation."

"So, back to the drawing board."

"Yep. The Kid came back home, opened the files and started all over again."

"When did the case start to move from the unsolved column?"

"John went to interview Brent Inman again. This was John's second interview with the man. Inman was sitting by his pool watching his two sons and their friends having a good time over the Labor Day weekend. Inman was as cooperative as he had always been in the past so his demeanor didn't set off any alarms, but there was something different about him."

"What had changed?" queried the host.

"Inman had acquired a tattoo of a cross on his upper chest since pictures had been taken of him the day after Waters went missing. Not just any cross, but one like those often seen in a Christian church."

"People get religious tattoos all the time. What was it about this one that Hutsell found suspect?"

"It was the Bible reference that was written on the horizontal timber of the cross; Matthew thirty-seven, verses one through twelve. You have to remember, John was educated in a school where every classroom had a crucifix. He had attended religion classes for twelve years and he couldn't place Matthew, chapter thirty-seven, let alone verses one through twelve.

"Back at the department he conducted an online search and found the last chapter in Matthew is twenty-eight. Something in Denmark was starting to stink. One of Hutsell's high-school friends was with the Secret Service and in Springfield at the time. John consulted with Greg Baptiste about the case while Baptiste was home visiting family."

The next scene showed a handsome black man sitting on the bleachers of a high-school football stadium. Next to him sat a news correspondent, Lauren Tomboc.

"John Hutsell and I have been friends since kindergarten," Baptiste informed the woman interviewing him.

"What was he like growing up?" Tomboc asked.

"Dependable—had a good work ethic—a live by the golden rule kind of guy," answered Baptiste. "He's always been a visual learner. If he reads or sees something, for the most part he's 'got' it. Yet, when it came to the real world, he was oblivious to nuance—especially concerning humor. He's got a sense for it but back then it was almost like he couldn't be bothered with subtleties. He's worked hard to overcome that little imperfection in order to become a better investigator. We—his friends and family—don't have to say, 'Hut-one, hut-two' nearly as often as we used to."

"'Hut-one, hut-two'?"

"In high school, John's sport of choice was wrestling. But like a lot of athletes, he lettered in more than one sport. He had the moves that made for a good defensive end—probably due to the fact his grandmother owned a dance studio and she had him doing the waltz by the time he could count to three. In the end it worked out well for John. Girls like to dance, and they love guys who can. He rarely asked girls out. He didn't have to—they asked him."

Baptiste leaned back on the bleachers and smiled.

"'Hut-one, hut-two' is sort of a play on words concerning his last name," Baptiste continued. "We were sophomores in high school when a senior girl interviewed John about the wrestling team for an article in the school paper. Soon after the story appeared, she started showing up at meets. She also began sitting with us at other school events. One day, after a backyard football scrimmage, several of us went to get something to eat. We were sitting at a table outside a fast food restaurant—I was beside John—when she walked up and squeezed in between us. We all stared at her—well, with the exception of John. He went right on talking football. Finally, one of the guys tried to get John's attention to what was going on and said, 'Hey, Hutsell, hut-one, hut-two', and he moved his eyes back and forth between the girl and John. Finally, John *got it*."

Baptiste, dimples showing, shook his head from side to side and reiterated, "The term stuck. But, like I said, we don't have to, or should I say, 'get' to say it as often as we used to."

Tomboc was smiling as she brought the conversation back to the show's main topic.

"How did you get involved with the Josenda Waters case?"

"I was in Springfield for my grandmother's birthday. John attended the celebration. Later, we were sitting on my grandmother's front porch when he laid out the particulars of the Waters case. He'd been working on it off and on for about two months. We started listing all the ways numbers could be used—birthdays, pin numbers, GPS coordinates, codes, cyphers."

"And highways," added the reporter.

"And highways," Baptiste concurred. "John kicked it around before landing on an intersection southwest of Springfield in Barry County. Missouri State Highway 37 connects to Missouri Highway 112 in the town of Seligman, Missouri.

"Matthew: chapter *thirty-seven*, verses *one through twelve*," said Tomboc.

"Yes. And a few miles east of Seligman is the Mark Twain National Forest."

"A national forest," said the interviewer. "That's a big area to cover in hopes of finding a body."

"Exactly. Where to look?" questioned Baptiste. "John felt the answer would be found if he could remember what had been inscribed on the vertical timber of Inman's tattoo. But how was he going to find out without alarming Inman of his suspicions?"

Baptiste leaned forward and put his forearms on his knees before continuing.

"Turns out one of the dispatchers knew a woman who was friends with Inman on Facebook. His settings didn't allow just anyone to access his Facebook page, but since the dispatcher was friend of a friend, she could send a friend request. She did, he accepted and wouldn't you know, there was a picture of a shirtless Inman on the site. It took some enhancing but John now had another piece to the puzzle: the numbers five-point-five, eight-point-eight, and three-point-three."

"Very cryptic," Tomboc observed.

"Yes, ma'am, it was," agreed Baptiste.

After a commercial break, Tim Bower was back on the screen. He was sitting at a picnic table in the Mark Twain National Forest. Across from him sat an elderly man named Clayton Roberts.

"Mr. Roberts, how did you meet Deputy John Hutsell," Bowers asked.

"I was sitting in my jeep next to Sugar Camp Tower, drinking from a water jug I'd filled at home. You young guys might go for that bottled stuff, but that's 'cause you've never had well water,"

Roberts said. "Anyway, I was thinking back on how this spot was one of the tallest around and about the man who used to sit in this tower all day long with his wife and look for fires, when a black SUV drove up. He introduced himself as a Greene County Deputy and wanted to know if it was okay if he asked me a few questions about the area. I've lived here most all my life and figured if nothing else, I would enjoy telling him a good yarn or two.

"Deputy Hutsell told me all about a teacher who'd gone missing several years back. I remembered hearing about it on the news at the time, so I knew some of the particulars. He told me about some new evidence dealing with a cross tattoo and how he figured out some of the numbers on one of the timbers of the cross stood for roads. He'd noted the mileage when he turned off Highway 37 onto 112. And exactly five-point-five miles later was the turn-off for the Sugar Camp Scenic Drive. Five-point-five was one of the numbers on the other timber."

"Did the other numbers lead to turn-offs as well?" asked Bower.

"Well, Hutsell said he'd traveled another eight-point-eight miles down the road with nothing to show, and he hadn't had any luck with the number three-point-three, either. So, he just came right out and asked me if I wanted to hide a body in these woods, where would I hide it. I told him to hop in my jeep and I'd show him."

"And you brought him to this scenic overlook?"

"Yep. But to get to the hiding place, you've gotta take a trail that starts over there," Roberts said, pointing across the road. "I'm ninety years old and not fond of ticks, so I wasn't gonna take him to the spot. I just told him how to get there."

"I don't like ticks, either, but if I had come prepared, where would I find this 'spot'?"

"Right across the road there is a trail that leads down an embankment to Black Jack Cave. Not too far down, there's a sinkhole to the left. The hole is big enough for a man to get through but it's a vertical drop. As kids we would use a tree ladder to get down in there and back out."

"What's a tree ladder?" Bower asked.

"Well, you look for a tree with a lot of branches—sometimes we'd find one laying on the ground; if not, we'd cut one," explained Roberts. "Where the branches meet the trunk makes for a good place to put your foot. Kind of like those guys climbing up and down a telephone pole with metal spikes on the sides of the pole. Only instead of spikes, we stepped on branches. That way we could get down in the cave and back up again."

"The perfect place to hide a body," commented Bower.

"Dang if it ain't," Roberts agreed.

"Did you and Deputy Hutsell ever determine what the other numbers from the vertical timber referenced?" asked Bower.

"After Deputy Hutsell took a few pictures he asked if I would mind driving him to Highway112. We kept track of the mileage and it was exactly three-point-three miles from the trailhead to 112."

"Then eight-point-eight was the total of the other two numbers on the vertical timber?"

"Yep," answered Roberts. "Five-point-five miles to the turnoff. Three-point-three miles to the trailhead. Eight-point-eight miles all together."

The narrator did a voice over as video played of authorities, following up on Hutsell's work and Roberts' tips, brought what was left of Josenda Waters' body to the surface. The body of the young teacher had been wrapped in a magnetic gray winter car cover and dropped to the floor of the cave. Due to scavengers and conditions inside the cave, all that remained of Waters were bones, teeth, hair and clothing items.

Bower was back in Harlan Price's dining room as the deputy told about the arrest and trial of Brent Inman.

"The prosecutor got a break when Inman's childhood friend, Darren Knadler came forward to say he and Inman had vacationed with Knadler's grandparents in Cassville, Missouri, when the two friends were in high school. They had done a lot of hiking and camping the summer after their freshman year. One trail they'd hiked was the one that led to Black Jack Cave.

"But the district attorney still felt he needed more to put Inman behind bars," said Price. "So Hutsell visited Inman's wife, Brooke, and persuaded her to testify against him. Turned out Mrs. Inman had backed up her husband's story for three years out of fear. She admitted to John that Inman had been abusive throughout their marriage. John made her see that if Inman was sent away for life, she and her two sons would finally be free of him."

"How damaging was her testimony?" Bower asked.

"She was able to show he had an abusive personality through

medical records. She informed the jury her husband had always carried a magnetic winter car cover in his car's trunk but that it had disappeared around the time Waters went missing. She provided a picture of her sons smiling as each one attached the cover to the side windows of Inman's car the previous winter. She also testified she had been home when a new magnetic cover was delivered from an online purchase Inman had made in October 2010.

"You said earlier you had tested Inman's car. If he had been traipsing in the woods lugging a body, surely there would have been trace evidence in his vehicle," Bower speculated.

"Well, Brooke Inman provided the answer to that question, too," said Price. "Missing along with the car cover was a duffle bag Inman kept in his trunk. It had contained a set of clothes, including winter boots."

"You're not suggesting Brent Inman is another Dexter Morgan from the TV show, *Dexter*, are you?"

"Let's put it this way—Inman is a suspect in two other unsolved crimes in southwest Missouri and at least one in central Illinois where he'd spent summers with his father's family as a boy. *Dexter*—a kind of tongue-in-cheek horror show—was popular at the time. Who knows, maybe Inman was a fan."

The narrator informed viewers of Inman's conviction and sentence as video played of him being escorted to prison.

The program ended with a message of thanks from Josenda Waters' parents as photos of Waters and Deputy Hutsell filled the screen.

Hadley had read earlier that Hutsell had declined to appear in "The Cross Timbers Murder" episode of *Murder in the Fifty*— something he would have probably done in the same situation. The former Greene County Deputy had been described as a dog with a bone when it came to working a case. Hadley wondered if that tidbit about Hutsell might become an issue for him and the Shannon County, Tennessee, Sheriff's Department, because at this stage of the game, Rick Hadley wasn't ready to show all his cards.

10

Both Rankin and Hutsell were blowing steam off the tops of coffee cups in the detective squad room when Rankin's cell vibrated.

"Josh says to tell you good morning, John."

"Tell him it is a good morning but to bundle up. There's supposed to be a thirty-degree drop in temperature today."

"He says he will," said Rankin. "By the way, got some more information on Deputy Hadley."

"What kind of information? His relationship status for example?" Hutsell smiled and took a sip of hot coffee.

"Don't know about that, but I do know he's not just another pretty face." She flashed Hutsell a document she had composed the previous night and then began reading from it. "He's got a degree in criminal justice from the University of Tennessee at Martin."

"Oh, man, Hadley and I were almost classmates," Hutsell said. "I considered attending UT at Martin before deciding on John Jay."

"So why New York instead of Tennessee?"

"Don't get me wrong. My Mom's apron strings were never really tight. She was great to let me make my own way. But my family was/is in the public eye. Martin's about an hour across the Missouri–Tennessee line, and it just wasn't far enough."

"Understandable," Rankin replied. "After graduation Hadley landed in Oak Ridge, Tennessee's police department. He spent a few years on patrol, then completed the University of Tennessee's National Forensic Academy program and moved up to Oak Ridge's Criminal Investigations Division."

"That's a pretty intensive course, Trish."

"I know. He's also a member of the International Association for Identification," Rankin added. "Hadley stayed four more years in Oak Ridge before signing on as a detective with Knoxville's Forensics Unit."

"Tennessee?"

"Yes, John, Knoxville, Tennessee."

"Hey, don't judge too quickly, Trish. There is a Knoxville,

Missouri."

"Yeah, don't tell me . . . you know a cute . . . oh, hell, just fill in the blank when it comes to towns you know cute girls from, John."

Hutsell leaned back in his chair, put his hands behind his head, looked up and said, "She had a cute sister, too."

"You know I don't believe half of what comes out of your mouth, right?"

"Moving right along . . . .." Hutsell sat up and placed his elbows on the arms of his chair. "When did he sign on with Shannon County?"

"He was in Knoxville from 2010 to 2013," Rankin said. "To answer your question, he signed on with Shannon County in January, 2013, to be precise."

"Kerry Donlan killed herself November 28, 2012," he reminded his partner. "Interesting timing."

"Yes, it is. And here's another interesting bit for you. Daddy wasn't elected Sheriff of Shannon County until 2014 in a special election. So, Hadley's made his own way."

Two of their colleagues walked in and headed straight for the coffee pot. Hutsell wheeled his chair closer to his desk.

"I worked on the case last night, too. Gail wants convincing evidence so I comprised a list of tie-ins for the three primary victims. I sent it to you late last night. Look it over and see what you think. We can add, take away, or present as is," Hutsell stated. He rose and made his way to the investigation room.

Rankin turned to her computer and brought up Hutsell's email. She opened the attached document.

Janssen, Donlan, Newkirk Cases
Three stalked (primary) victims; six murdered (secondary) victims

MO
1. Greeting cards sent every traditional holiday.
2. Greeting cards are always Halloween cards, regardless of which holiday is being observed.
3. Cards arriving on or about October 31, depending on mail service:
   a. Reference Day(s) of the Dead.
   b. Reference an anniversary; first, second, third.

c. Include a photo of a murdered friend, family member, etc. of the primary victim.

d. The murder victim's death is in accordance with each anniversary; paper, cotton, leather.

Motive: Drive primary victims to suicide?

1. Kerry Donlan. Death: November 28, 2012. Method: CO_2 poisoning, car in garage.
2. Jenny Newkirk. Death: March 17, 2015. Method: Drug overdose, self-induced.
3. Lydia Janssen. Has considered suicide. In her words, ". . . have come close a time or two."

Rankin closed the document, refreshed her coffee and walked to the bull pen to join Hutsell.

"It's a pretty compelling document, John. We've got a big case here," she said.

"Yeah, we better have our act together at every turn," he responded. "I feel a lot better knowing Hadley's got the education and experience needed to assist."

"Well, we need to make it clear he is *assisting* in this investigation." Rankin said.

"You know what the big problem is, right?" Hutsell asked.

"Yes. Ours is a stalking case. Tennessee, Nevada, and Arkansas are homicide cases," Rankin answered. "But it's here in Missouri where the killer is anteing up. He's pursuing a St. Louis resident and starting to make mistakes, so we stand the best chance of catching him. We have jurisdiction. We own this one, John."

"I just hope our stalking victim doesn't go the same route of his previous victims."

"Janssen's considered suicide, but so far dismissed it," said Rankin.

"Yeah, she's held it together longer than any of the others, Trish. But be realistic. How much more can she take? If she commits suicide, he's accomplished his goal. Then we lose him, and he's off looking for another victim."

"Oooh, if that ain't a pretty evidence board," came a voice from the doorway.

"Hello, Joe, how's your morning going?" questioned Rankin.

"Can't complain. Your case is crossing state lines, huh?" Kleeman asked as he continued to study the board. "I couldn't help but overhear—you really think this guy's motive is to get women to 'off' themselves?"

"Two out of three have, Joe," said Rankin.

"He's one sick son-of-a-bitch," declared Kleeman. "Don't envy you two this one. Good luck."

"Time to present our case, partner. Let's see if Vashon is free," said Rankin.

Rick Hadley walked into St. Louis Police Department's University District building at 8:50 A.M. Two men were standing at the hallway leading off the lobby's entrance. One was in plain clothes; the other sported a police uniform. The uniformed officer turned to Hadley and asked if he needed assistance.

"Yes, sir, I'm Deputy Sheriff Rick Hadley from Shannon County, Tennessee, here to see Detectives Rankin and Hutsell.

"You're the guy who brought in the Juliet Case from Tennessee," said the man in street clothes.

"'Juliet Case'?" questioned Hadley.

"Yeah, there's beautiful young women around the country being driven to suicide, right? 'Juliets'. Get it?"

Before Hadley could answer, the man in uniform said, "Right this way, Deputy. Let's get you signed in, and then I'll escort you to the detective division."

Once on their way and out of ear shot, the officer spoke, "I'm Gabe Fenske. I was in charge of making sure your files were handled properly."

"Who's the guy you were talking to? Is he working the Janssen Case in addition to Rankin and Hutsell?"

"Detective Joe Kleeman and no, he's not. In fact, John Hutsell's not going to like the 'Juliet' label one bit. He feels such designations dehumanizes victims. Kleeman's got a tough shell. I call it a cop's armor. He's a good investigator, though."

The two men entered the room that housed the detective unit. The place was in full swing with detectives working their own, separate cases. Fenske spied Rankin and Hutsell in Lt. Vashon's office. He caught Rankin's attention. She acknowledged him with a nod.

"Detectives Rankin and Hutsell are in a meeting right now," Fenske informed Hadley. He led the deputy to a desk and motioned to a nearby chair. "If you'll have a seat, they will be with you shortly."

"Thank you, Officer Fenske."

"My pleasure," Fenske replied. Hadley dipped his head to hide a smile. "I see they have Chick-Fil-A in Tennessee, too," he said, referencing the restaurant chain's signature 'you're welcome' phrase.

"That they do, sir," said Hadley. "That they do."

Hadley sat down and surveyed the scene. He was reminded of his days in Knoxville. It had been an adjustment, moving from a big city law enforcement agency to that of a rural county. He hadn't been involved in near as many major cases in Shannon County as he had during his Knoxville tenure. One advantage rural had over big city was that residents didn't just go to work, come home, and lock the world out. They paid attention to the comings and goings of their neighbors—and strangers stood out. There were residents who stood out, too . . . one in particular came to mind . . . .

Hadley knew he was thought of as a hometown boy by many, even though he hadn't moved to Eagle Ridge, Shannon County's seat, until the age of fifteen, when his father had retired from the army. This worked in his favor for the most part. But with amity came familiarity, and if there's one thing Hadley had learned since his return, it was that gossip dies a slow death.

Lately, Hadley'd been questioning his decision to return home. Had the move been worth it? He'd spent the past five years investigating his friends' deaths, and still had nothing to show for his efforts. Then, unrelated to the case, there was the personal cost— one issue in particular that never took a holiday—one that was there every moment of every day.

Rick Hadley leaned forward in the chair, clasped his hands between his knees and stared at the floor. He thought of St. Jude, the patron saint of desperation and wished he could remember more than just a few lines of St. Jude's Novena that had brought him peace and comfort as a child.

"Penny for your thoughts, Deputy," said Rankin as she and

Hutsell approached him.

Hadley stood up and replied with a smile, "Sorry, but due to inflation, it's going to cost you two-bits."

"You were in deep thought there, Rick," observed Hutsell.

"Just wondering what the common denominator is between the primary victims," Hadley said. "How does he choose them? Where does he meet them? Social media? Through his work?"

"Our lieutenant just agreed that the three cases are related and so the investigation is now at full throttle. What do you say we head to the investigation room and look for that connection?" suggested Rankin.

"I'm going for coffee first," said Hutsell. "Anyone with a like mind can get in step."

"Right behind you," said Hadley.

"You've got good credentials, Rick," said Hutsell as he handed Hadley a Styrofoam cup. "I visited the UT campus at Martin when you were a senior. We were almost schoolmates. It's got a good reputation."

Hutsell poured coffee into Hadley's cup, then refilled his own as the deputy responded with a smile, "John Jay's not bad, either." He took a sip, testing the temperature. "Glad that's out of the way."

Hutsell turned his head toward Hadley, "Yeah, you gotta know who you're working with . . . especially when the first Hadley who pops up on the Shannon County Sheriff's website is named Mike."

Rick smiled. "Hadley is a familiar name in law enforcement in eastern Tennessee. The question, 'Who's clinging to whose coattails?' has been asked more than once." The two men headed for the investigation room. "You had to move out from behind a well-known shadow yourself, John."

"You saw it, then?" Hutsell said, referring to "The Cross Timbers Murder" episode of *Murder in the Fifty*.

"Streamed it last night," Hadley admitted. "And, John, my mom has a request."

Hutsell stopped walking and looked at Hadley, "And that would be . . .?"

"She's a Joe Kenda fan. Are you familiar with him?" Hadley asked. Using the index finger on the hand holding his cup, he pointed to their destination and began walking again.

"Yeah, my Aunt Jean is a huge fan."

"Mom needs some one-liners so she can create a new meme for a Kenda group on Facebook," said Hadley as they entered the bull pen. "She's hoping you've got a few to pass on."

"Ask Trish. She's got a page book-marked online she refers to if I don't show up bright-eyed and bushy-tailed," Hutsell said.

"Ask Trish what?" said Rankin.

"For law enforcement one-liners for Rick's mom."

"Okay, here's one. 'I'm *glad* the Chief of Police is a personal friend of yours. At least you know *someone* who can post your bail.'"

Hadley's chest heaved as he stifled a laugh.

"Pretty funny, huh?" asked Rankin.

"Yep, especially when you consider my dad was Chief of Police in Eagle Ridge before he became Shannon County Sheriff."

"Oops," said Trish.

"Nah, she'll love it," Rick assured her.

The room went silent as all three law enforcement officials studied the display board.

"He hasn't got a type," Hadley said after several minutes. "Hair color and style, height, age—all different."

"One thing that is the same is that they are all beautiful," observed Hutsell.

"That's true. And he's not like the Green River Killer from the Seattle area where all were local victims—our guy is all over the map," added Rankin, leaning back against the table. "Rick, did your investigation ever develop a suspect?"

"There was a guy we looked at early on, but we could never put him in the right place at the right time."

"What was it about him that caught your attention?" asked Trish.

"Kerry heard a noise outside her window one night and told her dad. He investigated and found footprints. Two nights later, her brother, Kelly, was taking the trash bin to the curb when he saw a figure between his house and the neighbor's. Kelly pretended to go back in the garage, but instead sneaked around and tackled the guy."

"Who was he?" questioned Hutsell.

"A guy we'd gone to school with. He's a couple years younger than me," said Hadley. "He's different, you know what I mean? He has some medical problems and poor social skills. He's been made fun of most of his life. Kelly gave him a black eye that night and he didn't bother Kerry again. That was in 2004 when I was at UT."

"What made you drop him as a suspect?" asked Rankin.

"He worked at a hotel in Gatlinburg. Kelly's body was found in an Eagle Ridge cemetery at 8:30 A.M. on October twenty-ninth, two days before Halloween of 2012. Witnesses said our guy worked a double shift on the days in question. He normally worked evenings from 4 P.M. to midnight. But on October twenty-ninth, he'd agreed to stay and take over the midnight shift for an employee whose daughter had been hospitalized. He couldn't have been the doer for two reasons. Kelly's autopsy showed he had died the night of October twenty-ninth, and that picture on your board was taken before dawn. Everyone agreed it wasn't him."

Hutsell walked over to the evidence board and looked closely at the murder photo of Kelly Donlan. Next, he studied that of Zach Rydell.

"Notice anything different about these two photos compared to the other victims?" he asked.

"The Tennessee bodies have wooden crosses above their heads," observed Rankin.

"He's not Catholic," said John.

"What makes you say that?" asked Trish.

"They're empty crosses," answered Hutsell.

"What's that got to do with it?" she continued.

"A Catholic would have put a crucifix," said Hadley. "A cross with the body of Christ."

"You Catholic, Rick?"

"Yep. Lapsed, but it's the religion I would check on a questionnaire."

"Okay, if he's not Catholic, then why the Day of the Dead reference with each murder photo?" Trish questioned.

"Rick, you want this one?" asked Hutsell.

"Prejudice might be one reason. And like most prejudices, the animosity shown toward Catholics stems from ignorance," answered Hadley.

"'Splain, Ricky," Trish said out of habit. All three of them smiled.

"Damn, Trish, you finally have a real 'Ricky' to ask," said Hutsell.

"Guess that means I've got some ''splainin'' to do," said a still-smiling Rick Hadley. "Anti-Catholic prejudice stems from myths and misconceptions for the most part," he said. "Catholics don't worship Mary for example. We revere her, we honor her, but we don't worship her—or any saint for that matter."

"What about the Hail Mary thing?"

"John?" said Rick, passing back the buck.

"It comes from scripture, mostly from Luke," reported Hutsell. "But I think you might be asking if Catholics don't worship Mary, why do they pray to her? The simplest way to put it is to ask the question, 'Do people ask others to pray for them?' Of course they do. All the time. So what is wrong with asking the same of Mary?"

"There are a host of other reasons people site to justify their prejudice against Catholics as well as Muslims and other religious groups," added Hadley. "And don't forget entities like the KKK, who include Catholics in their hate rhetoric. Maybe our unsub is anti-Catholic, maybe not. But it is something we need to consider."

"What about the primary victims?" asked Trish. "Janssen is Catholic, what about the others?"

"Kerry was," said Rick.

"Guess I need to make another call to Nevada," said John.

"While you do that, I'll touch base with Janssen," Rankin added.

"How much does she know about the investigation—is she aware of Kerry and Newkirk?" questioned Hadley.

"John and I decided to keep mum about other victims until we got approval from Lieutenant Vashon. Janssen doesn't need all the details, but she needs to be kept in the loop. After all, there's more to go on now. We've got a better chance of catching him than anyone ever has. Besides she may be able to come up with a link between her and the other two."

"So at this stage, background only, right?" asked Hadley. Rankin nodded. "I know I'm not officially a part of your investigation, but for my two cents worth, I agree."

"Ummm, Deputy Hadley?"

"Yes ma'am?"

"I believe that will be four bits in today's market.

11

Batter up! He had just spied his next mark. A man akin to him in age and physical attributes. One who had three kids and a wife in tow. One who wanted to save fifteen percent by opening a store credit card. His two oldest kids, probably seven and five in age, were playing tag and other customers were already giving him dirty looks.

"Honey, what's my Social again?" the man asked his wife as she struggled with a fussy infant.

The wife rattled off the number as he recorded the man's Social Security number on his cell while pretending to compose a text. Dad had just put his driver's license back in his wallet when his kids knocked over a display, and the chase was on. Daddy went in pursuit, leaving his wallet on the counter. Easy as pie. Walk up, place clothes on the counter, lean in, interrupt the clerk and palm the wallet.

"Excuse me, ma'am, where's your bathroom?"

The clerk glanced at him and pointed to her right and said, "That way, behind the elevators."

"Thank you."

He headed for the restroom, placing the clothes on a chair in the shoe department on his way. Inside the second stall, he removed the license only, leaving the man's credit cards in their appointed slots. *Don't forget the finishing touch.* He turned and flushed the toilet before exiting.

Back in shoes, he picked up the clothes and walked to the counter. Once again, he leaned in, interrupted the clerk and asked directions to the bathroom, depositing the wallet before walking away. Four minutes later, someone made an announcement.

"Would Mr. Trent Tolliver please report to the shoe department? Trent Tolliver, to shoes, please."

From his vantage point, he watched Daddy make his way to the shoe counter where the clerk handed him his wallet. Daddy immediately opened it and heaved a heavy sigh seeing that his credit cards were all in place. *How lucky can you get?* The beauty was, the man's driver's license was an afterthought. Odds were Daddy wouldn't notice it was gone until he was asked to present it for some transaction, and that might not happen until he went to the bank. Then he'd rack his brain for the last time he'd seen it. He might remember having it out when he applied for today's credit card. Then again, he might not. If he did, he'd also recall the incident with his kids and figure he had neglected to put it back in his wallet. Before long he would just throw up his hands, go to the DMV, report it lost and apply for a new one.

On his way home, he hoped Tolliver hadn't arranged for notification every time his Social Security number was used to apply for a credit card. He would wait about a month before applying for one online in Tolliver's name. He smiled, remembering how things always seemed to fall into place for him. Here he was, in need of another identity as he only had a few 'appropriated' ones left. And low and behold, God had provided him with an opportunity to acquire one.

The rain promised by a phone app began to fall. He switched on his wipers and smiled at the sun shining through gaps in the clouds. As he turned down his street, he noticed a rainbow off to his right— God truly was pleased with him.

12

"I can't reach her," blurted Rankin as she stuck her head in the doorway of the investigation room.

"Did you try the hotel where she's staying?" Hutsell asked.

"Yes, they said she's checked out."

"Damn! Get your coat, Trish."

Rankin followed Hutsell's thought. "I hope to hell she hasn't . . .."

"I'm a licensed EMT," said Hadley.

Rankin looked at Hutsell with her eyebrows raised. Hutsell nodded.

"Come on. We'll drop you at your vehicle, and you can follow us."

John Hutsell drove while his partner continued to try to reach Lydia Janssen by phone. A few blocks from the station, he checked the clock on the dash. The trip to Janssen's would normally take twenty minutes at this time of day; he was determined to cut it in half. He pulled down the car's visor and hit the controller on the back of the visor light bar. Red and blue lights began flashing moving motorists out of way.

"Is he keeping up?" asked Rankin.

"Yes," answered Hutsell. Nine minutes later, he rounded the corner onto East Redbud Drive. "Everything looks tranquil."

"That can be good *or* bad," said Rankin. She pocketed her cell phone.

The unmarked car had barely stopped when the occupants exited the vehicle. Hadley parked on the street.

Rankin called out, "Deputy—."

"I got it—backup status," he said.

Rankin and Hutsell moved quickly and positioned themselves on either side of Janssen's front door. Hadley lagged behind.

Rankin pounded on the door and yelled, "Ms. Janssen, are you there?"

When there was no answer, Hutsell stepped up.

"Ms. Janssen," he shouted, "if you are there, please open the door."

"There's movement behind the curtain," said Hadley, peering in the bungalow's kitchen window.

Rankin tried again. "Ms. Janssen——."

"I can see her," Hadley said. "Can't tell for sure, but she seems to be alone. No visible signs of injury. Just a blank stare."

"Ms. Janssen. Open the door or we *will* break it down," Hutsell said loudly.

"What's going on?" called out a lady from across the street.

"Go inside, ma'am, and stay until further notice," instructed Rankin.

"She hasn't moved, detectives," Hadley added.

Hutsell took up where he'd left off. "Okay, Ms. Janssen. On the count of three, this door is coming down."

"Go away!" yelled Lydia.

"One . . . two . . .."

"Okay! Okay! I'm coming."

"Can you see anyone else, Rick?" Rankin asked.

"No, but she *is* moving towards the door. No weapon that I can see. Her hands are empty."

Lydia Janssen opened the front door and without even a casual glance at the investigators, turned her back on them and walked back toward the kitchen.

"We couldn't reach you," said Rankin as they gathered round the dining table. Janssen took a seat across from the sink. Hutsell and his partner moved to either side of her. "The hotel said you were no longer a guest."

"I couldn't stay there indefinitely."

"You didn't answer your phone." Rankin looked at Janssen's cell on the table.

"It's turned off. I don't want to be disturbed. So, you've come, you've seen, you've conquered. Now you can leave."

There was movement at the entryway. Lydia turned her head and saw a tall man clad in a white shirt and jeans.

"Who're you?" she asked with contempt.

"Deputy Sheriff Rick Hadley from Shannon County, Tennessee."

"You allowing drive-alongs now, detectives?" she said without taking her eyes off Hadley. She watched as his gaze shifted to the six pill bottles she had lined up next to the sink. "None of your business, Tennessee."

"In a way it is," responded Hadley. "I knew someone like you once."

"Oh, really? You knew a woman who was being stalked by a madman who murdered her friends and family and then presented their bodies as anniversary presents?" she said. She turned away from him and stared straight ahead.

"Yes, ma'am, I did. Her name was Kerry Donlan. And she did what you are thinking about doing now."

Both Rankin and Hutsell watched as Janssen closed her eyes and slowly dropped her head.

"May I come in?" Hadley asked.

Janssen nodded yes. Rick Hadley walked into the kitchen, stopped a few feet in front of Lydia, and crouched down. She looked at him and saw the same pain in his eyes she'd felt for the last three and a half years.

"Who was she?"

"A friend. So was her brother and former boyfriend. He paused and watched Janssen clasp her hands tight enough to stop the blood flow. "Please . . . help us stop him, Ms. Janssen."

Lydia's eyes drifted back to the orange bottles with the white caps, "I'm tired, Tennessee."

"I know."

"I want it over, but it never will be . . . not even when he's dead and gone."

"I know that, too."

"Then why are you here?" she asked, still focused on the pill bottles.

"The pain and hurt he has caused is almost unbearable. But what is even more unbearable is the thought of him causing more."

"I can't fight him anymore."

"You have the three of us now."

"Others have tried. Nothing has worked."

Hadley stood and looked at Rankin and Hutsell and mouthed, "Can I tell her?" The partners turned to each other. There was no denying Hadley'd had a positive effect on Janssen. She'd gone from kicking them out to carrying on a conversation. They gave their permission for him to continue.

"May I sit down?" he asked.

Lydia nodded, and Hadley took a seat in the chair to her left.

"Due to the efforts of detectives Rankin and Hutsell, we know of at least one other victim in addition to you and Kerry."

Lydia turned to face him. He felt somebody smarter than him needed to invent a new word to describe the look on her face. She abruptly rose and rushed out of the room. Rankin followed while Hutsell and Hadley hoped Janssen made it to the bathroom in time.

Blue and red lights were still flashing through a slit in Lydia's kitchen curtains.

"If you'd like, I can go turn off the lights," Hadley said.

"Yeah, thanks Rick," said Hutsell. "I'll check on things in the next room and meet you back here."

Hadley made his way to the unmarked car, opened the driver's door and switched off the visor emergency lights. He walked to the curb and surveyed the bungalow, looking for vulnerable spots a stalker might make use of.

"Are you Detective Hutsell?" It was the woman from across the street who had spoken to them earlier.

"No, ma'am. He's inside. I'll get him for you."

Hadley entered the house and met Hutsell in the hallway that led to Lydia's bedroom.

"The lady across the street is asking for you by name."

"Thanks. I left a card on her door Wednesday. Maybe she's got some information for us. Janssen's lying down and is asking for her anxiety med," said Hutsell. "Would you mind getting *one* pill for her—you know where they are. Tell Trish where I've gone."

"Will do."

Rick Hadley went to the kitchen. He picked up the bottles in turn until he read one labeled "For anxiety". He dispensed one pill. Next, he took a glass from the cupboard and filled it with water from the tap. Rick carried both items down the hallway and gently rapped on the door jamb.

"Yes?" It was Trish's voice.

"The lady across the street wanted to talk with Detective Hutsell," Hadley told her. "He asked me to deliver these." He handed the blue colored pill and glass of water to Rankin. "Is there anything else you need?"

"Does Sheriff Matthews know about your friend and the other lady?" Lydia asked Hadley as she sat up in bed.

"I'll defer to Detective Rankin since she's heading the

investigation."

"Yes. We have forwarded copies of Deputy Hadley's files as well as those from Nevada," said Trish. She handed the pill and glass of water to Janssen.

"Is that where the other lady's from?"

"Yes."

"Does she still live there?"

"No, Ms. Janssen.

"She moved then. Is that how she escaped him?" Lydia asked.

"No, she didn't move," Trish answered.

Lydia looked from Rankin to Hadley and back again. "What was her method of choice?"

"The same as yours."

"He doesn't leave us many options," said Janssen. She swallowed the pill. "What's next?"

"Well, that's something I want to discuss with my partner."

Lydia turned and looked at Hadley. "What about you?"

"I'm here strictly in an advisory capacity, Ms. Janssen. There are at least four law enforcement agencies involved. Sharing information and theories is what will lead to his apprehension."

"You can sound just like the rest of them when you want to," Lydia said.

"Ma'am?"

"Professional cop talk. Very detached," she replied. "So, which one is the real you?"

Hadley looked down before he answered. "Ms. Janssen, like you, I've seen and experienced things I hope to God others never have to—both professionally and personally." He paused and gave an almost imperceptible shake of his head before continuing. "I'm just a man. When I'm cut, I bleed." Hadley brought his eyes to hers. "But I'm no good to you or anyone else if I can't forget about that cut when I need to and focus on the job. The scar from that cut will be there when the job is done."

Lydia allowed a few beats before responding, "Fair enough . . . now, would you get me a sleeping pill? I need to be at work before eleven tonight." She held out the glass for Hadley to refill.

"Isn't your normal bedtime 1 P.M.?" asked Rankin, checking her watch. "It's only eleven."

"Right now, I don't want to think about anything. Sleeping is the only way to accomplish that detective." Janssen nodded at Hadley. "He can get it for me, or I'll get it myself."

"Deputy, if you would . . .," Rankin conceded.

"I'll be right back," Hadley said. He took the glass from Lydia and headed for the kitchen.

"Cold water from the fridge door, please," called out Janssen.

Rick had started back to the bedroom with Janssen's sleeping pill and water when Hutsell opened the front door. He carried a tablet at his side like a young boy would carry a library book.

"Good news," Hutsell said as he held up a flash drive. "We've got video from Wednesday morning." Noticing what Hadley had in his hands, he asked, "You just now getting Janssen's' pill?"

"No, she's already taken the one for anxiety. She wants to go to sleep earlier than usual." He held up a white pill. "Can't say as I blame her."

Hadley turned in the direction of the bedroom. Hutsell fell in step behind. Rick entered and as before, gave the items to Rankin. Hutsell held back so Janssen wouldn't see him and held up the flash drive and tablet.

"You going to be here when I wake up, Tennessee?" Janssen asked Hadley without looking at him.

Before he could answer, Rankin interjected, "Someone will be." She held out her hands containing the sleeping pill and water glass. Lydia downed the pill and set the glass on the nightstand. Rankin sat down in an upholstered chair by the wall across from Janssen's bed.

"Please, just go. You said you needed to have a discussion—so go have it," Janssen said, dismissing the sitting Rankin. When Rankin hesitated she added, "Empty the bathroom of razor blades and get me a plastic cup instead of the glass one if that will make you feel better." Janssen turned her back on Rankin, lay down, and adjusted the covers.

·14·

John Hutsell powered up the tablet and slid the flash drive into a USB port. He positioned the device so Rankin and Hadley could view the video.

They watched as on the morning of February fourteenth, two days prior, a white panel van had pulled up in front of Lydia Janssen's bungalow just after her landlords had departed for work. A minute later a man dressed in gray coveralls and wearing a gray cap exited the back of the van. He was carrying a container commonly used to spray for pests. The man was visible for only a few moments before he disappeared behind the vehicle. Twenty-two minutes later he could be seen walking from the backyard of 6821-B East Redbud Drive to that of 6821-A, all the while pretending to spray insecticide. Another twenty minutes lapsed before he emerged from the north side of the house. He moved along the front, continuing to 'treat' the foundation, then finally on to the back of the van, where he had begun. In total, it was fifty-four minutes from the time he'd parked the van until he got back behind the wheel.

"No logo on the van, coveralls or cap," observed Rankin.

"Looks like he's sporting a dark-haired ponytail," added Hutsell.

"At least we now know what he used to transport the snake," said Trish. "And I'll bet the bottom of that container has the same shape and dimensions as the one Martelli's working on."

"If so, it's what he used it to break the bedroom window," said Hutsell. "Rick, got any ideas?"

"It's a standard panel van so from the looks of it, he's about six foot. He's also wearing gray work gloves so no tattoos, scars or telltale birthmarks. Your crime scene techs have their work cut out for them. No department of transportation—federal or state—markings on the van that I can see and from the camera's angle the license plate won't yield much, either."

"What about posture and body language? Does he remind you of anyone?" Rankin asked.

"Not really . . . and just a thought, considering his obsession with

Halloween, he might not actually have a ponytail. He could be wearing a novelty hat with a ponytail extension," suggested Rick.

Trish Rankin's cell signaled a message from Gabe Fenske. She opened it and silently read, "You've got another one."

"It's getting close to lunch time. You like Italian, Rick?" Trish asked.

"Sure do."

"If we order by phone app, would you mind going to pick it up?"

"Not at all."

"John, pull up Rossano's menu for Rick, will you? Let me know when you two have made your selections," she said. "Everything is good, by the way," she added for Hadley's benefit.

Ten minutes later, Hutsell watched as Hadley pulled away from the curb. "Nice job, Trish. It'll take 'Tennessee' at least thirty minutes. What was in the message?"

"Kathryn Bryce. New Haven, Connecticut, 2009. Predates Hadley's case by two years. They're sending the files. Gabe will forward when they come in and print out photos and pertinent info for the board."

Hutsell stood up, walked over to the counter and leaned against it from behind. "Damn, Hadley's good," he said. "He puts you at ease by telling you he's only here as back-up, then he swoops in and manages to take over where the victim's concerned."

"I know what you mean. He deferred to me when Janssen asked about the investigation and yet he's the one she wants to be here when she wakes up," Rankin said.

"Well, he *won't* be the one," stated Hutsell. "Vashon would have our hides—she might anyway."

"He did talk her down, John. She was in the middle of throwing us out when he got her to reconsider. If he hadn't, we would've had to do the 'protective custody' thing and where would we be then?"

"So where do you want to go from here?"

"I'm not comfortable with her being alone. It's Dan's weekend with the kids, so I can stay this evening. If it's okay, you and Hadley can work on the case from the bull pen. Make sure to ask him about the wood working angle. I'll need the power cord from the car so I can study the Bryce files from here," she said, tapping the tablet. "We can touch base later today."

The three investigators chit-chatted through lunch.

"What do you do in your spare time, Rick?" John asked.

"Listen to music and shoot pool," he answered. "Yourself?"

"I enjoy good music," Hutsell said.

"And dancing—don't forget dancing, John," added Trish.

"What about you, Trish?" questioned Hadley

"Get to play Mom to a nine-year-old boy and a five-year-old girl. You got any kids, Rick?"

"No. If you two are finished eating, I'll make a trip to the trash bin," Hadley said as he began clearing the table.

Hadley seemed preoccupied upon his return to the kitchen. He moved to the sink and peered through the slit in the curtains. Trish finally spoke. "Oh, by the way, Rick, while you were getting lunch we got confirmation of another primary victim."

Hadley turned to face the two St. Louis detectives.

"Authorities in New Haven, Connecticut, are sending their files. John's going back to the station to look for a connection linking all four cases. You want to join him? I'll work from here till Janssen leaves for work."

"Sounds good. What about in the morning when she clocks out at the hospital?" Hadley asked. "Will someone be able to make sure she makes it home okay? And what about after?"

"Haven't got that far yet," answered Trish. "There's always protective custody but that's usually reserved for trial witnesses or for someone in eminent danger."

"I can hear Vashon now, 'Define *eminent*, detective'," said Hutsell.

"Well, you can just disabuse yourself of that notion right now, Detective Rankin."

All three investigators turned to see Lydia Janssen leaning against the kitchen door jamb.

"I'm not going into protective custody. You want my help, find another way."

"Ms. Janssen, we have—," started Rankin.

"What about him" Lydia asked, nodding at Rick Hadley.

"Ms. Janssen, Deputy Hadley is not part of our department. We would never get approval for him to serve in such a capacity."

"Well, when it comes right down to it, you have no say concerning who I invite into my home," stated Lydia. "What about it, Tennessee? You in?"

"Deputy Hadley, we need to step outside," Rankin said.

"Yes, ma'am."

Once she had closed the bungalow's front door, Rankin directed Hutsell and Hadley to the end of the driveway.

"Deputy Hadley, you have us in a tight spot, here," Rankin said.

"Not intentionally, Detective," he replied.

"Intentional or not, 'Tennessee'," Hutsell said, mimicking Janssen's nickname for Hadley. "Here we are."

"I can stay with her when she's not working," Hadley said. "I've got vacation time I can use if need be."

Trish Rankin bowed and shook her head as Hutsell put his hands on his hips.

"Here's your out, detectives. When your lieutenant starts in, remind her at least this way you're still invited to the party."

"As opposed to *your* party, Deputy," countered Hutsell.

Hadley waited a few beats. "It's not about you or me, John. It's about Lydia Janssen."

The two men continued to hold eye contact. Rankin cleared her throat as a signal for both to stand down. Rick Hadley turned and took a few steps down the sidewalk. He put his hands in his pockets and looked at the bungalow. Janssen was watching from the window. Rankin followed his line of sight.

"It's got to be done in a way that we have plausible deniability," she insisted.

"That can be accomplished," stated Hadley. "Record video of Janssen giving a verbal disclaimer."

"John?" Rankin looked at her partner. "Are we together on this?"

"Until we come up with something better."

This was his weekend to work. At least that's what he'd told her. Not his regular job mind you, but on the handcrafted religious items he constructed from broken stained-glass pieces to sell on a well-known website. It was important he not be disturbed at their second home on the river as he was backed up on orders for mosaic crosses. She didn't like the idea of him missing Sunday Service, but she had to admit God had given him this talent and he *was* using it to do God's work. He even donated half the proceeds to their church. She was not to worry though, he'd arranged for Poet to deliver his meals and while the two ate he would witness to the nonbeliever.

A reservation on the red eye to St. Louis in the name Logan Hale had been booked using a prepaid phone. Hale's was an identity he'd commandeered four months prior. Ooh, what a sweet word commandeer was—kind of like an eminent domain kind of thing. Well, he'd 'needed' Hale's identity and he'd taken it—just like the county had taken the church he'd been baptized in for a new road.

He'd used Hale's social security number to apply for a credit card several months later and now with Hale's driver's license, he would make the trip. He would rent a car under the name of Aaron Cagle —but not at the airport. He'd wait for the metro and take it to within a few blocks of a car rental agency. The credit card bills would be sent to commercial mail boxes he had rented in a neighboring county. Always wary of cameras, he would have Poet collect them and then pay them off with money orders purchased at a convenience store. He always paid his bills—his motive had never been to rip off the ignorant. But his personal life was nobody's business—especially people like Sheriff Jimmy Matthews out of Benton County, Arkansas.

He was enjoying a bag of bar-b-que potato chips and a Mountain Dew on break when he couldn't stifle a grin any longer. Yeah, he wasn't Mensa quality but he wasn't dimwitted either——a description he'd heard others whisper about him ever since he was a kid. They were getting *theirs*, though. They—the kind of people who were born talented and beautiful; the jocks and the cheerleaders. Those that never had to work for anything 'cause everything was always handed to them. Some of them tried to act like they weren't entitled. His Dad called them do-gooders and there was one particular do-gooder he despised more than all the others put together.

Growing up all he ever heard was Richard *this* and Richard *that*. His cousin Richard was the perfect child, the perfect student, the perfect athlete—the perfect everything! In high school Richard had "taken him under his wing" as others had described it. "Man, that Richard's a great guy," he'd heard them say. But he knew the truth. Richard had only been play acting so people would heap even more praise upon him. Richard could have beat the crap out of any of those who'd bullied him in school. But no, Richard didn't dirty his hands. He'd have his friends do his 'scut work' for him, as his Dad had called it. Richard and his friends would even let him hang around with them from time to time to show how great *they* were.

He'd grown to hate Richard even more than his tormentors. At least the bullies were real, not pretending to be something they weren't. He looked up and whispered, "Sorry." He'd been taught that God didn't like the word hate. Instead of wishing harm on others, he needed to be patient and wait for a judgment day. He needed to remember that God would provide. Richard's day would come, just like Lydia Janssen's day was about to.

· 16 ·

Rick Hadley pulled up outside the St. Louis University District Police Station and dropped John Hutsell off at the front door. This way he could park and have privacy when he made a follow-up call to his dad in Tennessee. Hadley had known at the time the real reason Rankin had asked him to make the lunch run—she wanted him out of earshot. Not a problem. He needed a chance to catch his dad up to speed and didn't particularly want them over-hearing him, either. He parked, pulled out his cell, and placed a call to his dad.

"How's it going?" asked Sheriff Mike Hadley as he leaned back in his chair and crossed his feet on his desk.

"Touch and go," replied his son. "Since our conversation at lunch, there's a report of another victim. Kathryn Bryce of New Haven, Connecticut, from 2009. That's all I know about Bryce right now, but I'm getting ready to head to the investigation room where I should learn more. I will forward information as soon as I can. Have you been able to determine the whereabouts of our guy on the days in question?"

"The weekend Rob Prasser went missing was the same weekend he was in the auto accident. He was laid up in the hospital for three days, and then his leg was in a cast for six weeks. Rick, I know your instincts are good, but I really think you're off base on this one."

"I'm telling you, Dad, he's involved someway. If he's not the doer, he's assisting."

"Beware of tunnel vision, son," warned the senior Hadley. "What about Janssen? What is St. Louis going to do to keep her safe after today?"

"Funny you should ask," replied Rick. "I got the assignment."

"What?" Mike Hadley's voice was loud enough that Deputy Larry Timbrook turned in time to see his boss bring his feet down and sit straight up. "How did you manage that?"

"Actually, Lydia Janssen set it up."

"Damn, Rick, be careful. She's vulnerable, and putting yourself alone with her for a considerable length of time makes you vulnerable, too."

"Look, Dad, I know the risks. I'll keep a safe distance."

"Well, I'm not telling your mother," Mike Hadley declared. "There'd be *Big Trouble in Little Eagle Ridge* if I did."

Rick laughed at the reference to the movie, *Big Trouble in Little China*.

"I can always take vacation time," said the son. "What I do on my own time is my own business."

"Ain't gonna work, kid. Lydia Janssen is Shannon County business and you know it. By the way, you can't tell me Hutsell and Rankin are happy with this arrangement."

"Like I said, touch and go . . . and right now, I've got to go."

"Call me tonight."

"Will do. We're getting close, Dad. I can feel it."

"Dad gum that fortune teller in Germany anyway," cursed Mike Hadley. "Telling your mom on the train to Wiesbaden when she was pregnant with you that you were going to be born with 'the sight'."

Rick Hadley laughed. "Mom doesn't really believe that; it just makes for a good running gag."

"I'm not so sure, Rick. In your mom's eyes, when it comes to you—."

"Yeah, I can do no wrong."

"And Rick?"

"Yes, Dad."

"In the words of Lori McKenna and Tim McGraw . . .."

"'Always stay humble and kind'," Rick finished his dad's thought.

"Take care, son."

Rick Hadley walked into the detective squad room in time to see John Hutsell's lieutenant "ream him out." He recalled how Kelly Donlan had looked confused when the center from their high school football team had used the term as he exited the coach's office.

"Reamed out?" Kelly asked.

"Yeah, he tore me a new one."

Hadley watched as Vashon finally dismissed Hutsell with a wave of her hand. The detective's jaw was already set tight when he noticed Hadley standing by his desk. Hutsell walked by him and nodded toward the investigation room.

"Hey, it could be worse," Hadley said once they were inside.

"Oh yeah? Tell me, Deputy, how could it be worse?"

"Janssen could have seen Missouri's *Murder in the Fifty* episode and chosen you."

"Damn, Hadley. How do you come out smelling like a rose all the time?"

"My aunt says I have the face of a sad puppy dog that everyone wants to take home."

"Well, she's on to something 'cause you sure got yourself invited into Janssen's." He waited a few beats, put a grin on his face and said, "Hope you like kibble."

Hadley laughed and with the tension broken asked, "You ready to get started?"

"Yeah. Let's see what 'we've' got."

The St. Louis detective powered up the computer, picked up the file labeled Kathryn Bryce and laid out its contents.

Trish Rankin was opening the same file on the tablet sitting on Janssen's kitchen table. Kathryn Bryce had been a costume designer working at a community theater in New Haven, Connecticut, when she received a Halloween card on April Fool's Day 2009. She thought nothing of it—in fact, it was a pretty good joke considering its day of arrival. Another Halloween card was sent in time for Cinco de Mayo, May 5. Again, Bryce was not alarmed. The figures were clad in traditional Hispanic dress and she had several friends who would celebrate Halloween all year if they could. Halloween cards continued to arrive for subsequent holidays. Postmarks were from all over the United States. Her friend was quite the traveler.

Tragedy stuck Kathryn Bryce when the body of Judson Warner had been found on the Chelsea Theatre stage the morning of October 18, 2009. The face of Warner was obscured by a Phantom of the Opera papier-mâché death mask. The autopsy determined that Warner had been smothered. Left over strips of the water, flour and paper mixture used to construct the mask were found stuffed into Warner's nostrils and throat. Kathryn Bryce was visiting her mother in Susquehanna, Pennsylvania, when she received word of Warner's death.

Initial suspicion had fallen on Warner's wife, Camille, as she had become aware of Bryce's affair with her husband two weeks prior to his murder. Mrs. Warner was cleared when she produced photos of her alongside her husband's brother taken during the Florida Keys Pirates in Paradise Festival on October 17. A major airline manifest showed Camille and Elliot Warner were passengers on a flight from Bradley International to Miami on October 16. It turned out that Mrs. Warner was having an affair of her own. When the death photo of Warner arrived inside a Halloween card addressed to Bryce on October 31, 2009, the pieces started to fall into place.

With few clues and no viable suspects, the investigation went cold. Rankin wondered if Hutsell and Hadley were having any luck at the station. She dialed Hutsell on her cell.

"Any progress?" she asked.

"Just a lot of new questions. Have you had a chance to look over the information on Bryce?"

"This guy is pretty creative. Who knew there were so many ways to kill by paper?" Rankin said. "Do you know what became of Bryce after she moved to Pennsylvania?"

"New Haven didn't have anything on her after November 17, 2009, so I contacted the Susquehanna Police Department. Hold on a second. Rick hand me that latest print-out."

Rankin heard Hadley reply, "Here you go, John."

"So are 'we' past addressing him as 'Tennessee'?"

"Yeah, I figure he's always going to land on his feet, so I might as well accept it. He's actually damn good at this. I'll 'splain later."

Hutsell chuckled.

"What's so funny?" asked Rankin.

"I do believe Deputy Hadley's blushing."

Trish heard Hadley's response in the background, "I'm just gonna go stretch my legs for minute . . . or two."

"The women around here will love that," joked Hutsell. "Anyway, back on track. Bryce was awarded a graduate assistantship in the theatre department at Winbridge College in Scranton in January 2010. Her mother passed away on June third of 2010 of kidney failure. In fact, her mother's illness was the reason behind Bryce's visit the weekend Judson Warner was murdered and it factored heavily in her move to Susquehanna, Pennsylvania."

"Are we talking a natural death, John?" Rankin asked. "Could our guy have been involved?"

"It was natural. Her mother had a living will, and life support had been removed, resulting in her death."

"And Bryce?"

"Well, that's where it gets interesting. Bryce died from an apparent suicide on May 31—Memorial Day—three days prior to her mother's passing. Her mother was still on life support. Bryce and the doctors were waiting for her brother to drive in from Indiana before shutting down the machine."

"Apparent?"

"Kathryn Bryce was found hanging from the ceiling fan in her bedroom at her mother's home. The coroner ruled it an apparent suicide but Bryce's brother wasn't having it. Turned out there had been some words the week before over the mother's will. Prior to Bryce's move to Pennsylvania, her cousin, Erin Smallwood, had been Mrs. Bryce's caretaker."

"John—."

"Hold on, Trish. The deal had been upon Mrs. Bryce's death, Smallwood would inherit Bryce's home. But Bryce changed her will and made Kathryn the main beneficiary. Long story short, Smallwood was arrested and eventually convicted for the murder of Kathryn Bryce. Motive —the niece would claim her former status in Mrs. Bryce's estate."

"Was there a Halloween card for Memorial Day? If so, it could have been the last straw for Bryce."

"Don't have an answer for you. We just got this information."

"Smallwood could be innocent, John."

"I know. Hadley and I had just started discussing it when you called," Hutsell said. "How's Janssen?"

"Lightly snoring when I checked fifteen minutes ago. How'd it go with Vashon?"

"She had a few choice words, but what can she do? It's a done deal with Janssen's video absolving us of any responsibility. And Hadley had a good point—."

"He's actually had several," interrupted Rankin.

"Yeah, but he pointed out it could have been me on the top of her bodyguard list. Truth be told, I'm probably at the bottom."

"Guess you need to work on your boyish charm, partner."

"Not my style," Hutsell said.

I know, John. You always keep them at arm's length.

"When do you want to hand the reins over to Hadley?" Hutsell asked.

"I'd like to talk to him first. Why don't you two swing by here with dinner, and we'll discuss it?"

Hutsell checked his watch. "How about seven-thirty?"

"Sounds good."

"What are you hungry for?"

"I was afraid you were going to ask that question. Surprise me."

"No problem. I'll just put it on Hadley. Make him earn his keep," Hutsell said as Rick Hadley walked back in the room.

The last thing Rankin heard before she disconnected was, "What are you . . . .." She smiled, stood up and went to check on Janssen.

·18·

John Hutsell and Rick Hadley were sitting at the bar of the 10–7 when a pretty brunette walked up.

"As I live and breathe, if it isn't John Hutsell," said the woman.

"Hi, Stacy. Anything new?" asked Hutsell.

"Nope. Still walking the streets, busting 'johns'—pun intended," she said jokingly.

"You always know what to say to make a guy open his wallet and give you twenty bucks," returned Hutsell.

"Make it one hundred, sailor, and you get the whole night. How much cash do you have on you?" she asked as her hand went for Hutsell's back pocket. He put his hand on hers, stopping her before she made contact.

"Rick, meet Stacy Parisi. Stacy works vice. Stacy, this is Deputy Rick Hadley from Tennessee."

"Hello," said Parisi just before she leaned in and whispered in Hutsell's ear. When she was done, she looked at Hadley. "Enjoy your time in Missouri, Deputy," she said before walking away.

"Grab your drink, and let's move to a booth," Hutsell said, snagging a couple of menus on the way. "Don't ask," he said once they were seated.

"None of my business," Hadley responded. He opened the menu. "What do you recommend?"

"Close your eyes and pick one. It's all good. I'm going with the classic burger. They'll cook it to your specification."

"Sounds good."

The waitress came and took their orders.

"Nice place," said Hadley. "Reminds me of a cop bar in Knoxville. We don't have anything like this in Eagle Ridge."

"Shannon County's in the Smokey Mountains, right?" asked Hutsell.

"For the most part. When I tell people I'm from Eastern Tennessee, they think of Dollywood and Gatlinburg. Shannon County is a little farther east."

"You ever been to the Ozarks?"

"No. I've been over most of the U.S. and parts of Europe, but never made it to the Ozarks," answered Hadley. "That's where you're from, right?"

"Yeah. Concerning tourism, the Ozarks and the Smoky Mountains are a lot alike. We've got Silver Dollar City, you've got Dollywood. Our Branson is like your Gatlinburg. And for those into nature, there's The Mark Twin National Forest and The Great Smokey Mountains National Park."

"Then you learned to drive on winding roads, too?" Hadley asked with a smile.

"Yeah, I loved watching my relatives from Kansas press their feet on the passenger floor board as I rounded corners," Hutsell said.

"Yeah, wishing they had a brake pedal," added Hadley.

"But you're not a native of Shannon County?"

"No. I lived on army bases till my sophomore year in high school. Dad was career army, and mom was a contributor to The Stars and Stripes. Both my parents grew up Eagle Ridge—high school sweethearts as a matter of fact. When dad retired from the army, they moved our family 'back home' as they described it. Dad had been military police and continued to work in law enforcement on the civilian side. He was Chief of Police in Eagle Ridge for years before he became sheriff."

The waitress stopped and refilled their drinks. "Won't be long, John," she informed Hutsell.

"Thanks," he said. "Oh, we're going to need take out for Trish."

"Hawaiian Chicken?"

Hutsell smiled. "Yeah, she said surprise her, but I'm going with the tried and true."

"Smart move. Signal me ten minutes before you're ready to leave and I'll make sure it's ready to go when you are."

Trish Rankin had just finished talking with her kids when she saw lights flash through the slit in Janssen's kitchen curtains. Dinner had arrived.

John Hutsell walked in carrying two bags. He set the big one on the table and put the smaller one in the freezer. He turned around and was met with a questioning look.

"You said to surprise you."

Trish started toward the fridge.

"No, not yet. You have to eat your vegetables first," he chided.

Trish sat down and opened the container holding her evening meal.

"So what's the latest on the case?" she asked the two men sitting at the table with her.

"Bryce did receive a Halloween card for Memorial Day—the day of her death," Hutsell said. "The Susquehanna Police Department is unaware of any other Halloween Cards that she might have received from the time she arrived in the city to the time of her death. And of course, they're not too keen on some outsider suggesting they got it wrong, and that Bryce's death was in fact a suicide."

"Who inherited the property after Mrs. Bryce's death? The brother?"

"Yes. The brother now holds the title," her partner replied.

"What does Susquehanna PD think of the cards Bryce received while living in New Haven, the Warner murder and the similarities to the other three primaries?"

"They were unaware of what took place in New Haven," Hutsell answered. "They said they would take it 'under advisement'. What exactly they mean is your guess as well as mine. Complicating the matter is that the Bryce family came under scrutiny eight years prior after Kathryn's father, who worked in the city's purchasing department, had been caught under-cutting bids. The father's illegal activities made it rough on his family—sling and arrows, you know—and they guarded their privacy thereafter. His wife divorced him and, in fact, inherited her family's home after the divorce."

"What do you think, John? Was Bryce's death a suicide or was she murdered?" Rankin asked.

"Don't have enough information to make a call. All I could do was suggest they look into the possibility that it was suicide. And right now, our hands are too full to even think of other options where Susquehanna is concerned. Oh, and neither Bryce nor Jenkins were Catholic."

Rankin checked her watch. She knew Lydia Janssen had set her alarm for 9 P.M. The three investigators had thirty minutes in which to develop a plan whereby Rick Hadley would be providing her with protection. But first things first. Rankin walked to the freezer and took out the bag Hutsell had placed there earlier. She looked inside.

"Cheesecake flavor with raspberries?"

"Yeah, but don't you dare let anyone know I made a Cold Stone Creamery run just for you," warned Hutsell.

Rankin leaned her back against Janssen's kitchen counter and scooped a spoonful. "Guess we better discuss what happens next," she said. "Rick, you're the chosen one. What are your thoughts?"

"If it's okay with you, I would like you to stay until it's time for Ms. Janssen to leave for work," Hadley began. "Then I'll drive her to the hospital and accompany her inside. I'll spend the night at the hotel and pick her up in the morning when she gets off work—meeting her inside the lobby and walking her out."

Hadley rose from his chair and made his way to the counter adjacent to Rankin. He placed his hands on the edge of the counter and leaned back.

"We really don't know if the suspect will try anything, but this way, she won't feel as alone as she has been. Maybe she'll even begin to feel optimistic. As we found out today, that's the biggest problem she faces right now," Hadley continued. "I know, it's a lot to ask with all she's been through. But I tell you both, for the first time in five years, I feel there's a chance to catch him. We just need to find the connection, and the more time we spend with Ms. Janssen, the more we get to know her, the better chance we have of doing just that."

"I agree," came Janssen's voice from the entryway. All three looked in her direction.

"Were you a librarian in a previous life?" Hutsell asked rhetorically. "You're so dang quiet."

Rick Hadley began clearing the table of the paper and plastic items left from Rankin's meal.

"Have all of you had dinner?" Janssen asked.

"Yes," answered Hutsell.

Lydia walked to the refrigerator and peered in.

"Deputy, would you hand me a can of chunked chicken from the last cabinet on your left?" she asked without turning to look at him.

"Yes, ma'am."

Janssen pulled several items out of the refrigerator and placed them on the counter.

"After the chicken salad is prepared, I'll set it in the fridge to chill while I take a shower. Then we can discuss what happens next," she said.

Rankin looked at her partner. She and Hutsell were officially the ones in charge of this investigation, yet in some ways, it looked like the St. Louis detectives were just there to decorate the set. And as long as progress continued to be made, she would allow Janssen and Hadley a place at the table.

Lydia Janssen emerged from her bedroom dressed in jeans and a Rogers, Arkansas, High School T-shirt with the Mountaineer team mascot on the back. She was preparing a chicken salad sandwich when Trish Rankin spoke up.

"Ms. Janssen, concerning tomorrow, what are you plans?"

"After Hadley—," she turned to Rick, "That is your name, right?"

"Yes, ma'am," he answered.

"After Hadley picks me up, I'd like to come home and work on the foot locker for Sheriff Matthews' son. I'm not scheduled at the hospital again until Monday night, so I can get a lot accomplished. There's a stool Hadley can sit on in the work room while we try to find a connection between—what was the term you used—the three primary victims?"

And again, the three investigators went mum.

"There's another one, isn't there?" asked Janssen after registering their collective silence.

"Yes," answered Rankin. "New Haven, Connecticut. 2009."

"Is she living?"

"No, Ms. Janssen."

"Suicide?"

"Up for discussion at the moment," said Rankin. "Initially, yes. But due to a family dispute, authorities settled on murder."

"Was there a conviction?"

"Yes."

"So, someone is likely serving time for a crime he or she didn't commit?"

"Could be. Detective Hutsell has made contact with the proper law enforcement agency. It's up to them on how to proceed with the new information."

"Why are all these cases coming to light now?" asked Janssen.

"He screwed up," Rankin said. "He hand-delivered the Valentine card, and he included a note that talked of other victims. Detective Hutsell requested and received permission to send out a nationwide bulletin since the suspect's method of operation is so unique. It went out Wednesday night. Deputy Hadley contacted us the next morning. Nevada and Connecticut followed."

Janssen looked at Hutsell, "So you're the one who finally put it all together?"

"I—we had more to go on than other investigators have had," replied Hutsell. "I know Jimmy Matthews. If this had happened in Benton County, he would have been the one sending out the bulletin."

Rick Hadley checked his watch. "What time do we need to leave, Ms. Janssen?"

Lydia looked at the clock on her microwave.

"In about forty-five minutes." She stood and picked up the plate holding her untouched dinner.

"Ms. Janssen, I know you have an empty—," Lydia interrupted Hadley, anticipating the rest of his sentence.

"Don't go getting bent out of shape, Tennessee. I'll bring it along and eat it at my desk."

"Yes, ma'am."

"Deputy, this 'Yes ma'am' stuff has got to stop," she said as she placed the sandwich in a plastic container. "I understand the need for professionalism, but I'm not your grandmother."

Trish Rankin turned her head so the others wouldn't see her smile. Lydia opened her fridge and brought out a bag of baby carrots. Next she slid open a drawer and pulled out a small plastic bag. She selected several carrots as Rick Hadley picked up the baggie and held it open for her.

"Ms. Janssen, where I come from the term is used to show respect. Age isn't a requirement," Hadley explained. Lydia placed the carrots in the bag. As Hadley zipped it shut he said, "Let's see . . . how about I just call you . . . Arkansas?"

"Works for me," replied Janssen. She put the sandwich container in her lunch tote. Hadley followed suit with the bag of carrots. She turned and headed toward her bedroom. "I won't be long," she said over her shoulder.

Hadley took a step toward the table, picked up an apple from a small basket of fruit, gently tossed it in the air and caught it as gravity pulled it down. He was putting it in Janssen's lunch bag when Rankin heard the bedroom door close.

"There's something I'd like to know, Hadley," she said. "Just how many women are in love with you?"

Rick gave her a puzzled look.

"I've observed you for only twenty-four hours, but I can tell you that, when it comes to what a lot of women want, you're damn near the whole package."

"Not a one, Detective Rankin," Hadley said matter-of-factly. He grabbed his jacket from the back of a chair and left the room.

At least not the *right* one, thought Rankin.

Hadley continued until he was outside. Hutsell looked out Janssen's window and saw the deputy walking down the sidewalk with his collar turned up and his hands in his pockets. He moved so his partner could also take in the scene. Hutsell slightly shook his head.

"You're no better off, John. They're in love with you, too. Just for a different reason."

At ten-thirty, the three investigators went their separate ways.

Deputy Rick Hadley drove Lydia Janssen to the Madison University Medical Center. After walking her inside, he headed for his hotel. Two blocks away, he pulled into a convenience store and purchased a liter of beer. Once in his room, he hit his computer's power button. As it warmed up, he took off his boots and belt, then pulled out the tail of his shirt. He typed in *"Lone Star*, "My Love" on YouTube. Sitting in the dark with light from the city dimly illuminating the room, he opened the beer and watched as actor Chris Cooper drove through the night listening to Little Willie John sing about a love like, "the deep blue sea." One ". . . so deep that I'll never be free."

Trish Rankin dropped her partner off at the station and turned in the department's unmarked car. Instead of going straight home, she chose a different route. She drove to an older housing development and pulled into a parking spot across the street from a small white house. A porch with wrought-iron trim ran the width of the home. It had a wide center door and windows on either side. She could see the flickering of a television screen behind the drapes and knew the owner was still awake. Trish entertained the idea of pulling into the driveway, but had second thoughts and drove on to an empty house.

Detective John Hutsell got in his red BMW sports car and drove a familiar route. Finding a parking spot at the apartment complex was easier than most nights, as it was the beginning of the weekend and many residents were out enjoying the night life. After parking across from the third building, he climbed the steps to the second floor and knocked on the door of Apartment 328. The door opened, revealing a pretty woman framed by a soft light from down the hall. She was wearing a white, thin-strapped camisole over an identical black one. The contrast of the black and white straps and low cut had the desired effect on Hutsell that the wearer intended.

Hutsell walked inside and shut the door behind him. The woman took a step towards him so their bodies were touching. She wrapped her left arm around him, placing her hand in the slight curve above his waist. Hutsell stood his ground as she pressed tightly against him and slowly ran her hand down his frame. This time, he didn't stop her. "Hello, sailor," she whispered.

·19·

Hadley was a few minutes early. He parked and walked into the lobby to wait for Lydia Janssen to get off work. A newspaper was lying on a side table. He picked it up and sat down. He smiled, thinking of the many film noir detectives who needed a cover and had done the same thing he was doing at the moment—pretending to read a newspaper while actually conducting surveillance. He glanced around and smiled again. If one compared the three people seated in the lobby, he would be the one that stood out. The other two were busy with their cell phones.

A little after seven, Lydia walked out of one of the elevators on the right. Hadley put down the paper and stood. As was his habit, he stuck his hands in his front pockets. Janssen couldn't miss the six-foot-four deputy and turned in his direction. A few seconds later, a sudden movement from behind her caught his eye. A man had entered the area beyond the elevator bay and was walking toward Janssen. He was a few steps behind her when he immediately stopped, referred to a paper in his hand and did an about face.

Rick Hadley made his way to the elevators and asked Lydia to stay put. He turned sideways and maneuvered around her. By the time he rounded the corner, the man was out of sight. Hadley joined Janssen by the elevators.

"Everything okay?" Lydia asked.

"I think so. A man did an abrupt turn when you started walking toward me. He did refer to what could've been a hospital map, like the ones provided at the information desk, and might have realized he was going in the wrong direction."

"It's a big place. I'm familiar only with the section I work in. It wouldn't take me long to get lost in another wing."

"Anyway, good morning, Arkansas. Ready for some breakfast? I'm buying."

"Thanks, Tennessee. I really don't feel like cooking this morning."

"Any place close where you can get eggs over easy without the cook breaking the yokes?"

"Loretta's Diner," she suggested. "Two blocks east, three blocks south."

"Loretta's it is."

· 20 ·

No, NO, NO, NO, NO! What in the world! It had never entered his mind that if a connection was going to be made it would be Deputy Rick Hadley making it. But there he was, standing in the same lobby as Lydia Janssen. All six-foot-four of him in full Technicolor. Odd choice of words since Hadley seldom wore anything but jeans and a white shirt. It was those damned icy blue eyes of his—they could see right through you. He rarely cursed, but sometimes emphasis was needed, and this was one of those times.

He tried to calm himself. He needed to remember who was really in charge. In times like this, his dad would always say, "Fall back on your faith, son." So, he'd looked for the silver lining and had actually found several.

He'd been smart enough to have and to use the hospital map as a decoy. Almost anybody observing him would think he was trying to find his way. And if Hadley had seen him, he was betting five seconds wasn't time enough for the deputy to put two and two together.

The hospital was undergoing a shift change, and he'd been lucky to exit the west entrance in time to catch the shuttle to the employee parking lot. The shuttle doors had begun to close when he'd called out for the driver to wait. He'd disembarked at the second stop and made his way to his rented car. And what a stroke of genius it had been not to rent the car at Lambert International Airport, but instead, to take the metro to within a couple of blocks of another rental agency and get a car there. For an added safeguard, he'd used yet another identity for the transaction.

But now, it was time for damage control. First, he needed to check out of his hotel and return the rental. Next, take the metro to a rental agency across town and use a different identity—the third one for this trip. Then, check into another hotel and spend the day dreaming up a new strategy because right now he was feeling pretty good—for he'd found the blessing in what some would have called a disaster. When he'd calmed down and his mind was clear, he'd remembered that Deputy Rick Hadley was one of 'them'—the beautiful ones.

Another opportunity was at hand and this trip could end up being a two-fer—two for the price of one. Oooh . . . and if he played his cards right, Hadley's bon-voyage party would be one he'd actually get to attend.

21

Rick Hadley pulled his truck into the parking lot of Loretta's Diner.

"Ready?" he asked after shutting off the engine. When she didn't answer he turned to look at her. She was staring out the windshield.

"Ms. Janssen?"

"Do you think the man at the hospital could have been him?"

"Maybe . . . I really don't know," he answered truthfully. "But, to be on the safe side, I'm going to ask Detectives Hutsell or Rankin to get video of him." Janssen continued to look uneasy. "Look at it this way. If it was him, he made another mistake by calling attention to himself and he'll keep on making them. It's just a matter of time."

"It's almost too much to hope for."

"I'll make the call as soon as we get you inside."

Lydia recalled Hadley's comment from the previous night, how that for the first time in five years, he had hope of catching the killer. Was he accurate in his assessment? Were the stars finally aligning? Maybe . . ., maybe not. He'd been right about one thing. Right now, she didn't feel alone. She closed her eyes and took a slow, deep—almost cleansing—breath.

"Eggs over easy, right?"

"To begin with," he replied with a smile.

John Hutsell had just walked into his own apartment when his cell signaled a call.

"Hello, Deputy. How's it going?"

"Pretty good. I'm standing outside Loretta's Diner. I can see Janssen in a corner booth studying the menu. But there's something I think needs checking out."

"Shoot," said Hutsell as he plopped onto the sofa.

"Janssen had just stepped off the elevator when a man appeared behind her. He looked in our direction and did an about-face. He tried to give the impression he was consulting a hospital map but something was off."

"How so?"

"He didn't give himself time to actually look at the map," Hadley said. "He sees Janssen, and he's fine. He catches a glimpse of me, and he's gone. Janssen was between us, so what I saw of him amounted to only a few seconds. By the time I got around her, he was gone. But I would like to look at video of him."

"Hold on while I get something to write on," said Hutsell. "Okay, describe him for me."

"About six-one, jeans, St. Louis Blues stadium jacket, black baseball-like cap. There was a logo on the cap, but I didn't catch it."

"St. Louis Blues? You know hockey?" asked Hutsell. "Oh, hell, forget I asked," he said remembering his resolve to accept Hadley's abilities at face value. Hadley's motives . . . now that was another question. "Approximate time?"

"About five after seven in the east-west hall beyond the elevators at the hospital's main lobby."

"Anything else?"

"Big black glasses," answered Hadley as he continued to watch Lydia Janssen.

"Still going with your plans for the day?"

"Yeah. After breakfast I'll take Janssen home. She'll work on her project, I'll sit on a stool, and we'll talk. Hopefully, we'll find the one thing that ties all four cases together."

"Okay, I'll touch base as soon as I have the video," said Hutsell.

"Thanks, John."

"Later," signed off Hutsell.

Rick Hadley walked in, sat down across from his charge, and picked up a menu.

"How'd it go?" she asked.

"Detective Hutsell is going to see about getting video."

The waitress arrived with their drink orders. "Do you need a few more minutes before you order?"

"Would it be okay, to save time, if I just tell you what I want? It's fine if you need to write it all down à la carte," he said.

"Not a problem. What would you like?"

"I'll let the lady order first."

"The American Omelet with ham."

"Toast, pancakes or biscuits, and gravy?"

"Toast, thank you," answered Lydia.

The waitress turned to Hadley, "Sir?"

"Two eggs, over easy. Four slices of bacon, hash browns, two pancakes, and two slices of toast with orange marmalade."

Both women stared at him.

"What?" he asked, feigning ignorance. "My mom says I'm still a growing boy."

"How tall are you, mister? Six-three, six-four?" the waitress questioned.

"Six-four."

"How much taller is your momma figurin' on you gettin'?" the waitress asked rhetorically. "Still a growing boy . . .," she muttered as she left to give the cook their orders.

Rick looked around. "This place is for real, right? Not just a back-to-the-fifties theme restaurant, right?"

"The story of Loretta's is on your placemat," said Lydia. "Loretta and her husband opened the diner in 1958. She was twenty-five at the time. That's her sitting by the jukebox. Her two daughters run the place now. Granddaughters show up every now and then, but customers are worried they won't want to continue the family business, and that the diner will become a thing of the past." Janssen went on to explain, "Women today have more options than Loretta and her daughters had when they were younger."

They had almost finished eating when Hadley watched Loretta put her hand on the jukebox and boost herself to a standing position. She maneuvered so she was in front of the machine, then reached into her pocket. Hadley heard several coins fall in. He nodded in the direction of the jukebox as the older woman began to make her selections.

"Oldies, right?"

Janssen nodded yes.

"Want to play, 'Name that Tune'?"

"You're on," she said.

They both heard horns, a rhythm guitar and the sound of soft drums.

"Oh, I know this one," Lydia said. "It's . . . It's . . .."

Rick provided the rest of the title, "Up to You," then added the artist's name, "Ricky Nelson."

Hadley noticed Loretta swaying to the music. He got up, walked over and tapped her on the shoulder.

"May I have this dance, Ma'am?"

Loretta, at the most five-foot-four, tilted her head back far enough so she could see his face and said, "Yes, young man, you may."

Rick led the smiling woman in a small two-step circle. Halfway through the song, he started singing along with Nelson. Loretta joined in. They danced and sang in harmony until the song ended. The cook, who had poked his head out from the kitchen when he'd heard Rick and Loretta singing, started clapping when the record finished. Loretta's daughters added their applause.

Lydia stared at Rick as he made his way back to the booth and sat down.

"I really had an unfair advantage," he said.

"What do you mean?"

"I was actually named after Ricky Nelson."

"Were you really?"

"No, I'm just kidding," he confessed with a broad smile. "I wasn't." Then gently said, "But you should see your face, Arkansas."

She didn't need any explanation because for the first time in years, she was smiling. And then it hit her—she shouldn't be smiling. She didn't have the right to smile. She got up and ran to the restroom.

The waitress walked over, "Is she all right, Mister?"

"She's had some stomach issues," lied Hadley.

"By the way, breakfast is on us."

"No, ma'am, I couldn't—."

"Your money's not welcome here," she interrupted. "But you are any time." She turned to walk away and said over her shoulder, "Tell your momma I said, 'hi'."

Rick Hadley slid thirty dollars under the sugar container and checked his watch. He was starting to worry. It had been over seven minutes since Lydia had raced to the restroom. Seven minutes wasn't really that long, but considering the bottles Lydia had lined up yesterday, she might literally be in a life-or-death situation. He called the waitress over.

"Would you mind checking on her?" he asked. "Her name is Lydia."

"Sure," she replied and made her way to the restroom. It wasn't three seconds later when she emerged, her face drained of color. "Mister, you better——." She vomited before she could finish.

Hadley rushed in and was hit with a foul smell. He found Lydia lying on the floor in a small, dark red bloody pool. He recognized the grainy, black like coffee ground substance and knew she was in trouble. Another waitress was now at the door.

"Call 911," he shouted.

"Doing it now," she replied.

"Lydia?" No response. "Lydia?" He gently shook her arm.

"Tennessee . . .." was all she managed to say.

Hadley heard the siren a few minutes later. He stepped aside so the paramedics would have room to assess Lydia's condition.

"What can you tell us about her, sir?" asked the female EMT as she took Lydia's vitals.

"She's been under a great deal of stress. I'm concerned about the amount of blood loss."

"Yes, sir. Anything else?"

"Several meds; depression, anxiety, sleep aid, blood pressure. She's been contemplating suicide," he said as he washed his hands. He checked the two stalls and found them empty. There were no windows.

Soon Lydia was on a stretcher and being wheeled to the ambulance. Rick pulled out his badge and ordered the restroom sealed until further notice. On his way out, Loretta handed him two paper bags, one containing Lydia's belongings and the other his Shannon County Sheriff's Department jacket. He quickly caught up with the stretcher carrying Lydia. When he attempted to follow her inside, the male EMT stopped him.

"I'm sorry, sir, but you can't accompany her——."

Rick flashed his badge for a second time. "This woman is under protective custody and I *can* and *will*."

The paramedic moved aside, let Hadley in and closed the door. The ambulance took off with lights and sirens.

22

Rick Hadley, with his badge pinned to his shirt pocket and two paper bags at his feet, stood in the hallway outside an emergency room and watched through a sliding glass door as a doctor and two nurses tended to Lydia Janssen. His cell was to his ear. He was getting ready to leave a voice message for John Hutsell when the detective picked up.

"Sorry, I was in the shower. What's going on?"

Hadley relayed the events at the diner.

"They're working on her right now. It's bad, John."

"I'll call Trish and be there as soon as I can."

Another doctor had been summoned to help with Lydia Janssen. Hutsell and Rankin, with badges on display, joined Hadley outside the room housing her. The first thing the St. Louis detectives took in was the dark red blood staining Hadley's white shirt and jeans.

"What do we know?" asked Trish.

"Her stomach lining is perforated and there's internal bleeding. They've called in a gastroenterologist," reported Hadley.

"Prognosis?" questioned Rankin.

"Don't know yet."

"Rick, is this something she could have brought on herself or might someone—?"

"No, Trish. What she has is commonly known as a peptic ulcer. It might be caused by an infection or overuse of anti-inflammatory drugs such as ibuprofen. Anxiety disorder exacerbates the condition," Hadley explained. "Could someone have caused this to happen? No one entered or exited the restroom once she went in. I checked the stalls—they were empty—and there was only one entry. The room had no windows. I ordered it sealed. I thought you might want to check it out."

"Thank you," said Rankin. "So, right now, it's a wait-and-see situation?"

"Correct."

The doctor walked out of Lydia's room. Hadley introduced the two St. Louis detectives.

"She's being given epinephrine to stop the bleeding," he said. "The patient is weak but responding well."

"Doctor, is there a determining factor as to why today, of all days, Ms. Janssen ended up in the emergency room?" Rankin asked.

"Not really. I can tell you there is some scaring on her esophagus, and I believe she's had problems with acid reflux. We're going to admit her."

"How long a hospital stay are we talking about?"

"If there are no further complications, a few days. She'll be extremely weak. Does she have someone who can stay with her?"

"Yes," answered Rankin. She nodded in Rick's direction. "Deputy Hadley has medical training, and Ms. Janssen has previously requested his presence at her residence."

"What kind of training, Deputy?" asked the doctor.

"Licensed EMT."

"Then I'd say she's one lucky lady. And Deputy, if you'll follow me, I'll show you where you can get out of those clothes and clean up. We'll get you some scrubs for the time being—they'll probably be high waters—but I would prefer you not present in bloody clothing when she wakes up."

"Sounds good."

Hutsell waited until the doctor had gone before addressing Hadley. "Rick, Trish will remain with Janssen while I go check on the video we talked about earlier."

"I'll call and get a uniform at the diner and request a crime scene team to take samples and look things over," said Trish.

"Okay. I'll see you later," Hadley said. He picked up the paper bags, turned and followed the physician down the hall.

"What do you think?" Rankin asked her partner.

"Make it a couple of uniforms and have them interview people at the scene."

"Absolutely."

·23·

He was sitting in a new rental in the parking lot of a new hotel. He had completed all his tasks except for one—a plan. But before he could accomplish it, he needed more information.

He texted Poet. "Anybody come by the house looking for me?"

"Nope."

"You had lunch yet?"

"No. Starting to get hungry."

"Go ahead and get something to eat. Use that online order-and-delivery app on my phone. It will ask for special instructions. Tell them to deliver to the side door—the one that opens to the carport. Don't you go outside the door, okay?"

"Okay. Can I get something to drink and a dessert?"

"Yeah, if you get Mountain Dew," he answered. "Oh, and give a good tip."

"Will do."

"And Poet, keep an eye out. I think she might have a friend drive by to check on me."

"Okey-doke. If I see anything suspicious, I'll let you know."

At least one worry he'd had was now out of the way. If Deputy Hadley had recognized him, someone (or "ones") from the sheriff's department would be "patrolling" the road that went by the family home. He felt reasonably assured he hadn't blown his cover, for if there was one thing Poet was good at, it was ferreting out members of the constabulary.

Next step. Find out the actual reason Deputy Rick Hadley had been at the hospital. There wasn't much the guy could do, since he had no jurisdiction in St. Louis. At the least, he'd become a glorified taxi driver, and, at the most, he was acting as her bodyguard. Oh, how he hoped it was the latter. He smiled at the old saying, "A bird in the hand is worth two in the bush." If Hadley was acting as her protector, there was definitely two in his hand—or was it there "were" two in his hand? It didn't really matter at this stage of the game—ha, ha, ha.

Whichever capacity Hadley was serving in St. Louis, he would know soon enough. First, he would discretely drive by Lydia's home. If Hadley's vehicle was there, he was babysitting. If not, his fancy truck was nothing more than a cab.

This trip was turning out to be a lot more fun than he'd hoped.

Rick Hadley looked at himself in the physicians-lounge mirror. Janssen's doctor had been right. There was about three inches of exposed ankle beneath the hems of the scrubs he'd been given. Hadley had cleaned off his boots as best he could, still he felt that they were not suitable for a woman recovering from a stint in the emergency room. So he'd opted for blue booties instead. He put his soiled clothes in a Madison University Medical Center plastic bag and sat down to make a phone call.

"I believe he's here, Dad."

"What makes you say that?"

"I saw a man this morning for only a few seconds, but I think it was him," replied the son. "You know there are certain aspects about him . . .."

"I know Rick. It's why he was bullied for most of his life."

"One reason of several," Rick reminded his dad. "I'll be viewing video sometime today but it may be a while." He filled his dad in on the day's happenings then asked, "Would you check around and see if he's in the area?"

"I'll call Caleb Murray over in Pigeon Forge to do some surveillance. He used to be with Sevier County and Gatlinburg PD before that, which makes him a local, concerning places *your* suspect might be. He retired before you came back to Shannon County and prior to my becoming sheriff, so hopefully, no one will connect him with us. For as we all know, we have to avoid even the 'hint of harassment', thank you very much J. Evan."

Yeah, J. Evan.

"Talk to you later, Dad," Hadley said and hung up.

The scrubs had no pockets. He adjusted the cell's ring tone and returned it to his jacket pocket. Carrying the bag with his soiled clothes, as well as the two Loretta had handed him earlier, he left the doctor's lounge and started back to Janssen's room. Barring complications, she would make a full recovery and maybe soon they would stumble on a tidbit that would bring this case to a close.

The bed Lydia was in had just been wheeled out of the room in emergency when Hadley arrived. He fell in step with Rankin who was following the orderly as he navigated the corridor to the patient transport elevators. Once Janssen was settled in her new room and sleeping, the two investigators got a chance to talk about the case.

"I've been thinking . . .," said Rankin as she tapped her fingers on the arm of her chair.

Hadley, who had been leaning forward in his, staring at the floor, raised his head and looked at her.

"You and John have different styles but in a lot of ways you two are alike," she said, purposefully easing him into a discussion.

"'Splain, Lucy," he said, cabbaging Hutsell's *I Love Lucy* line.

She wagged her right index finger and said, "But, I want to know something first."

"O-kay," he said tentatively, drawing out the word.

"You recognized the guy this morning, didn't you? You know who he is?"

"He reminded me of someone, yes," Hadley answered. He sat straight back in his chair.

"Who?"

"I'm not at liberty to say."

"Liberty about what?" asked Hutsell as he walked in the room carrying the tablet. He tapped it. "We've got video . . . for what it's worth."

"Gentlemen, we need a place to talk," Rankin said.

"There's an unoccupied family waiting room at the end of the hall," Hutsell suggested.

"Let's go," Rankin said.

"First of all, what did I miss?" Hutsell asked after the three had carved out their physical space.

"Deputy Hadley's got a name," Rankin said.

Rick's phone sounded. The volume was so low, Rankin and Hutsell barely heard it. Hadley checked the screen.

"I'm sorry, but I have to take this," he said and walked into the hall.

"What's going on, Trish?"

"Our Tennessee deputy has a suspect, but he's not sharing."

"Well, we've both felt from the beginning that he's been holding back. With him, we're damned if we do and damned if we don't."

"I know. And it's not just professionally. He's got a personal story he's guarding as well."

"His little walk down the street outside Janssen's," recalled Hutsell.

"We protect our personal lives, too, John," said Rankin, remembering her side trip from the night before. "It becomes a problem only if one interferes with the other."

Rick Hadley walked back into the room. "What do you say we look at the video?"

"Deputy, you've got a name, and I want it," Detective Rankin said.

"I understand," replied Hadley. "Let's look at the video, and then we'll talk."

Rankin and Hutsell looked at each other. They needed him, and they both knew it, if nothing else than for the link he'd carved out with Janssen. Hutsell put the tablet on a table and sat down in front of it. Rankin and Hadley moved behind him so they could view the screen.

"There's not much," Hutsell told them as he clicked "play."

The man Hadley described had spent a few minutes window shopping at the hospital's gift shop before turning to his left and walking toward the elevator bay. He stopped just short of the elevators, paused for a minute and then turned the corner. He took one step in Lydia's direction, quickly put the map in front of his face and immediately double-backed. Keeping his head down, he went out the side door, hopped onto the employee shuttle and was gone.

"Well?" asked Rankin.

"Anything from the parking lot?" Hadley asked.

Hutsell keyed up the next video. They watched as the man, along with several employees got off the shuttle at its second stop. He disappeared behind the vehicle. The three continued to watch for him, but he did not resurface.

"No pony-tail," observed Hadley. "Any images before he enters the hospital?"

"Not yet. Hospital security is working on it," replied Hutsell.

"Is your guy short-wasted?" Rankin asked.

"Yes," answered Hadley.

"Does he wear glasses?" Rankin again.

"Never seen him in glasses."

"They could be for show," suggested Hutsell. "There's so much action with other employees, walking to their cars and then driving off, he gets lost in the shuffle. Hold on a second." Hutsell backed up to where the suspect moved behind the shuttle. "He got lost on purpose. I'll lay you money he crouched down and moved between trucks and cars, parked and moving, until he was able to reach his own vehicle or the metro."

"Okay, Deputy. Truth time. Who is he?" Rankin demanded.

Rick Hadley walked to the other side of the room. With his back to Rankin and Hutsell, he put his hands in his pockets and took a deep breath. He let it out slowly before he turned around.

"You have to understand, I'm walking a thin line here," he said. "I moved back to Shannon County because of this case. From the start, I had my eye on him. All leads had dried up, so we went back to the beginning, which meant he was brought in for another round of routine questioning. Within thirty minutes, a lawyer stormed into the interview yelling at him to be quiet. Our guy hadn't even called a lawyer. The lawyer showed up on his own."

"I've got to ask, Rick . . . had he been advised?" Rankin asked.

"The suspect *had* been advised of his rights. He said he had nothing to hide—even signed off on it. This was in late January 2013. I hadn't even been with the department for two weeks."

"Why was he brought in in the first place?" Hutsell asked.

"History. He was the one caught peeping in Kerry's window in 2004. I—we couldn't produce any evidence. Yeah, we were fishing, but that's what you have to do sometimes."

"Were you in on the questioning?" Rankin asked.

"No. Jim Russell was sheriff at the time and smart enough not to assign anyone with local ties. He chose a guy originally from South Carolina."

"You were involved with her, right?"

"Had been . . .." Hadley closed his eyes a moment before continuing. "We both moved on."

"Go on," Rankin prompted. She took a seat next to her partner.

"It wasn't just any lawyer who showed up that day. It was Eagle Ridge's own J. Evan Litle," said Hadley. "Litle had applied to be

Eagle Ridge's city attorney six months earlier and had asked Chief of Police Mike Hadley for support. Dad denied the request. Litle didn't get the position and blamed Dad."

"Okay, that was what, 2013?" Hutsell said. "So, what's the problem now? What's got you and your dad walking on eggshells?"

"J. Evan Litle is now the Shannon County District Attorney," Hadley said. "And if he can't find any mud to sling, he'll manufacture some. If that guy on the video is who I think he is, he's from a well-known religious family. At one point, Mom and Pop served as missionaries in South America. When it comes to a lot of people in Eagle Ridge, they are beyond reproach."

"Well, 'sonny boy' isn't. He was a peeping tom," Hutsell asserted.

"But he made amends," Hadley countered. "And, to quote his lawyer, 'Kerry's a beautiful woman. What man wouldn't want to catch a glimpse of her?'" He paused. "I hate that 'boys-will-be-boys' cretin defense." He paced around the room. Finally, he came to a stop. He looked at the man and woman before him. "Kerry was one of the sweetest, most caring persons I've ever known. Yet, Litle began a successful smear campaign. Good Catholic girl isn't really 'good'. Former boyfriend is home from college for the summer. Three months later, good Catholic girl, abandoned by boyfriend, goes to live with relatives in Virginia where she gets an abortion. Truth? Good Catholic girl did get pregnant. Did go live with relatives. Had a miscarriage."

Hadley brought up his left hand, palm up. "One hand; she broke God's laws." He brought up his right hand. "Other hand; window peeper repents." He paused before making his final point concerning Kerry and her stalker. "Keep in mind, some people's God is not forgiving, and they have appointed themselves his judge, jury and executioner here on Earth."

"And the boyfriend?" asked Trish.

"Yep, yours truly," Hadley replied.

"Did you know about the baby?"

"You know what, Trish. It's none of your business, but you want my cards on the table, so here they are. I knew about the baby. But it wasn't my baby."

Hadley picked up his jacket, walked around the table and out the door.

"Next time you're the bad cop," she told Hutsell.

Rick Hadley went back to Lydia Janssen's room. He had two main thoughts. Ask Janssen if she'd ever been to Tennessee and get his truck—he wanted clothes that fit, and he wouldn't mind wearing his athletic shoes for a while. Janssen was sleeping, so he picked up the bag holding his jacket along with the Madison University Medical Center bag, went to the lobby and put on his boots. The five-block walk would do him good—he hadn't had any physical activity since he'd left Tennessee.

Hadley's jaw was set and his head was down as he headed out on the first leg of his journey. Anyone observing him would see a man so preoccupied with his thoughts that if he met a person looking at a cell phone—oblivious to his or her surroundings—the phone guru would be the one to step aside to avoid a collision before Hadley would.

Detective Trish Rankin had wanted to know his story and she'd gotten it—well, most of it. Many in Shannon County felt that he was too close to the case. And why wouldn't they, he thought. There was more to the J. Evan Litle story than Kerry Donlan. Kerry died five years ago—the slash that had brought him to his knees was two years later. Litle hadn't been solely responsible, but his hand had been right there between the pommel and cross-guard when the sword's blade had found its mark. Maybe he should take a page from Kleeman, the "Juliet" guy, and surround himself in "cop armor".

In so many ways, he was just going through the motions. His dad knew it. So did Chris, his brother. But it was his mom who felt it. Every now and then, he caught her looking at him in such way he knew she wished she could take his pain and carry it for a while. They all knew there was no future for him in Eagle Ridge. He wondered if there was a future at all.

Thinking of his mother brought thoughts of another—Faith Donlan—Kerry and Kelly's mother. Mrs. Donlan was a woman who had lost everything and it showed. Frail and off course, the woman had never blamed Rick for anything. She'd known he wasn't the father of Kerry's child. He remembered sitting beside her one night last August and holding her hand as she rocked for hours without saying a word. Kerry and Kelly would have been thirty-two years old that day. He felt she kept hanging on in hopes of seeing her children's killer brought to justice.

Hadley brought up the image of the man who had stood behind Janssen for only a moment this morning and with his head still down, repeated through clinched teeth the words from an Eagle's tune. *"Coming right behind you; swear I'm gonna find you, one of these nights."*

Rick Hadley was opening the door to his truck in the parking lot of Loretta's Diner when the woman who had waited on him earlier called out.

"Hey, Mister. How's she doing?"

Hadley walked over to her. "She's resting."

"She gonna be okay?"

"Doctor thinks so," he replied. "Thank you for your help this morning."

"I wasn't much help," she said. She carried something in her hand. She held the item out to him. "By the way, mom missed the lady's cell phone when she was putting things in the bag earlier. I was going to give it to one of the officers inside when I saw you. Figured it would get to her faster if you had it. Found it on the floor. The lady must have had it in her lap when she got up and ran to the restroom."

"Thanks. I'll make sure she gets it. How's it going in there?"

"We made sure no one went near the restroom till the uniform guys showed up. Didn't want any looky-loos—know what I mean?" Hadley nodded yes. "Even blocked off the booth you two sat in."

"I'm sure the officers appreciated it." Hadley reached in his jacket pocket for his wallet. He pulled out a business card. "May I borrow your pen?" referring to the one behind her ear. "I'm Deputy Sheriff Rick Hadley from Shannon County, Tennessee. I'm consulting on a St. Louis case with detectives Trish Rankin and John Hutsell," he said as he wrote the names on the back of his card. "If you think of anything else, please give one of us a call."

"Sure thing, Deputy."

Hadley got in his vehicle and drove to the parking lot's exit. He was waiting for a break in traffic when his cell vibrated. Rankin had sent him a message. "She's asking for you."

He typed, "Just got my truck. Be there as soon as I can."

25

Hmmm . . . not there. No fancy white Chevy Silverado parked at Lydia Janssen's home. Where are you Deputy? There're only two more places you would be: the hospital or the police station. Hospital first—maybe Lydia was working a double shift. It would take a long time to drive down every row in the hospital's several parking lots and garage, but a truck stood taller than cars so it would be like skimming for a certain word on a paper—it would go more quickly than one might think.

He was on his second pass when he'd spotted a tall guy in a Shannon County Sheriff's Department jacket on the street between the hospital and its southeast parking lot.

"Oh, say it *is* so, Joe," he said right out loud, using his dad's take on the famous 1920s line connected to Shoeless Joe Jackson. He and his dad would sit on the couch and watch *Eight Men Out,* and every time it came time for a kid in the movie to say, "Say it ain't so, Joe," he and his dad would say, "Say it *is* so, Joe." And right now, it *was* so. There he was, Deputy Sheriff Rick Hadley walking across the street.

Almost didn't recognize you there, buddy. Where're your jeans? Hadley turned south and he got an even better look. *Oh, and no white shirt? Maybe it's a special occasion. No, if it was, you'd be wearing a blue shirt. You are so predictable.*

He wondered why Hadley was walking with his head down. Why wasn't he taking in the scenery?

What's wrong Deputy? Did J. Evan Litle rain on your parade again?

He took a minute to appreciate Litle's abilities. The lawyer had sure known how to make Hadley and his dad sit up and take notice. What a stroke of genius Litle'd had when he'd started that rumor about Hadley and Kerry years ago. Oh, but it had been nothing compared to the stunt he'd pulled a few years later.

He drove through the second row nearest the street Hadley was walking on. The two were on a parallel course. He exited the lot a block later, driving slowly behind until he spotted Hadley's Silverado in a parking lot ahead. He picked up speed, passed Hadley, drove to the next stoplight and turned right. He went around the block and parked on a side street, so he could watch his prey.

Rick Hadley was talking to a waitress just outside the diner's entrance. She handed him an object. Wonder what that is, he thought. Hadley pulled something small and white from his wallet. He watched as the woman handed the deputy a pen from behind her ear. *He's writing something on the card for her. Or is he getting her phone number? Ha-ha-ha.* He recalled how former lover-boy Hadley hadn't had a girlfriend since the last time Litle had stretched his muscles. He gauged this woman to be twenty years Hadley's senior, but what the hey, he'd once heard a song by an Elvis impersonator that claimed older women understood younger guys. In fact, they knew "how to please a man". In his mind, he encouraged Deputy Rick Hadley to "go for it". After all, it might be Hadley's last chance to enjoy the company of a woman.

"I crack myself up sometimes. I really ought to 'take it on the road'—oooh, double entendre. Dad would have been proud of that play on words."

26

Rankin and Hutsell stepped into the hall outside Janssen's room so the nurse could take vitals.

"You know, John, he never did give us a name."

"He'll be here soon. I'll take lead for the next round."

"Do you think we got the truth?" Rankin asked.

"I don't think he lied, but the question is, did we get the whole truth?"

"With him, I don't think we'll ever know," she answered. She shook her head before saying, "He *is* good. Wonder what his solve rate is."

"I'm betting it's high," Hutsell said. "You know we could use someone like him."

"Why don't you wait till this thing is over before you go making suggestions."

The two were still outside Janssen's' room when Hadley, carrying a backpack, rounded the corner. He had exchanged his boots for cross-trainers.

"How is she?" Hadley asked.

"Very weak. How's it going at the diner?" Rankin asked.

"The uniforms are still there," Hadley said. "I gave the waitress my card with both your names on the back. Excuse me." He squeezed by them to enter Lydia's room. He dropped the backpack on the floor as he made his way to Janssen.

"How's it going, Arkansas?" he asked with an easy smile.

"Thirsty," she whispered.

Rick spooned a few ice chips from a cup and brought them to her lips.

"Maybe this will help," he said.

When Janssen asked Rick what the doctor had to say, Rankin moved further into the room while Hutsell remained at the entry.

"Here's Detective Rankin. She can fill you in," Hadley said and stepped back.

"Where're you going?" Lydia strained to ask Hadley.

He put his hand on the bed rail and said, "I'm going to get out of these scrubs. Three people have already stopped me and said, 'Doctor, it hurts when I . . .'."

"Funny guy," Rankin commented as she maneuvered Hadley out of the way.

"Rick, you want to meet me back in the waiting room after you change?" Hutsell asked as Hadley picked up his bag.

"Yeah, no problem."

Hutsell was leaning on the wall outside the family waiting room when Hadley, wearing Wrangler jeans and a blue shirt, approached.

"Just a few minutes, John. I've got something I need to check," he said and started for Janssen's room.

"Hadley, what's—?"

Rick held up his right index finger as a signal he wouldn't be long. Hutsell shook his head and followed.

Hadley tapped twice on the door jamb to Janssen's room and stepped inside. He walked over to the bed.

"Ms. Janssen, have you ever been to Tennessee?"

Hutsell arrived in time to hear the question. He looked at his partner as she pushed herself out of her chair. Janssen nodded.

"What part?"

"Nashville," she mouthed. She was having a hard time vocalizing. Hadley tried to stay with questions that could be answered "Yes" or "No."

"Any place else?"

She nodded.

"Have you ever been to the Smokey Mountains?"

Lydia nodded again.

"Did you just drive through, or did you stop somewhere?"

"Stop."

"Did you stay in Gatlinburg?"

She shook her head. "B&B in Maryville," she whispered. "Dollywood . . .magic show in Gatlinburg."

"When?"

"June," she paused trying to remember the year. "2015," she finally said.

Hadley reached over the bed rail and squeezed Lydia's hand. "Thank you." He turned and walked to the entryway. He nodded at Hutsell and pointed down the hall. Once inside the waiting room,

Hadley closed the door.

"John, you've got to call New Haven and Elko. Find out if Bryce and Newkirk were in *or* around Gatlinburg, Tennessee, prior to the first anniversary killing for each."

"Is that where he's from?"

"No. He's from Eagle Ridge, but he works in Gatlinburg."

"Damn. We're at fifty percent, Hadley. It's enough to get a search warrant for a stash of Halloween cards."

"No, it's not. Not in Shannon County with his former lawyer, J. Evan Litle as district attorney." Hutsell looked puzzled. "One, he was working the night Kelly was murdered. Two, he was in the hospital at the time of the Prasser murder. Three, his car was under the carport at his family's home this afternoon, and there was movement in the house. And four . . .."

"He hates the Hadleys," Hutsell finished. "He's not working alone, Rick."

"I know. But how are we going to prove it? If there's a Gatlinburg connection with the others, it will help, but—."

"Check his cell phone records? If he's here in St. Louis, he's probably communicating with someone in Tennessee?"

"Warrant, John," Hadley reminded Hutsell. "J. Evan won't issue one on him."

"Not if it comes from you," Hutsell said.

"Won't work. Litle will think I put you up to it."

"Oh, it'll work," Hutsell asserted. Now it was Hadley who looked confused. "Let's just say I know a 'guy' . . .."

John Hutsell pulled out his phone, pressed an icon, hit speaker and waited for the person on the other end to pick up.

"We've got a guy not playing by the rules," he said.

"Guess we better find one who will," replied State Senator Claire Nelson Hutsell.

27

As soon as Rick Hadley had moved his truck, he'd spied the police cruiser that had been behind the Silverado. Hey, even police have to eat, he thought. He'd followed Hadley from a safe distance as he made his way back to the hospital. Figuring he had some time, again there were only so many places the deputy would go, he returned to the diner for dinner and to find out what he could.

The cruiser was still in the parking lot when he shut off the rental's engine and sauntered into Loretta's Diner. To his surprise, the officers who belonged to the vehicle were not eating but had positioned themselves by the restrooms instead. He selected the closest empty booth to them, sat down and tried to overhear their conversation. But the most he could manage was a word or two due to a family with two bratty kids at the cash register. The waitress walked up with a glass of water and a menu.

"You may want to move to the other side of the diner, Mister," said the waitress. "When that bathroom door opens the smell will knock you over."

"Aw, that's okay. I've changed a few messy diapers in my time. I'll be fine," he told her.

"Suit yourself. Today's special is pork tenderloin with salad and your choice of vegetable," she said. "I'll be back in a few minutes for your order."

"Thank you."

He took a sip of water and opened the menu while watching the officers out of the corner of his eye. The bell above the door dinged as the noisy family left the restaurant.

The tall officer was an older, dark-skinned black man with a toothy grin. He'd already nicknamed him, Smiley. The other was a younger, shorter female with masculine mannerisms. He liked the name Butch for her.

"That Vaseline under the nose trick worked," said Butch.

"I know," Smiley said. "You ever heard of a gut wagon—'cause that's what it smells like in there."

"No," Butch answered.

"Back in the day, before vehicles, it was a horse-drawn wagon used to haul away scraps left over from butchering."

Ha-ha-ha—he's talking to Butch about 'butchering'.

"I was in the back seat of my grandparent's car when I was about six and smelled something really bad," continued Smiley. "I asked what it was. Grandfather said, 'It's a gut-wagon.' I looked over the seat as best I could and saw a trailer being pulled by a truck. I asked him if it was carrying guts, and he said it was."

"I don't envy the people who have to clean up that mess."

"I'm glad I'm not part of the crime scene team." There was that toothy grin again.

Butch checked the clock on the wall and said, "It's already past our end time. Hope they finish soon, so we can head back to the precinct."

"Yeah, too bad they were tied up at the park this morning where that jogger found a man hanging in a tree."

'Tied up' 'cause of a 'hanging.' These guys are funny.

The door to the women's restroom opened, and two men walked out. One carried a satchel. It took a few moments for the stench to reach the booth he was sitting in.

So that's what a gut-wagon smells like.

"We're done. Thanks for your help officers."

"That didn't take long," Smiley said.

"'Bout the only thing we had to do was collect a specimen of the vomitus," said the one with a neatly trimmed beard. "Don't know the full history on the woman who spewed, but Detective Rankin was concerned she might have ingested something that could have brought it on."

"Take it easy," said the other man as both techs made their way to the exit.

Smiley and Butch walked over to an old woman sitting near the register, said a few words, then they were out the door, too. The waitress was carrying a tray across the room. He picked up the water and menu and met her, "Believe I *will* move," he said.

"Let me clean off a table and I'll take your order." She went three booths down and piled dirty dishes and silverware on the tray. A young boy walked up, took the tray and carried it through the door leading to the kitchen. The waitress wiped down the table, pulled the pen from behind her ear and poised it above a notepad. "Have you decided, sir?"

"I'll go with the special," he said after sitting down. "What happened in there?" he asked, nodding at the women's restroom.

"A woman got really sick in there this morning. We had to call an ambulance."

"Why the police?"

"I'm not sure. There was some deputy with her. From Tennessee, I think. He had her under protective custody. Don't know why he was the one doing the honor 'cause I know she's local––seen her in here several times. What salad dressing would you like?"

"French. She going to be okay?"

"The deputy stopped back by about twenty minutes ago and seemed to think so. He was a real nice guy. He sure charmed my mom. Choice of vegetable?"

"Green beans with ham."

"I'll be right back with your salad."

He looked out the window, smiled and thought that the real nice guy's charming days were about to come to an end.

28

"Get down to the waiting room ASAP," read the text from Hutsell. "And bring the tablet."

Rankin hurried down the hall and was soon standing next to her partner.

"How is she?" Hadley asked Trish Rankin, his phone to his ear.

"Resting," Rankin answered. She handed the tablet to Hutsell. "What's going on?"

"Sorry, Dad, come again," Hadley said into his cell.

"We've got a name," Hutsell told Trish. "And even more important, we've got the connection."

"We think," said Hadley as he covered his other ear and walked to the far side of the room.

"Come on!" Hutsell barked at the small computer. He watched the screen. When the little spinning circle disappeared he said, "Finally."

"John! Talk to me," Rankin said

"Hadley's suspect lives in Eagle Ridge, but he works at a hotel in Gatlinburg." Hutsell opened the Bryce Case file. "Trish, tell your android assistant to take a note and read off this information. It's the contact info for the Bryce Case."

"Where's your notebook?"

"In the BMW."

Rankin did as instructed. Hutsell clicked a few more times. "Now, do the same for Newkirk."

"Got it."

"While I make the calls, sit down here and do a search for Kathryn Bryce. See if you can find a connection to Gatlinburg, Tennessee." The two switched places.

"Oh, and the guy's not working alone," Hutsell said.

"What?"

"He's got alibis for at least two of the murders."

"Then it's not him."

"There's a reason he's short-waisted, Trish. It's him," Hutsell said. "Go on, do the search for Bryce."

"Thanks, Dad." Hadley turned to tell the two investigators that information was coming via email, but each was busy with a task. He decided to check on Lydia Janssen. As he was about to enter her room, a woman in scrubs called out.

"Are you Rick?"

"Yes ma'am. How may I help you?"

"Ms. Janssen asked me to find you. Who's Tennessee? She's asking for him, too."

"I'll make sure he gets the message," said Hadley. He walked into the room and over to Lydia's bed.

"Hey, Arkansas. How're you doing?"

"Something's going on. Please tell me," she begged in a low voice.

"I've got to let Detective Rankin or Hutsell do that. Please try and understand." She closed her eyes. When they opened again, she wouldn't look at him. "There is something *you* can do, though."

Janssen turned toward him and mouthed, "What?"

"If I get pen and paper, would you write down anything you can remember about your time in Dollywood and Gatlinburg? Shows, restaurants, dates, times, incidents—anything?"

Janssen nodded. Hadley went to the nurse's desk and requested paper and pen. He returned to Janssen's room as his cell vibrated. He handed her half of the writing materials he'd collected and checked his phone. The email from his dad had arrived. He informed Lydia he'd be down the hall in the waiting room with the St. Louis detectives.

The room was silent when he entered. Both Rankin and Hutsell were immersed in the display on the tablet's screen. He made his way to the table, laid pen and paper on its surface and started reading over their shoulders.

"Three out of four. Seventy-five percent, Hadley," John Hutsell said. He raised up, "Here's what we've got. Bryce was a costume designer and had her own business, Costume Alley, in Gatlinburg in 2005–2008. And Hadley, read the name on the July 10, 2008 customer review."

"Judson Warner."

"Yeah, Warner had a murder mystery theatre in downtown Gatlinburg till he got a job in New Haven. Bryce closed the business after the 2008 peak tourist season."

"She followed him to Connecticut," said Hadley.

"Her job in New Haven didn't begin until February 2009, so that's what I'm thinking, too."

"Any results from your phone calls?" Hadley asked.

"Didn't raise anyone. Left messages."

"I've got the data we need from Shannon County," Hadley said.

"Forward to me, and I'll start the ball rolling on a warrant for his cell phone records," Hutsell said.

"John, the battery on this thing is about gone," Rankin said.

"I know. The power cord's in the car. I need to head to the station, anyway. What do you want to do?"

"Go with you and work on this. But somebody's got to stay here. You and Rick have the connections to get things done right now, so it's probably best that he be the one to go with you," she answered.

"Just a suggestion, but Janssen is writing down everything she can remember about her trip to Gatlinburg and the surrounding area. I know the place, and I know his routine," said Hadley.

"Good point." Trish powered down the tablet. "We'll stay in close contact."

"Oh, one other thing," Hadley said. "Janssen knows we're on to something. She asked me about it. I told her she would need to speak to one of you. Please give her something before you leave."

"Okay, I'll go down in a minute," Rankin said.

"I'm heading to the vending machines outside the emergency waiting room."

"Dang, Rick, that's no good," Trish said. "The hospital cafeteria is closed for the night. but there's a small deli across the street that delivers." She pulled out her phone, picked up the pen and wrote down a phone number. "Go for the premium roast beef, cole slaw instead of chips, cookie or brownie—your choice. They'll meet you at the employee entrance used by our suspect this morning."

"Thanks, Trish."

"John, I'll see you at the precinct after I talk to Janssen," Rankin said. "And Vashon needs an update."

"Will do. See you in a bit," Hutsell replied. He carried the tablet to the doorway, stopped and turned. He caught Rick Hadley's eye. The two men exchanged a respectful look. "I'll be in touch."

Hadley nodded. He sat down at the table and started making

arrangements for his dinner. Rankin got his attention and pointed toward Janssen's room. He nodded.

Lydia Janssen appeared to be sleeping when Trish Rankin walked in her room. There was a paper with hand-written notes under Janssen's hand, her fingers still holding a pen. Rankin hated to disturb her. She tried to gently pull the paper free when Janssen opened her eyes. The patient looked at the St. Louis detective.

"I'm sorry," Rankin said. "Were you sleeping?"

"No . . . I'm just so tired."

"Deputy Hadley said you had some questions for me."

Janssen nodded.

"We do have a suspect we're looking at. The tourist industry in eastern Tennessee may be the connection. May . . . be," Rankin stressed. "Detective Hutsell and I are leaving for the station. Deputy Hadley will remain with you."

"Where is he?"

"Getting dinner. He'll be back soon. May I borrow this paper to make a copy from which Detective Hutsell and I can work?"

Again, Janssen nodded. When Rankin returned to the room, Janssen's breathing was slow and steady, a sign she was sleeping. The detective placed the paper on the bed tray for Hadley before leaving.

· 29 ·

He was lounging on the queen-size bed, staring over his folded hands at his wiggling toes. He thought of all the players in his little production.

Thinking of himself first, he began, "This little piggy went to St. Louie." The next line was Lydia's. "This little piggy got sick." Then the new character, Hadley. "This little piggy met a floozy." Don't forget Poet. "This little piggy's a sidekick." He paused, trying to think of a comparable last line. After a minute, he gave up and said, "And this little piggy is one happy camper." He laughed so hard he almost fell off the bed.

If his dad were still alive, he would have given a thumb's up to the new words his son had come up with for an old nursery rhyme. People loved his dad, not only because he was a great man, but because he made them laugh. His dad had taught him how to tell a joke, and when he'd started making people laugh, the bullying decreased. His dad's favorite type of humor was the "play on words." He'd worked hard to increase his vocabulary, so he could please his dad with a new joke every now and then. He still read the "Word Power" section of *The Reader's Digest* every chance he got.

He knew he needed to be formulating a plan. Lydia was in the hospital, and he would have to wait until she got back home to secure the win, so he felt like he had all day tomorrow to come up with one. Besides, he'd had a big day, and believed he deserved a little down-time.

He looked over at his wallet and pocket contents laying on the night stand. He picked up the Ober Gatlinburg key chain that held Lydia's two keys and rubbed the circular piece of plastic before holding it between his index finger and thumb for a closer look. He wasn't a skier, but he liked the picture of a bear hugging a snow-covered tree. Not that he was a nature lover either, but it was on clearance last summer at a truck stop/travel center outside Sevierville, Tennessee, and the price was right. He'd been in a hurry that day. He'd stopped in to get a double order of the potato wedges he loved, when he'd spotted the key chain by the cash register, and tossed it on the counter. He wouldn't need the keys after the next few days, but thought he might keep the chain. Maybe he'd start a collection . . ..

Before he dozed off, he thanked the man upstairs for his good fortune. He had faith that everything would work out, and that he would be on his scheduled flight Monday morning.

· 30 ·

Rick Hadley had received a text that Lydia Janssen was sleeping, and he would find Janssen's notes on the bed table. He collected the paper and returned to the waiting room with his evening meal. The third item on Janssen's list caught his eye. Although she had misnamed the place, he felt he now knew where Lydia Janssen and his suspect had crossed paths. He called John Hutsell.

"John, I'm looking at Janssen's list of places she visited around Gatlinburg. One of—."

"Trish made a copy of the list," interrupted Hutsell. "She's getting coffee, but I know it's here. Hold on a sec." Rick crumpled up the bag that had contained his sandwich and shot it into the trash can by the door. "Here it is," Hutsell finally said. "Okay, what were you saying?"

"The third item down is The Underground Railroad Café. The actual name of the restaurant is The Underground Kitchen. It got its name from a skirmish over property owned by Governor John Sevier of Franklin, the proposed fourteenth state to the union. John, it's a block south of the Overmountain Hotel."

"His place of employment," Hutsell said. "I'm getting notes together for 'The Senator' to present to Missouri's Attorney General's office to pass on to Tennessee's AG with a request for our guy's cell records. When Tennessee's AG sees the national scope of this investigation, I think we'll get the warrant. We're asking only for his calls, messages, etc. right now—Litle won't even have to be informed. When it comes right down to it, Rick, Tennessee's AG can't take the risk. He won't want to be accused of dragging his feet in a serial-killer case by his opponent in the next election."

"I hope you're right."

"What does Janssen have to say about the café?"

"She's sleeping, but we know she was there the first week in June 2015. She received the first Halloween card on the Fourth of July, three weeks later."

"Can you hear it, Rick?" Hutsell asked.

"I hear you snapping your fingers."

"Nah, it's not my fingers. It's the sound of the pieces falling into place."

"You've come a long way from 'Hut-one, hut-two Hutsell,'" said Hadley.

Detective John Hutsell had reviewed the email sent by Sheriff Mike Hadley from Shannon County, Tennessee. He had a name, two addresses, a cell phone number, and a place of employment. Attached to the email was the suspect's criminal history, mugshot, and current photo. The latter was a taken from a church directory. He'd passed it on to his mom, The Senator. She would present it with circumstantial and video evidence the next day in a meeting with a Missouri assistant district attorney in Jefferson City. Hutsell had included a photo of the display board in the investigation room and an updated document he'd originally prepared for Lt. Gail Vashon, showing primary and secondary victims, modus operandi, and motive. He had yet to hear from law enforcement in Connecticut or Nevada. It was a waiting game now. At 11:45 P.M., he climbed in his red BMW and drove home.

Trish Rankin had spent most of her evening on the computer. She'd been unsuccessful in linking Jenny Newkirk to Gatlinburg. Rankin had been the one to make the call to Lt. Vashon about the eastern Tennessee connection for three of the primary victims—what she and Hutsell were officially calling a break in the case. Vashon had never been the excitable type, but she always made sure her ducks were in a row. Rankin knew the odds were good that Vashon would show up tomorrow to start preparing a presentation for her boss. Around 8 P.M., she called her kids to see what exciting news they had to share. Josh had made it to a new level in a video game, and Sophie was coloring pictures her father had downloaded from the computer. At 10:30, she texted Deputy Hadley, saying she had nothing new to report, and that she and Hutsell would touch base in the morning. She went home, poured a glass of wine and streamed *Bosch*, a cable TV series based on author Michael Connelly's Hieronymus Bosch character.

Lydia Janssen woke up to a quiet, dimly lit room. She saw a

dozing Deputy Rick Hadley sacked out in a short-legged recliner with the paper containing her notes on his lap under his right hand. She wasn't feeling much pain, but she was thirsty. She pressed the nurse call button.

"What time is it?" she asked the nurse upon her arrival.

"About 2:30 A.M. Is there something you need?"

"Water."

The nurse held a small cup of water to Janssen's mouth. "Small sips," she said. When Lydia motioned she'd had enough, the nurse checked the IV drip and asked if Lydia needed anything else. Lydia shook her head from side to side.

Janssen looked at Hadley and wondered what progress had been made while she'd been sleeping. She wished they would tell her more—like who their suspect was. The few days she'd spent in the Gatlinburg area had been fun but uneventful. She'd tagged along with her sister and 12-year-old nephew on a historical vacation to Virginia. They'd called it their Colonial America Tour. The three had visited Jamestown, Williamsburg, Jefferson's Monticello and Washington's Mt. Vernon.

One night the television was on in their hotel room, and her nephew saw a commercial for Dollywood. He asked if they could go. At the suggestion of a co-worker they'd already arranged to stay in Maryville, Tennessee, at a B&B, so Lydia and her sister had checked an on-line map and found the amusement park was only an hour out of their way. Why not, they thought. They liked roller coasters just as well as the next person. They'd even managed to take in dinner and a magic show the night before in Gatlinburg. She didn't recall any run-ins during their time in Tennessee—no road rage incidents or persons thinking they had cut in line at a ride. She didn't recollect anyone trying to flirt with her—nothing.

She fell asleep hoping her mind would be clearer in the morning and she would remember what on Earth she'd done to get the attention of a psychopath?

Lydia Janssen was reclining in her hospital bed after having a breakfast of fruit juice, vanilla custard and honey-lemon tea. It had been a little over twenty-four hours since Rick Hadley had found her lying in a pool of her own vomit. The nurse had just informed her that a doctor was making rounds and would be in to discuss her condition within the hour. The nurse exited the room as Rick Hadley entered. He was clean-shaven and wearing a fresh, medium, blue shirt. He glanced at her breakfast tray.

"Glad to see you've got an appetite."

"Want to help catch him," she said, her voice revealing how weak she still was. She tried to raise herself in bed by pushing her elbows on the mattress, but was having little success.

"Hold on a minute there, Arkansas."

"Keep sliding down."

Hadley moved the bed tray aside, picked up the call button and asked for assistance in repositioning the patient. His cell vibrated in his pocket.

"I'll be right back," he said and stepped into the hall.

"Good morning, John," he said. "Anything to report?"

"I was about to ask you the same question," replied Hutsell. "Too early on a Sunday morning. I doubt we hear anything till late afternoon or early evening, and that's if we're lucky. How's the patient?"

"Weak, but eating well. She's anxious to assist in any way she can. She's been racking her brain for an incident or a face that stands out from her time in Sevier County, but she keeps coming up blank."

"Speaking of faces, I'm thinking of putting together a photo line-up."

"Sounds good—the doctor is here. Talk to you later."

The doctor looked up from his patient's chart. "Good morning Ms. Janssen. How are you feeling?"

"Tired."

"That's to be expected for a while," he said. "Your vitals are good." The doctor picked up the breakfast tray covering. "Did you eat all your breakfast or did you hand it off to your friend?" he asked, only half-joking.

"I did. He had breakfast in the cafeteria. When can I go home?"

"You're eating well, up and walking to the bathroom with assistance—all good indicators of a speedy recovery, but I'd like to keep you for another day."

The doctor turned toward Hadley. Rick stuck out his hand, "Deputy Sheriff Rick Hadley, sir," he introduced himself.

The doctor shook Rick's hand. "Looking at notes from yesterday, I understand you are a licensed medical professional in addition to being a member of law enforcement. And you're planning on staying with Ms. Janssen once she's released?"

"Yes, sir."

He turned his attention back to his patient. "A clerk will bring you a list of 'do's and don'ts' I'd like you to get familiar with." He smiled and asked, "You promise to follow them?" Lydia moved her head up and down. "And to follow-up with your regular doctor?" She nodded again. "Let the good deputy wait on you, okay? Don't overdo it."

Janssen looked at Hadley and nodded once more.

"I'll see you tomorrow morning, then. If you continue to improve, we can talk about discharging you."

"Thank you, doctor," she said.

When she was sure the doctor had gone, Lydia looked at Rick. "We're going for a walk down the hall, Tennessee. Come over and assist please."

The statement was somewhere between a request and a demand. Rick Hadley felt that the Lydia Janssen he'd met Friday was back in charge. He wasn't sure it was necessarily a good thing.

By mid-afternoon, John Hutsell had called with a status report. A Missouri DA had agreed to contact the Tennessee District Attorney's office in Knoxville. Elko authorities were checking with Newkirk's friends and relatives about a Gatlinburg connection. Lt. Gail Vashon had alerted upper management that two of her detectives were working on a nationwide serial killer case. And thanks to Trish Rankin and a computer program, a photo array, including the picture of a certain Eagle Ridge, Tennessee, resident, would soon be ready for viewing.

Deputy Rick Hadley touched base with his dad. There had been movement at the suspect's family residence until 11:40 P.M. It took up again at 8:25 the next morning. Lunch had arrived via a food ordering and delivery service at 12:15. Rick and his dad found it encouraging that the occupant had forgone Sunday Services—could it be he was in St. Louis instead of Eagle Ridge? And if so, who was the person making it seem like he was home? Both men hoped cell phone records would point to his unnamed accomplice, as known associates and family members had been accounted for.

At five in the evening, Lydia Janssen announced she was leaving the hospital, AMA—against medical advice. No pleading or cajoling on the part of nurses and/or Rick Hadley could dissuade her. As she put it, Hadley could take her home or she would have hospital personnel wheel her down to the entrance and a cab could do it for him.

With little recourse, Hadley texted Hutsell about the change in plans and asked if it was possible for a uniformed officer to check out Janssen's residence for signs of her stalker. Hutsell said he would do it himself and remain until they arrived. Hadley then used his cell to place an order with a discount store as Lydia Janssen's menu needed to be filled with liquids and soft foods, and he needed supplies of his own. On the way to East Redbud Drive, he stopped by the store and an employee carried out the ordered items.

· 32 ·

He'd already made two runs by the hospital, and Deputy Rick Hadley's truck was still parked in the same place as the night before. Time was starting to run out. His scheduled flight was set to depart at 7:50 in the morning, and he needed to be at Lambert at least two hours earlier—he couldn't take the chance of arriving late to the airport in this day and age.

He'd thought about calling in sick, so he would have an extra day, but Poet had texted that his family home was indeed under surveillance. He guessed Hadley must have recognized him after all. If Hadley and his "peeps" continued to run reconnaissance on him, he'd just sic J. Evan Litle on them.

One good thing; he did have a plan. But to execute it, Lydia Janssen would have to be home. The groundwork had been completed at 2:30 A.M. In the wee hours of the morning, he'd driven to Lydia's, parked a block away, and staying in the shadows, made his way to her back door. Shining a small pen-light on the lock, he'd pulled out his tree-hugging bear keychain and entered Lydia's workroom. Although he'd been in Lydia's house several days ago, he'd not been afforded the time to become familiar with the entire floor plan. So, he'd used a small flashlight and given himself a tour.

Wow, he thought—what he could do with all these fantastic power tools at his fingertips. Ha-ha-ha. Finger . . . tips . . ..

But first things first.

He walked through the garage and up the two steps to Lydia's kitchen door, where he used the second key. Once inside, he propped open her refrigerator door for extra light. The kitchen was in good order. He checked the cabinet under the sink and knew Lydia, or whomever, had found the snake venom he'd left. Last Wednesday, he'd actually turned on the water to wash it down the drain but had changed his mind. It would become one more "thing" Lydia would have to worry about.

The kitchen's entry was directly across from the bathroom's doorway. Moving clockwise, he took two steps to his right and stopped just shy of the front door. He turned left and shined the light inside the small room Lydia used as an office. No greeting card this time, my sweet, he thought. Those days have come to an end. He smiled. "The End." He preferred the term "The Big Finish," used by his father.

He leaned against the door jamb and thought of the time his mother, the church soloist and choir director, had been asked to help out with a high school musical. The choir teacher's appendix had burst the previous weekend, and mom was happy to help. A couple of times, he and his dad got to attend the play's rehearsals. One night, the drama teacher announced it was time for the big finale. His dad had leaned over and quoted baseball player, Frank Thomas, "I want to thank these guys for pulling my big butt across the finish line." They had snickered a little too loudly, and his mom had given them a disapproving look. In unison, they'd both used their hands and given the "My lips are sealed" gesture.

He didn't really have time for reminiscing, so he did an about-face, and with the flashlight shining the way, took a step forward, placing him back in the hall. He walked past the sliding double-door closet, took one step to his right, and entered the bathroom. He stopped and retraced his steps. He noticed the front door was not in a direct line with the entry to the bathroom or to Lydia's bedroom. The closet jutted too far out in the hallway, creating a "blind spot." Good to know, he thought.

He picked up his tour with the bathroom. Again, nice and neat. On to the bedroom. The bed was at the far wall. He noticed the wardrobe to his right. He opened the doors. The right side had drawers; the left was designed with a rod for hanging clothes. He started pulling out drawers for a look-see and picked up an item he felt would come in handy later. He slid his back pack off his shoulders and placed the garment inside. He closed the wardrobe, exited the bedroom and moved back into the kitchen-living area.

The furniture was on a small scale. No way would Hadley be comfortable in this room, which raised a question concerning sleeping arrangements. Only one bed—would Hadley dare? Whether he did or didn't, if things went even the least bit sideways J. Evan Litle could make a case that Hadley *had* dared. After all, think of the deputy's previous encounters with the opposite sex. But then again, what could go wrong? Pre-planning and reconnaissance pointed to a successful outcome.

A few paces left and he noticed a light radiating from behind him. The refrigerator was still open. Oh, can't forget that, he thought. He closed it, and made his way to the garage door, never once entertaining the thought that he just might be getting a little cocky. He shut and locked the door, then down the steps and into the wood shop.

He shined the light around the room, focusing on all the power tools. He had similar ones in his shop at the family home. Thinking of the coming event, he gleefully made another round with the flashlight, saying, "I'll take one of those . . . and one of those . . . and one of those." Finally he locked Lydia's backdoor and made his way back to his hotel.

Between runs to check on Hadley's location, he'd placed several twigs he'd brought with him from the yew plant back home on the bathroom counter. Next, he'd set-up a new mini-chopper—he wanted everything to be nice and fresh. He'd plugged it in and snapped the twigs into smaller pieces. While he chopped them to little bits, he'd thanked the United States Department of Agriculture for its website that had told him how much foliage (after all, it was the fourth anniversary—flowers and plants) to body weight he needed to do the job. Then he'd put the poisonous chippings in a zip-lock baggie.

He planned to tell Lydia how she could put an end to it all by having a little "snack." She might resist at first, but she'd beg for it once he put one of her tools to use on Rick Hadley. He'd cleaned up what little mess there was, stored the chopper in the back pack and put the baggie in his coat pocket. With everything in place, he decided a nap was in order. He set his alarm, lay down, and went to sleep.

· 33 ·

"All clear," said John Hutsell as he climbed out of his red sports car. He'd been sitting in the running BMW to stay warm.

He took Lydia Janssen's house keys and opened the door so Rick Hadley could carry her inside. While Hadley made sure Janssen was comfortable, Hutsell brought in the grocery bags and stored perishables in the refrigerator. He ran a cursory check through the small home, returned to the kitchen, and waited for Hadley.

"Got the results of the warrant just before you pulled up. His cell is in Eagle Ridge at the family home and has been all weekend."

"I had a feeling that was going to be the case," replied a disappointed Hadley. "Caleb Murry, a friend of my dad's is helping out with surveillance. He pretended to walk by the residence as food was being delivered. He struck up a conversation with the delivery guy saying 'something smells good'. He was told it was a pasta dinner with all the trimmings. Murray walked a few steps down the street, waited for the kid to return to his car and asked, 'How do you get something like that delivered?' He was told by a phone app that stored name and method of payment. The kid was still holding a copy of the receipt so Murray asked if he would download the app for him."

"And he got a look at the name, right?" Hutsell asked. Hadley nodded yes. "Everett Ryan Highley."

"Yep."

"So, if that was him yesterday morning, he's back home, now" Hutsell said.

"Looks that way."

"Well, for what it's worth, hospital security sent over more video. It shows our hockey fan entering the hospital at the same place he exited. I've sent it to you. Let me know if you see anything new."

"I will."

"Oh, where's your computer?" Hutsell asked.

"Stored in my truck with my duffle bag.

"Why don't you get it. Trish sent you the photo line-up. Might as well have Janssen look at it."

While Hadley retrieved items from his vehicle, Hutsell knocked on Janssen's bedroom door.

"Yes?"

"Ms. Janssen, do you feel strong enough to look at a photo line-up?" he asked.

"Yes."

"We'll need your Wi-Fi password."

"It's on the back of the modem in the office."

"Thanks."

Hutsell caught Hadley as he entered the front door.

"In here," he told the deputy. Hadley walked into the office, powered up his computer, and hooked up to the internet. He opened the computer-generated photo line-up and carried his computer to Janssen's bedroom.

"There's a TV tray behind the headboard," she told the two men.

Janssen took her time looking at the six-photo array. On her fourth round, she indicated that the second man on the top row was familiar. She stared at his picture for a long time, but couldn't say what it was about him that had captured her attention or where she might have seen him.

"Is it him?" she asked Hadley.

"Ms. Janssen, it would be inappropriate for either of us to answer that question," said a stoic John Hutsell.

"How about I warm up some chicken broth," Hadley said. "And there's butterscotch pudding for dessert."

"Yum," responded Janssen flatly.

Hadley picked up his computer and carried it to the kitchen table.

"Wish she could have positively said it was number two," said Hutsell.

"There's a reason he looks familiar, John. She's just got to figure out what it is and then we've got him. Figuring the logistics is the main problem now—and identifying his partner.

"Not too many serial killer duos," Hutsell said. "A lot of times it's a family member. LA's Hillside Strangler cousins. A husband-wife team from Canada. We even have a famous husband-wife team from here in Missouri—Ray and Faye Copeland. They lured men from Springfield's homeless shelters to their farm and set them up with bank accounts to purchase cattle at sale barns. When checks bounced, the men couldn't be found. The victims were drifters, so good luck finding them. Their bones were finally discovered buried in the Copeland's barn. Any chance Highley's partner is a relative?"

"Could be," answered Hadley. "But known family members in Eagle Ridge are accounted for."

"Where's Eagle Ridge?" came Lydia Janssen's voice from the hallway.

"What are doing up without help?" Rick Hadley asked.

"I have to go to the bathroom," she replied. "So, you think he's working with a relative of his?"

"Detective Hutsell, you want to spoon up some broth and bring it to the bedroom while I make sure Ms. Janssen gets to the bathroom and back?" Hadley asked.

"I do believe you are annoyed with me, Tennessee."

"Wouldn't do me any good if I was. So, bathroom and dinner—in that order."

After Janssen was served dinner, Hadley accompanied Hutsell to the front door.

"Don't envy you this one, Deputy," said the St. Louis detective.

"She'll be asleep before long. She's still very weak and needs the rest. I'll review the video from yesterday morning. If I find anything, I'll let you know. Are you going to be free tonight if something should come up?"

"What was it you said the other night . . . none of your business?" Hutsell grinned.

Rick Hadley smiled back, "Have a good evening, Detective."

·34·

Lydia Janssen fell asleep around 8 P.M. Hadley viewed the latest video from hospital security. From the man's build and gait, he had no doubt it was Highley.

At 9:15, a car alarm down the street started to blare. Rick Hadley checked on his charge and saw she was still sleeping. The alarm ceased, and Hadley went back to the kitchen to prepare his own dinner. He had just finished a turkey sandwich when his cell vibrated.

"Just heard from Elko, Nevada," said John Hutsell. "Jenny Newkirk attended a craft show at the Gatlinburg Convention Center in spring 2014. Her friend, Victor Arhens, was murdered that fall."

"The Liquid Paper drowning," added Hadley. "Highley sells crafts online and attends the area's local craft shows. You know John, I've been racking my brain as to why he's changed—why he's actually making contact with his victim."

"And . . .?"

"Highley and his dad were very close. Kenneth Highley was a successful photographer. His photographs were used in calendars, tourism brochures, even puzzles. He had a studio at the family home we have under surveillance, but he also traveled a lot. He often took his son with him. Kenneth passed away from pancreatic cancer in December. Everett took it really hard."

"What you're intimating is pretty depraved, Rick."

"Yeah, a father-son duo. But it's one avenue we haven't looked at. I'll suggest it to my dad in the morning. Of course that doesn't explain who he might be working with now."

Rick heard another car alarm. It was weaker than the first—probably farther away.

"That's the second car alarm that's gone off in the last twenty minutes," he told Hutsell. "John, see what's going on around here."

"I'll call you right back."

Hadley had just finished washing and putting away the dishes when Hutsell called.

"Looks like we've got some vandalism in the University District. So far four cars have had their windows smashed. Police are patrolling the area."

"Thanks, John. I'll talk to you tomorrow."

"Night, Rick."

Hadley sat down and reflected on John Hutsell's comment to Trish Rankin when she'd expressed skepticism that Highley might not be the man they were looking for, "There's a reason he's short-waisted, Trish."

Everett Ryan Highley was diagnosed with Klinefelter's Syndrome, a genetic disease, when he was in elementary school. He carried an extra X chromosome that manifested in certain physical features. Long legs and a short torso were just a few. Other characteristics, such as enlarged breasts and wide hips on a male, almost guaranteed he'd be the butt of jokes growing up. Hadley had to admit, Highley had endured a lot of ridicule throughout his life.

Rick began to wonder if it was the facial features of the man in photo two that had triggered an elusive memory for Janssen. He did a search for distinctive facial features of Klinefelter's but the closest he found was for Trisomy—disorders with an additional chromosome—of which Klinefelter's was one. He was in the process of comparing listed features when his truck's alarm went off.

Hadley went to the front door. He was tall enough that he could look out the decorative elliptical window over the door. The light from an outdoor fixture allowed him to see that the windshield of his vehicle had been shattered. He wondered if he should go out and shut off the alarm or just wait for it to die on its own. Six of one, half dozen of the other, he thought. Hadley decided he didn't want to leave Janssen alone for even a few minutes, so he pulled out his phone. He didn't feel the incident was worthy of an emergency, so he called the University Heights Police Station instead of 911 to make a report. He kept an eye out for any movement while he reported the incident.

Thinking she was most surely awake because of the alarm, Hadley headed for Janssen's bedroom. He never made it. As he passed the bathroom he was struck on the head from behind and went down on all fours. Another blow put him prone.

Hadley was vaguely aware of a weight on his back, and then his arms and hands became fixed. Next, something opaque was pulled over his head. As his mind started to clear, he realized he was in real trouble. His hands were tied behind him; he couldn't see, and his head was pounding. To make matters worse, his truck's alarm was still blaring, compromising his hearing. Hadley tried his best to concentrate and realized he could feel the vibrations of an intruder's footsteps as the man walked down the hall.

His first thought was to yell a warning to Janssen, but it was no use. Even if he could yell loud enough to be heard over his truck's alarm, she had nowhere to run or the strength with which to do it. Finally, the alarm went silent. It wasn't much comfort for the next thing he heard was a panicked Janssen.

"Rick!"

Hadley's ears continued to ring as he made it to a sitting position. He could hear voices coming from Janssen's bedroom but couldn't make out what was being said. Then he felt the floor vibrate again and knew the intruder was walking in his direction.

"Put me down." It was Lydia Janssen's voice.

"Now, my dear sweet Lydia, you might as well save your strength for the party," came a familiar voice.

"Hello Everett."

"Hello, Cousin Richard," said Everett Ryan Highley. "And don't call me that."

Richard . . . Rick . . .. Lydia's fear ratcheted up another notch. Could it be true? Could the man she had placed her faith in be cousin to the one who had terrorized her for over three years?

"I hardly recognized you with that hood," said Highley. "So nice of you to come to our little farewell party."

Highley let go an eerie laugh as Lydia entertained the thought that Rick Hadley had been part of the conspiracy to destroy her all along. From her position, she couldn't see Hadley or the so-called "hood." She envisioned a ritualistic one and wished she'd dismissed Hadley along with the two St. Louis detectives last Friday and carried out her original plan. At this moment, she welcomed death, but not the kind these two envisioned. She stopped struggling. She needed to save what little strength she had. If she was going to die, she was going to try to take one or both of them with her.

"Richard, the festivities will take place in Lydia's wood shop. It will make a fine play room, don't you think?" asked Highley rhetorically. "You are going to have to get there on your own. I'll guide you, so listen carefully. Are you ready?"

"And if I'm not?" said Hadley as he used his fingers to determine what kind of hand restraint his cousin had applied.

"I'll return with one of Lydia's toys and we can play a scene from Stephen King's *Misery*."

"I don't have a choice then, do I?"

"Not really," said Highley. "You've always been the athletic type. Of course it's been a long time since you did the Fosbury Flop thing in high school—or college for that matter—but I'll bet those long legs of yours are still strong enough to get you to your feet. So upsa daisy."

The nylon rope wrist restraint used by Highley had been fashioned using a "handcuff knot." Good old, over-confident Everett, Hadley thought. Knowing his cousin like he did, Hadley guessed Everett had done a search and assumed the "handcuff knot" would restrain a person in the way police handcuffs would just because of the name. The knot had actually been designed for water rescue, and some hunters used it to haul harvested deer from the woods. The truth was, the rope handcuff was a poor excuse for a wrist restraint for anyone trained in tactical escape. Little by little, Rick begun to increase the slack in the rope. Eventually, he'd work his hands free. Now at the direction of his captor, while continuing to stretch the rope, he pretended to be cooperative and used the wall behind him as leverage to get to his feet.

"See how easy that was, Richard?" asked Highley. "Walk forward until I tell you stop."

Rick did as he was told. As he got closer to the garage he felt a slight draft and knew the door was open.

"Stop, and ease your foot forward till you reach the metal strip where the flooring ends," instructed Highley. "Now, you've got to go two steps down to the garage floor. Be careful; you don't want to fall and damage that pretty face of yours."

After Hadley had successfully navigated the steps, Highley, carrying Lydia Janssen over his shoulder, made his way to the entryway.

"Turn right and take three steps," continued Highley.

With Hadley safely ahead of him, his cousin made his way down the steps into the garage.

"The shop door is open. Go inside. Once you have cleared the door, put your back to the wall and slide down to a sitting position," said Highley. "And I do mean sitting—cross your legs like they were in that picture of all of us taken at Aunt Cora's in 1993. You know, the one with you in the center of all us kids—the one where half my body is *cut* off. By the way, remember that word—cut."

Again, Rick followed Highley's instructions. When Hadley was seated, Everett Ryan Highley proceeded into the shop where he stopped and shifted Janssen on his shoulder. Lydia saw an opportunity and grabbed a tool off the storage board. The tool had just cleared the top of a small storage cubby when Highley laughed.

"Nice try, Lydia. Hand it over," he said, reaching over his left shoulder. Lydia placed a pair of pliers in his hand, pretended to lose her balance and palmed a small bottle of decorative art varnish from the nearest cubby.

"Be careful Lydia. You're not much more than skin and bones right now but it wouldn't take much for me to drop you on this concrete floor."

Highley walked over to a stool near the work bench that ran along the west wall and sat Lydia down. She doubled over, held her sides in pain and leaned on the bench. With Rick Hadley in full view, she realized the covering over his head was actually a pair of her black leggings. Good enough for who it's for, she thought.

Everett Highley clapped his hands together and said, "Let the party begin." He put his hand on Lydia's shoulder. "I've got an idea for a unique piece of furniture," he told her. Then he looked at Hadley, pretended to be a movie director and placed his hands in front of him as if framing a camera shot. "I'm thinking a table or chair. Not just any table or chair, mind you, but one made with the limbs and torso of the perfect male specimen."

With Hadley's eyes covered, his hands tied behind him and his legs crossed, his cousin walked over and pulled the leggings off his head.

"Well?" he said. "He's about as *perfect* as they come, don't you think?" Then as an afterthought, "By the way, do you want these back?" He tossed the leggings at her and laughed again.

Classic, Everett, thought Hadley of his cousin's grandstanding. It's all about you, which means you aren't paying attention to detail.

Highley made his way back to Lydia. Standing beside her, he reached in his pocket and pulled out the baggie containing the chopped yew twigs. He dangled the bag in front of her face.

"What's a party without snacks?" he asked. "Unlike my cousin Richard, you've got a choice on how you go. Not very tasty, but these tidbits will do the job." He tossed them on the bench to her right. "It's a little chilly in here," he said as he took a couple of steps and turned on the electric space heater. "An older model, but it will take the chill off."

"You won't get away with this, Everett," said Hadley.

"I told you not to call me that," he said through clinched teeth. "Only two people can call me by that name. One is dead and the other worships the ground I walk on. I'm Ryan to you—just like you're Richard—not Rick—to me."

While Highley was berating his cousin, Lydia Janssen lifted the small levered opening of the varnish bottle. He was one step away when she pointed it at him and with both hands squeezed its contents into his face. Highley screamed and took a step backwards, falling over the heater. He immediately scrambled to his feet and unplugged the device, saying, "Not going to be that easy, Lydia. Nobody's going up in flames tonight."

Highley used the sleeve of his shirt to wipe the varnish from his face. "So kind of you to use one that's not irritating to the eyes," he said. The first thing he saw when his eyes focused was a finishing nail gun. Lydia Janssen was holding it with both hands and it was pointed at him.

"Don't come any closer," she warned.

"Lydia, come on," he chided. "You and I both know that gun has two safety features. It has to actually make contact before it shoots a nail."

"Not this one," she said.

Highley didn't believe her. Lydia Janssen pulled the trigger and a nail flew through the air and embedded itself in his hip. Highley screamed and went down a second time. Rick Hadley was immediately on his feet, his hands almost free.

"Stay where you are *Cousin Richard,*" she said.

Lydia Janssen was very weak. She knew it, and so did Rick Hadley. In a few moments, he would be able to physically disarm her but he chose another way instead.

"I understand," he said, knowing she was confused about his role in this scene. "How about this?"

Lydia was leaning heavily on the work bench.

"My hands are almost free. Let me finish freeing them. I'll take out my phone with two fingers, dial 911 and put it on speaker. Is that okay?"

She nodded yes and then turned to the moaning man on the floor and stated, "Be still and shut up before I shoot you again."

"911, what is your emergency?"

"This is Deputy Sheriff Rick Hadley from Shannon County, Tennessee. You are on speaker. I am at the home of Lydia Janssen, at 6821-B East Redbud Drive. Send police and an ambulance. There is an intruder wounded on the floor in Ms. Janssen's wood shop at the back of the garage. Ms. Janssen is understandably unsure of me in this situation and has a nail gun aimed in my direction. The nail gun's safety features have been disabled, and it can shoot a nail through a distance. Also, please contact St. Louis detectives, Trish Rankin and John Hutsell out of the University District Precinct. Tell the officers all parties—the intruder, Ms. Janssen and I are in the shop."

"Miss Janssen, can you hear me?" asked the 911 operator.

"Yes."

"Is the information Deputy Hadley given correct?"

"Yes."

"Police are on their way."

At that moment, Everett Ryan Highley grabbed Lydia Janssen's foot. She adjusted so the nail gun pointed at him. She fell from the chair and landed on top of her attacker. The nail gun fired driving a second nail into Highley. He yelled out in pain. Rick Hadley sat his phone on the floor on his way to Lydia.

"Ms. Janssen, what's going on? Can you hear me?" yelled the operator.

"Lydia, it's going to be okay," Hadley said as he pulled her free of his cousin. He grabbed the nail gun and threw it in the garage.

"Deputy Hadley, speak to me."

"Make that two ambulances," he said. "Ms. Janssen left the hospital AMA earlier this evening. She has not sustained further injury but is very weak and needs medical attention."

"The intruder?"

"His name is Everett Ryan Highley from Eagle Ridge, Tennessee. He has two nail puncture wounds. One in his left hip, the other in the upper right inner thigh. His face has been splashed with a decorative varnish."

"I know where I've seen him before," whispered Janssen.

"Don't try and talk now, Arkansas."

"Deputy, are you armed?" asked the 911 operator.

"Yes ma'am. I have a gun in an ankle holster."

"Keep your hands in plain view when the police arrive."

"They're almost here. I can hear the sirens," he said.

"Do not hang up," she added.

"Yes, ma'am."

Lydia Jansen was sitting upright in her bed watching for the third time, a press conference that had been conducted earlier in the day by The St. Louis Police. The Police Chief had just turned over the microphone to Lt. Gail Vashon of the University District Precinct. With Trish Rankin, John Hutsell, and Rick Hadley standing behind her, Vashon addressed the citizens of St. Louis.

"Thanks to the unrelenting work of St. Louis Detectives Trish Rankin, John Hutsell, and Shannon County, Tennessee, Deputy Sheriff Rick Hadley, at least eight homicides throughout the United States have been solved. The work of these three investigators led to the discovery of a cache of photos of serial killer, Kenneth Highley with his victims. Highley of Eagle Ridge, Tennessee, died in December, 2018. His son, Everett Ryan Highley, also of Eagle Ridge, had taken up where his father left off in the stalking and terrorizing of a St. Louis resident."

The Anniversary Killer Case was now national news. Janssen clicked off the television and proceeded to wait for a visit from the man she called, Tennessee. At 6:30 sharp, his Silverado pulled into her driveway. The knock on her door was answered by Benton County, Arkansas, Sheriff Jimmy Matthews.

"Deputy Hadley, please come in. She's waiting for you in the bedroom."

"Thank you, Sheriff Matthews."

Rick Hadley made his way down the hallway and rapped his knuckles on the open bedroom door.

"How's it going, Arkansas?" he asked.

"Not bad. I'll be heading back to work soon. What about you, Tennessee?"

"Not sure yet," replied Hadley. He walked into the room and stuck his hands in his pockets. "I'm going to take some time off to figure out my next move, but before I do, I want to be sure you know what's going on behind-the-scene."

"Have a seat," Janssen said, indicating an upholstered chair,

"What's the latest?"

Matthews' phone sounded. "It's my son," he said and disappeared down the hall.

"As you know, Everett Highley is my third cousin and has Klinefelter's Syndrome. His mother, Elise Highley is first cousin to my mom."

"I still can't believe all this started because my nephew noticed his physical appearance was similar to our uncle's, who has the same genetic condition. All my nephew did was mention it to me."

"Well, the story is Everett didn't actually hear the conversation that took place at The Underground Kitchen. Supposedly his father overheard what was being said and told his son that you and your nephew were making fun of him for having Klinefelter's. It was just another example of what his father called the 'superiors' persecuting the 'inferiors'. The 'superiors' had used their God-given beauty, talent and wealth to oppress and bully 'inferiors'."

Jimmy Matthews returned with a kitchen chair and sat down.

"Like many people of faith, Kenneth Highley had taught his son that God worked through his 'believers' to make a better world," continued Hadley. "That concept was reinforced by what he heard in church and read in the Bible. Only Kenneth left out the part in Romans where God says 'vengeance is mine'. Instead, Kenneth taught his son that they'd been 'chosen' by God to set things right on Earth—that doing away with those who tormented God's people was a sacred mission they'd been given. And because one was not to be prideful, the 'chosen' must carry out their task in secret."

"He bastardized the Bible's teachings," Janssen said. "As a child, I can see where your cousin would fall for this line, but as an adult ...?"

"You have to realize, people who teach that you should follow blindly do so to cement their own power," Hadley said. "Their 'sheep' are never taught to critically think and are admonished for questioning."

"You've got something there. I remember talking to a neighbor about what it was like to go to a Catholic school. She was surprised to learn our religion instructor allowed us to question the church's teachings. When I thought about it, I started to wonder, too. I knew a lot of Catholics who fell back on the old, 'we are not to wonder why' platitude, so I asked my teacher why she let us question. Her answer: faith.

"She had faith in us and in the Church training we'd received. She felt that once we'd explored other viewpoints and positions, we would come to feel that the Church's teachings had set us on a path on which we would do our best in our endeavors and our personal lives as well as serve others along the way. And therefore, we would indeed be servants of God."

"Along the line of, 'If you love something, set it free'," said Matthews.

"Okay, back on topic," Janssen said. "So, your cousin wasn't taught to question or think, then how was he able to get to the point where he almost killed the both of us?"

"As long as he followed what his dad taught him, he was okay," replied Hadley. "For example, Everett knew how to steal and use identities by emulating his father. But he went off script. His dad was gone. He started to freelance and in not having the ability to think critically, he made mistakes. Think about it. He wrote a note on a card—something that had never been done before. Detective Hutsell sent out a bulletin, and in less than twenty-four hours, we knew you weren't the only victim."

Hadley shifted his weight in the chair.

"Also, he knows his way around a work shop. He's done crafts most of his life. Trish Rankin wondered if there was a wood-working connection, and, in a way, she was right."

"I have one question left," Lydia said. "What is Highley actually being charged with?"

"I'm not very happy about this," Matthews said.

"None of us are," said Hadley. "Right now, there is no evidence that Everett took part in any of the murders. He knew about them, and what other jurisdictions will decide to charge him with, we don't have a clue, but conspiracy to commit murder is in there. As far as St. Louis goes, a deal has been made."

"Do I want to hear this?" Janssen asked.

"Stalking."

"What happened to attempted murder and assaulting a member of law enforcement?"

"When Elise Highley showed up, the situation changed," Hadley said.

"You should have seen the video of him crying to his mom,"

Matthews said. "Saying, 'I promised Dad. Mom, I'm sorry. I thought I was doing the right thing.' Then his mom, *comforting* him. 'It's my fault son. I should have known. I should have protected you. I was the one who asked him to take you on his business trips'."

"In exchange for photos Kenneth Highley had taken of himself with his murdered victims, which meant the chance to solve eight murders, including one in Sweetleaf, Mississippi, we didn't know about, St. Louis dropped the attempted murder and assault charges."

"Jimmy, what about Benton County?" Janssen asked.

"With the older Highley being dead, no evidence on the younger one—in fact a foolproof alibi for Rob's murder—Benton County's DA's office signed off on conspiracy charges and closed three unsolved murders."

"Bottom line, what's he getting?" Janssen asked.

"Nine months with the possibility of parole in six," answered Hadley.

"What about his accomplice in Eagle Ridge?" asked Matthews.

"Poet is an old hippie, nothing more. He thought Everett was gay, and he was covering so his mother, the staunch evangelical, wouldn't be a problem. He cooperated fully with an affidavit, and by turning over Everett's cell along with the back-up with which they used to communicate when Everett was out of town."

Deputy Sheriff Rick Hadley stood and said his goodbyes. He was at the bedroom door when Lydia Janssen spoke up.

"Hey, Hadley."

Rick turned around, "Yes, Janssen."

"Why did he get so angry when you called him Everett?"

"From the beginning, his parents had planned to name him Ryan. The name Everett came about when one of his Mom's clients—Elise worked for a maid service at the time—offered her a riverside property in exchange for naming her son after the client's husband. The client was a wealthy woman who was unable to have children. Everett's parents agreed. The property became a photo studio for Kenneth Highley and a craft shop for Everett."

"Have you always called him Everett?"

"Our family always has, but in school I, like everyone else, called him Ryan. I knew using Everett would irritate him. I needed to rattle him any way I could."

"Well, it worked," Janssen said. "Thank you for all you've done,

Tennessee."

"I should be thanking you, Arkansas," Hadley said. "You're the one who took him out."

Deputy Sheriff Rick Hadley sat in a booth across from Detectives Trish Rankin and John Hutsell at the 10–7.

"What do you think Hadley, do you believe Elise Highley? Was she ignorant of what her husband and son were doing?" Hutsell asked.

"No way of knowing at this point. She claims she found the pictures in a safety deposit box her husband had arranged for her—that it was in *her* name only to stave off law suits by his half-brother over an inheritance. She said he gave her envelopes of money periodically and she would deposit them in the box."

"And she didn't look inside the envelopes?" asked Rankin.

"Not until she needed money for Everett's defense," replied Hadley. "That's her story anyway. Me, personally? No, I don't believe her, but she's got a lot of support in Eagle Ridge in the religious and business communities."

Trish changed the subject by saying, "John's already been contacted by a cable station to bring the Anniversary Killer to TV. The producers are keen to feature him in the show."

"And . . .?" asked Hadley.

"I gave them your number," Hutsell told Hadley with a smile.

"Careful, Detective. You know what they say about karma," Hadley warned.

"Don't worry, you're safe," Hutsell said. "But Trish and I think the department might order us to give interviews—good PR and all that . . . .."

"My dad's on the hook at home when it comes to the media. I won't even be in town. And I don't plan on heading back soon," Hadley said. "I'll finish my report tonight from my hotel, then I'm taking some time off to sort through the last five years. I really feel the need to distance myself from Eagle Ridge."

"A vacation, huh?" Rankin asked. "Where you thinking of going?"

"Haven't got that far, yet," answered Hadley. "Maybe I'll start by taking a trip up the Gateway Arch."

"Make sure it's not a windy day," said Rankin. "Unless you like to sway, that is."

All three investigators smiled as Trish Rankin slid out of the booth.

"It was good working with you, Deputy," she said and reached over to shake his hand. "Look us up if you're ever in town again."

"Yes, ma'am."

Rankin smiled and slightly shook her head. "You can take the boy out of the country but you can't take the country out of the boy," she acknowledged. "Good night, gentlemen."

Trish Rankin checked the time on her cell while the clerk was ringing up her purchases. She had three hours before she was scheduled to pick up her kids. After storing her packages, she closed the cargo door. She spotted her daughter's tiara in the back seat on the way to the driver's side door. She got in, pulled out onto the street and as she drove, played back the memory of the day Sophie had worn it into the station.

"That's a pretty fancy crown you've got there, Miss Sophie," a co-worker had said.

"You can try it on if you want?" Sophie'd offered. "But you have to give it back. If you don't, my mom will make you. She's a policeman."

"Oh, I'll give it back," the man replied.

"But I have to put it on," Sophie said.

The man had looked at Trish for permission to pick up her daughter. She'd nodded her approval.

"Take a picture, Mom."

While stopped for a red light, Trish pulled up the picture on her phone and looked at her daughter in the arms of a smiling Gabe Fenske, sporting a tiara. When the light turned green, she put on her blinker and pulled her car into the left lane. Twenty minutes later, she entered the driveway of the white house she had parked across from last Friday night. She made her way up the steps and knocked on the door.

"Hi, Trish," Fenske said. "Everything okay?"

"Sophie can't find her crown and she wondered if you might have it."

"I don't think so, but you're welcome to come in and look," Fenske said with a smile.

"I don't have a warrant."

"You don't need one."

Gabe Fenske walked Trish Rankin to her car. When she turned to say goodbye, he cleared his throat and nodded at Sophie's crown in the back seat.

"Oh, that's where it is," she said, sheepishly. "Sophie will be very relieved to see it when I pick her up."

"Feel free to stop by if she misplaces it again," he said with a smile.

"I will. She does it quite often you know?"

"I think she gets it from her mother."

Stacy Parisi spied John Hutsell and Rick Hadley. She walked over to the booth they shared and sat down next to Hutsell.

"Saw you on TV."

"Yeah, couldn't be helped."

"Lori Chandler and I are heading over to the Quicksilver. Why don't you and the fine deputy join us?"

"What do you think, Rick? Paper work versus a night on the town?"

"Well, when you put it that way . . .."

John Hutsell and Rick Hadley descended the stairs that led to the Quicksilver night club. There were tables and chairs arranged on three sides of a recessed dance floor. On the far side, a live band was doing a mic check. Stacy Parisi stood when she saw the two men arrive and waved them over to the table she shared with Lori Chandler, a pretty woman whose blonde hair was styled in a low bun updo. On their way, Rick was happy to see the club had several pool tables. Where his favorite pastime was concerned, Hadley felt like he'd been going through withdrawal.

"You got here just in time," Stacy said. "The first set is about to begin."

Introductions were made for Hadley and Chandler. A waitress soon arrived and took their drink order. A whistle came from the bandstand followed by a rhythm guitar. The crowd knew their part and sang, "That . . . that . . . dude looks like a lady." Then the lead singer took over as the patrons made their way to the dance floor, Stacy and John leading the way.

Hadley watched as Hutsell executed a hand slide move and led Parisi in a triple twirl.

He raised his voice so he could be heard over the music. "I heard he was good, but I had no idea he had those kinds of moves."

"Yeah, John's pretty popular. How about you, Rick? You like to dance?"

"I've been known to two-step across a few dance floors."

"Want to try this one?"

Rick stood up, extended his arm and said, "After you."

Halfway through the second set, John Hutsell took his phone out of his pocket. He looked at the screen, told those at the table he'd be back in a few minutes and walked up the stairs and outside. There was a solemn look on his face when he returned.

"Everything okay?" Rick asked.

"What do you say, we go play a game of pool."

"What's going on?" questioned Hadley once the two men were alone.

"Just got a message from my Aunt Jean in Springfield. My cousin Elle may be in trouble."

For the next few minutes, John told Rick the story of his cousin Elle Wyatt. Elle's life hadn't been an easy one. She'd been sexually molested by her step-father at the age of eleven. Elle told her teacher, and authorities removed the step-father from the home. While he was under investigation, he returned, killed Elle's mother and attempted to kill Elle before shooting himself.

Elle was adopted by her and John's aunt and uncle in Springfield. Elle abruptly discontinued therapy when she turned nineteen and had been on a path of self-destruction ever since. Things had started to improve. Elle was spending more time with her best friend from high school and had picked up sewing again. She had real talent when it came to putting fabric to a sewing machine. The family was holding its breath, hoping Elle was on her way to becoming a responsible adult.

John had just been informed by his Aunt Jean that his cousin was missing, which in of itself didn't set off alarms—Elle often took off for places unknown. But Jean insisted that this time was different. A lady in town had seen Elle that morning and reported that Elle was covered in bruises and had a cut lip. Aunt Jean was asking for John's help.

"She was a bright spot at family gatherings when she was a kid—she was so much fun," John said. "I hate the son-of-a-bitch who took that kid away."

Rick Hadley remained quiet, letting his friend talk through his emotions.

"I'm not proud of it," Hutsell said, "but I've got to tell you, Rick, there've been times I've thrown up my hands in disgust at some of the stunts she's pulled."

Hutsell paced the width of the pool table, finally stopped and said, "The Janssen Case is over and like you, I've got some time coming . . .."

Hadley waited a few beats and then asked, "What do you want to do, John?"

"She's family, Rick."

"Then let's go find her."

PART TWO
HIS AND HER DEMONS

Forgive sounds good
Forget, I'm not sure I could
They say time heals everything
But I'm still waiting

From the song, "Not Ready to Make Nice"
by
Martha MaGuire, Natalie Maines, Emily Robison
and
Dan Wilson

· 1 ·

Elle Wyatt drove into the parking lot in front of the small building. The area was well lit, after all it was a commercial property. He'd told her to park in any space she wanted as the office had closed three hours earlier.

She'd met him online early last week. They had exchanged messages and pictures in the beginning and had graduated to talking on the phone several days ago. He wasn't what one would call handsome, but Elle liked his rugged look and was impressed with his ability to carry on a conversation. She'd laughed when he told her about a couple who had been in the office recently.

"They were in their sixties, I think. Anyway, the man, who was in a wheel chair, passed gas. His wife tried to deflect the blame by asking, 'Was that a car backfiring?' The husband said, 'No, honey. That was a left cheek sneak.'" He laughed and then continued, "The last time I heard that line was on an *X-Files* rerun."

"I remember that one. Mulder and Scully were outside a house on Christmas Eve."

"Yeah, they were. You like the *X-Files*?"

"I had a poster like the one in Mulder and Scully's basement office once upon a time," Elle said.

"'I want to believe.'"

"That's the one."

"Did you see the new episodes that aired last year?" he asked.

"No, I missed them."

"I still have them on my DVR. Would you like to come over Friday evening and watch them?"

Elle didn't answer right away.

"I guess it's a little premature to talk about being alone together. What do you say about a coffee date instead?"

"I can drink coffee anytime, but how often do I get a chance to see the latest *X-Files* episodes? I'm in," she'd told him.

His place was attached to the office of a storage facility in eastern Springfield. He was the onsite manager. Elle got out of her car and walked up a small incline so she was standing on the porch when he opened the door.

"Charles?"

"Guilty," he said with a smile. "Please come in."

Elle entered the front office.

"That leads to the kitchen," he said pointing to an opening in the far wall. "The living area is just beyond. The place is small, but it's all I need. Come in and I'll show you around."

Elle followed him through the kitchen that opened onto a nicely decorated living room. He motioned to the only interior doorway in the place.

"That's the bedroom. The bathroom is inside on the right."

"I had no idea some storage facilities had living quarters on site."

"Yeah, it's actually a pretty good gig. Sure makes the customers feel better." He pointed to the kitchen and said, "Would you like to join me while I make some popcorn?"

"Sure."

Elle took off her coat and placed it on the back of a chair as Charles opened the cabinet above the stove and reached up. Instead of coming down with a package, he twirled around and struck Elle full force in the face. She fell hard against the refrigerator, its handle digging into her back.

"I guess we're not going to watch TV," she smarted off as she wiped blood from her lip.

"Oh, hell no," he said.

Elle was pushing herself off the refrigerator when he twisted his hand around her hair and pulled her into the living room.

Charles punched her in the stomach, knocking her to the floor. Elle's left side hit the corner of the coffee table as she went down. She doubled over with pain. He grabbed her shirt and pulled her to her feet. He punched her in the face again before shoving her to the floor a second time. Her head bounced off the table this round. She rolled from her back unto all fours and tried to crawl away.

"Where do you think you're going?" he said.

He went for her hair again but never made it. He heard a click and looked down to see he was bleeding from the abdomen.

"What the fuck!" he yelled as Elle struggled to her feet, still holding the switchblade she had pulled from her ankle sheath moments earlier.

"Take one more step and I'll kill your ass," she snarled.

He made a move forward.

"Oh, please do," she said. "It's taking everything I've got not to cut you six ways from Sunday as it is."

He looked down at his hand covering the wound. Blood was seeping through his fingers.

"If I were you, I'd get to an emergency room pronto," she said.

"They'll come after you for attempted murder."

"Send them. They'll take one look at me and you'll be the one behind bars. You're good at making up stories, so you better come up with a good one that doesn't include me."

He started to feel weak. With difficulty, Elle pulled her car keys from her pocket as he collapsed on the sofa. She grabbed her coat on the way out.

"Cal, I'm hurt."

"Elle, where are you? What do you need?" Cal Davies said into his cell.

"The corner of East Mill Cross and South Gillian. I need medical attention . . . but, Cal, no emergency rooms, got it?"

"Damn, Elle. You've been warned over and over! Who did it? Can he still get to you?"

"He's in worse shape than I am. Just come and get me and take me to your place."

"What about your car? Oh, hell, I'll get Lance. He can drive your car back here."

"Bring a couple of blankets."

"So there's blood. Are you still bleeding?"

"I don't think so. Just hurry."

There was little traffic at the intersection of the parking lot Elle had chosen to pull into and call for help. She closed her eyes and leaned her head against the seat's head rest, wincing as the pain spiked from an open gash. She put her hand on the back of her head and felt the congealed blood that had collected from the collision with the coffee table. She changed tactics and rested her forehead on the steering wheel instead. Elle cradled her left side with her right hand and waited for Cal to arrive.

Davies pulled his restored 1980 GMC Jimmy next to Elle's 2016 Caddy so the driver's windows of both cars were across from each other.

"How bad is it?" he asked.

"I'm not sure. Bruises, a busted lip, head gash . . . maybe a fractured rib."

Cal and Lance Geraghty jumped out of the Jimmy. Lance collected two blankets from the rear seat as Cal opened Elle's car door and knelt down so they were facing each other. In the ambient light he could see the red beginnings of a black eye accompanied by swelling. The cut on her lip was no longer bleeding.

"Can you move?" he asked.

"With great difficulty."

"Let me help you up so we can get you to the passenger seat."

Elle cringed at the pain as Cal reached in and moved her legs in unison from the floorboard to outside the car. He waited till she nodded her willingness to proceed. Cal reached for her right arm as Lance did the same for her left. Both men carefully lifted her from the seat. Her friend lent his support as Lance retrieved one of the blankets he'd placed on the Caddy's roof and positioned it around her shoulders. The night air was cold and Elle was glad for the covering. Cal picked her up and carried her to the far side of the car. Lance opened the door and Cal gently sat her down in the passenger seat.

"You okay?" he asked.

Elle nodded. He closed the door and walked to the driver side.

"What do you want to do?" Lance asked Cal.

"From what I can tell, the bleeding has stopped and she's not having trouble breathing. I'll get her home, call Sean, get his take and then decide the next move."

"Okay. You lead, I'll follow."

Cal covered the Caddy's driver's seat with the remaining blanket, got inside and the two vehicles made their way to North Trenton Avenue.

"Thanks for coming, Sean," Cal told his friend as he walked through the front door.

Lance stood up from his seat and the two men nodded at each other as a greeting. That was as good as it was going to get. Lance hadn't liked Bychowski since the good doctor had left Cal several years ago for a closeted state politician.

"Where's the patient?"

"I put her in my room," Cal said.

Sean followed Cal to the master bedroom. Elle was lying on his bed with her eyes closed.

"Elle, this is Dr. Sean Bychowski."

"Doctor," she replied in acknowledgement of the introduction.

"Let's see what we've got here," Bychowski said.

He set his medical bag on the night stand and went to work.

"Get your razor, Cal, she needs a few stitches." He turned toward Elle. "Ms. Wyatt, you really need some pictures. You may have a few broken ribs, and x-rays are the only way to know for sure. You need to go to the emergency room."

"My family is well known in this town. I'm tired of the whispered comments beginning with, 'I don't know why they continue to put up with her . . ..'"

"Tell them you were in a car accident," Bychowski suggested.

"There are just so many accidents a person can be in. Can we just say I have my reasons for handling things this way and get on with it?"

"It's your funeral," he acquiesced.

"Sean said there's not much he can give you for pain, Elle," Cal told her after Bychowski had gone. "Heavy-duty pain killers mess with pupil response, which I've got to keep an eye on since you may have a concussion. And no matter what, if I think things are going south, you are going to the emergency room."

"Okay, fine," she said. She hurt too much to argue.

"I can load you up on over-the-counter pain relief meds, but that's about it. Go ahead and sleep if you can, but Lance or I will be waking you up every few hours to make sure you can answer basic questions. And if you can't, you're taking a ride to Melcher Memorial North."

Elle closed her eyes, resigned to the fact that Cal would follow through with his promise to get emergency treatment if he was convinced she was deteriorating. All she wanted right now was some blessed sleep. She managed to get down several pain reducing capsules. She felt they must have helped because she soon fell asleep.

· 2 ·

Elle opened her eyes to a snoozing Lance. He was occupying a chair that had been moved close to the bed. He was halfway lying down with his legs propped up on the mattress. He stirred when she tried to move.

Lance opened his eyes. "How you feeing?"

"I need to use the bathroom."

"Okay, let's get you there."

Lance helped her to the bathroom. He stood outside the door until she was ready to return. She glimpsed her face in the mirror on her way out. There was quite a bit of swelling and a hint of blue coloration to her left cheek and eye. She knew that, in a few days, most of her face would be deep purple. At least Bychowski had used steri strips for the cut on her lower lip rather than the conventional stitches he'd used to close the gash on the back of her head. She wondered how much area had been shaved, not because she would have a bald spot, but more in terms of how noticeable the spot would be to inquiring minds.

"You hungry?" Lance asked after she was back in bed.

"I don't know what I am."

"Well, you need something in your stomach with all the pain relievers you're popping."

"Plain toast will work."

Elle looked at the clock on the night stand. It was 9:40 A.M. She closed her eyes. She hurt all over.

Trying not to be consumed by pain, she went back in time to when she'd first met Cal. It was seven years ago in a group therapy session for people like them—victims of sexual assault. She hated that description: sexual assault. Hell, it was like "they"—society— was sanitizing what had happened to them. Call it what it is. RAPE! *It makes you uncomfortable to say the word rape? Well, too fucking bad! It's pretty damn uncomfortable to be raped!*

She was fed up with the word "victim," too. Victim: a poor, pitiful, cowering thing. Well, she might have been a victim at one time, but she wasn't anymore. She'd proved it last night, and that son of a bitch didn't know how lucky he was.

So much for getting last night off her mind. She was thankful when Lance appeared and interrupted her thoughts. He placed a tray with two pieces of toast and a bottle of water on the bed.

"Thanks."

"No problem," he said.

"When will Cal get home from work?"

"Probably about one. You need him to bring anything? I can text him."

"I'll give it some thought."

"The TV remote is on the night stand. There's a *Doctor Who* marathon on BBC America," he said.

"How do you know I like *Doctor Who?* I don't remember us ever talking about it."

"Tardis cell phone case." He nodded to her phone on the night stand. "So which doctor is your favorite?"

She gave him a look.

"Okay, I get it. You don't feel like talking. So, I'll just answer according to what I think you'd say."

Elle wasn't one for small talk, and most of her time in Lance's company had been spent laughing. Maybe after what had happened to her, he'd decided on a different approach.

"Number nine, Eccleston, was the sexy one. And Tennant, the tenth doctor was the one companions fell in love with. Well, except Donna Noble. Matt Smith, number eleven, was the kid everyone wanted to go exploring with. But the latest one, Capaldi . . . his Doctor Who is somewhat crabby. I think he's your favorite. You can identify with him."

So much for not laughing.

"Damn, Lance. You know it hurts . . .."

Lance smiled and didn't miss a beat. "Well, as for me, I'm going with Eccleston. It was during his reign they introduced Captain Jack Harkness and eventually the spin-off, *Torchwood*. Women loved Captain Jack, but he was also a 'man's man', if you know what I mean."

Lance was smiling from ear to ear, and she couldn't stifle a laugh. She groaned and begged, "Please Lance . . .."

"Good medicine often has its side effects, Elle," he said, causing her to groan again. "So, if it's okay with you, I'm going to hop up on the other side of this king-size bed you've been hogging all night and binge watch *Torchwood*."

She nodded her approval.

They were both asleep when Cal walked into the room. Last night had been a long one for all of them. He went to the living room, took off his shoes, and lay down on the sofa. "Three can play this game," was his last thought before his breathing became slow and measured.

Lance left for home around six in the evening. When Cal checked on Elle, she seemed to be resting comfortably. He turned to leave.

"Cal?"

"Yes."

"Have you ever wanted to kill your rapist?"

Cal walked over and sat down in the chair by the bed.

"Yeah. Even planned it out. There're a lot of hog farms in southeastern Missouri. And hogs will eat anything."

"You never told anyone you'd been raped at the time, did you?" she asked.

"No. There were already rumors floating around I was gay. I was artsy-fartsy in a rural community at the time AIDS was considered to be God's vengeance on homosexuals. He was the bank president. I was fourteen. I wouldn't have been believed."

"I couldn't kill mine. He took that away from me by doing it himself." She paused. Her voice was low and full of hate when she spoke again. "Last night I saw my step-father's face, and I wanted to stab that guy *again* and *again* and *again* . . . once for every time my step-father had raped me."

Cal waited several seconds before asking, "What stopped you?"

"You know, Cal," her voice now more measured. "The first thing that came to mind was, 'So this is how it's finally going to end'. And if I'd thought all he'd wanted to do was kill me, I think I would've been good with it. But it was the way he was going about it that was unacceptable," she said. "If he'd chosen a quick, easy method, I would have let him."

Cal had been where Elle was right now. Lance was the one

who'd given him a "safe space" from which he could voice what he was feeling. Elle needed that now. But he was keenly aware that he needed to make sure she was safe from herself.

"So why did you call me, Elle?" he asked. "Why did you reach out for help last night?"

"My mother. If I'd died sitting in my car that would have been by my own hand. My mother died saving me, Cal. Suicide would be a betrayal."

"Elle, if the next guy wants to kill you and you let him, isn't that an indirect way of suicide?"

"Perhaps. But it's a distinction I'm willing to live with," she said. "Is that an oxymoron statement? 'Indirect *suicide* is something I'm willing to *live* with.' Doesn't matter. Maybe the correct term is 'assisted suicide'. After all, we're talking about quality of life, here, aren't we?"

"How long since your last session with Sarah?"

"I don't go anymore."

"Maybe it's time you reconsidered."

On the morning of the fifth day following Elle's brutal attack, she received a phone call from a cousin on her father's side.

"Cal, I need to get to Melcher Memorial South," she said after disconnecting the call.

Normally, Cal would be at work, but he'd taken the day off for a doctor appointment. Cal held a contract with the US Postal Service to transport mail from one post office to another, so taking a day off meant he had to arrange for someone to fill in for him. Enter Lance. Lance, like many Americans, worked two part-time jobs to make ends meet. Some days would find him selling jewelry at a department store at The Battlefield Mall, and other days, he functioned as a process server. When Cal needed time off, he would plan it for a day Lance was not scheduled for either job.

"What's going on?"

"You remember my cousin, Myles Stafford?"

"On your dad's side, right?" Cal said. "He's the one who has a liquor store and tavern in Galena."

Elle nodded. "His daughter was air-lifted to Melcher Memorial South yesterday. She's asking for me. Will you drive me?"

"Sure, my doctor's office is a few blocks away. I can drop you off on the way to my appointment and pick you up after. What do you say we leave early enough we can get a pork chop and gravy biscuit?"

"I like the way you think."

"Glad your appetite is back," he said. "You need help getting ready?"

"No. I'm okay with short easy tasks. I'll be out in a few minutes."

Elle put on the new clothes Lance had purchased for her two days after she'd been assaulted. He'd offered to get what she needed from the guest house she had inherited from Grandpa Nelson, but he would've had to drive past the main house on the Wyatt Estate to do so. Still wanting to leave inquiring minds in the dark, she'd gone online and selected a couple of outfits and then given him cash to pick them up at the store's local outlet.

Once in the car, Cal asked about the emergency that had brought Elle's second cousin to a hospital in Springfield.

"Kaela's been estranged from her family for a couple of years. Yesterday she showed up at the package store in a lot of pain with vaginal bleeding. She wasn't coherent so Myles called 911 and the operator dispatched an air ambulance. Turns out she was twenty-three weeks pregnant. The placenta had detached. The doctors couldn't save the baby."

"That makes for a rough family reunion," Cal said.

"Nothing you can really say at a time like this. Just be there . . . .."

"I didn't know you and Kaela were close."

"She saw me as someone to confide in at an early age, because I knew how to keep my mouth shut."

"That's a fine line to walk."

"Yeah. I remember when she started belting out songs—she was in middle school at the time. Myles began pulling her on stage with his band at events like Crane's Broiler Festival."

"Wait a minute," said Cal. "Did she appear with her father's band on a local news station a few years back?"

"Yes."

"Dang, Elle, she's good."

"I know. When Kaela was sixteen, her dad hired a group out of Oklahoma to fill in for his own band while he was recovering from knee surgery. The lead singer's name was Lonnie Marcum. She was allowed to attend Marcum's practice sessions. Marcum asked her if she had any requests. Instead of just giving him the name of a song, she sang the title. He invited her to sing harmony with him as his band performed the song. Her parents thought it good experience for her—at least they did at the time."

There was a break in conversation as they placed their breakfast order at Hardee's drive-thru. While they sat in Cal's Jimmy and ate, he asked why the relationship between Kaela and her parents had become strained.

"A little over a year later, Kaela's maternal grandmother was in the hospital in Tulsa. After being discharged, the grandmother needed assistance at home. Both Myles and his wife, Adsila—Sila— went to stay with her for a week. It was during fall semester finals at Kaela's high school so, Myles and Sila arranged for Kaela to stay with their drummer's parents. Myles booked Marcum's band to fill in during their absence."

"Sila's got a voice on her, too, as I recall."

"She's full-blood Cherokee, and you should hear her sing 'The Cherokee Morning Song'. She would sing it for Kaela when she was a baby, and they often performed it together at Cherokee music festivals."

Cal gathered up their trash from breakfast, got out of his vehicle, and deposited it in a nearby bin. Elle picked up the conversation after he pulled out onto Battlefield Road.

"Myles knew Marcum was no longer with the band when he signed the contract. What he didn't know was that Marcum 'occasionally' traveled with them. Maybe if he'd known that little bit of information, he might have stayed in Galena."

"Why the air quotes?" Cal asked.

"The story was Marcum had landed a good paying job and was no longer available for most out-of-town gigs. In reality, he didn't 'occasionally' accompany the band—he went everywhere with them."

"Why the subterfuge?"

"He'd developed a reputation as a sexual predator."

"Damn, Elle, the world's full of them. If he was a teacher, I can see where it would cost him his job, but lead singer in a band? How does that happen?"

"His taste ran on the young side. The band's booking agent received so many complaints about Marcum's predatory behavior that he was black listed. Of course, all this came to light after Marcum had convinced Kaela to run off with him."

"What?"

"He was a slug, but he had talent, and he looked like that guy from the TV show, *Supernatural*."

"Jensen Ackles?"

"Yeah, that's the guy. Anyway, he fed her head full of ideas of making her a 'star'—that he knew people in the business who could make it happen and after all, he *loved* her."

Cal pulled up outside the hospital's front entrance.

"You going to be able to make it on your own?" he asked. "I can park and help you inside."

"If I take it slow, I'll be fine."

"I'll text you when I'm out of the doctor's office."

"Don't forget to cough for the man," she joked.

"Glad your humor's back, too . . . I think . . .."

Elle took her time getting out of the vehicle. She told him she'd see him later and slowly walked to the hospital's entrance.

"Cal, I need to get some cash—pronto," Elle said as soon as she was back in the Jimmy.

Cal drove Elle to the ATM outside the nearest branch of her bank. And that's where the cat got out of the bag. Cal had just inserted her debit card when two bank employees walked up to service the cash machine—one of whom recognized Elle. The woman was not an Elle fan. As Cal collected her money, Elle imagined the woman making a special trip to Wyatt Interiors just so she could rub it in her aunt/adoptive mother's face that Elle had messed up again. "How many accidents have there been now, Jean?"

"Damn, it's only a matter of time now. I've gotta move quickly. Pull over to the next bank—any bank you see."

Cal did as he was asked. Once the vehicle was in park, he swiveled in his seat and looked directly at his passenger.

"Okay, what the hell is going on?" he asked.

"There's something I've got to take care of and I need money to do it."

"Kaela needs money for medical bills?"

"It's more than that," she said. "Let me go in and—."

"Your trust fund only allows you to withdraw so much at a time, Elle. What do you plan to do in there?"

"Get a cash advance on one of my credit cards."

"Elle, I'm sure if you explain the situation to Jean and Pat, they'll help."

"That's not what this is about," she said. "As soon as I'm done here, we'll go back to your place. I'll pack my stuff, get my car—."

"You're in no condition to do anything. Elle Wyatt, you try my patience sometimes."

"I know Cal," she said. "It's best right now if you don't know the particulars because, sooner or later, a member of the Nelson or Wyatt family will come knocking. I'll be in touch in a few days."

"Elle—."

"Please, Cal . . . ."

"You have to promise me one thing first," he said, knowing she would do just what she wanted anyway, but he felt the need to try.

"What?"

"You'll make an appointment with Sarah when this is over."

Elle waited a few moments before responding. Cal always came running when she needed help and never asked for anything in return.

"Okay. I'll call her next week."

Once on North Trenton Avenue, Elle Wyatt looked for another bank. She had one more credit card she could use for a cash advance. What little adrenaline she'd had after leaving the hospital was gone, and she was feeling wiped out. She thought she really should have confided in Cal. He could've helped her, but she didn't want to put him in a position where he'd have to lie.

Thanks to Lance Geraghty, Elle knew exactly where to go and what to say to get what she needed.

Elle parked as close as she could to the entrance of the department store at Battlefield Mall where Lance was employed. She walked to the jewelry counter and asked for Lisa Fremont.

"I'm a friend of Lance Geraghty's, and I understand you have Le Vian designer jewelry on clearance with an extra twenty-five percent off."

"That's true," confirmed Fremont. "We have a wide array of rings, pendants, and earrings. If you'll step right over here . . . are you interested in a signature chocolate diamond piece?"

"I'm not sure about chocolate diamonds but I would like to purchase several pieces—a couple of rings, a pendant, earrings, and a watch."

"Do you know what size ring you wear?" Fremont asked.

"A seven, I think."

"Let's find out for sure."

Fremont went to a drawer and pulled out a ring sizer. She selected one of the rings. "Try this."

It was a perfect fit. "Lucky seven it is," Fremont said. "You won't need to have one sized."

Elle hadn't even considered sizing; she just needed to set the stage. Designer jewelry was one way to do it, but she had to be careful and *not* overdo. Elle selected two white gold rings, one with a huge blue topaz stone, surrounded by a halo of small diamonds. Designer, but could still be considered casual—in other words, great with jeans. She went with a bezeled diamond pendant and matching earrings that paired nicely with a second ring. A Bulova watch rounded out her purchases.

"It's my understanding that I can apply for a store credit card and get an additional twenty percent off. Is that correct?"

"Yes, ma'am."

"Let's do it. Oh, and since Lance referred me, can we make sure he gets commission on a few of the pieces."

"Not a problem."

Next Elle walked over to the Sephora counter and explained to the attendant she'd been in an accident and needed make-up to cover as many bruises as possible. She was thankful to sit as the associate showed her useful make-up techniques. Elle was amazed at the finished product. Color corrector, foundation, and concealer had taken care of most of the discoloration, and she liked the natural look the make-up artist achieved with a pink-mauve-brown combination in eye shadow, blush, and lipstick.

Elle needed a few clothing items, but her strength was gone. She barely made it to the restaurant just outside the department store's mall entrance. She ordered lunch and took ninety minutes before paying the bill. Next, she walked across the center aisle into a clothing boutique. Elle knew what she wanted from visiting the store's website during lunch. She selected a pair of girlfriend jeans, a white camisole with a bit of lace trim, and an elongated jacquard denim jacket that hit below the thigh. It was tailored so it swayed with her hips when she walked. Slightly sexy was so much better than in-your-face trashy. Elle had learned a long time ago to leave something to the imagination—men so loved to unwrap the package.

Everything else would have to wait. She texted her cousin and told him she was on her way.

·4·

John Hutsell and Rick Hadley left St. Louis an hour after John had talked to his aunt and arrived at the Wyatt Estate at 1:30 A.M. There was hot coffee on the kitchen table when they sat down and listened to why the Wyatts were so concerned for their daughter.

"You remember Angie's mother, Roberta?" Jean had asked her nephew.

"Yes."

"And how she always blamed Elle for you and Angie not getting together?"

"Elle had nothing to do with it, but yeah, I remember," John answered.

"I was at the bank just before closing today when she told me to wait—that she was worried about Elle and wanted to walk out with me. She said Elle had been at the ATM mid-morning and was in bad shape. She didn't realize it was Elle at first, because she was in the passenger seat of an older GMC Jimmy. The man driving was getting money out of the ATM."

"How did she know it was a Jimmy?" John asked. "They stopped making them in the early nineties."

"She described it as being like the one Tom Selleck drove on the TV show, *Magnum, P.I.*"

"Cal Davies," said John.

"Had to have been."

John turned to Rick and said, "Cal's a friend of Elle's."

"Roberta said Elle's face was covered in bruises, and she had a cut lip," Jean continued.

"Cal's a good guy, Aunt Jean. He wouldn't hurt her. Did you contact him?" John asked.

"I left a voice message for him just before I called you. He hasn't returned my call."

"Aunt Jean, if Elle's been hurt, Cal would take good care of her."

"I don't think she's with Cal anymore."

John looked at his Uncle Pat for confirmation. "Here's what we know, John," said Pat. "Since Friday night, the only person Elle has talked to on the phone has been Cal—that is until this morning. At 7:40, she got a call from her cousin, Myles Stafford. She sent him a text at 3:30 P.M. and then shut off her phone."

"I know Myles. He's a pretty good guy, too," John said. "Beside the bruises, what has you two so worried?"

"In between the call from Myles and her text to him," Pat said, "Elle withdrew as much as she could from the bank, got cash advances on two credit cards and opened a new card at a department store."

"Could her identity have been stolen?" John asked.

"We contacted Vince Gardner with SPD," Pat said. "He didn't have a warrant and didn't view the video himself, but was assured by the store's security people that there was footage that confirmed it was Elle in the store. She had bruises and she was alone."

"Excuse me," Rick Hadley interrupted. "She's thirty-two, right? How do you know all of this?"

"Our grandfather set up a trust fund for Elle before he passed away in 2008," John said. "She wasn't very responsible at the time, so he put Jean in control. Jean's name is also on Elle's credit card and phone accounts. If Elle keeps her nose clean, she gains control when she turns thirty-five."

"John, she has been doing better," Pat said, defending his adopted daughter.

"I know Uncle Pat. You're right. I'm sorry," John apologized.

"John, she's never ever tried to get cash advances or open a credit card independently before today. For the most part, she's been responsible where money's concerned, and that's why we're so scared. Why does she need all this cash? Why has she turned off her phone? Why won't Cal Davies call us back?"

Tears fell down Jean Wyatt's face. Her husband took her hand.

"She doesn't want you tracing her," answered the nephew. "When was the last time you saw her?"

"Last Friday morning at breakfast," Pat said. "She actually came over and started the coffee before we came downstairs. She was shredding potatoes for hash browns when I walked into the kitchen. She got on to me because the coffee wasn't decaf."

"Could she have been setting you up?" John asked. "You know, trying to throw you off guard for some reason?"

"She doesn't operate that way, John. She never has. You know that," replied Pat. "She doesn't feel the need to lie. She'll tell you to your face when something is none of your business."

"Okay, you two go on to bed. First thing in the morning, Rick and I will visit Cal."

John turned to Rick as Jean and Pat left the kitchen's alcove.

"We need to hit the sack, too," he said. "Cal's job requires him to be on the road most of the day. If we don't catch him before he leaves for work, we won't have another chance to speak to him until early evening."

"What time do you want to leave?"

"I'd like to be at his place by six-thirty, so let's plan on getting out of here at five-forty-five. We'll grab breakfast on the way."

· 5 ·

Elle was in her cousin's guest bedroom when she awoke the next morning and thought of her visit to Melcher Memorial South. She closed her eyes and mentally brought up the feel of running her fingers over the letters of her mother's memorial nameplate: In loving memory of Sharon Nelson.

After a visit to the bathroom, Elle made her way to the kitchen.

"Have you heard from Sila this morning?" she asked her cousin.

"Yes. Kaela is doing better physically, but mentally . . .." Myles trailed off. Elle remained silent while her cousin took a deep breath. "If I ever get my hands on him . . .."

"Right now, Kaela needs you with her."

"I wish it could be done a different way, Elle. I just didn't know who else to call," he apologized.

"I've got the means to get it done," she said.

"Yes, but you're recovering from a bad situation yourself."

"Can't be helped, so let's get this show on the road."

After breakfast, Elle showered and applied her new make-up as she'd been instructed. She emerged from the bathroom carrying an overnight bag and found Myles still sitting at the dining table staring into space.

"Well, what do you think?" she asked.

"In the right light . . .."

"Yeah, not bad. The cut on my lip can't be helped, though. People will notice, but I've got time to come up with a good story before I hit Tulsa."

"Cut or no cut, Elle, you are beautiful—always have been," Myles said.

"Let's hope he thinks so."

"He will."

"I'm a little old for his tastes, but that's where the money comes in."

Myles Stafford stood up and went to the hutch. He opened a drawer, brought out a black caddy, and set it on the table in front of Elle.

"Just in case you need it," he said.

Elle opened the box. It contained a Rohrbaugh r9 pistol.

"I bought it for Sila several years ago. It's small but has real stopping power. How long since you've been to the range?" he asked as he handed her a thigh holster.

"A couple of years."

"Let's go out past the shed and get you comfortable with this model."

Forty-five minutes later, Elle was standing inside the driver door of her Cadillac.

"'Must Be Doin' Somethin' Right'?" she asked over the top of the car.

"Yes."

Elle held up a throw-away phone and gave it a couple of shakes. "I'll be in touch," she said.

It took fifty minutes to drive to Mt. Vernon, where she merged onto I-44 on her way to Tulsa, Oklahoma, via Joplin. She planned to stop in Joplin to pick up a few more items, including a pair of two-and-a-half-inch navy heels. Before leaving the city, she got a manicure. But, no fake nails. They wouldn't fit with the persona she was trying to cultivate. She went with a basic oval shape with clear polish.

Elle crossed into Oklahoma and settled in for the one-hundred-thirteen-mile trip. Myles had reserved a Brownstone in the Cherry Street District. He'd arranged payment through a credit card for which she'd given him a cash reimbursement. She would be within walking distance of After Midnight, a club named for Tulsa singer/songwriter J.J. Cale's song made famous by Eric Clapton. Myles had schooled her the night before in the Tulsa Sound—a mix of three musical styles: rock 'n' roll, western, and jazz. Elle needed to make Lonnie Marcum sit up and take notice and one way to accomplish that goal was to know the Tulsa music scene.

According to Kaela, Marcum hit After Midnight every week to

sing karaoke, since his performing days on stage had been curtailed. Marcum would probably be in the company of Jamie Rabern, who, up until two days ago, was billed as Marcum's cousin. The truth that Rabern was Marcum's ex-wife was discovered thirty minutes before the two had dumped a bleeding, semi-conscious Kaela on the sidewalk in front of Myles' liquor store Tuesday afternoon.

Elle had also learned yesterday morning that this had been Kaela's second pregnancy with Marcum. She'd given birth to a daughter ten months prior who'd been given up for adoption. Kaela was barely eighteen at the time, and Marcum had assured her that he loved her unconditionally, but that they weren't in a position to provide for their infant daughter. He convinced Kaela that, if she truly loved their child, she would let a loving couple adopt the baby and give her all the things they couldn't.

Thinking Kaela was unconscious, Rabern and Marcum had argued over how to handle Kaela's medical emergency. Rabern advocated an emergency room run, but Marcum refused. It was during the altercation, that Kaela learned the true relationship between the two, and that the baby she'd given up had actually been brokered to the highest bidder. Making matters worse was that Marcum had lined up another baby sale, and he wasn't the least bit concerned over what was happening to Kaela. All he cared about was the lost revenue, because the pregnancy wouldn't see full term. Marcum argued that he could always get another baby-maker. After all, Kaela wasn't the first, and she wouldn't be the last.

Everyone involved thought Marcum needed to be stopped, but not before they knew for sure what had happened to Kaela's baby. Who had "adopted" her? And had she actually been adopted by a loving family or . . .? No one wanted to consider the alternatives, and they were in agreement that, if the authorities were brought in, there would be lawyers and delays. Time was wasting, and, one way or another, the family was going to find the answers to their questions. Sila was Cherokee, and most of her family lived in Oklahoma. The Cherokee Nation had a network. Marcum would talk. Elle was just the bait to bring him to a place where he'd beg to tell all he knew.

Elle thought that finding Marcum would be fairly easy. Marcum had believed Kaela to be more or less comatose for the ride to Galena, and so was still clueless concerning the true nature of what had taken place since she'd given birth. Marcum had even congratulated himself for being a "good guy." After all, he hadn't dumped Kaela in a field or left her in a dumpster to die—he'd dropped her off at her father's business for help. It might be touch and go legally for a while, but in the end, it had been an of-age Kaela who'd signed her name right next to his.

It was 2:45 in the afternoon when Elle walked into the rented apartment. She still hurt from the beating she'd taken last Friday night and so took her time climbing the stairs to the second floor. She hung her new clothes in the closet, slipped into a nightshirt and set the alarm on her cell for 5:00 P.M.

·6·

With Rick Hadley standing beside him, John Hutsell knocked on Cal Davies front door at 6:25 Thursday morning.

"Where is she?" Hutsell asked, when Elle's friend answered the door.

"Good to see you, too, John," said Davies. He stepped aside. "Come in for some coffee?"

John and Rick walked through the threshold and followed Cal to the kitchen. Cal turned, extending his hand to Rick Hadley.

"Cal Davies," he said, introducing himself. Rick shook his hand.

"Rick Hadley."

"Have a seat."

Davies stood in front of the coffee pot and asked if either man desired cream or sugar. Both declined. He filled two cups and set them on the table. He carried his empty breakfast plate to the sink and refilled his own cup.

"John, I don't know where she is," Cal said. "You know Elle. If she doesn't want to tell you something she's not going to. And no cajoling will get her to change her mind. To tell you the truth, I'm glad you're here."

"What's going on?"

"Last Friday night, she called me to come and get her. She'd been beaten. She wouldn't go to the emergency room. I called a doctor friend. She's been recuperating here—that is until yesterday."

"When she got a call from Myles Stafford."

"Yes."

"Just a minute gentleman," interrupted Hadley. "What were Ms. Wyatt's injuries?"

"My friend treated her for cuts and bruises. There's a cut on her lip that's pretty bad. He stitched a gash on the back of her head. Not sure if she's got any broken ribs. She may have had a concussion."

"Who beat her?" John asked.

"Don't have a clue," answered Davies.

"Why did Stafford call?"

"All I know is his daughter was air-lifted from Galena the day before. She was pregnant. The placenta detached, and she lost the baby. Myles called, because his daughter was asking to see Elle."

"What about?" asked Hutsell.

"I don't know. I dropped her off at the hospital on my way to an appointment. When I picked her up, she said she needed cash. I took her to the bank, brought her here, and she took off."

"Mr. Davies, how is Ms. Wyatt doing?" Rick asked. "She took a pretty bad beating. She must still be hurting. How was she getting around when you saw her last?"

"She was moving pretty slowly. She tired easily, but was doing better than I would have in the same situation."

"Which hospital?" questioned Hutsell.

"Melcher South," said Cal. "And now I need to ask you to leave. I've got to get to work."

Just outside the door, Rick Hadley looked at Cal Davies, "Mr. Davies, is there anything else you can tell us that will be helpful in finding Ms. Wyatt?"

Cal hesitated, then finally spoke up, "Kaela Stafford became estranged from her family a few years ago when she ran off with a singer from Oklahoma. It's my understanding that he dumped Kaela at her father's liquor store in Galena Tuesday afternoon."

"Do you have a name?" Hadley asked.

"Lonnie Marcum."

"Thank you, Mr. Davies," said Rick as he reached out to shake Cal's hand.

Rick followed John off the porch. He was on the next to last step when Cal read the words printed on the back of Hadley's jacket: Shannon County, TN, Sheriff. Unlike John, Hadley's questions had shown concern for Elle's condition rather than just her whereabouts.

"Mr. Hadley?"

"Yes."

"Marcum's been branded in the music industry as a sexual predator. Elle's savvy, but occasionally bites off more than she can chew. Please find her."

"We'll do our best."

As John pulled away from the curb, Rick asked, "Well, what do you think?"

"Marcum has hurt someone Elle cares about. She's after revenge."

"I don't know, John. Seems to me the timing's off. Okay, let's say revenge is her motive. Why now? It makes more sense to wait till she's stronger physically to make him pay for his actions. There might be more to it . . . of course, I don't really know her."

"Yeah, maybe. But Elle usually does what she damn well pleases. She's put herself in dangerous situations in the past, regardless of potential consequences, especially where men are concerned. It's like she's going for the thrill."

"Maybe not. Maybe she's still trying to slay the demon that was her step-father. Like you said before, she's wanting to gain some semblance of control. She just hasn't realized that the way she's going about it won't bring what she seeks."

"Let's head to the hospital and see if Stafford's there. If not, we'll go on to Galena."

The two men rode in silence. After several minutes, Rick Hadley spoke up.

"John, you were a little hard-boiled back there. Kind of like last night when your uncle objected to your comment about your cousin keeping her nose clean."

"Where Elle's concerned, I guess I'm not very objective. I seem to have run out of sympathy."

"You're here, aren't you?"

"Yeah, but is it out of a sense of family duty, instead of a feeling of concern for my cousin? I don't know how to reach her, Rick. I've tried for years. It's like I'm here only to pick up the pieces."

"Picking up the pieces is a lot easier than putting them back together, John."

Elle woke up fifteen minutes before her alarm was set to ring. She stayed in bed, contemplating the situation until the alarm sounded.

The apartment was even better than the pictures online had portrayed. It was an older brownstone that had been restored and so retained the charm of a bygone era. She believed she would revisit the place again after completing her mission. Music was central to her soul and usually entered into her plans whenever she took off running. Elle had learned of a new genre named for this city, so it would be an ideal destination in the future.

After consuming a deli sandwich she'd had delivered for dinner, Elle hung her new clothes in the bathroom, so the steam from the shower would encourage the wrinkles to fall away. She took more time than usual getting ready to spend an evening sitting in a bar. On her way out, Elle checked her image in the mirror. She looked at the finished product. Upper middle class on the way to wealthy. The only thing out of place was the cut on her lip. She turned out the light. Better, she thought. She went over the story line to explain the cut. Better, still. Elle carried her belongings to her car and stowed them in the trunk. If things went according to plan, she wouldn't be staying the night.

Elle entered After Midnight and chose a table in the second row a little to the right of the stage. Not obvious, but visible. The performers were eclectic. She was enjoying a cover of Nick Waterhouse's version of a sixties song, when Lonnie Marcum showed up with Jamie Rabern in tow. Twenty minutes later, he stepped to the microphone. Two lines into a hard-hitting rockabilly tune, Elle took off her jacket revealing her lace trimmed camisole. In the dark room, the white color drew attention. She sat back in her chair, and when Marcum's eyes found her, she leaned into him laying her left forearm on the table parallel to her body. She held his eyes in hers, slowly brought up her right arm and placed her chin in the palm of her hand.

Elle politely clapped with the rest of the patrons as he made his way back to his table. She picked up a coaster, turned it over and signaled the waitress. Using the server's pen, Elle wrote a note and handed both items to the woman, who then delivered the coaster to Marcum. He didn't acknowledge her, but when it was his turn to take the stage again, he keyed up, "Must Be Doin' Somethin' Right". Halfway through the sexy country song, Marcum took the mic from its stand. He had a rich baritone voice and a way of slightly inhaling and exhaling before and after delivering lyrics. He was exactly the bad boy type some women loved. As he continued to sing, he moved to his left, so he was closer to Elle. She leaned back in her chair and folded her hands at her waist. By doing so, she ever so slightly increased the distance between them.

Not going to be that easy, Marcum. You're going to have to come to me.

When the song was over, he started for Elle's table. She used her foot to scoot a chair out giving him permission to join her. He tossed the coaster on the table.

"Why, this particular song?" he asked, sitting down with confidence.

"It's your signature song, isn't it?"

"How do you know?"

"I've seen you before."

He just smiled.

"Did you mean it when you sang 'Anywhere you wanna go, baby, show me the way'?" she asked.

Marcum leaned closer and repeated another line from the song, "'. . . umm, whatever you say'."

"Get your jacket," she said.

"What about my cousin?" he asked.

"She's not invited."

"What you got in mind?"

"Gambling in Miami." Before he could object, she added, "My newly ex-husband is footing the bill."

Elle stood up. Marcum hesitated for effect only, then rose to his feet.

"I'll meet you at the door," she said.

Elle waited by the entrance as Marcum left a bewildered Rabern standing alone at the table. She hadn't expected it to be this easy. But then again, he was just a con artist looking for his next mark.

The driving time to Miami, Oklahoma, was one hour and twenty minutes. Most of the time was spent talking about music. Marcum seemed impressed with Elle's knowledge on the subject and occasionally she "let" him dazzle her with his. When there was a lull in the conversation, he asked the question she'd prepared for.

"How'd you get the cut on your lip?"

"My ex-husband's former stepson felt I was taking part of his inheritance. He paid me a visit last week, and now I will be," she answered with a sly grin.

Elle wasn't much on gambling, but she acted the part. After dropping hundreds of dollars in a casino, the two took a break to listen to a live band and have a few drinks.

"It's going to be a long trip back to Tulsa," he said.

"They have a hotel," she replied.

Marcum had just ordered another drink when a drop-dead gorgeous brunette walked in. She was wearing a leather midriff bra and top combination trimmed in lace. Her skirt was of the same leather with a surplice hemline that afforded a peek inside to her inner thigh. The left side had a tie lace-up feature that he immediately wanted to untie. The white of the leather was in contrast to her copper-brown skin. When he finally brought his eyes up to her face, he wondered how she'd gotten by the sentries—she didn't look old enough to gain admittance. Maybe she had a fake ID, but he didn't know where she would carry it in the outfit she was wearing.

The woman sat at a table making sure she was in his line of vision to the stage. When she knew he was watching her, she uncrossed and crossed her legs the way Sharon Stone had done in the *Basic Instinct* interrogation scene. Elle dipped her eyes and looked in his lap. The woman definitely had his full attention. That was her cue. Elle excused herself and went to the restroom. When she returned, he was gone.

· 8 ·

The volunteer at the hospital information desk would neither confirm nor deny that Kaela Stafford was a patient, so John Hutsell and Rick Hadley stopped by the Wyatt Estate to drop off Hutsell's car and pick up Hadley's vehicle. A red sports car would attract attention in a small town, where a Chevy truck would not.

Stafford's package store was attached to his bar, The Hideout, just outside the city limits of Galena. Three nights of the week, you could dance to live music, courtesy of Stafford's band, The Street Outlaws. The band's repertoire included classic country and oldies rock 'n' roll. For added fun, they threw in a little rockabilly every now and then. It wasn't uncommon to dance to songs made popular by Sam Cooke, Merle Haggard, Credence Clearwater Revival, and Delbert McClinton, all in one night. The dance hall days were over in Springfield, and those wanting a live band and a nice size floor were happy to make the fifty-minute trip. John Hutsell had been one of them before he'd moved to St. Louis.

John and Rick decided to have lunch while they waited for Stafford to open for business. At 1:00 P.M., Rick Hadley pulled into the parking lot of The Silver Flask. He followed John Hutsell to the store's entrance. A bell over the door chimed as they entered.

"Hello," a woman said over her shoulder as she put beer in a cooler. "May I help you?"

"Is Myles Stafford around?" asked John.

"No, he won't be in today. Is there anything I can do for you?"

"How about Sila?"

"No, sir," she answered. The woman stopped filling the cooler and looked at Hutsell. "Do I know you? You look familiar."

"The name's John Hutsell."

"Well, hello John. It's been a while. You probably don't remember me. My son Eddie plays drums for Myles. I'm Bev Smith."

"Nice to see you again, Mrs. Smith," said John. "Do you know where Myles is?"

"Myles and Sila are out of town. I've been instructed to contact them only in the case of an emergency," she explained. "I'm sorry."

"Are they open for business next door?" Hutsell asked.

"Sure are. Go on over, take a load off and have a beer. That way it won't be a wasted trip."

"How about it, Rick?" he asked Hadley. "They serve tap beer in frosted mugs."

"I'm driving, but I'll hold up the bar while you have one."

The two men went outside and walked next door. John held the door open for Rick and then led the way to the bar. They had just claimed two stools when a woman walked through the door that led to the back room.

"May I help—." She didn't finish her sentence. One look at John Hutsell and her body tensed. Having no other recourse, she walked over, grabbing a towel on the way.

"Hello, John," she said without effect. "What do you want?"

"Carolyn, I really need to talk to Myles. Where can I find him?"

A man, with a load of clean glasses walked through the same door the waitress had. He immediately sized up the situation, and gave John an indignant look.

"We serve beer here, not information," she said.

"I'll have the usual then."

The waitress took a frosted glass from a small freezer and filled it with beer from the tap.

"Here's your beer, Hutsell. Drink up and get out." She turned and walked off.

Hadley kept quiet as John sipped his beer. The waitress leaned on the bar near the register, picked up a pen and involved herself in paperwork. The male employee arranged the glasses on the lower counter, stealing glances at Hutsell while he worked. He returned to the back room when he'd finished his task. John had a few sips left when the waitress started making her way toward him. He finished his beer and tossed a twenty onto the bar.

"Keep the change," he said.

She placed her body between the bar and the service door, picked up the twenty and deposited a piece of paper. She lifted the empty glass and wiped down the bar as John palmed the paper.

Once they were in the truck, John read the note. "She says to meet at her place at four," he said.

"That's a little over two hours from now. What do you want to do till then?"

"Might as well drive out there, pull around behind the trailer and take a nap."

At three-fifty-five, Rick drove his truck to the front of the house trailer and the two men waited for the waitress.

She arrived ten minutes later and, without a word, unlocked the door and walked in. John and Rick followed. With her hand, she indicated they should take a seat in the living area.

"She's in Tulsa," she said after they were seated.

"Is she in trouble?" asked John.

"I don't know. Could be. She left this morning. She's booked an apartment at least through tonight."

"What can you tell me, Carolyn?"

"Myles' daughter Kaela, was dumped at The Silver Flask Tuesday afternoon by her boyfriend, Lonnie Marcum. She was in bad shape and taken by helicopter to a hospital in Springfield. She was pregnant, but lost the baby."

Carolyn broke eye contact with John, looked off into the distance, and went quiet.

"Why Tulsa?" John prompted.

"That's where Marcum lives."

"So, she's gone after Marcum," he said.

Carolyn nodded.

"Why?"

"Kaela had a baby by Marcum last year. He convinced her to give it up for adoption. He told her they couldn't financially support a child. Kaela learned Tuesday that Marcum had actually sold the baby. She also learned his 'cousin,' Jamie Rabern, is his ex-wife."

"So, what does Elle expect to accomplish by going to Oklahoma?"

"Find out who purchased Kaela's baby."

"Are they thinking black market?" John asked.

"Or human trafficking."

"Damn," he said. The situation had just gone critical. "Where in Tulsa?"

"He frequents a bar called After Midnight. And that's all I

know."

John rose to his feet. Rick and Carolyn followed suit. He walked over to the waitress and mindful of distance, stopped several feet in front of her.

"Thank you, Carolyn," he said sincerely.

She remained silent until both men were almost out the door.

"She's got a gun."

"Damn," Hutsell said for a second time.

"Why not go to the police?" questioned Rick as he put the Silverado in drive.

"Timing and history. They don't want to wait for an investigation to run its course—they want answers now. And in Elle's eyes, the authorities can't be trusted. She went to them once before. They didn't protect her or her mother then, and she's got a scar on her left side to prove it."

"Can she handle a gun?"

"Yes. She was on the Rifle and Pistol Team at MSU for two years, before she dropped out of college."

"Well, that's something positive. What do you want to do now?"

"Head back to Battlefield, pick up mom's SUV, and head to Tulsa. It's less conspicuous than the BMW."

"We can take my truck," Hadley offered.

"I think it's best if we have two vehicles. That way, if need be, we can carry on two searches at once."

Rick glanced at Hutsell with a questioning look.

"I've been here before, Rick. Elle often seeks the comfort of live music and dim lights. She may not stay at the bar Carolyn mentioned. If need be, you can handle clubs down one strip as I check another."

"There's got to be a lot of clubs in Tulsa, John."

"We'll start with those featuring country bands."

"Harlan Howard, 'Three Cords and the Truth'," quoted Rick as to Elle's choice of genre.

"Pretty much."

With their cell phones hooked to the USB ports of their vehicles, the two men discussed tactics on the drive to Tulsa. John was a go-for-the-jugular kind of guy; Rick liked the bees-and-honey approach. Both agreed to see how the initial request was received at After Midnight to determine which strategy was best served. If the reaction was congenial, Rick would take lead. If not, John would do the honors. Men like Marcum made enemies and he would cause a scene if need be and maybe a friendly patron would step up.

The male bartender was polishing glasses when Rick and John walked in a little after 9:00 P.M. Both canvassed the room. Each man had studied Marcum's Facebook photos and felt they would recognize him if he was in the club. When they failed to find him, they strode over and stood by the bar. Rick assumed his custom position by putting his hands in his pockets.

"I'm looking for a guy who's in here a lot," John said.

"What's his name?" asked the bartender.

"Lonnie Marcum."

"Don't know who you're talking about?"

Not, "I don't know him." or "He isn't here." With his exact choice of words and demeanor, Hutsell and Hadley knew the man was telling them he knew Marcum, and that the two men asking about him could go to hell. A waitress came up and started placing dirty glasses on the bar.

"Look mister," John said. "I know Marcum comes in here all the time. He's been after my wife—singing love songs over the phone—you know, shit like that. He needs to back off."

"Can't help you," replied the bartender.

Rick stepped up. "Maybe you've seen his wife."

"What's she look like?"

"Real pretty blonde, thirty-two years old," Rick said. "Her hair is straight and hits below her shoulders. Occasionally with soft curls. Sometimes she wears it up—nothing tight, mind you. Nice figure, more shapely than skinny."

The bartender laughed and looked at John. "Sounds like he's the one you need to worry about," he said, indicating Rick. "From his description, I wouldn't mind meeting up with her myself."

While the bartender talked, the waitress stepped back out his view and mothed slowly to Hutsell, "Go, sit. Table, far wall."

"Asshole," John muttered. "C'mon," he said to Rick. "I'm thirsty."

After the two men were seated, the waitress, knowing she was being watched, took their orders in a no-nonsense manner. When she delivered the drinks she positioned herself where the bartender couldn't see her face.

"They were both here. I go on break in fifteen minutes. Meet me out front."

John gave her a generous tip and leaned back in his chair.

"Good description you gave of my cousin, Rick," he said as they nursed their beers. "Sad she doesn't see herself that way."

"Seeing won't do it, John. She has to feel it."

Rick and John left the bar ahead of the waitress's scheduled break so it wouldn't appear they were following her outside. She showed up several minutes later wearing a jacket. She carried a lighter and a pack of cigarettes.

"Your wife and Marcum left together about forty-five minutes ago."

"Did you happen to hear any of their conversation?"

"No. The only thing I heard was Marcum bragging to the bartender that he had a 'live one', and she was taking him to Miami to gamble."

"Thank you," said John as he handed her a hundred-dollar bill.

She pocketed the money and responded, "Hope you find the son-of-a-bitch."

· 9 ·

Rick messaged John from the parking lot, "I found her."

Elle watched as the band left the small stage for a break. She put her feet up in an empty chair and began stacking the coins in front of her. She glanced up as the door opened. Lights from the parking lot flooded in and silhouetted a man in the entryway. He stepped to the side, letting the door close on its own, and then stood still. She figured he was probably waiting for his eyes to adjust to the darkness before continuing farther inside the tavern.

She was fully aware she wasn't the only woman in the place staring at him when his eyes began scanning the room. They landed on her and stopped moving. He discontinued his canvasing, and in two steps, closed the distance from the entrance to the bar. He chose to stand instead of taking an empty stool. While the stranger waited for the bartender, the door opened again, and in walked a second man.

Damn! Someone's called in the Cavalry.

She moved her feet from the chair, sat up straight, and readied herself for the confrontation that would soon follow. She was surprised when, instead of coming toward her, her cousin, John Hutsell, joined the man at the bar. The two shared a few words, and then John looked in her direction.

Elle finished her drink as both men made their way across the room.

"Hello John. What brings you to this locality?"

"I like these little out-of-the-way places. You meet the most interesting people in them."

"Wish I could say the same."

"Elle Wyatt, meet Rick Hadley. Rick, this is my cousin, Elle."

"Ma'am." Rick nodded in her direction.

"'Ma'am'?" Elle said. "That line is often accompanied by the tip of a cowboy hat, Mr. Hadley."

Hadley didn't miss a beat.

"That gesture might have helped my dad get elected sheriff, but all it ever got me was laughed at," he said with a genuine smile.

"May we join you?" John asked.

"Suit yourself," she said.

After they were seated, John pulled a couple of twenties from his wallet and placed them on the table. Addressing his cousin, he asked, "What you drinking?"

"The usual; Diet Coke with a twist of lime." She looked Hadley up and down, then said, "You look like a draft beer kind of guy to me."

"I've been known to down a few."

The waitress arrived to take their drink orders.

"Would you like another, Elle?" John asked.

"Sure."

"Rick?"

"Tomato juice will be fine."

"And I'll have ginger ale," John said.

John waited for the waitress to walk away before he picked up the conversation. "What are your plans, Elle? You going to stay in Oklahoma or drive back to Battlefield tonight?"

"Haven't decided. What about you and your compadre?"

"We haven't discussed it yet."

"Why don't you while I hit the restroom." She stood up and headed to the back of the bar.

"She's going for the rear exit. I'll follow her and meet you in the parking lot," John said.

"I believe I'll stay right here."

John gave his friend a puzzled look and headed for the door. Rick got up and made his way to the jukebox. Elle, who had watched the scene play out from the shadows, walked over and stood next to him. She pointed to a particular song and he touched the corresponding buttons.

"Where'd John go?"

"To the parking lot. He thinks you're sneaking out the back," he said without taking his eyes off the jukebox screen.

"And what about you? What do you think?"

"It's more a question of what I don't think." He stepped aside for her to choose the remaining selections.

"Okay, what is it that you *don't* think?" Elle pressed the screen with her finger.

"I don't think you need a babysitter."

They continued to stare straight ahead.

"You dance, Hadley?"

"Not as good as John. You shoot pool, Wyatt?"

"Not very well. But I do know what *English* is."

"You rack, I'll break."

They had cleared half the balls from the table when John walked back into the bar. Rick nodded at him and Elle waved.

"You know, sooner or later, he's going to ask where Marcum is."

"I don't know where Marcum is." She chalked the tip of her stick. "How much does he know?"

"He knows about the apartment in Tulsa, and that you and Marcum were gambling earlier tonight." He paused as he lined up a shot. "And he knows when you get in the light, that cut on your lip will be more noticeable."

Elle jumped at the cracking sound made by the cue ball as it slammed another ball in the right corner pocket.

Rick pulled out Elle's chair and scooted it in just as she sat down. Elle's eyes went wide as she mouthed, "What's with this guy?" to John at the same time Rick mouthed to him, "Play nice."

The band returned to the stage and opened with Jackson Browne's "Running on Empty" for their last set. John tapped his fingers on the table in time to the music as he watched couples dance.

"C'mon on Elle, Let's show 'em how it's done."

"Ah, I don't know John. I pulled a couple of muscles last week and I'm still a little sore."

"Are you as good as he is?" asked Rick, diverting the subject.

Continuing to look at her cousin, she replied, "Better."

"In your dreams, my dear cousin," said Hutsell.

Elle turned to Rick. "I always made him look good."

"Who was leading?" John asked. "I determined where you went on the dance floor.

"Who executed all the fancy turns? Who was there to meet you after each move?" Elle countered. "What was it Ginger Rogers said?"

"Something about doing 'everything a man does, only backwards and in high heels'," interjected Rick.

"I think I'm going to like you, Hadley," she said.

"Where do you come up with this stuff?" John asked Hadley about the Rogers quote.

"My parents have this same conversation every few years. They started dancing together when they were cast as the leads in their high school's production of *Camelot*. The only way Dad could win the argument was to sing 'their' song from the play, which is why I think Mom would start the fight in the first place."

"'If Ever I Would Leave You?'" guessed Elle.

"I think I'm going to like you, too, Wyatt," Rick said.

"You from St. Louis?" she asked.

"Nope, Shannon County, in eastern Tennessee."

"How'd you meet up with John?"

"We worked a case together."

"Rick's a deputy sheriff," John said.

"How long you going to hang around?" Elle asked Rick.

"Haven't decided yet."

"Tennessee's not calling you back?"

"Let's put it this way . . . Shannon County, Tennessee, isn't."

"Interesting . . .." Elle mused.

"Yeah, it is," Rick said with a smile.

"Oh, brother," said John.

The three decided to head back to Battlefield instead of staying the night in Miami. Elle had keyed open her car and was about to get in when John walked up beside her.

"I need the gun," he said.

"Well, you're not going to get it."

"I'm not trying to be an ass, Elle," he said. "It's 1:00 A.M. You're leaving a bar. There's libel to be DUI checkpoints between here and home. You don't have a permit."

"I don't need one in Missouri."

"You're not in Missouri. You can carry in Oklahoma if you have a valid permit from the state you reside in. You don't. I'm law enforcement. If we get stopped it won't be a problem."

Elle hated it when John Hutsell was right.

"How about him?" She nodded at Hadley. "He's law enforcement." She looked at the Tennessee deputy. "What do you say, Hadley?"

"Sure."

Elle brought the pistol from under the driver's seat and opened the trunk. She retrieved its case, placed the gun inside and handed it to Rick. As Hadley stored it in his saddle truck box, Elle slowly turned and faced her cousin.

"Guess Myles has a traitor in camp. Carolyn, maybe . . .?"

"Elle, don't go making trouble," John said.

"What's in it for me?"

John Hutsell thought for a moment. Finally, he said. "You don't talk, and neither will I. Aunt Jean's questions go unanswered. No mention of Marcum or Oklahoma."

"John, either you get this show on the road, or I'm going to start without you," Rick said. "If I have to get a hotel room, so be it."

"You can stay at my place," Elle offered.

"Well Miss Wyatt, how kind of you, since we've only just met and all. Tell you what I will do. I'll trade you pool lessons for dancing lessons next week."

"Deal."

He not only lands on his feet, thought Hutsell, he owns the damn sidewalk.

"So, John, what is it?" asked Rick. "We staying with your aunt and uncle tonight or . . .?"

"Elle, you lead and I'll bring up the rear," John said.

"See you boys in the morning for breakfast." Elle twirled her keys. "By the way, John's cooking. How do pancakes sound, Hadley?"

"They'll work . . . for starters."

·10·

Elle looked in the mirror. She hated it, but there was nothing she could do, so she concealed her bruises with make-up once again and made her way to the main house on the Wyatt Estate. She walked through the French doors leading to the family room and followed the smell of freshly brewed coffee. Rick Hadley was pouring himself a cup as she entered the kitchen.

"Good morning, Wyatt. Care for a cup?" he asked as he held up his steaming mug.

She hesitated, nodded at her cousin and mouthed, "Did he make it?"

Hadley slightly shook his head from side to side and pointed to himself.

"Yes, I would. Thank you," she replied and then whispered, "He makes it way too strong."

"No, I don't," John said as he whipped a bowl full of eggs.

Rick handed her the cup he was holding and grabbed another for himself from a mug tree hanging on the wall.

"Where's Jean and Pat?" she asked.

"Jean's in the shower, and Pat's on his morning walk," said John. "Why don't you make yourself handy and set the table?"

"How may I help?" Rick asked.

Elle wanted to say, "Just stand there and look pretty" but instead said, "Got it covered, Hadley."

As she went about her task, she engaged Rick in small talk. "How long have you known, John?"

"A little over a week."

Elle stopped what she was doing and looked at him. Rick smiled and said, "I know, not very long, right? And we really didn't hit it off to begin with. But, he's a good investigator. He gets results."

Jean Wyatt walked in the room and added, "John, his partner, and Rick just solved a national case."

"Good morning, Jean," said Elle. "I'll check it out on the internet this afternoon."

"Smells good, John," Jean said. She briefly hugged Elle from behind on the way to her chair.

John saw movement out of his peripheral vision and turned his attention to the window. "Here comes Pat."

"Now that's what I call good timing," Elle said when Pat entered the nook.

"Good morning, Retha," Pat said and then kissed Elle on the top of her head.

"I know what you're thinking, Rick," Jean said at the quizzical look on Hadley's face. "There's got to be a story there. When Elle was a toddler, Pat went looking for the perfect nickname for her. But it had to be very special—no regular princess name would do. So, Pat looked up the real names of Disney princesses and settled on Snow White's given name, Margaretha. Retha for short."

"Everyone have a seat and join hands while grace is given," Pat said. When all were seated, he gave the blessing. "For food in a world where many walk in hunger; for faith in a world where many walk in fear; for friends in a world where many walk alone; we give you thanks, O Lord. Amen."

After breakfast, Jean headed to Wyatt Interiors. Elle collected the dirty dishes as Pat asked John and Rick to join him in the family room.

"If it's all right with you sir, I'll help Miss Wyatt in the kitchen first," Rick said.

"See you in a bit, then."

"Nice couple," Hadley said as he stood beside Elle at the kitchen sink.

"Yes, they are." She handed him several items to put in the refrigerator. "So, what are your plans, Hadley?"

"I'm heading out a little after noon."

"Where to?"

"A few hours up the road to Ft. Leonard Wood. A friend is stationed there. His dad and mine served together while we were in Germany. Both were career army."

"And after that?"

"Well, it seems to me I made a deal last night I need to make good on," he answered. "When would be a good time to instruct you in the difference between a kiss-shot and a kiss-out?"

"Excuse me?"

"I'm talking about pool."

"Oh."

Rick slowly pulled a towel from Elle's hand, causing her to stop what she was doing and look directly at him.

"You're still moving slowly," he said. "I don't want to interfere with your recovery."

"At least you're up front," she said about his approach. "Kind of nice for a change."

"John's up front."

"No, John's judge and jury." She turned her head and looked out the window. "Problem is most of the time he's right, and I'm guilty as charged. It's just none of his business. Hang around here long enough, Hadley and you'll see it."

"See what?"

Elle took the towel back from Rick.

"The way they look at me," she answered. "Sadness, bordering on pity."

"I don't think they pity you. They just don't know how to make it better."

"'It'?" she questioned. "How much do you know? What did John tell you to get you to join him in his little quest last night?"

"I know what was done to you."

"They want to change it—change me. They can't, and so they've decided the best they can do is manage me."

Elle threw the towel over her shoulder.

"Well, that will never work," he said. "You're not a woman to be 'managed'."

He waited a few beats before continuing.

"Here, let me help you with that." He reached up and removed the towel. "It's covering a pretty big chip and that's something we just can't have."

Rick Hadley draped the towel on the handle of the oven door, walked over to the refrigerator, pulled a pen and page from a magnetic note pad and carried them both to the counter. He jotted something down and slid it across to her.

"Get in touch when you're ready, and I'll introduce you to Sneaky Pete." He turned to leave. He took three steps, then called out over his shoulder, "Google him first."

Elle made sure the kitchen was spotless before leaving. She chose a different route for the return trip home, passing through the mud room and out the garage side door instead of the family room. On her way she stopped as she often did to admire the lines of what used to be the Wyatt guest house before she'd inherited it from her Grandpa Nelson. The house was of the Usonian style, made popular by Frank Lloyd Wright. She loved its open design and how it seemed to blend with nature. It was like the home belonged to the landscape rather than the other way around.

Elle closed her front door, and as usual went to her home audio system. She selected Gail Davies—a safe and true artist for pure enjoyment. She was lounging on the sofa, tapping one foot against the other when she laughed out loud.

"Early in the morning all alone at my place. Black coffee, dry toast, and egg on my face."

Oh, what the hell, she thought. Elle went to her desk, powered up her computer and typed Sneaky Pete into the search bar. Several suggestions popped up for her to choose for more information. She looked down the list and found two that pertained to Rick Hadley. Sneaky Pete holsters and Sneaky Pete pool cues. Speaking of holsters, Hadley still had the gun that went in the one Myles had given her.

Elle reached in her pocket and pulled out the note Hadley had written. She made her way to the window facing the Wyatt Estate's main house and saw Hadley's Silverado still parked in the drive. She keyed in his number and typed a message.

"You have an item that needs to be returned. Please do so before you leave town."

Rick Hadley gave apologies to Pat Wyatt and John Hutsell and made his way to the guest room he'd occupied the previous two nights. He had a new message from a number not in his contact list. The first few words of the message were visible but didn't offer clues to the identity of the sender. He tapped the screen, read the entire message and then typed a reply.

"I'll drop it off on my way out of town."

Rick placed his phone on the night stand and was on his way to check for items he might have left in the bathroom when his cell signaled a new text. He walked back to his phone.

"Holsters or pool cues?"

He smiled.

"Pool cues."

John Hutsell carried Rick's bag to his friend's truck.

"A few days at Ft. Wood, and then what?" he asked his friend.

Rick tossed the bag to the passenger floorboard.

"Maybe a week in the Pacific Northwest. I'm having trouble deciding if I want the ocean or the mountains. Up there, you don't have to choose. They've got both within a few hours of each other." Hadley retrieved the gun case he'd placed in storage.

"You want me to give that to Elle?" John asked.

"That's okay, I'll take care of it," Hadley said. "What about you? When are you going back to St. Louis?"

"Mom will be here next weekend so I'll stay through then. I'll be leaving in a few hours to stay at her place until I head back."

Rick looked at the case in his hand. "I might even opt for a few more days in Missouri before I go."

"You like her that much?"

"I like her. She's got a quick wit."

"Go in with your eyes open, Hadley," cautioned John.

"I'm not interested in anything physical or emotional, John. She'll learn how to 'run' a table and I'll be able to challenge you on the dance floor."

"How long you talking about, Rick? The former will take years, and the latter will never happen."

"I'm messing with you, John. Your cousin and I struck a bargain last night, and I'm about to find out if she wants to carry it through. Neither one of us needs to be thinking about anything other than becoming good friends."

John recalled Trish's remarks about Hadley's personal life. He agreed there was a story but Rick hadn't pried into John's while they were in St. Louis or Galena, and John didn't have any business prying into Rick's now. He kept his mouth shut and hoped that in some way, Rick and Elle might be good for one another.

Rick Hadley knocked on the wood-encased glass door. A few seconds later, Elle came into view. He watched as she walked through the gallery of windows that led to the entryway. She opened the door and motioned for him to come in. He carried the gun case to the living area.

"I understand you shot in college," he said before placing the case on the coffee table. He sat down in one of two chairs separated by an end table.

"Everyone should have a sport," she said before sitting in the matching chair. "Friday."

He gave her a puzzled look.

"You, me, and Sneaky Pete. Next Friday."

"Where?" he asked.

"I'll text you the details."

"What are you doing Thursday?"

"Don't know yet. Why?"

"Want to do some target shooting?"

"We could do that. There are several indoor ranges in and around Springfield," she said, thinking the ranges at Ft. Wood were probably better. "What do you carry?"

"Glock 17 and a Beretta 9mm."

"I'll make reservations for Thursday afternoon."

Rick closed his eyes and slightly turned his head. Elle knew he was concentrating on something, maybe he was looking for a certain word.

"Who's singing?" he finally asked.

"Rhonda Vincent,"

"That's why she sounds familiar," he said. "She collaborates with Dolly now and then."

"Eastern Tennessee . . .," Elle recalled where Hadley was from. "Dolly Parton . . . it makes sense. If you follow Dolly you've probably heard Vincent."

"No way not to follow Dolly," he said with a smile. "Is that Keith Urban?" he asked of the male voice that had joined Vincent's.

"A discerning ear," Elle said. "Don't know what I'd do without music."

"What CD are we listening to?"

"It's a playlist I compiled several years back during my placid period."

Rick smiled. "And she has a good vocabulary, too."

Elle shook her head and returned the smile. "Sometimes I come home, throw everything in a chair, lie down on the sofa, close my eyes, and just listen."

"It's great background music," Rick commented.

Elle got up and walked over to the media player. She reached in a drawer and slipped a new flash drive into a USB port and copied the playlist. She faced him and asked if he would like something to drink.

"No, I really need to get on the road." He rose to his feet. "I'd like to get there before dark to have some time to visit before dinner."

Elle detached the thumb drive.

"Hold on a minute," she said before placing the plastic cover on the device. "Mood music for your trip. Dolly's on there with a couple of selections from the *Trio* album with Ronstadt and Harris."

"Thanks, Wyatt." Rick leaned over and tapped the gun case sitting on the coffee table and said, "See you Thursday."

"I'll send details."

She walked him to the door.

"Goodbye, Wyatt."

"Goodbye, Hadley."

She closed the glass door and watched him walk to his truck. He opened the vehicle's door and held up the flash drive just before he got in and drove away.

Elle went to her computer and typed Deputy Sheriff Rick Hadley into the search bar. The first item that popped up was a St. Louis news report with video. While she'd been recuperating at Cal's, Hadley had worked with John and his partner to solve a national serial killer case. She copied the link and sent it to her best friend. Then she dialed Chelle Thomas, hit speaker, and sat back in her chair.

"Well, what do you know," Chelle said. "She's in a talking mood."

"Funny," commented Elle. "What you doing?"

"Updating software. Yourself?"

"Go check your email."

"What's up?"

"There's someone I want you to check out."

Michelle Thomas was founder and CEO of Safety-Net, a Springfield-based company specializing in background checks.

"Since when did you care enough to do a background check on anyone?"

"Just look at the email, please."

"Oh, yeah," she said after clicking the link. "John's gone to national hero status. But John's not—oh, wait," said Chelle as she watched the video. "Oh, he *is* nice," she commented about Rick Hadley. "Why don't you ask John to introduce you?"

"He already has."

"Ooh, the plot thickens. John can fill in the details so why do you need me?"

"C'mon, Chelle. Don't make me work so hard, here."

Chelle laughed. "So, when did you meet him and why do you want to know about him?"

"Last night and . . . oh, I don't know. Let's just say he's different."

"Must be to get Elle Wyatt to sit up and take notice."

"And, Chelle?"

"Yes?"

"Nothing to Greg, okay?"

"Okay."

"I'll see you Monday morning."

"Make it noon—and bring me lunch."

After disconnecting with her best friend, Elle typed a message to Cal Davies, "I'm home."

"Sarah?" came the return.

"Getting ready to call now."

"Good."

After calling her therapist's office, Elle made her way back to the media player, highlighted "The Water Is Wide" and replayed the song that had captured Rick Hadley's attention.

.

Between bites of a pick-two Panera Bread combination lunch, Chelle Thomas laid out the highlights of Deputy Sheriff Rick Hadley's professional life.

"Impressive guy, detective, crime scene investigator, current emergency medical technician license. If he makes your heart pitter-patter just a little too much, he can give you CPR," Chelle said and laughed at her own joke. "Oohhh, you could feign getting the vapors like my great-granny used to do."

"I don't know why I put up with you."

"Because without me, there would be no 'Elle and Chelle'. I complete you," she said with a satisfied smile.

Elle knew her friend was right.

Elaine and Michelle. *Elle and Chelle*, as they had been known from the sixth grade on. Chelle had come up with their nicknames one day in the school cafeteria. They had laughed for years at the look on people's faces when, instead of seeing twin girls after their names were called, they saw a reserved, blue-eyed, blonde white girl and an outgoing, tall black girl come running. Chelle was one of the few Elle believed cared about her for who she was—unlike family, who *had* to love her.

"But, my dear friend, I wouldn't say you are exactly his type."

"What the hell does that mean?"

"Take a look." Chelle swiveled her computer's monitor so they could both see the screen. "Here he is at a charity event in Shannon County, Tennessee."

Elle saw a picture of a smiling Rick Hadley standing next to a beautiful brunette. The woman looked nothing like Elle. Where Elle might be considered pretty, there was no denying the woman on Hadley's arm was gorgeous—walking-the-runway-gorgeous.

"Wow. She's wrapped a little too tight," Elle said. "Know what I mean?"

"Yes. The hair. The make-up. The clothes. Definitely not your style," observed Chelle. "For example, you'd never wear your hair in a classic chignon—yours would be 'messy.'"

"Who is she? Maybe it was just a, 'Hey, I need a date for this event' kind of thing."

"Meredith Embry. She's a lawyer. And from photos on her mom's Facebook page, she and Hadley were together for two years." Chelle made a series of clicks. "Here, check this out. For the next two years, she was with this guy."

The new photo showed Embry with a man who, judging from the height of the dining table the two were standing in front of, was much shorter than Rick Hadley. He had a receding hair line, and his lips were taut. It reminded Elle of how young girls pursed their lips when taking selfies.

"Must have a great personality," Elle said.

"Nah, he's a dick."

"How do you know?"

"He's the Shannon County District Attorney, and, from reading his comments in the media, he's got a big mouth. He's bombastic, like many of today's politicians."

Chelle turned the screen back to its original position and sat back in her chair.

"So, tell me, *why* is he different?"

"Besides the obvious part where his legs go on forever."

"Yes, I need more, please."

"Well, you'll like this," she said. "He has a way of telling me off that doesn't make me mad." Both women laughed. "Besides you and Cal, there's only one other person who can do that."

Elle's eyes went wide, and she sat up in her chair when she realized the implication.

"Oh my god!" Chelle shrieked. "He's a male Sarah Bennett."

"Not funny, Chelle."

"Add psychoanalyst to his repertoire. Oh, when can I meet him? Please say I can meet him."

Chelle's office door opened, and Greg Baptiste walked in.

"Ladies, you are disturbing the clients," he said. "Besides, lunch time is over." He tapped his wrist where a watch would be if he wore one.

Elle got up to leave.

"Talk to you later," said Chelle.

· 12 ·

Elle was sitting on a stool at the bar that divided her kitchen from the dining area, trying to decide what to do. It was Wednesday, early evening, and she needed to write a text. She'd composed several in her head but wasn't happy with any of them. Of course, it might help if she would make up her mind if the text was to be one of confirmation or cancelation.

She picked up her cell and went with short and sweet.

"Tomorrow, 3 P.M. Cherokee Firearms. 1500 W. College Ave."

The reply was almost immediate. "See you then."

Elle went to change her clothes. She was meeting Cal and Lance for dinner.

"Habanero fried pickles?" questioned Lance. "Really now, Elle."

"Fine. Shredded onion rings, then," she said. "If that will make you happy."

"Now, children," admonished Cal.

Elle and Lance turned in unison and looked at him.

"We're going with the truffle 'n' parmesan non-gmo fries," he said with authority.

Elle looked at the waitress. "Bring all three," she said. "And I've decided I will have a beer after all. Blue Moon draft."

"You're looking good, Elle," commented Lance once the waitress had gone. "Oh, and thanks for the Le Vian commission."

"Fair is fair." She held up her hands and wiggled them in a reverse jazz hands motion. "What do you think?"

"Careful, you'll give Shellie Matheson a run for her money," said Lance.

"I'll never have *that* many Le Vian rings," she said.

After dinner, Cal walked Elle to her Cadillac.

"Saw Sarah today," she said.

"How'd it go?"

"Not bad. I've got another appointment next week."

"John visited me last Thursday morning," he said, changing the subject.

"He showed up with a friend at the Copper Canyon in Miami that night."

"Elle . . . you were—."

"I know, Cal. Don't worry about it."

"His friend seemed like a nice guy."

"Yeah, he does."

"'Does', not did?" he questioned her word choice. "Is he still in town?"

"No, but he'll be back tomorrow."

"And you know this because . . .?"

"Don't pry, Cal. It's not attractive."

"Elle's got a date with tall, dark and handsome."

"Don't know about the dark part. His hair is light brown, and his eyes are blue."

Cal gave a hearty laugh.

"Oh, shut up and go home. Don't you have to get up early in the morning or something?"

He leaned down and kissed her cheek. "Have a good time with tall and whatever," he said.

·13·

Rick Hadley's Silverado was in the parking lot of Cherokee Firearms when Elle pulled in. He got out and walked over to her Cadillac.

"Hello, Wyatt.

"Hadley."

"Beautiful day. Must be close to sixty degrees."

"It is nice for this time of year. How was the trip down?"

"Relaxing . . . you see I've got this new playlist . . . ."

Thirty minutes later, they were packing up to leave and he asked if she had plans for dinner.

"Haven't had lunch yet."

"Well, we need to fix that," he said. "Any suggestions?"

"The Springfield Brewing Company is close. They serve a varied menu."

"Lead the way."

Once they'd ordered, Elle turned the conversation to Rick Hadley's plans.

"How long are you planning on being in town this time?"

"I'm leaving Saturday morning for the Pacific Northwest. I need some time and solitude to decide my next move."

"In terms of . . .?"

"Career and location."

"You thinking of leaving law enforcement?" she asked.

"No, but I signed on with the Shannon County Sheriff's Department five years ago with a specific goal in mind. With the help of John and Trish Rankin, that goal has been accomplished," he explained. "Other than family, there's nothing in Shannon County, Tennessee, for me anymore."

"Options you're looking at?"

"Knoxville's Forensics Unit has a door open. I was there for three years prior to Shannon County."

"But . . .?"

"In some ways, it's still too close to Eagle Ridge, the town I live in."

"How about St. Louis with John?"

Rick smiled. "They've extended an offer."

"Again . . . but?"

"Don't want to make any hasty decisions," he said. "And yourself, Wyatt? What's on your horizon?"

"I've got a few projects in mind," she answered. "I like to sew."

"Do you have a business?"

"I've been asked to construct custom designs, and that wouldn't be a problem, except that it would require I work on a timeline." She laughed. "And that would make it too much like a 'real' job. I don't need the money, so I work on what interests me and donate or give away the finished product—except for Jean. I do make pieces for her interiors boutique."

"What are the projects you're looking at?"

"Items for friends and family. I see fabric and/or a pattern, and I want to create. I've got a fifties vintage apron pattern that's calling me right now. It will be perfect for my best friend for Sunday dinners at her house. She always looks like she stepped out of a fashion magazine. And for years, she actually did."

"How so?"

"Michelle Thomas was a model for an international make-up company. It's how she paid her way through college and had enough capital to start her own business here in Springfield. Her boyfriend works with her part time—when he's not working as a flight instructor or chartering some big-wig somewhere. He was with the Secret Service but resigned when Obama left office to come home and convince Chelle to marry him. So far, he's been unsuccessful in putting a ring on her finger. He's actually John's best friend."

"Would that be the man interviewed in "The Cross Timbers Murder" episode of *Murder in the Fifty*?"

"Yeah, Greg Baptiste," she answered. "We were like the Four Musketeers in high school."

"Speaking of John, I'm supposed to meet him in a few hours."

"You staying with him at his mom's?"

"No, I got a hotel room. In a lot of ways, I really need some time to myself right now. But he's offering a cold beer or two . . .."

"I understand. When it comes to cold beer . . .."

They both smiled.

"We still on for tomorrow?" he asked.

"Yes. T-Bairz on Chestnut Expressway. I'll text you the address. The have a separate room with several pool tables. Time?"

"3 P.M. again?"

"Works for me."

Hadley paid the bill, and together, they started for the exit. She was almost to the door when he rushed ahead of her. She stopped and looked at him.

"Just getting the door, ma'am," he said as he reached out and held it open.

"You really get into that stuff, don't you Hadley?" she asked once they were out the door.

"A sign of respect where I'm from, Miss Wyatt."

"That's *Ms.* Wyatt."

"Got it," he said with a grin.

At a stoplight on the way home, Elle looked at her image in the rearview mirror and asked. "What are you getting yourself into?" The light turned green as the answer came, "Nothing. He'll be gone in a couple of days. Enjoy the view until then."

Rick Hadley walked into Earhart's Tavern and spotted John Hutsell sitting at a corner table with a man he recognized as Greg Baptiste.

"Hello, John," he said when he reached the two.

Both men at the table stood. John introduced Greg as his oldest friend, and the two new acquaintances shook hands.

The three exchanged career histories, with a few personal stories of Hutsell and Baptiste thrown in for comic relief.

They'd just left the bar when Greg began a new topic of conversation.

"Saw Elle Monday. She dropped by with lunch for Chelle. They were laughing so loud I could hear them in the reception area. She was definitely in good spirits."

"And she will be until the next incident," said John as they walked to their vehicles.

"Well, I do know she had an appointment with Sarah Bennett

this week," Greg said.

"We've been down this road before Greg. How long will this round of therapy last?"

"Even one session is better than none," said a hopeful Greg.

"Yes, if she's not just going through the motions," John said.

They reached Hadley's vehicle first. He opened the door of his truck, leaned on it and said, "You know, I heard a song on the way to Springfield this morning, and there was this one lyric that has stayed with me: 'Sometimes she's caught between the woman that she is and the one she's expected to be'."

He got in the Silverado and drove off. Hutsell and Baptiste remained silent for several moments. Finally, Greg spoke up.

"It often takes someone from the outside to point out the truth."

"And you've got to hand it to him for the way he does it—like, he's almost in your face, but not quite." John added.

"Makes you think, doesn't he?" Greg said as a statement rather than a question. "You know John, I'd be willing to bet he's had Elle on his mind since they met."

"I've been hoping he'd be good for her. Little did I know he would take me along on the ride," said John."

"Too bad he's only passing through."

"St. Louis PD has offered him a position."

"So, you two could end up working together?"

"I don't know Greg," John said. "I like my partner—we really work well together—but in a way, I'm like Hadley. I'm thinking I need a change. I might not be long for St. Louis."

"With your recent exposure, you could probably do whatever you want in law enforcement," Greg said.

"I don't like the exposure, Greg. It hampers me. It gets in the way."

"Maybe it will be one of those 'fifteen minutes of fame' deals."

"We'll see . . .."

·14·

Elle stood in her small walk-in closet trying to decide what to wear for her 'date' with Rick Hadley. Using that term where Hadley was concerned made her uneasy. She'd actually called it a 'meeting' Wednesday morning, sitting in Sarah Bennett's office causing Sarah to grin. When Elle asked why the smile, Sarah had said, "It's not a meeting, Elle. It's a date."

Elle had been on lots of dates, so it wasn't the word itself that had caused concern, it was the context in which Sarah had used it. 'Date'—as in boyfriend-girlfriend. It implied an emotional investment. Emotions complicated things. So, by her own design, the men in her life had never been around long enough for an 'entanglement' to begin. Elle reminded herself there was no need to fret. Come Saturday morning, he'd be out of Springfield, Missouri, and therefore, out of her life.

But, just to be on the safe side, she settled on a comfortable pair of jeans and rejected a blue Henley top in favor of one in dusty green. She then allowed only two buttons to go unfastened, rather than her usual three or four. She looked in the mirror and satisfied with her choices, headed for her 'appointment' with the deputy from Tennessee.

Elle made it to the tavern before Hadley. She texted him she would meet him inside the pool room. He walked in looking fresh. His hair was shorter than yesterday, making him look younger.

"How's it going, Wyatt?"

"Can't complain, Hadley. Yourself?"

He placed his hands on a pool table from behind, leaned back and smiled. A dimple appeared on his left cheek. One dimple, she thought. So he *isn't* perfect, after all.

"Feeling good," he answered. "Would you like a beer, or wait . . . what is it . . . a Diet Coke with a twist of lime?"

"Think I'll compromise and have a Corona with a twist of lime."

"You going to one-up me all afternoon?" he asked, dimple still showing.

"If you keep setting yourself up, I'll oblige."

"I'm an officer of the law. I'm observant by nature," he explained, concerning his knowledge of her preferred drink.

"Well then, pick up a pool cue, and let me observe you for a while," she said.

The waitress appeared, and he gave their drink order.

"Shall we start at the beginning?" he asked.

She nodded. He selected a couple of cues, and the lesson began. Things were going well, until she missed three shots in a row.

"You have a steady grip, and you're good with identifying your contact point. Now, concentrate on your follow-through. Here, let me show you."

Rick Hadley stood to the left and a little behind Elle. His arms were long enough to go around her and still manage the angle needed.

Concentrate, my ass, she thought and wondered if he'd noticed that her heart rate had increased.

Once they were fully standing again, Elle laid her stick on the table.

"Hungry?" she asked, and without waiting for a reply, said, "BBQ wings sound good. I'll be right back."

While she placed the order at the bar, Rick made his way to the jukebox. Elle soon joined him, and reminiscent of the night they'd met, helped him make the final selections. Most of the wings were gone, and the cue sticks back on the rack when Elle excused herself to go to the restroom. Upon her return, she found Hadley standing at the jukebox for a second time.

"Since I'm leaving tomorrow, you want to hold up your end of the bargain and give me a dance lesson?"

"Sure."

He pressed the screen and took her hand as a mandolin played the first few notes of a song she immediately recognized. Elle stopped and looked at him. He brought his finger to his lips. She took the hint and remained silent while he led her through the opening to the pool room where they would be alone.

Rick Hadley brought her into his arms in a classic slow dance stance. He then led her in a small two-step. When Urban's voice joined Vincent's in harmony, Rick pulled her arm to his chest, encased her hand in his and leaned his head down so her forehead was against his chin. He broke their embrace a few moments after the song ended.

Without meeting his eyes, she said, "You've been holding out on me Hadley."

"What do you mean?"

She raised her face to his.

"You can dance."

"I can't do the fancy steps John does."

"With a song like that, it's not about fancy steps. It's about the way you hold a woman."

Before he could respond, two men entered the room laughing. "Rack 'em, Jim. I'm gonna show you how it's done."

Rick picked up Elle's jacket and held it open for her. He escorted her to the exit and made sure he was in the lead, so he could open the door for her. They were almost to her car, when he heard the lock click open. She turned to face him, and watched as he stuck his hands in his pockets.

"Have a good trip," she said. "Hope you find the answers you're looking for."

"Thanks, Elle," he said.

"That's the first time you've called me Elle."

With his hands still in his pockets, he leaned in and kissed her cheek. "Take care," he said.

Rick took a few steps back, so she could open her door. Once she had backed out her Cadillac, he waved and walked to his truck. It was near the end of rush hour traffic, and Elle was still waiting to pull onto Chestnut Expressway, when he drove up behind her. Finally, a break in traffic allowed them both access. She turned right. He turned left.

Chelle was driving her friend home when Elle received a text message. She tapped the screen, read it, dropped the phone, and her hands to her lap.

"It's from him, isn't it?" asked Chelle.

Elle looked at Chelle with a questioning look.

"I thought he might get in touch with you," Chelle said.

"And why did you think that?"

"Because John called and asked him to stop by on his way back to Tennessee. So, what did the message say?"

"He wants to know if I want to play a 'game or two' of pool Saturday evening."

Chelle pulled into the circle drive of Elle's home. "Well you do, don't you?" she asked and turned off the ignition.

"Why does John want him to stop in Springfield?"

"Don't know. I just got in on the tail end of a conversation John and Greg had Wednesday in our reception room. Everyone else had gone for the day, and as soon as they saw me, they went mum."

Elle didn't respond.

"Well, you want to see him again, right?"

"Chelle, I'm trying to get my life together. I don't need Rick Hadley complicating things."

"Then, at least have the decency to tell him the truth."

"Why? He's just passing through."

"There's something I haven't told you."

"Oh, hell."

"Don't go getting all bent out of shape, Elle," Chelle said. "Last Thursday, when he met Greg and John at Earhart's, Hadley set your cousin straight about how he treats you."

"What do you mean?"

"He let John know he passes judgment on you. After he'd gone, John admitted to Greg that Hadley was right. He stuck John with the sharp end of the truth, and John accepted it."

"Yeah, Hadley's good at the 'mic drop,'" Elle said.

"Well, the man needs an answer. He's done well by you Elle, so think carefully about your response," advised Chelle. "Part of getting your life together is considering the feelings of others."

"I'll think about it."

At 8:30 P.M., Elle texted Rick Hadley and accepted his offer. She suggested a pool hall on East St. Louis Street—no place for slow dancing there. She was making mental notes on her 'Let's-be-friends' speech when her phone rang.

"Good evening, Hadley."

"Ms. Wyatt. Wanted to touch base about Saturday evening. Concerning a time, it's up in the air at the moment. John wants to meet late afternoon, and he can't give me a time when the meeting will likely end. Is it okay if I text you as soon as I'm free?"

"I guess that will work. Where are you now?"

"Battle Mountain, Nevada. I should roll into Springfield around noon on Saturday."

"Will you be staying with John?"

"No. He and I will part company, and then I'll meet you. Not knowing what time you and I will end our evening . . .." Hadley struggled to find the right words, while Elle held her breath and hoped he wasn't hinting for her to offer accommodations. Finally, he gave up and said, "It just didn't seem right to ask for a key to his mom's house. I'll get a room and head to Tennessee Sunday morning."

"Have you come to any decisions concerning the offers you have?" she asked.

"No. Neither one really appeals to me. I'll send out feelers when I get back home. I can hang out with the Shannon County Sheriff's Department a while longer."

"I'll see you Saturday then."

"Goodnight," he said and disconnected the call.

Looking for escape from the Hadley situation, Elle streamed *Miss Fisher's Murder Mysteries* and got lost in the fashions worn by the female detective of a bygone era. Before turning in for the night, she went online and purchased a pattern for a vintage beaded flapper dress of deco design.

· 16 ·

Rick Hadley texted Elle after checking into his hotel room in south Springfield. He had almost three hours before his conference with John. She didn't ask about the topic up for discussion but surmised John might be acting as recruiter for the St. Louis Police Department.

Hadley apologized for not being able to provide a time for them to meet. She responded by saying she understood, and from that point on, it became a waiting game. When she hadn't heard from him by six-thirty, she got in her Cadillac and drove to the Blue Room Comedy Club that adjoined the pool hall. Laughing was a better way of marking time than checking her phone every five minutes for messages.

Elle had just locked her car when her phone signaled Hadley's call.

"Elle, I'm sorry," he began.

"I'm already here. I'll meet you inside."

"Elle, if it's okay, I'd like to show you something first," he said.

"What is it?"

"It's going to take some explaining. I'll text you the address. Oh, have you had dinner?"

"No."

"What's the best pizza place in town, and what are your favorite toppings?"

"There are several good ones, but I'm partial to Garbo's Pizzeria."

A text arrived. The address he'd given her was on Booneville near the Green County Courthouse.

"Style and toppings?"

"Rick, Garbo's is in the wrong direction."

"Don't worry, I've got it covered. Somebody here owes me a big favor and is going to play delivery boy."

"Not funny," came a familiar voice from Hadley's end.

"What's John doing there?" she asked.

"Waiting for your order. You're on speaker. Order anything you want. He's footing the bill."

"Is he joining us?"

"No. He's intruded on our time too much as it is," Hadley said. "Order, Ms. Wyatt?"

'Our time'.

And there it was—the one line that always showed up when things got uncomfortable—*To hell with it.*

How easy it would be to forget the whole damn thing and go into the comedy club—better yet, go to a neighborhood bar and see what was available in terms of disposable men. So what if she went backsliding? This 'trying to change your life' and 'thinking about other people's feelings' crap was for the birds.

"Elle Wyatt, are you still there?" She didn't answer. "Elle?"

"Yes."

"I'm looking at their menu now," he said. "So, we going for the combo deluxe or what?"

"She'll want Canadian bacon and pineapple," John said in the background.

"Pineapple? Are you sure?" Hadley asked John. Then to Elle, "Is that right, Elle? You like fruit on your pizza?"

"As a matter of fact, I do." Maybe she should just start a fight. That would end it fast enough. "What's wrong with pineapple on pizza?"

"You know, come to think about it, nothing," he answered. "It's got anti-inflammatory and anti-cancer properties. The Vitamin C helps prevent cataracts, and several researchers feel it increases fertility."

"Oh brother," said John.

"Yeah, you're welcome for the warning, John. Now Elle, is that all?"

Hadley knew how to deliver a line, all right. She wished she knew what he'd said to make her cousin admit his treatment of her needed revising.

"Hey, John," she said.

"Yes."

"Add a house salad."

"Make that two," said Rick. "How long till you get here, Elle?"

"Ten minutes."

"Drive around back. I'll meet you there."

The building at the address Hadley had given her was a vacant two-story storefront. Elle pulled in next to his Silverado. The light at the top of the external staircase blinked off and then on again. She looked up and saw Hadley start down. She got out of her car and met him at the base of the stairs.

"Okay Hadley, what's so important you'd forego a game of pool?"

"Come up, and I'll show you."

Ever the gentleman, he indicated she should go before him. When she got to the top, she didn't step aside for him to open the door, even though she caught a glimpse of his arm as he started to reach around her. They both walked into to an empty room.

"Well, what do you think?" he asked.

"Look, Hadley, it's already been a long day . . . .."

"You're right. You deserve some answers. Pat and Jean own this building and they, along with John's mother, want to set him up in business."

"What kind of business?"

"Private investigations."

"Okay, so he's consulting with you. Wants to know your opinion. I get it. You could have given me this information during a game of pool."

"It's a little more than that," he said. "Come over here and sit with me."

He selected a spot between two windows on the street side of the room where the wall would provide back support. Elle sat cross-legged on the floor while Rick bent his legs upward. He put his forearms on his knees and interlocked his fingers.

"Here's the proposal. The Nelson/Wyatt Group not only wants John to run an agency out of this building; it wants to eventually set up a private forensic lab somewhere in Springfield." The pieces were staring to fall into place. "John wants a partner and—."

"You have experience and background in both areas," she interrupted.

"Yes."

"Is this what you want?"

"I admit, I've thought about it," he said. "Elle, I don't know if this is the answer, but it's an opportunity I never thought I'd have for another ten years."

"The Nelson/Wyatt Group will follow through on their word, Rick. You can trust what they tell you."

"They've even sweetened the deal," he said. "They offered to turn all of this into a loft apartment. What do you think? 'A little paint, some flowers . . .?'"

She laughed and finished the quote from *Young Frankenstein*, "'A couple of throw pillows . . ..'"

"Best comedy ever made," he said.

"I beg to differ," she countered. "It's number two. Number one is *Some Like It Hot*."

There was a knock at the door.

"Open up," came John Hutsell's voice from the other side of the door. "I've got places to go and people to see."

Elle and Rick looked at each other and smiled.

"Okay, on the count of three," he said. "One, two, three."

"'And a lot of livin' to do!'" they yelled in unison.

"Very funny," came the response.

Hadley jumped to his feet and opened the door. He unloaded John of two pizza boxes and two plastic bags. He thanked him, closed the door and returned to his spot by Elle. He handed her the top box.

"Not mine," she said after peering inside.

"Sorry, Elle. I just can't do fruit on pizza," he said with a smile and exchanged boxes with her. "But first things first."

Rick opened one of the bags and brought out a six-pack of beer. He handed Elle one of the bottles.

"Here's to new friends and new beginnings," he said and clinked her bottle with his.

Halfway through dinner Elle picked up her phone and brought up a YouTube video. Rick heard the sound of a motorcycle and then music.

"You're kidding me," he said. "Hold up the screen."

Rick snapped his fingers with the man in the video and then sang along.

"'There are chicks just right for some kissing. And I mean to kiss me a few.'"

Elle smiled and shook her head.

"'Man, those chicks don't know what they're missing. I got a lot of livin' to do.'"

"Dang, Hadley." She paused the video.

"What?"

"I didn't know you could sing like that, but by all rights, those words are more likely to come out of John's mouth than yours."

"You don't think I'm right for the part of Conrad Birdie?"

"Hold on as minute." She tapped the screen of her cell and said, "Jesse Pearson" into the mic. "Okay, Pearson was six-three. I thought your legs resembled his."

He gave her a look.

"You know—long," she explained. "How tall are you by the way?"

"Six-four. I'd say you're five-seven?"

"Yeah, said the man who is 'observant by nature.'"

"Until last Friday, it was only a guess."

Rick and Elle went silent. They both knew he was referring to the dance they'd shared.

"Elle, you know we've been flirting around for a couple of weeks now."

"Yeah, I know."

"I've put a lot of thought into the past eight days, and I think I've figured out why we get along so well. We're new on the scene where each other is concerned. We don't have any preconceived notions––no expectations of one another. As a result, I feel free to just be me when I'm with you."

"Rick—."

"Just a minute," he interrupted. "There's more." He paused. "I've got baggage, Elle."

"You hide it well."

"If I move to Springfield, some of it will come along. What I'm getting at is right now I need a good friend. Nothing more, nothing less."

"Oh, thank God," she said. "I've been working on the same speech for two days. What a relief."

"So, if this room becomes my new home, we can spend time together as friends—it's not going to be a problem?"

"Rick, I don't feel the need to explain myself to you either."

"People will assume we're an item."

"And therein lies the beauty," she said. "As long as they think we are, they'll stop trying to set us up with other people."

They both laughed.

"Okay, so tell me why you know all these old movie quotes," she said.

"Mom, dad and family movie night. We watched our favorite ones over and over. Half the time I respond to comments with quotes from movies. Most people never catch on. What about you?"

"Knowledge of movie quotes and a lot of song lyrics came from my Grandma Nelson. Where the performing arts were concerned, she made sure her grandkids knew their stuff," Elle said. "On the Stafford side, my grandparents took turns with friends hosting country music parties. They'd play instruments and sing while I danced. I inherited the Nelson rhythm but not the Stafford ear. Couldn't sing on key if my life depended on it."

"So, if I do come to Springfield and set up shop with John, will we continue with our respective lessons?"

"We can. When do you think you'll make a decision?"

"I told John I'd have an answer for him in a week."

Hadley leaned his head against the wall and tried to stifle a yawn.

"Okay the party is officially over," she said as she got to her feet. "Take yourself to your hotel room and get some sleep."

Rick stood and picked up what was left of dinner. He followed Elle down the stairs. He placed the pizza boxes on the hood of his truck and put the trash in his truck's storage compartment. He leaned in and hugged her.

"Be careful going home," he said. "I'll be in touch."

He picked up the top box and handed it to her. She was about to shut the door when he called out.

"Oh, Elle?"

"Yes."

"You remember the name of Bogart's character in Casablanca?"

"Rick." She smiled and added, "As in Blaine, not Hadley."

"You remember his last line?"

"Yes."

"Good night," he said.

The next morning, Rick Hadley left for Tennessee. The following Saturday, Elle attended an event hosted by Senator Claire Nelson Hutsell on the Wyatt Estate for funds to update Greene County's 911 system. Sunday evening, Hadley called.

"It's official. I'm moving to Springfield," he said.

"When?"

"My dad asked me to stay for six more weeks. My last day will be April twenty-seventh," he said.

"That gives Pat time to remodel your new digs," she said.

He laughed at her choice of words.

"Gives me time to decide what I want to do with my place here. I've got a house sitting on ten acres. My mom thinks it would be wise to hold on to it. She says urban sprawl will make its way here soon, and I'll be able to sell to a developer for a 'tidy sum', as she put it."

"You going to let Jean handle the loft's interiors?" Elle asked.

"I don't know," he said. "I'm not very fancy-schmancy."

"She's a professional, Rick. She can tone it down to your liking."

"I was thinking maybe you would help."

"Not a problem."

"I'm putting Eagle Ridge in my rear-view mirror, so I'll be selling most everything here. The only pieces of furniture I'll bring are my maternal grandmother's three-piece coffee table set and a wardrobe I've commissioned from Lydia Janssen in St. Louis."

"The lady from the case you and John worked?"

"Yep. Oops, gotta go. My brother just pulled up. Talk to you soon."

On Sunday, April twenty-ninth, Rick Hadley moved into the loft apartment on Booneville. John and Greg helped him unload and carry what little he'd brought with him. Chelle, sporting a new apron trimmed in green rick-rack, got her wish, and finally got to meet

Hadley late that afternoon when all gathered at her home for dinner. That evening, Rick and Elle sat in his new apartment on a portable air mattress with their backs against the bedroom wall. Her computer was on her lap.

"Take a look at these and tell me what you think," she said of the pages she'd bookmarked. "King size. Low, or no footboard, Mr. 'I Still Can't Believe How Long Your Legs Are'." She interrupted herself and asked, "What is your inseam, anyway?"

"Thirty-six."

"Gotta be hard buying off the rack," she said. "Sleeve length's really out there, too, huh?"

He looked at her.

"I'm a seamstress. I notice these kinds of things." She smiled knowing he would pick up on her take of his observant law enforcement comment made weeks ago. "By the way, any other colors besides white or blue when it comes to shirts?"

"Wine. My mom bought one when I moved back to Shannon County five years ago. She was trying to encourage me to branch out, so she said. It's still in the package," he said. "Speaking of sewing, did you make the apron Chelle had on today?"

"Yeah, came out pretty cool, huh?"

"But you don't like taking special orders, right?"

"I do for friends," she asked. "What do you need?"

"Something similar for my great aunt. She'll be seventy-eight on Christmas Day and is the only one in our family who still wears an apron. I'm her favorite, and I'd like to keep it that way."

"You have pictures of her from past Christmases?" He nodded. "Send me a few, and I'll see you remain the 'chosen' one."

The computer screen had gone dark while they'd talked. Elle tapped the keyboard, bringing it back to life.

"What do you think of this one? It's a bookcase headboard with panels that slide back and forth to hide the contents—not exactly dust-free, but close. The frame has built-in drawers underneath for storage."

"I like it. How soon can it be delivered?"

"Next week sometime. Matching night stands and dresser?"

"Yes."

"Okay, that takes care of the bedroom. Now for the living area. You'll want a style that compliments your coffee table. Hold on, I'll be right back," she said as she got to her feet.

Rick was on the phone when she returned.

"Rick, that's a great set. It's Early American—oh, I'm sorry. I didn't realize you were on the phone."

"Yes, Mom, I do have company. I'm putting you on speaker. Mom, meet Elle Wyatt. Elle, meet my mom, Sylvia Hadley."

Both women exchanged 'How do you do's.'

"Elle is John's cousin. Her mom has an interior design business, and Elle is helping me set up house."

Elle's eyes went big; her mouth dropped open.

"You got a bed picked out yet?"

"Yep, we decided on one tonight."

Elle shook her head from side to side.

"Elle, don't let him go with those microfiber sheets. Cotton all the way, okay?"

"I'm with you, Mrs. Hadley. Natural over man-made any day. I think sheets should 'breathe.'"

Rick mouthed, "Breathe?"

Elle mouthed back, "I'll explain later."

"Sounds like you're in good hands, son."

"Except for one thing, Mom. She thinks *Some Like It Hot* is funnier than *Young Frankenstein*."

"Well, she's right. Go to the American Film Institute's website. I'll leave you two alone. Send pictures when you've got the place the way you want it. Good night."

"'Night, Mom."

Elle sat down beside him and hit him on the shoulder.

"Ow! What was that for?"

"'Setting up house'? We 'picked out a bed tonight'?"

Rick laughed, "Yeah, she didn't miss a beat, did she?"

Sylvia Hadley rarely did. She'd closed her eyes after talking to her son, caught between wanting him to be happy and knowing he'd just made himself vulnerable again.

· 18 ·

Gambit Investigations opened for business on the first Friday in May. Southwest Missouri businessmen and women along, with members of the law community, enjoyed food and wine with Springfield's two newest private investigators/crime scene consultants.

Noticeably absent from the festivities was Elle Wyatt. Rick Hadley hadn't seen his friend since Monday when they'd gone furniture shopping. She'd been about to disembark from his truck when she'd inquired about his wardrobe plans for Gambit's opening. He'd smiled and told her he'd step it up a notch. Her last words were that she'd see him Friday, if not before. It had been a busy week and they hadn't connected since.

Wondering when she might arrive, Rick disappeared for a few moments and texted her, warning that if she didn't hurry, there was no telling when she'd get the chance to see him in a suit jacket again. When the message went unanswered for over an hour, Rick inquired of John if he'd seen his cousin.

"From past experience, I'd say something's going on, and she's running. She goes dark, Rick. It may be several weeks before you hear anything."

That night Rick carefully composed a new message.

"Whew! Glad today's over. Ready to resume lessons. Text when you've got time."

He read it over. Although he was concerned, the message didn't show it and he'd successfully put the ball squarely in her court. Rick hit send and hoped she was finding the answers she was looking for.

Elle resurfaced on Tuesday, the eighth of May with a message.
"Billiards of Springfield, 7:30 tonight."
"Dinner?"
"They have food," she replied.
"See you then."

After placing their orders, Rick and Elle snagged one of the few booths outside the adjoining Blue Room Comedy Club's entrance. Both were reserved in their approach to conversation. The discussion centered on Rick's activities since they'd last seen each other rather than Elle's. He finally found a way to bring her in personally.

"The sofa was delivered yesterday," he said. "You were right, you know?"

"About?"

"The color of leather. With the hardwood floors, slate blue was the best choice."

"A 'muted' splash of color," she said. "Oxymoron if I ever heard one."

"Yeah, Wyatt, talk grammar to me."

Elle choked on her beer.

"Damn, Hadley," she said, finally giving up a smile. "Actually, it's not grammar, it's a literary term."

"Yeah, that's it. Keep talking."

She rolled her eyes.

"Missed me, huh?" he teased.

Bantering was their normal, and the question was out of his mouth before he knew it.

She looked at her glass and placed both hands around its base. Keeping her eyes down, she said, "Yes."

"The elephant just left the room," he said with relief.

She brought her eyes to his. "Rick, I . . . .."

She was struggling.

"No explanation needed, Elle. When and if, okay?"

Elle watched Rick as he went to pick up their orders. She placed a napkin in her lap and thought Meredith Embry'd been a fool for letting Rick Hadley get away.

When time allowed, the next several months found Rick and Elle making good on the bargain they'd entered into on the night they'd met. Elle could now scatter balls with her strong, measured break, and Rick was executing east-coast swing moves on the dance floor. And, he'd been right—people did take notice.

When the two had begun making the rounds in Springfield,

women had blatantly asked Rick to dance, but not anymore. Men had openly watched Elle line up a shot, hoping to catch a glimpse down her shirt, but now they did so from afar.

On Tuesday, August twenty-first, Rick returned from an Arkansas business trip earlier than expected. He rolled into Springfield at noon, and after lunch with John, headed to his loft. He tossed his overnight bag in the corner, set the alarm for three, and threw himself on the bed for a nap.

A police siren woke him at 2:30. He knew Elle would be at The Swingin' Door in an hour. She was scheduled to give a dance lesson to a friend of John's who'd been told by the woman he liked to come back when he'd learned how to dance. Rick and Elle had made arrangements to meet after the lesson. He showered and shaved, then headed out the door forty-five minutes early.

Not wanting to disturb Elle and her pupil, Rick slipped quietly into the tavern. Fifteen minutes later, the student checked his watch, walked Elle to a table and left the bar.

Rick slid his debit card into the jukebox and summoned a Randy Rogers Band tune he knew would appeal to Elle. She was tapping her toes on the floor while Rogers sang, ". . . if things don't work out by the next song, and you're looking for someone who can dance, I'll be right over there by the jukebox . . . trying to buy myself a chance."

Out of curiosity, she turned and looked in the corner and saw Rick leaning on the wall next to the machine, arms crossed and a big smile on his face. She stood and gave a come-hither motion with her finger. With his long strides, he made it in time for the second chorus.

When the song ended, Elle started back to the table. Rick took her hand and said, "Wait."

The next song was one she'd heard her Grandfather Stafford sing dozens of times. Rick pulled her close like he'd done for their first dance. With his chin touching her forehead, he sang, "'You give your hand to me'." He moved his hand from the small of her back all the way around to her right side bringing her closer. "'. . . and anyone can tell, you think you know me well, well you don't know me'."

Elle closed her eyes and allowed herself to get lost in the music and the movement of their bodies. He continued to hold her for several moments after the song had ended.

Not going to happen. She patted him on the back, breaking their embrace and said, "C'mon, let's go have dinner."

After they'd eaten, Elle begged off the rest of the evening and texted Cal.

"You busy?"

"Busy procrastinating."

"Want some company?"

"Love some."

Cal opened the door and said, "Come in and tell me the latest."

When she entered the room, he saw her expression and said, "Hard liquor it is."

She gave him a puzzled look. He turned her around by the shoulders and brought her a step to their left, where she could see herself in the mirror.

"Look," he said. "That's not a coffee-, beer-, or wine-face, my friend. Go sit down. Rum and Coke coming up."

Cal handed Elle her drink, sat down next to her on the sofa, and said, "You going to get to it or him-haw for twenty minutes, until I prove I know you better than you know yourself, and tell you why you're here?"

"By all means, let's skip the preliminaries. Why am I here?"

"How long did you think the two of you could pull it off?" he asked.

"Cal, he's one of the best friends I've ever had. I don't want to lose that."

"Who says you have to?"

"Because you and I both know I don't do the couples thing. I never have, and I don't want to start now."

"He's never come on to you, right? Not even when he's leaned over, put his arms around you and helped you line up a pool shot?"

"Nope. Not during any of the dancing lessons, either."

"Maybe he likes guys," Cal suggested.

"Nah, I know what side he dresses to."

"Then you've been dancing a little closer than friends should be. Has he done anything that makes you think he's moving in that direction?"

Elle laid out the afternoon's events and ended by saying, "He knows my family's history with that song, Cal. Yet, he didn't choose a classic version. No, he went with Michael Bublé."

"Damn, Elle, he made the song about you and him. No way is it ever going to be about Grandpa again." Cal smiled and added, "Yeah, the 'just friends' thing is over. Just a matter of time now."

"I don't want it to change," she insisted.

Cal laughed which made her set her jaw.

"Don't give me that look. You both have been playing with fire for months."

"You're not helping, Cal."

"Okay, try this on for size. There are couples who continue to be best friends even after they become lovers."

"There's the problem, Cal. My lovers have never been friends."

"So, you're still out there?"

"I'm more selective," she said defensively.

"Well, you've got a decision to make then, don't you?"

Rick Hadley lay on his bed and tried to figure out why he'd crossed the line with Elle—especially now. He was afraid it was the same reason he'd downed six bottles of beer in an hour last Saturday night. If someone had asked him two and a half years ago what he'd be doing on August 18, 2018, he sure wouldn't have said getting drunk in a hotel room in Russellville, Arkansas. He wished August eighteenth could be stricken from the calendar—just skip it and go from the seventeenth to the nineteenth—like his hotel had skipped the thirteenth floor.

The date was a reminder that, in his thirty-five years, there had been two men he'd wanted to kill—only the term that really applied was murder. He'd been successful in holding his own, and even though he'd been thinking of broaching the subject of taking their relationship to a higher level, it wasn't fair to Elle to do so now.

And her reaction—talk about slamming on the breaks.

He closed his eyes and played back the few minutes they'd shared. He knew she'd felt his body react to hers, yet she had allowed him to pull her even closer and had waited until the song ended before jumping ship.

His cell vibrated against the shelf of the headboard. The message's sender knew him well.

"I love you, son."
"I love you too, Mom."

·19·

The last Saturday in August, Elle decided she needed a hiatus from Springfield and the people in it. On the drive to Galena, she stayed away from country music and listened to rocker, and former *Voice* contestant, Terry McDermott.

She walked into The Hideout in time for The Street Outlaws second set. Elle was surprised to see Myles walk on stage and sit down behind the drums. She wondered if Eddie Smith, the man who usually occupied the seat, had quit. Myles saw her and pointed the drum sticks in her direction before clapping them together signaling the other band members it was show time.

Sila was strapping on her guitar when Kaela and Eddie took center stage. The harmony of the two youngest band members was spot on. Elle realized Myles had taken a back seat to showcase his daughter.

Three songs in, Carolyn arrived with a drink.

"His name is Ellis. Blue denim shirt. Last stool on the left," she said as she sat the drink on a coaster.

"Can he dance?"

"Yeah, but he's an ass," Carolyn said.

"So am I. We'll get along just fine."

Elle looked in the man's direction and raised her glass.

Carolyn had been right on both counts. Two dances later, Ellis walked Elle to her table and sat down uninvited.

"That chair's taken," she said.

"You expecting someone?" he asked.

"No. Please get up."

He did so and Elle put her feet in the chair. "There, that's better."

On her break Carolyn walked over, pulled a chair from the table next to Elle's and sat down.

"Where's your usual partner—Hadley, isn't it?" she asked.

"I don't have a clue."

"Too bad. He's *not* an ass."

"He's available. John can introduce you to him."

It was a cheap shot, and both women knew it.

"Elle, I know you and John have had your differences, but you should know what happened between him and me was my fault, not his. He told me from the beginning, he wouldn't be around long. I'm the one who didn't keep my emotions in check. And to tell you the truth, I wouldn't give up one minute of the time I had with him."

"And you're telling me this because?"

"You're like that Pam Tillis song—the one about the woman who hits the bars and ends up in a different man's arms every night. Concerning John, yeah, I got hurt, but in the long run, it was worth it." She stood up and said, "Quit messing with the likes of Ellis. Take the chance, Elle."

· 20 ·

It was Labor Day. Elle and Chelle were standing outside Hammons Field, home of a minor-league baseball team, waiting on the rest of their party. The clouds had finally cleared, and the Springfield Cardinals would take the field in thirty minutes for the last game of the season.

Chelle stood near the gate, looking chic in her new Roberto Cavalli sunglasses, while Elle reached in her bag for her retro SojoS shades. Greg and John drove by and honked before turning into the parking lot across the street. Elle looked up after putting away the case for her sunglasses and saw a familiar figure walking toward them. She nudged Chelle, who followed her line of sight.

"Just look at him," Chelle said. "Shirts always starched and pressed. The same with his jeans. Do you see that crease down the front of each leg? And I swear, I've never seen him when he wasn't clean shaven. What is it with him?"

"I wish I knew," Elle said.

Something in her voice made Chelle look directly at her friend. "Are you having second thoughts?" she asked.

"Maybe."

"That's all I needed to hear."

Elle shot her friend a questioned look.

"Hello, Rick," Chelle said as Hadley stopped in front of them and put his hands in his pockets.

"It's been a few weeks, Chelle. How was Vegas?"

"Came back with more money than I went with. What's new with you?"

"Business is good. Defense attorney Carver D'Orsay just put us on retainer as crime scene investigators."

"How about a personal life? Making any headway?" Chelle asked.

"Not enough hours in the day for that. Starting a new business requires a lot of time and attention."

"Yes, but take it from someone with experience in that

240

department. Carve out a few hours here and there or you'll burn a fuse."

"Planning on doing just that as soon as John gets here with the tickets. Where is he anyway? I'm starting to get thirsty. 'Peanuts and Cracker Jacks' were good enough when I was a kid, but now I want a nice cold beer in my hand." He paused. "How about you, Elle?" he asked bringing her into the conversation.

"I could go for a cold beer."

"Here he comes," Chelle said as John and Greg crossed the street to join them.

Once inside the stadium, Chelle grabbed the tickets out of John's hands.

"Let's see . . . three in front, two in back," she said as she looked at the tickets. "Rick and Elle, here you go," she handed the back two tickets to Rick. "You two can expand your topics of conversation from billiards and two-stepping to baseball. Have a seat and discuss."

"At least I'll get a word in edgewise since I won't be sitting next to you," Elle said.

"C'mon, Wyatt. I'll treat you to that beer we were talking about," Rick said before anyone had taken a seat. "Anybody want to send an order with us?"

"Yeah," said John as he made himself comfortable. "Two hot dogs with all the fixings and a cold beer."

"Chelle? Greg?" asked Rick.

"Nachos and iced tea, thank you," Chelle said.

"Two hot dogs, no onions," Greg said as he winked at Chelle. "With iced tea."

Rick held out his arm for Elle to lead the way.

"What would you like, Elle?" Rick asked as they stood in line.

"A soft pretzel and a beer. Think we'll have to make two trips?"

"Nope."

"One pretzel, one hot dog and two beers," he told the attendant.

"What a—?"

"It'll be okay," he said.

Rick handed Elle the food items, and he carried the beers. He nodded to a seating area nearby.

"We'll eat here, so there will be two less orders to take back."

Once they were seated, he took a sip of beer and said, "Elle, I'm sorry . . . I know I crossed—."

She interrupted him. "Rick . . .." She dropped off the conversation.

"Close your eyes," he said. Her eyes went wide instead. "No, that's what I've got in mind." Elle did as instructed. "Now respond to the next line like you would have before I came back from Arkansas."

He gave her a few moments.

"Sorry, I've been so busy, Elle. I'm afraid we'll have to start all over where the waltz is concerned. Darn the luck."

With her eyes still closed she said, "Rick Hadley, if I didn't know better, I'd think you were flirting with me."

"And if I am?"

Elle smiled and said, "You'll make Chelle Thomas one happy woman."

"It's not Chelle I'm thinking about." She opened her eyes. He wasn't smiling.

Elle's cell signaled receipt of a text. She waited a few moments before checking on the sender.

"Well, she's thinking about you?" she said showing him the message.

"What's taking so long? LOL"

"Tell her the lines are really long, and we'll be there when we can," he said.

"We're busted. She's got Greg's binoculars."

"I'll go place their orders. You can wait here till I need help."

As Rick walked away, Elle texted back, "Don't get excited just yet . . . oh, hell, too late for that, isn't it, Ms. Bond?"

"Ms. Bond?"

"They're talking about casting a woman as the next James Bond. You've been spying on us. Might as well be you."

"Are you playing nice up there?"

"Yes, I am."

"Took you long enough," John said as he reached for his order.

"The line was long," Chelle and Elle said at the same time.

"Oh," John said, oblivious to the fact Rick and Elle were empty handed after all items had been delivered.

There was a loud crack and a collective, "Oohhh . . ." from the crowd.

"It's gone," predicted John.

Halfway through the sixth inning, Chelle nudged her friend. "Powder room, Elle."

The two friends climbed the steps to the restroom.

"So, tell me. What did he say?" Chelle begged to know.

"He was classic Hadley. He took an uncomfortable situation and turned it around."

"So, what happens now?"

"I'm thinking on it."

After the game, the five friends stopped outside to say goodbye before going to their vehicles.

"Rick, you want to get something to eat before heading home?" Elle asked.

"Sounds good."

"Hey, great idea. Those hot dogs just didn't cut—." Chelle jabbed John in the side and kept him from finishing his sentence.

"Nice going, Slick," she whispered out of the corner of her mouth. "Now hush, and drive Greg and me home, please."

"See you later," Rick said.

Chelle waved, and Greg nodded. As the threesome crossed the street, Rick and Elle could hear John.

"What was that for? Man, you have one bony elbow, Michelle Thomas."

"Just shut up and walk," she said.

"So, what are you hungry for?" Elle asked.

"I know it's late, but how about we stop at the store, get a couple of steaks and the makings for a salad, and I'll cook dinner?"

"Your place or mine?"

"I've got a stovetop grill I haven't even taken out of the box. Let's see if it's all it's cracked up to be?"

With Rick sitting beside her, Elle drove to the nearest grocery store.

"You okay with steamed broccoli and cauliflower?" he asked as they walked into the store.

"Yes."

"Cheese sauce?"

"Even better."

They'd made their selections and were headed toward the check-out lane, when a little boy rounded the corner and ran into Rick. His mother made the turn just in time to see her son fall on his bottom.

"I'm sorry," she said as she helped her son to his feet. "He just got his second wind."

The boy looked up at Rick and started moving his fingers and hands to communicate. His mother translated as her son spoke.

"Look Mommy. It's a giant."

Rick squatted down and spoke to the boy, using sign language, "I'm not really a giant. I'm just tall for my age."

The boy grinned.

"How old are you?" Rick asked as he continued to sign.

The boy held up five fingers.

"It's been a long time since I was five," signed Rick. "But I think I've stopped growing. You've still got time to catch up with me."

The boy's grin got bigger.

"It's getting late, honey. We need to get you home and into bed."

"Take good care of your mom," Rick said.

"I will," signed the boy. "Bye."

"Bye."

After mother and son had disappeared, Elle said, "Pretty impressive, Hadley."

Rick shrugged his shoulders. "I worked at the 'Y' when I was in college. They had a strong deaf-ed program. I've kept up with it, because it's something I don't want to lose. I'd like to volunteer in Springfield, but with the business, availability is a problem right now."

Rick put his hands on the cart next to Elle's. "What do you say we head to the check-out?"

Rick carried the two grocery bags up the steps to his apartment. Once inside, he deposited them on the bar that framed the kitchen.

"How can I help?" she asked.

"You can wash the vegetables.

Rick did most of the cooking. After dinner, they sat next to each other on the sofa.

"How about going with superheroes tonight?"

"Only if I can watch Steve Rogers and Tony Stark at the same time," she said.

"*The Avengers* it is."

Rick slouched on the sofa and propped his legs on the coffee table. Elle sat next to him and drew her legs up under her. She placed her right arm on the back of the sofa just above his head. Halfway through the program, she detected a slight snore. Elle watched Rick for several minutes as he slept before she tapped him on the shoulder. He jolted awake.

"I'm sorry."

"It's after 1 A.M. You're entitled."

"Hold up a sec," he said as she picked up her bag. "Let me walk you to your car."

Rick followed Elle out the door and down the stairs. She keyed her locks, turned to face him, and with her back against the door, said, "Would you call this a date, Hadley?"

"I'd say it qualifies." He leaned on the car beside her, arms at his chest.

"And how do you usually end a date?" she asked.

"Elle Wyatt, if I didn't know better, I'd say you were wanting to be kissed."

"Well . . . you going to do it or not?"

Rick pushed himself off the Cadillac and turned so he was facing her. He put his forearms on the car's window, framing her head. "So, you want to be kissed, huh?"

She placed her hands on his shirt collar, slowly pulled him to her and kissed him.

"You are something else," he said.

"You want to come to my house Saturday night? This time I'll cook."

"Isn't Saturday when Jean and Pat are having their big charity event?"

"Oh yeah," she said.

"You planning on going?"

"I'll make an appearance."

"Then, I'll see you there."

Rick leaned in and kissed her again, making sure he was in

control this time.

"Things are about to change, Elle," he said, taking on a serious side.

"They already have."

·21·

"Spill!"

The two friends were in Chelle's office, and she wanted to know all the details of the night before.

"He can cook," Elle said as she sat down in the chair in her friend's office.

"We already knew that. Can he kiss?"

"He had to be primed, but yeah, he can."

Chelle shook her head, leaned back on her desk, and said, "Damn Elle, what did you do?"

"He was taking too long, so I kissed him."

"Oh, Elle . . .." Chelle shook her head from side to side. "Couldn't you let him have control just once?"

"Don't worry. He returned the favor."

"You going to see him again—and I don't mean as his dance teacher."

"He'll be at the Wyatt Summer Fling."

"That's not what I mean."

"Baby steps, Chelle," Elle said as she slouched further in her chair.

"Does he know what to expect?"

"He knows it's a fund raiser."

"But does he know what part you'll play?" Chelle asked.

"I doubt it. Why don't you take my place?"

"Sorry. Can't break with tradition."

Chelle went serious with her next question.

"Elle, what made you change your mind about him?"

Elle stood and pulled up her shirt exposing her midsection.

"Oh, Elle, not again. When did it start?"

Elle moved her fingers over the cuts on her midriff then dropped her shirt.

"Almost two weeks ago," she answered.

"Are you still seeing Sarah?"

"Yes."

"Does she know?"

Elle nodded.

Greg walked in the door. "Sorry, ladies. Chelle, our one o'clock is here."

"See you Saturday," said Elle.

Thursday evening Rick texted Elle. "What you doing?"

"Sewing."

"Have you had dinner?"

"No."

Her phone rang.

"The Deli got my order wrong. I ordered a steak sandwich, they handed me turkey. They made good and then gave me the turkey anyway. You want it?"

"You could have it tomorrow for lunch."

"The bread will be soggy by then. I'm on South Campbell. I can jump on James River and be there before you know it."

"Beverage?"

"I guess you're worth doubling back a few blocks," he said. "A peach Arnold Palmer, it is."

Rick got up to leave shortly after dinner. Elle walked him outside.

He put his arms around her.

"Mmm, I like the way you fit."

Elle laughed.

"What's so funny?" he asked as he nestled her neck.

"I was just wondering how well you would," she said.

"Would what?" He kissed her ear.

Elle pushed away and looked down his body, stopping just below his belt.

"Fit."

He smiled and said, "I walked right into that one, didn't I?"

"Not yet you haven't," she joked. "But it will happen, right?"

Still smiling, he answered, "We'll see."

Rick turned and headed for the Silverado. He was reaching for the door when Elle called out, "Hey, Hadley."

He leaned against the truck, slowly crossed his arms and said, "Yeah, Wyatt."

"In anticipation of that day . . . to save time and all . . . concerning 'protection'. . . it's taken care of."

"O-k-a-a-a-y . . .," he said.

"Oh, don't look at me like that. You'd stop right in the middle of things just to ask."

Rick smiled and shook his head.

"You know it's true. You're such a Boy Scout."

· 22 ·

The caterers had just finished setting up when Chelle posed a question.

"White or blue?"

"Huh?" asked John.

The four longtime friends were sitting around a table inside the air-conditioned pavilion on the Wyatt Estate.

"She's taking bets on what color shirt Hadley will wear tonight," Elle said.

"White for business," John said. "Blue for other occasions."

"Blue it is," Chelle said.

"I don't know—he could see a fund raiser as a business obligation," John pointed out. "What does it matter anyway?"

"For a detective, you are so slow sometimes," Chelle said.

John looked at Greg and shrugged his shoulders.

"John, your mom's trying to get your attention," Elle said.

"Later." He stood and headed in his mother's direction.

"You look great tonight, Elle. New dress?" Chelle asked.

"Yeah. Thought I'd branch out. You like the color?"

"Yes. Peach goes great with blue," teased Chelle.

"And with that comment, I think I'll get some fresh air," Elle said and walked outside.

She made her way to the pool, took off her shoes and dangled her feet in the water. She was glad to have a few minutes to herself before the evening got into full swing.

Pat walked up and sat in a lounge chair beside his adopted daughter.

"How's it going, kid?"

"Pretty good."

"You make your dress?"

"Yeah. I think it will flare out nicely on the dance floor."

"Jean looks forward to this night all year, you know. Too bad she had to go and fall for a guy with two left feet," he said, describing himself.

"She didn't get cheated, if that's what you're thinking."

"Dancing's a Nelson family tradition. Every kid who ever sat on a Nelson hip got be-bopped throughout the house. Then they were off to actual lessons once they could walk."

"Well, we may have rhythm, but none of us can carry a tune," she said. "So, when they play her favorite song tonight, just walk her to the dance floor and sway while you sing in her ear. Don't worry about the steps. She'll close her eyes and be happy in the moment."

"Pat? Elle?" Jean called out. "Our guests are starting to arrive."

"On our way," Pat said over his shoulder. He tossed a towel that had been lying on the chair to Elle. "Show time."

"I'll be right there."

Elle dried off and reached for her Capezio dancing shoes. She hadn't spent much time on her appearance for past Summer Flings, leaving the details to Jean instead. But this year, she'd created a one-of-a-kind dress and taken the time to style her hair in a Messy French Twist. Maybe she was finally growing up.

Elle was carrying a short glass with Diet Coke and a lime twist when she spied Cal and Lance. She got their attention and waved them over.

"Looking dapper there, Cal," she said.

"Well, check you out Elle Wyatt. Belle of the Ball, if I ever saw one."

He leaned in to kiss her check.

"'Taffeta, darling.'" She smiled and batted her eyes.

"Shellie Matheson would be proud of you," Cal said.

"Elle, your dress isn't taffeta," said John.

"It's a line from *Young Frankenstein*, John."

"Oh, yeah . . . .."

"Cal, you know Shellie's coming tonight, and she's bringing her significant other," Elle said.

"It'll be good to see her again," Cal replied.

"And John, she's a good dancer, so make sure she gets her money's worth," Elle added.

"Her significant other is Jonathan Starr. Gambit Investigations has several new clients, thanks to Starr." John stretched out his arms and brought them down on the backs of his friends' chairs. "I'm gonna dazzle her."

"Oh, brother . . .," Elle muttered.

"Blue. I win," Chelle said. She stood up and waved to someone across the room. She tapped Greg's arm. "Move over."

Greg slid to the empty chair on his right.

"Hello, Rick. I saved you a seat." Chelle moved to the chair Greg had vacated.

"Thanks," Rick said. He sat down, leaned back in his chair, placed his hands on his upper legs, and looked at Elle.

"Wyatt."

"Hadley."

John looked from his partner to his cousin and back again. "I am slow," he finally said "Hut-one, hut-two . . .."

"Nice crowd," Rick commented.

"Always a good turn-out when Dizzy Monk is performing," Greg said.

"Dizzy Monk?" Rick asked.

"Dizzy Monk is a jazz vocal quartet," Greg explained. "The members met while attending MSU about ten years ago. They tour all over the world now."

"Jazz. Okay, I get it," Rick said. "Dizzy Gillespie and Thelonious Monk."

"You hungry, Rick?" asked Elle.

"As a matter of fact, I am."

"Dinner isn't scheduled for another half-hour. Follow me," she said.

There was a loud crash as Rick got to his feet. He pivoted and saw a waiter picking up an empty tray. Elle was standing when he turned back. It was the first time he'd seen her in a dress. He took a few moments before replying, "Lead the way."

"You can leave your jacket here if you'd like. The humidity outside is pretty high."

Elle picked up two glasses of water on a sidebar near the pavilion's entrance. Once outside, she handed the glasses to Rick. She stopped a server carrying a mostly depleted tray of hors d'oeuvres.

"I'll take care of this for you," she said.

Elle led Rick to the far side of the deck. They climbed the

stairs, stopping two steps before its surface. Elle placed the tray on the deck; Rick followed suit with the glasses. They both sat on the first step down.

"What are you smiling at," she asked.

"Nice dress."

"What? This old thing?"

They both laughed. Rick leaned against the railing and patted the empty space beside him. Elle took the hint and moved so she was reclining in the curve created by his chest and upper arm. He closed his eyes and breathed in slowly.

"How do you do it?" he asked.

"What are you talking about?"

"Have you ever detected a scent so fresh and clean you wanted more? Like the smell you get from walking in the woods after a rain?" Rick took a deep breath. "And the only way to hold onto it was to block out all your other senses—like you were compelled to close your eyes, so you could drink in as much of the scent as you could before it was gone?"

"Something's 'gone' all right. Your empty stomach to your head. I believe you've become delirious." She picked up a canapé and handed it to Rick over her shoulder. "Here, have a cheese stuffed mushroom on a cracker."

"This could work," he said in a teasing voice as he took the snack. "If I make this a two-bite caper, I could drop a few crumbs on your shoulder . . . then I'd have to remove them . . . and brushing them off with my hand would be too indelicate." He kissed her upper arm.

"Well, I guess that leaves only one way then."

"Yeah, you're right. I'll just have to eat the whole thing in one bite."

Elle turned around and laughed as he stuck the entire appetizer in his mouth.

"You know you let a lot of opportunities fly by, Hadley."

"Right time, right place, Wyatt." Rick smiled.

"Caper?"

"Sam Spade or Phillip Marlowe would have used the term. And they always got the girl."

"Yeah, well they would have taken two bites."

Elle was nowhere in sight when Chelle slipped a card into Rick's hand.

"I signed you up. You've got the last slot on Elle's dance card. By the way, you owe me a thousand dollars."

"Dance card—?"

The big screen behind the stage came to life. The video showed adolescents, Elle and John, in a dance competition.

Jean was on the stage when the video ended. "And here they are, reprising their award-winning performance, Elle Wyatt and John Hutsell dancing to Bobby Darin's "More".

There was a round of applause as John led Elle to center stage.

The song was nearing its end, when Rick shook his head and said, "I'll never be that good."

"You don't have to be," Chelle said. "Just love her, 'simply love her'."

Rick looked at her. "Goulet or Burton?" he asked of the men famous for singing the song she'd just quoted.

"Richard Harris."

With the Nelson cousins standing next to her, Jean said, "Ladies and gentlemen, check your dance cards as Southwest Missouri's celebrities prepare to sweep you off your feet. Please welcome Dizzy Monk to the stage."

Rick turned to Chelle as guests made their way to the floor and asked, "Does this mean I have to wait till the last song to dance with her?"

"Yes," she answered. "Wait a minute." Chelle held her hand out to Greg. "Give me your pledge card for Elle." She scanned it and handed it to Rick. "Dance nine, 'The Thrill Is Gone'."

"Damn, Chelle. I love B.B. King," muttered Greg. Chelle whispered in Greg's ear who then turned to Rick and said, "Go with my blessings."

"Do I now owe you a thousand dollars, too?"

"No. Always glad to help out Harmony House."

Shellie Matheson caught Cal's eye from across the room and motioned him and Lance over. She hugged both when they arrived and introduced Jonathan Starr.

"Nice to finally meet you, Mr. Starr," Cal said.

"Same here." Starr shook hands with both men. "Have a seat."

"Who's the tall drink of water?" Shellie asked Anne Lacey, Jean's business partner and wife of Shellie and Jon's friend, Jesse James Golden.

"Rick Hadley."

"Rick Hadley of Gambit Investigations?"

Anne nodded.

"What a nice young man," mused Shellie.

"Isn't he though . . .," commented a smiling Anne.

"Is he about to tame her?"

Anne looked at Davies. "Well, Cal, you know the situation better than anyone here. Is he?"

"Hadley's not about taming."

"He might just do it then," said Shellie, only half joking.

Lance was admiring Shellie's jewelry when he blurted out, "Shellie Matheson, is that a new Le Vian on your left hand? Oh my, did you two finally tie the knot?"

Jon and Shellie looked at each other and smiled.

"I haven't asked," he said.

"And neither have I," she added.

"But rest assured," Jon said. "As long as there are Le Vian trunk shows and two-years free financing at JCPenney at Battlefield Mall, there will always be a new Le Vian ring."

When the laughter died down, Shellie asked Cal to accompany her to the bar.

"How long has it been now—seven years?"

"As of last January," Cal said.

"I remember a very angry young woman that first session."

"Well, she didn't want to be there—didn't feel she *needed* to be there."

"Remember the joke she made that put us all in stitches?"

"Yeah," he said with a smile, "She was telling about being admitted to the center. The nurse had asked, 'Have you ever wanted to harm anyone?' and followed with, 'Have you ever wanted to harm yourself?' Then Elle said, 'What do you know—mental illness is like a belly button. It's either an innie or an outie.'"

They both smiled at the memory.

"She looks happy, Cal."

"Not sure she believes there's such a thing as happiness. Rick

Hadley could help her find it, but she's got tunnel vison. She's convinced another shoe is going to drop."

A member of Dizzy Monk announced the last song by saying, "Here's hoping everyone here finds 'Romance in the Dark'." Rick Hadley stood, walked over to Elle, and without a word, put his arms around her. They were swaying to the slow, sexy jazz tune, when a female voice began singing. "In the dark . . . it's just you and I."

The song had the effect on Elle and Rick that the composer had in mind when it was written.

"But soon . . . this dance will be ending . . .."

Elle didn't wait for the song to end. She took Rick's hand and led him out the door. She didn't stop till they were pressed against her back door exchanging desperate kisses. She touched him, letting him know what she was thinking. They were pressed together so tightly she felt the phone in his pocket vibrate.

"Let it go," she whispered.

The phone stopped and then started again. He pulled away but made no move for his pocket. She touched him again. Her took her hand and brought it to his chest.

"Not yet," he said softly.

"What's wrong?"

"I'm not ready."

She pulled her hand from his and said, "You feel ready to me. What's the problem?"

Before he could answer, they heard John call out, "Rick, where the hell are you? Answer your damn phone!"

They pulled farther away from each other.

"Give me a minute. Let me see what he wants, and then I'll explain."

Elle went inside. When he returned, he found she'd left the door ajar for him. She was standing in front of the living room window.

"Elle, I'm sorry, but Carver D'Orsay wants us on the north side."

"Did you get what you wanted?" she asked.

"It's not what you think," he said as he stood behind her.

"I only lowered the drawbridge a little Hadley."

"I know," he said. "I don't know how long this will take." Rick put his hands on her shoulders. Her body stiffened. "I'll call you in the morning."

"Yeah, why don't you just do that," she said, dismissing him.

· 23 ·

Rick welcomed Elle into his loft Sunday afternoon. They exchanged strained pleasantries before he asked her to sit beside him on the sofa.

"Elle, I want to show you something."

"Okay," she said apprehensively.

Facing her, Rick gently brushed the hair back from her face. As he positioned her curls behind her ear, she raised her shoulder and slightly pulled away. He adjusted so they were sitting side by side. He placed his hand on her leg just above her knee. Less than a minute passed before she fidgeted and moved so his hand fell away.

"Okay, Hadley. What's the big deal?"

Rick leaned in and kissed her, moving so he was on top of her. She put her arms around his neck and arched her back, thrusting her body into his. He broke the kiss and pushed himself up so their bodies were no longer touching.

"Do you see the difference?" he asked.

"The difference in what?"

"A loving touch and one that is sexual."

"Yeah, so?" She was starting to fume.

"I don't want us to be 'friends with benefits,' Elle. I want more."

"Whoa—wait a minute." She shoved him with both hands and sat up straight. "You're kidding, right?"

"No, Elle. I'm not."

Rick brought up his hand and gently ran the backs of his fingers down her cheek.

"You're not just a convenience, Elle."

She pulled away.

"Rick, I'm not looking for anything permanent, if that's what you mean."

"What I'm actually thinking about is an exclusive relationship."

"Ah, Rick . . . I don't know . . . that's a commitment. That's never been my strong suit."

Rick smiled and in an attempt at humor said, "Well, I don't think we're at the 'ring' stage, yet.

His comment fell flat. Elle wasn't in a bantering mood. He picked up the original conversation.

"I was engaged three years ago. It ended badly," he said. "You snuck up on me, Elle—not you personally, but the thought of being with you. I don't know . . . maybe we should take some time to make sure this is what we both want before . . .."

Rick tilted his head and closed his eyes. "If you only knew how much I want to pick you up right now and carry you to the bed—."

"Then do it!"

"You don't understand. I want to make love to you, Elle. That's completely different from having sex."

"Fine, Rick," she said. "Take all the time you need. Because I can tell you right now, I'm not the kind of woman a guy takes home to momma."

"Elle—."

"Save your breath, Hadley."

She got up, picked up her purse and headed toward the door.

"Elle, wait . . .."

She grabbed the door knob.

"At least let me walk you to your car."

"See you around," she said and shut the door behind her.

He watched from the top landing till she was safely out on Booneville and wondered how long it would be before she'd speak to him again.

24

Elle put five dollars in the jukebox and selected songs written in full or in part by Dean Dillion, whom she considered one of the best honky-tonk songwriters in the business. Back at her table, she propped up her feet and tapped them together as Vern Gosdin sang, "Set 'Em Up, Joe."

Three songs later, a guy who frequented the bar asked if he could join her. She nodded. He turned a chair around, straddled it, and placed his arms on its back.

"You and your friend not on speaking terms?"

"What friend?"

The guy nodded at the bar. Elle turned to see Rick Hadley sitting on a bar stool talking to a man on his right.

Damn.

"Not at the moment," she answered.

"So, is he gonna be in my face, if I ask you to dance?"

"He doesn't have anything to say about it."

Elle's last song selection began. George Strait sang, "Give me a bottle . . . of your very best . . .."

"Wanna dance?" he asked.

"Yep."

As they danced, Elle watched out of the corner of her eye. Halfway through the song, the man Rick had been talking to left, and Rick caught her eye in the bar's mirror. Elle held his gaze, then deliberately looked away. Jenna, the waitress, walked up to Rick, tucked her tray under one arm and leaned on the bar. They talked for a few minutes, then Rick stood, reached out and tapped the bar a couple of times. When the bartender looked in his direction, Rick gave a slight wave. He walked down the length of the bar and out the door.

Jenna went to the jukebox, pulled a dollar from her apron and slid it in the slot. Ronnie Dunn's unmistakable voice filled the room, "A man this lonely . . .." Elle's partner pulled her close for the slow song but it wasn't her partner she was thinking of as they danced.

Jenna placed a glass of draft beer on her tray. Instead of walking around the dance floor, her normal route to deliver an order, she made her way across the floor. As she passed Elle, she leaned in and said, "Go to hell, Elle Wyatt."

When the song ended, Elle walked over to the jukebox and deposited her own dollar. A mean fiddle with a bluegrass flavor came from the speakers. A feisty female voice followed. "Should have been different, but it wasn't different, was it?" Elle slid on her jacket and started walking as the song continued, "You keep seeing double with the wrong one . . . but you just keep holding on. There's your trouble." As Elle passed Jenna, she leaned in and said, "None of your damn business."

Chelle Thomas was shutting down her computer for the day when Elle barged into her office.

"Chelle, I tell ya, I've about had it with him."

"What's he 'supposedly' done now?"

"He's checking up on me."

"What makes you think that?"

"He followed me."

"Not Rick Hadley's style," Chelle said. "He's all about giving you your space."

"Then why did he show up at The Swingin' Door fifteen minutes after I did?"

"Was this about forty-five minutes ago?" asked Chelle.

"Yeah . . . how come you know?"

"He wasn't there because of you. He was there because Greg and I asked him to go there."

"You and Greg asked him to check up on me?"

"Dang, girl, you are losing it," said Chelle. "Like Hadley would even do that. You don't know him very well."

"Why did you and Greg—?"

"Did you see him talking to a guy?" Chelle interrupted.

"Yes."

"Did you recognize the guy?"

"No."

"Well, you should have. He's one of two we went to school with." Elle gave her friend a puzzled look. "Remember Nate and

Nick?"

"The Belson Twins. Yeah, so what?"

"How did we tell them apart?"

"Nate had a scar on his right eyebrow."

"Yes, from falling down when he was high. Nate did drugs, Nick didn't, remember?"

"Yeah . . . again, so what?"

Chelle sat on her desk and motioned for her friend to take a chair.

"Nate had a pre-employment drug test today. Greg waited outside the clinic to make sure it was Nate taking the test and not Nick. But whichever Belson it was, wears glasses now and Greg couldn't see if there was a scar. The Twins know I own Safety-Net, so neither John, Greg, nor I could 'accidently' run into him without setting off alarms. Greg followed the twin who took the drug test to The Swingin' Door, and called Rick to come down and check for a scar. Rick was there because he was doing us a favor."

"Oh . . .." murmured Elle.

"Yeah . . . oh . . .," Chelle said. "You know what I think?"

Elle let out a heavy sigh. "Go ahead and tell me. You will anyway."

"I think you were hoping he was checking on you so you could find something about him to actually be mad about," Chelle said. "Might as well give up on that little scheme Elle and admit he's damn near perfect."

"Chelle . . . I . . .."

"You what? Quit with the excuses. Hadley's a big boy, and he's one that sees the forest *and* the trees. He'll take you as you are. Better yet, he *wants* you as you are."

"I—."

"Hush! I'm talking," Chelle said. "Denial, they name is Elle. Get something straight. When this whole thing started three weeks ago, he didn't 'come on' to you. He showed you love. You've spent your adult life with men who only wanted to get you into bed, and you damn well ought to know the difference."

Elle went downtown to listen to some live folk music. At nine-thirty she got in her car and drove to North Booneville and pulled into the small parking lot across from Gambit Investigations. The upstairs light was on. She watched a shadow in front of a shaded window.

Elle knew all she had to do was knock on the door and she'd be welcomed inside. But she couldn't take Chelle's advice and climb those stairs. Elle watched until the lights went out. She remembered her conversation with Chelle as the lines of a Pam Tillis song echoed the 'excuse' she'd given herself for walking out on Rick several days ago. "You do what you gotta do . . . when you know what you know . . ." Elle started the Caddy. ". . . when it's all said and done . . . you let that pony run." Chelle didn't understand. It wasn't about what Rick could give her, it was about what she couldn't give him.

She put the car into drive and drove into the night.

After Rick Hadley made his report about the man at The Swingin' Door, he drove home, opened the refrigerator, and scanned the shelves. Leftover pizza and beer. He grabbed a bottle of beer, walked to his desk, powered up the computer, and logged onto an internet radio site.

Rick rested his legs on the coffee table, opened his beer, and wondered if Elle was still on a dance floor somewhere in Springfield.

Futile exercise. About as smart as drinking your dinner.

He opened a phone app to place an order for delivery when his dad's ringtone sounded.

"Hey, Dad. How's it going?"

"Rick, can you get a few days off?" Mike Hadley asked in a somber voice.

"Sure, what's going on?"

"Your Mom and I would appreciate it if you would come home for a few days."

Rick didn't ask why his parents wanted him in Eagle Ridge. Whatever the reason, it was important, or the request wouldn't have been made in such a manner.

"Okay. I'll get a flight out tomorrow. I'll text you the details."

"Thanks, son."

Rick logged onto his preferred airline's site, booked a departing flight to Knoxville and arranged for a car rental. He decided to forgo ordering dinner and headed to the kitchen to warm up the pizza. He was walking by the window facing Booneville when he stopped and texted his itinerary to his father. After two pieces of limp leftover pizza, he packed a carry-on bag. Rick returned to the sofa to relax and listen to a few more songs before turning in for the night. He slouched down, put his feet up, leaned his head back, and closed his eyes. The next few notes brought up a memory of his mother and a smile to his face.

Rick Hadley remembered sitting on the kitchen counter when he was a young boy as his mom peeled potatoes for potato salad the family would take on a Sunday picnic, when a song she loved came on the radio. She sang along with Mary Chapin Carpenter as she watched his dad and brother play with their dog in the backyard. Halfway through the song, his mom had stepped back and begun twisting on the balls of her feet. She'd taken his hands in hers and moved them in time to the music. "'It's been too long since somebody whispered, shut up and kiss me.'" He was grinning from ear to ear when she'd leaned in and kissed him on the nose.

Hadley transported himself back to that time. His dad was stationed at Ft. Lewis, Washington—long before he'd known what it was like to want to kill a man. The Hadley family had spent many Sunday afternoons picnicking at Johnson's Marsh, where the ant hills were taller than he was. His mom would spread a blanket and set out lunch as Rick and his dad and brother would skip rocks on the water. Unlike Elle, his childhood had been one of happy dreams instead of nightmares.

Rick was on his way to turn off the computer when he heard the notes of a familiar Brooks and Dunn song. He stopped and shook his head. 'Someone' had perfect timing he thought. Then he wondered if it was the man upstairs or the one below.

Rick changed direction and moved to the floor lamp by the window. He switched it off, and peered through the slit between the drapes, and saw Elle's car pull onto Booneville.

"Oh, Elle," he whispered and then repeated the song's last line, ". . . I am that man . . . .."

25

Elle was in a chair at the reservations desk at Hemingway's Blue Water Café waiting on Chelle and the rest of the gang. Her friend had promised an evening full of surprises for all those present. Truth be told, she really didn't want to attend the get-together, but Chelle had insisted Elle put on a bra, whether she wanted to or not, and get her butt there on time.

She watched the two hostesses as they marked off the names of the latest guests before leading them into the restaurant. She looked at her watch.

Five more minutes Chelle Thomas and I'm out of here.

"Oh, Elle, there you are. I was going to text you after we were seated to ask if you were running late," Chelle said as she entered the waiting area with Greg and John in tow.

"Late? I was here on time. Where have you been?" Elle asked as she rose to her feet.

"I sent everyone a message to meet in the parking lot, so we could come in as a group. Check your phone."

Greg navigated through the alcove to the check-in desk as three more bodies squeezed in. Elle nodded at Greg's half-sister, Teresa, and his brother-in-law, Seth. She didn't recognize the third face.

The group was steered toward a large round table on the far side of the room. Elle sat to Chelle's right and surveyed the seating arrangement. Greg was on Chelle's left, followed by his half-sister, her husband, and the unidentified woman whom Elle had mentally named, The Unsub. She allowed herself a slight grin at the moniker as her eyes continued past an empty chair and then full-circle to John on her right. Elle started perusing the menu. First things first, she thought as she looked over the selection of appetizers. She had just picked up her glass of water when she noticed a man walking toward them. He was wearing a blue shirt tucked into Wranglers.

I'm gonna kill her.

Elle sat her glass down, put her elbows on the table, folded her fingers in front of her face, and rested her chin on her thumbs. She closed her eyes and dipped her head.

"Hello, Rick. Glad you could make it," Chelle said.

"You're a hard woman to say no to," he replied as he sat down in the empty chair.

At least he's not in full view from this angle.

"I think you know everyone except for the lady next to you. Let me introduce you to Seth's sister, Blair Simpson, from St. Louis. Blair, meet Rick Hadley, John Hutsell, and Elle Wyatt."

"Hello, Rick," Blair said. "Nice to meet you."

"Ma'am."

"Please, call me Blair."

Blair finally drew her eyes away from Rick long enough to acknowledge John and Elle.

"How do you do?" she said.

"Pretty good," John replied.

"Fair to middling," Elle said, using a line she'd cabbaged from an old movie she couldn't remember the name of.

Elle turned her face toward Chelle, and with her hands shielding her eyes, gave her friend a look of, "How could you?"

The waitress arrived and took their orders.

"Elle, you've still got that headache, don't you? Come on, I've got some acetaminophen in the car."

"Not funny, Chelle," she told her friend in the lobby. "I thought he was in Tennessee."

"I didn't know he was back till earlier today. Okay, you weren't expecting to see him tonight. Big whup. He's here, so why don't you admit you've missed him. I never thought I'd see the day Elle Wyatt would be pining away for some guy. But, girl, that's exactly what you've been doing for almost two weeks.

"Did he know I was going to be here?"

"I didn't tell him, but he had to have had a pretty good idea. By the way, it really didn't take much convincing to get him here."

"Well, make my apologies to Greg. I'm gone," Elle said as she turned toward the exit.

"Afraid of him, huh? It *is* a night of firsts, 'cos I never thought I'd see the day you'd admit to being scared of a man in public. Because if you walk out, Missy, that's exactly what you'll be doing."

Elle stopped and looked back at her friend. "Let's just say it was fun while it lasted, but it's over."

"Then what's your problem? If he doesn't mean anything to you, then prove it," Chelle said, challenging her friend. "He's in business with your cousin. He's become a friend and colleague to Greg and me. He's infiltrated your inner circle, Elle. You're going to be around him, so suck it up." Then in a softer voice, "Besides, Greg and I have an announcement, and I want you sitting next to me when we make it."

Their salads were waiting, when they returned along with a couple of bottles of wine.

Halfway through dinner, Elle tapped her cousin on the arm.

"Hey, John, remember when Greg visited Harvard after getting his bachelor's degree, trying to decide what step to take next?" she asked.

"Yeah, he was looking at several universities, thinking of a master's, when he was notified he'd been accepted by the Secret Service."

"True. But do you remember what he learned from his guide as he toured the campus?"

"Remind me."

Elle was on a roll. She'd learned a long time ago if she made people laugh, they wouldn't look behind the mask.

"Greg's guide told him about Harvard alum, humorist Robert Benchley."

John was visibly trying to recall the story as Chelle choked on her water."

"Oh, lord, Elle that was eleven or twelve years ago," Chelle said.

"Yeah, it was. But it's still funny." She smiled and continued with the story. "Robert Benchley had arrived in Venice and sent a telegram to his editor in the U.S., 'Arrived Venice STOP Streets filled with water STOP Please advise STOP'."

"Oh, yeah, "John said. "'STOP' was used to end a sentence instead of periods." He shook his head and started laughing. "It's even funnier when you remember Benchley's grandson, Peter, wrote, *Jaws*."

"That's right," Elle said. "Greg called Chelle and told her the story that night. So Chelle gets up the next day and fires off a telegram to Greg."

Everyone at the table was smiling, while Elle recited the message. "It read, 'Miss your body STOP On second thought don't stop'."

Laughter took over, and other restaurant patrons looked in their direction. When the laughter died down, Chelle said, "Well, it's taken a long time, but Greg finally upped me. Last week, we were watching a movie, and without taking his eyes off the screen, he said, 'It's time we started making babies'."

Looks of shock were soon replaced with smiles all around. Greg pulled a box out of his pocket, knelt down on one knee and said, "Michelle Thomas, will you finally please just marry me already? Daylight is burning."

"Yes, Greg," she replied.

Greg rose, put his hand in the curve of Chelle's back and pulled her into him for the big kiss.

Seth stood, picked up his wine glass and toasted the newly engaged couple. "Here's to my future nieces and nephews!" Laughter erupted again.

"So, is Chelle going to Thomas-Baptiste or is Greg going to Baptiste-Thomas?" John asked with a grin.

"No name changes," Chelle said. "Our children will carry both names."

"Any tentative wedding dates?" asked Elle.

"Not yet. Stay tuned," Chelle answered.

"I'm for a beach wedding in the Bahamas," Teresa said.

"I like the idea, but you'd never get Hadley in a flowered shirt," joked John.

Elle followed John's thought. "Yeah, if he wore anything other than white or blue, I wouldn't recognize him."

"Well, the blue shirt does bring out the color in his eyes," said Blair. "That blue on blue combination really works, Rick. I wouldn't change a thing."

Damn, woman. You put the 'a' in biatch!

"Did I hear correctly—you're from St. Louis?" Rick asked Blair, changing the subject.

"Yes."

"What part?"

"I live in the University District. I'm a phlebotomist at Madison

University Hospital."

"Then you must be familiar with a case John and his partner solved about six months ago."

"The only big case I remember from six months ago was the Anniversary Killer Case. No—you're *that* John Hutsell?"

"Rick's just being modest," John said. "He—."

Rick cut him off. "Why don't we change seats," he said to Blair. "That way you and John can talk."

The two switched places.

Rick was harder for Elle to ignore from his new vantage point.

Elle turned to Chelle and said in a low voice, "My headache's coming back." She pulled out several bills and placed them on the table. "Congratulations on your engagement. I'll talk to you tomorrow."

She was barely out of the room when Rick stood and tossed a hundred dollars on the table.

"I'll make sure she gets to her car safely," he said.

Blair picked up her glass of water. "I may be the new kid on the block, but it would take a knife to cut the tension in the air around those two."

·26·

Elle couldn't see her Cadillac due to Hadley's Silverado blocking her view. She rounded the front end of Rick's truck and realized he had positioned his vehicle so his driver's door was adjacent to hers.

A woman squealed and her attention was drawn to a young couple near the parking lot's entrance. She watched as the woman grabbed her boyfriend's hat and took off running. She could hear the voice of Bruno Mars coming through an open car window, "Lucky for you, that's what I like . . .."

She watched the young lovers in their happy, carefree universe from her dark one.

She leaned her back against Rick's truck and hugged herself at the waist. She felt her knees start to buckle. As she slowly slid down the side of his truck, she turned her eyes to the sky. She couldn't catch a decent breath. Short, quick ones were all she could manage, and she felt she would lose those at any moment.

Dear God, not now . . . please not now.

Rick heard music coming from a nearby car. His plan since leaving the restaurant had been to make sure Elle arrived safely to her car and hopefully get a chance to speak with her. He was a row away when he saw her and immediately knew something was wrong. She was huddled down by his truck and seemed to be gasping for air. He knew the warning signs—she was going into panic mode. Rick picked up his pace and was soon crouched beside her.

"Elle, take a breath and count with me. One . . . two . . . three . . .."

He knew not to touch her without permission; it might add to her fear.

"You're not in danger. You're safe. Breathe with me . . . one . . . two . . . three. Again, one . . . two . . . three."

Her breathing became more even.

"I'm going to open the door of my truck and help you sit down, okay?"

She nodded. He helped her to her feet, opened the door and gently guided her until she was sitting sideways in the driver's seat. She continued to look straight ahead, not seeming to focus on anything. He needed something to capture her attention; something to get her mind off the fear she was experiencing

"I'll hold your head. I'll ease your mind," he said in a low comforting voice.

She slowly turned and faced him.

"Where did you hear that?' she asked.

"*Revelation Road.*"

"How do you know about *Revelation Road*?"

"You drove the night of the Cardinals game. Before hitting the ignition button, you removed a disk from the CD player." Elle was still hugging her body. "You don't eject any and all CDs whenever you get behind the wheel. But when you do, it's always the same one; *Revelation Road* by Shelby Lynne."

Rick paused, giving her a moment before he continued.

"*Revelation Road* was obviously important to you. And if it was important to you, it was important to me."

She closed her eyes.

"Elle, do you know what brought this on tonight?" he asked.

She nodded in the direction of the young couple, "I wonder what it's like."

"What?"

"To grow up in their world."

Rick remained quiet, giving her room for her thoughts.

"Whenever I let myself believe there might be a bridge from here to there, the demons pull me back."

In the distance, she heard Chelle's unmistakable laugh.

"Rick, I don't want to talk to Chelle or anyone else right now. I need to go."

"I don't want you to be alone tonight."

"I'm okay," she said.

"Elle, please——."

"I'll call Cal if you will just let me go."

Rick reluctantly turned and opened her door. "Text me when you get home."

She nodded as she slid in the driver's seat.

Rick got in his truck and drove to his loft apartment. He decided to wait until he'd heard from Elle before going inside. He popped in the soundtrack from the movie, *Lone Star*. He'd first seen the film when he was fifteen. Rick had modeled his professional and personal life after character Sheriff Sam Deeds. Deeds played it close to the vest. He didn't tell everything he knew. Instead he waited for the right moment to pose a question or make a comment. Rick had done it the night he'd met Elle in Oklahoma when he'd mentioned the cut on her lip just before he'd smacked the eight ball into a corner pocket.

In his twenties, Rick looked behind the camera at independent film-maker John Sayles, who had written and directed *Lone Star*. He felt a special kinship with Sayles, in that both men chose to do things their own way instead of jumping through other people's hoops. It was one of the reasons he'd left the Shannon County Sheriff's Department and gone into business with Hutsell.

"The Night's Too Long" by Lucinda Williams had just started when he checked his watch. It had been forty minutes since Elle had started for home.

"Don't let go of her hand. You just might be the right man," sang Williams.

Rick reached for his phone. He began composing a text when her message arrived.

"I'm home."

"Is Cal there?"

"Cal is in eastern Missouri visiting his grandmother."

"I'll be there in fifteen minutes."

"I'm fine," she typed.

"It's me, or I call someone else."

When she didn't respond immediately, he put his phone in the cup holder and started his truck. As he put it in drive, his cell vibrated signaling a text had been received.

"I'll probably be asleep when you get here. I took a sleeping pill. The door's unlocked."

Elle's phone rang.

"I only took one," she said.

Rick walked into Elle's house and locked the door behind him.

He dropped his jacket on the sofa and made his way through the living room to her bedroom. The lamp on the far night stand softly illuminated the room and he could see she was resting comfortably. He returned to the sofa, took off his boots and lay down. He set his cell to vibrate and noted the time. It was ten forty-five. Rick closed his eyes. He checked on her at eleven-fifteen and again at midnight, before allowing himself the luxury of sleep.

He was jarred awake several hours later, when Elle screamed. He ran to her room.

"Elle, wake up. You're having a bad dream," he said as he gently shook her.

She woke up, quickly raised to a sitting position, and pushed him away. She dropped her head behind her outstretched hands trying to keep the mental demons at bay. He retrieved a half-empty bottle from the night stand.

"Here, take a drink of water."

Elle took several sips and handed the bottle back to Rick. "You want to talk about it?" he asked.

"No."

She slid back down in bed, turned away from him, and pulled up the covers.

Rick went to the living area and picked up a couple of pillows. He returned to Elle's room and put them on the floor near her bed. He lay down and stared at the ceiling. He had just closed his eyes when Elle spoke.

"I want to go home."

"Elle, you are home."

"It's not working."

"What's not working?" he asked.

"Shelby knows."

"'I want to go back so I can run away again'," he quoted another Lynne song.

"I'm not doing it right," she said. She paraphrased the song, "I keep going back and running away all over again . . . and again . . . and . . .."

"Lynne writes it's because pain is what you know, Elle. Pain is your comfort zone. It's the one thing that's never deserted you."

Elle knew Lynne had found some peace through her music. She closed her eyes and reached out to the woman who understood. *Keep singing Shelby 'cos I'm not there yet.*

When Elle woke in the morning, she was on her side. She looked at Rick on the floor. His breathing was deep and regular, a sign he was still sleeping. She got up and headed to the bathroom. When she emerged, he was sitting with his legs drawn up, and his arms resting across his knees.

"Heads up," she said.

She tossed him a slender box containing a new toothbrush. He caught it before it hit his shoulder.

"Thank my dentist," she said. "Coffee in five minutes."

Rick used the facilities, making sure he put the seat down. Elle had left a clean wash cloth and towel on the counter. He washed his face, wishing she'd tossed him a disposable razor with the toothbrush. He brushed his teeth and stuck the toothbrush next to hers in the holder on the counter top.

A cup of coffee was waiting for him on the bar. He sat down on a stool and took a sip.

"What don't you like in your omelets besides onions?" she asked.

"Most everything. I like onions, they just don't like me."

"You have a big day at work?"

"In a way. I'm behind on paperwork, because of my trip to Tennessee."

"Everything good back home?"

"A few family issues, but for the most part, everything is fine. What about you? What's on your agenda?" he asked, directing the conversation away from himself.

"I'll be sewing today. Jean found a pattern for a throw pillow that includes a detachable ruffle. The point is to construct interchangeable ruffles for the different holidays and seasons. She asked if I would make a few for the boutique side of her business."

Elle walked the few steps to the refrigerator, opened it, and pulled out two jars. "Strawberry or peach?"

"Peach."

The toast popped up.

"Here," she said handing him the butter tub and a knife, "You can do the honors."

She put the toast on a small plate and placed it in front of him.

They continued small talk until they'd finished eating. Rick picked up his plate, carried it around the bar into the kitchen, and set it in the sink. He turned around and leaned against the counter.

"When was the last time you had a panic attack prior to last night?" he asked

Rick knew his question would make her uncomfortable. He expected Elle to go one of two ways—either project confidence or become confrontational. It all depended on which attitude best suited her needs.

He was wrong.

Elle had been resting her chin in her hand. He caught a glimpse of her eyes, and in them, saw a drowning woman who had no clue how to reach out for help. She quickly shut them as if she knew they were betraying her. She turned her head and buried her face in the crook of her arm.

Rick pushed himself off the counter and walked around the bar. He was a few steps from her when she put out her hand signaling him to stop. He stood beside her for a few moments. He started to move away when she reached out and caught part of his hand with hers. When he attempted to turn in her direction she stiffened her arm keeping him at bay. She was pulling him one way while pushing him in another.

"Your birthday is Saturday, right?"

She nodded and let go of his hand.

"Want to go to Copper Canyon in Miami?"

She remained silent.

"You don't have to answer now. You can text me when you decide."

Elle heard the door shut and then the sound of his truck's motor. She moved to the living room's picture window and watched him drive away. Elle went to the bedroom and began pulling up the covers when she stopped and sat down on the bed's edge. She could barely focus, and was almost thankful when she heard a knock on her door.

Rick's truck was back in the drive. She walked to the entryway and opened the door.

"I forgot my jacket," he said.

Elle held out her arm in the direction of the living room, giving him permission to enter. Rick picked up his jacket and carried it to where Elle was still standing by the door. There was very little room between them. She was taking a breath when he brushed her arm. Her breath caught in her throat before flowing into her chest. It was almost like two breaths—a short one interrupted by another. He reached for the knob.

"Yes," she said without looking at him.

"I'll pick you up at five-thirty," he said and then walked out the door.

27

Rick knocked on Elle's door a few minutes early.

"Come in," she called.

Her back was to him when he entered the room.

"Think I'll need a jacket tonight?" she asked just before she turned around.

"Maybe, just in case—." He didn't finish his sentence. His smiled, showing his one dimple, and then began wagging his index finger in the air.

"What?"

"Lizabeth Scott," he finally said.

"Toni or Coral?"

"Huh?"

"*The Strange Love of Martha Ivers* or *Dead Reckoning* Lizabeth Scott?"

"Oh, good or bad Lizabeth Scott," he replied. "Bad, but with a hint of good."

"You're takin' the center on a two-way street, Hadley."

"Bad, then."

"Good. That was the look I was going for."

Rick picked up her jacket and escorted her to his truck.

"Pineapple sound good?" he asked as he drove onto Missouri State Highway FF.

"Yeah, it does."

Even though the banter was there, Rick knew Elle was still anxious about the evening when they left Garbo's Pizzeria after dinner. They were halfway to the parking lot when Elle realized she'd left her phone. Rick handed her his keys and went back inside to retrieve it. When he returned, he saw a man standing in front of Elle.

"Well, well, well," said the man as he closed the gap between them. "I recognize you."

"Don't come any closer," she warned.

The man grabbed his crotch and said, "You want some more of

this, don't you?"

With his other hand he started to reach between Elle's legs but never made it. She hammered his left instep with her heel. He cried out and as he reached down in pain, she slammed her knee into his face.

"And don't you dare bleed on me," she said as she shoved him away.

The man's friend came running. He and Rick arrived at the same time.

"You just assaulted him. I'm a witness," said the friend.

"I don't think so," said Rick as he pointed to a camera. "He assaulted her."

"He didn't touch her."

"He didn't have to. Legally, he assaulted her. He threatened her verbally, then took action to follow through on his threat. She clearly had a right to defend herself." He turned to Elle, "You want to file charges?"

"I've got better things to do with my time. I'm ready if you are."

They were halfway to James River Freeway when she said, "You see now what you're in for, Hadley? There will be more incidents like this."

Rick slowed down and pulled into a convenience store parking lot. He put the vehicle in park and turned toward her.

"Elle, what happened back there isn't a reflection on you. It's all on him. He's a jerk."

"Is that the strongest word you've got? I'd say more like a son of a bitch or asshole. Come to think of it, I don't believe I've ever heard you cuss."

"If you've got a big enough vocabulary, you don't need to."

"Somehow, dirtbag and sleezeball just don't seem strong enough to get the message across."

"Okay, I didn't want to, but you've forced my hand. I'm going to the world's foremost authority on insults."

"Don Rickles? Lenny Bruce? Sarah Silverman?" she guessed.

"All amateurs."

"Who then?"

"Buggs Bunny. And I quote: 'What a maroon. What an ignoranimus. What a ta-ra-ra goon-de-ay.'"

Elle couldn't help herself; she laughed.

After dancing two sets at Copper Canyon, Rick and Elle decided to play pool during the band's break. They were putting away their cues when a man who'd just won a game a table over threw down five dollars and pointed to her.

"No, thanks," she said.

"Don't think you can beat me, huh?" he asked.

Elle looked at Rick who smiled and said, "You can take him, Elle."

"Make it twenty," she said.

Elle proved Rick right and as she picked up the money the man asked, "Don't I get a chance to win it back?"

"No."

"Double or nothing," he said.

"No."

He moved between her and the entryway.

"Move out of my way," she said.

"Mister, you're about to bite off more than you can chew," said Rick.

"You think you can take me?" asked the man gesturing to the exit.

Rick smiled and said, "It's not me you have to worry about," then nodded at Elle.

The man looked at Elle and stepped aside.

Once outside the tavern Elle surveyed the sky and said, "There isn't even a full moon. What's the deal?"

Rick walked her to the passenger side of the Silverado. He hadn't keyed the door so she stepped aside expecting him to do his thing and open it for her. Instead, he faced her and slowly moved her hair away from her face like he'd done two weeks ago. She watched as he took her hand, positioned it palm up and tenderly kissed its center. Rick moved his eyes to Elle's and saw the uneasiness she still felt with his 'lover's' touch. He let go of her hand and, without touching her, leaned in, and with her upper lip between both of his, gently kissed her. He stepped back and opened the door.

It was 1:40 A.M. when Rick stopped at a red light at the intersection of US Highway 60 and Missouri MM.

"Do you want to go home?" he asked.

"What are my choices?"

"I can take you home; we can have an early breakfast, or . . . we can go to my place."

The light turned green. After several seconds, the car behind them sounded its horn and pulled into the left lane to pass.

"Where do you want to wake up in the morning?"

She let the question hang for a couple of beats.

"In a loft on North Booneville."

Rick put his foot on the accelerator just as the light turned yellow.

28

Rick backed the Silverado into his usual parking spot at Gambit Investigations. He pulled a CD from the center console and met Elle at the steps leading to the second floor. They climbed to the top where he opened the door, then followed her inside. He flipped the switch on the wall and a soft light filled a corner of the room. Rick was standing beside her as she placed her purse on the bar that separated the kitchen from the living area. Elle watched as he slid the CD he'd carried from his truck into her bag's side pocket.

"Happy birthday," he said. She gave him a questioning look. "You have Shelby Lynne. I have Radney Foster. You're familiar with him, right?"

Elle nodded.

Rick took her hand and escorted her to the media player. He pulled the same CD he had just given her from a rack. She picked up the case and was reading song titles when she noticed he specifically selected track three, "Again."

"He can do heartbreak, humor, and social consciousness," he said. Elle heard the sound of a steel guitar before he finished his thought. "But most of all, he does love."

Rick encircled her waist with his arms. Elle put hers around his neck while Foster sang of a man who was being given a second chance at love. They swayed together in a small circle. She closed her eyes and listened carefully to the words, knowing this CD was Rick's *Revelation Road.* Foster's voice was heartfelt. He wasn't just singing the song, he was actually feeling it—so was Elle. She was on foreign soil. This was a dance she'd never learned, and Foster's lyrics were dead on; in this situation, she was clueless.

Rick stopped moving and kissed her slowly, deeply. He took her arms from around his neck and placed them at her side. With his finger, he traced the line of her shirt from her neck to the first button. This dance she knew. She brought her hands up and started to undo the button when he covered her hands with his.

"Let me," he whispered.

Elle dropped her arms. Rick unbuttoned her shirt and slid it off her shoulders. Her bra soon joined her blouse on the floor. He kissed the crevice between her breasts, then took her hand and led her to the bedroom. They were sitting on the edge of his bed when Elle moved her hand to his belt. She had begun to pull the leather through the buckle's frame when Rick stopped her.

"Tonight, it's all about you, Elle," he said.

Elle awoke to the sound of music. Rick had a repeat feature on his media player and Foster's CD had been playing throughout the night. She could hear the singer's words clearly as he challenged the listener to explain, "Why God put love in hearts if we're not supposed to try?" and then asked the question, "Baby, what are we doin' here tonight?"

Elle lay beside Rick and realized she didn't have an answer for Foster or Rick; most important, she didn't have one for herself.

She got up, grabbed her clothes and phone, went to the bathroom, and called Cal.

"I'm at Rick's. Please come and get me. I'll be on the curb in front of the building."

"Are you okay? Did he hurt you?"

"No, Cal, he didn't. Just come, okay?"

Rick heard his door close. He checked the time: 5:15. He got to the window in time to see Elle climb into Cal's Jimmy.

· 29 ·

Rick saw Elle's Cadillac in the carport as he entered the circle drive. Two days ago she'd left his loft before daybreak for places unknown. This morning he'd received a phone call and a text informing him she was finally home. It was time to put all his cards––and his secrets—on the table. He got out of the truck and walked to the door. Rick knocked and waited for her to appear. He took a few steps back, and trying to look as non-threatening as possible, put his hands in his pockets. He glanced at the main house. When he looked back, Elle was peering at him through the glass door. They stared at each other for a few moments, then she opened the door and stepped aside giving him permission to enter.

He walked through the door and asked, "How was your trip?"

"The scenery was beautiful and the air was clean," she said in a monotone as she started toward the living room.

He got in step behind her. Elle was leaving a fresh scent in her wake. He guessed she'd stepped out of the shower only minutes before. They were halfway to the main room when he asked, "And how about you, Elle?"

Her body tensed. He paused, then picked up where he'd left off. "Did you find any answers?"

Elle stopped in front of him and turned around. "Tell me, Rick, what do you think? Do you think I found any answers?"

"No, Elle, I don't think you did," he said with compassion in his voice.

"And why is that, Rick?" she said with contempt in hers.

"Because, this time, I don't think you went looking for answers. This time, I think you went looking for excuses."

"Hanging out your shingle again, Rick?" she said as she resumed making her way to the main room.

She walked into the living area and sat in a chair. He followed and took the sofa.

She crossed her arms in front of her. "So why are you here? Is it the challenge?"

"No," he said.

For the second time in a week, he saw fear in her eyes. It lasted only a moment, then she composed herself. When she spoke again, the harshness was gone. She'd changed tactics.

"Rick, this idea of you and me being together, it's just not going to work, okay?"

"And why is that?"

"There are things about me you don't know."

"I know all I need to know."

"No, Rick, you just think you do."

"You slept with him."

"I've slept with a lot of men, Rick. You're going to have to be more specific."

"It was the night of the 911 Center fundraiser—a week after John proposed he and I become partners."

She now knew where he was going.

"Don't do this, Rick."

"Most of the guests had gone. You were in Jean's office, listening to a CD and swaying to the music when Matt Reid walked up behind you, put his arms around you, and swayed with you. When the song was over, he was facing you. He leaned down to kiss you, and, at the last minute, kissed your cheek instead of your lips. Later, when you were outside, you heard someone wondering out loud where Reid had gone. Somebody said he heard Reid say he was going home to dance with his wife."

Elle got up and walked over to a window and braced herself against its ledge.

"But he didn't go home to his wife, did he Elle? He sat in his car and waited for you.

"Why are you doing this, Rick?"

"Because I know you see it as a reason to push me away."

"You bastard," she said, turning to face him. "You think you're so smart, then tell me, Rick, what happened next?"

Now it was his turn to be caught off guard.

"I warned you," she reminded him. "You don't know everything."

"I know his wife has Huntington's disease. I know all in all, he's a good man who stumbled like we all do."

"There's one very important part you left out, Rick. You think you've dotted all your 'i's and crossed all your 't's." Her voice was calm and measured. "Speaking of 'i's and 't's, you don't know shit."

"Then, tell me."

"I got pregnant that night."

"Elle, what hap—?"

"Shut up, Rick."

He waited for her to say more. She turned away from him a second time. "I lost the baby." She dropped her head. "Paybacks are hell."

"Payback for what? You think God was paying you back for that night by taking your baby away? How much guilt can you carry around, Elle? You've been piling it on since you were eleven years old. God is not that vengeful, but you sure are."

Rick now knew why Elle hadn't been at Gambit's opening. He walked over to her. Standing beside her, his chest perpendicular to her shoulder, he whispered her name and was surprised when she closed her eyes and leaned into him.

"Elle, I'm so sorry. I know how it feels to lose a baby you never got to see or hold."

She took a step back so she could see his face.

"I told you I was engaged at one time. What I didn't tell you was that there were some health issues, and her doctor advised against using the pill, so we opted for a less effective means of birth control. She got pregnant, but I was okay with it. I thought we'd just get a head start on our future plans."

Rick looked down and took a few moments before continuing.

"Six weeks later, I'd just pulled into my driveway, when J. Evan Litle, district attorney of Shannon County, pulled his car up to the curb. He wasn't alone. She was with him. The window lowered, and with Litle beside her, she told me she no longer wanted marriage, or a child, with me and that she'd had an abortion." Rick swallowed hard and took a deep breath. "She's a lawyer, and I guess she felt her career would be better advanced by keeping company with a DA rather than a deputy. Whatever the reason, it didn't really matter. I, along with our child, got dumped by the wayside."

Rick bought his eyes up and looked at her.

"That's why I needed time, Elle," he said. "I tried to convince myself I didn't want you in my life, but the truth is, I do. What you've told me here today doesn't change that. I discovered in the time we've been apart, that I really don't have anything left to lose."

He brought his fingers up and gently pushed her hair back from her face. "Don't you see? Even if you decide you never want to see me again, it's okay. You made me realize I wasn't living—that in a lot of ways, I was barely existing. And that's not how I want to live my life."

Elle dipped her head and hid her eyes like she'd done the morning after her panic attack. She couldn't look at him then, and she couldn't look at him now.

Elle was in her comfort zone as she took a rural route out of Battlefield when an old cliché came to mind: between a rock and a hard place. She'd always played one or the other, instead of allowing herself to be caught in between, so two days ago she'd taken off, and ended up in a cabin on Beaver Lake in Arkansas, thinking things through. What she discovered was that she'd spent a lot of time and effort on 'turning her life around' when what she should've been doing was accepting herself for who she really was. And in no way did that include being in an 'exclusive relationship'. Relationships came with strings, and it was time to sever the few Rick Hadley had managed to slip into place.

She'd found some peace with her decision, then he'd shown up, and within ten minutes, he'd managed to set her back two days, saying he would've helped her raise a kid; that he would've been a father to another man's child. Easy to say, when there wasn't going to be a child. Hell, nobody was that damn good. So, she'd excused herself, saying she was going to the bedroom for her phone, but had slipped out the back instead. And here she was on the road again with no destination in mind.

As she crossed the Blue Springs Bridge, she realized who Rick's source had to have been—911 operator Candace Gorman. Gorman had observed the scene in Jean's office and had been interested in Hadley since the day he'd moved to town.

Elle reminded herself to stop at her bank's branch in Nixa to replenish the cash reserve she'd depleted during her Arkansas leave of absence. She knew Jean would probably track her, so she planned to use a credit card for some things, but only for items that wouldn't give a true picture of what she was doing. Jean would know she'd gassed up in a particular town, but not what she'd done while there, or where she'd spent the night.

She wondered who'd told Hadley she was back, anyway. Maybe John—his BMW had been parked at the main house since early morning. John had a Jesus Complex where she was concerned, always arriving at the last minute to *save* her. John could *save* a lot of time and effort, if he'd just open his eyes to the fact she'd never much cared if she was saved or not.

In all probability, it had been Jean, who'd contacted him. Poor Jean and Pat. They'd been elected to take her in twenty-two years ago, when Daddy Dearest couldn't handle the thought of bringing his damaged little girl home to live with his new family. She'd long ago quit caring about the daddy thing. He was only some guy she'd spent a few weeks out of every year with anyway. She guessed it really didn't matter who had called Hadley; it was a done deal now.

She stopped in Nixa for cash and gas. She'd just passed the city limits sign when her phone rang. Chelle Thomas' name popped up on the dash display. She let it go to voice mail.

"You could've at least said 'hi' and 'bye' before taking off again. Happy trails. Send me a postcard."

Old school Chelle.

Elle wondered where she would wind up this time. She slipped in a CD and listened as Trisha Yearwood sang about a man who was unaware of what had taken place in his lover's past in the town of Memphis. Hadley didn't fit that mold—he seemed to know it all. That settled it. In honor of Rick Hadley, Memphis it was. She would walk into a bar, listen to music, meet someone—anyone, find a few hours of comfort and move on.

She turned off Missouri Highway 13 and headed east towards Kimberling City. There was a bridge off to her right, and she noticed there were no barriers in place to stop a vehicle from turning off on a side road, taking the hillside and plunging into the lake. She'd considered taking that kind of exit ramp before, but thoughts of her mother had always stopped her. However, things might change. Store that image for reference.

"It is five hours and thirty minutes from Kimberling City, Missouri, to Memphis, Tennessee," said the voice from her cell.

Not bad, she'd be there by six. She'd just pulled out of the drive of Duncan's Storage Units, where she'd stopped to get directions, when her phone rang again. This time, it was Jean. Unlike Chelle, Jean didn't leave a message.

"Ironic, isn't it?" she thought. They'd traded places. Rick was now the one between a rock and a hard place. She wondered how he'd explained the reason why she'd taken off again. How much of their conversation had he told them? She hoped he hadn't mentioned the part about her having been pregnant. But then again, what the hell; it really didn't matter. If they started making noises, she'd just tell them it was none of their damn business.

When the pregnancy test showed a positive result, she hadn't even told Chelle. Then, there was Matt Reid to consider; would she tell him? It was moot point, anyway. Baby or no baby, Reid had packed up and moved with his wife back to Iowa three weeks after she'd had sex with him. He sure hadn't wasted any time in plucking out that eye that had caused him to stumble like the Bible said to do. She allowed an acerbic smile that she'd even come up with an appropriate Bible passage.

Regardless of the outcome, it wasn't like she'd expected to enter into a passionate affair with Reid. For her, sex was a mental rush accompanied by a physical release. Nothing more, nothing less. She still didn't know how it had happened. She was so careful about birth control. Lord knew she had no business bringing a child into this world. But there had been a change in her when she thought she might. And disappointment when she found she wouldn't.

She hadn't been the only one giving up secrets today. Rick had one of his own, and it was after his confession that he'd told her he would've helped raise her child as his own.

Life had been so much easier before she'd met Rick Hadley. Before he'd entered the picture, she could say with little compunction that she didn't give a damn about anything. Seven months later, he had her believing she had a chance at a normal life. God, she wanted to stop thinking, and for all of *it* to just go away. She wanted to go home, but she didn't know where home was anymore. Maybe it was some nice, dark storage unit off Missouri Highway 13, where she could park her car, leave it running and just go to sleep . . ..

Rick Hadley got in his truck and drove the short distance to the main house on the Wyatt Estate. He had some business to attend to, but now there was a personal aspect to his visit as well. John Hutsell met him at the door.

"The papers needing your signature are in the den. Jean, Pat, and I will be in the kitchen if you have any questions."

"Thanks, John."

Rick headed for the den, signed the papers and made his way to the kitchen. Jean offered him a cup of coffee and started to get up when he put his hand out and said, "I'll get it."

Rick returned to the table, pulled out a chair, and turned it so he was facing Jean Wyatt.

"She's running again, isn't she, Rick?"

"I don't think she's running. I don't think she's done that for a long time."

"Then where did she go?"

"I don't know. But when she's out there, it's just Elle, her music, and the open road. All external distractions are here with us. I don't think she realizes that what she's actually doing is facing her fears, not running from them. The problem lies with us when we don't accept her decisions—and I'm just as guilty as anyone else."

Rick looked in Jean's worried eyes.

"She'll be back," he said. "We need to give her the room she needs."

"I just want her to be happy, Rick."

"I know," he said.

· 31 ·

Cal carried two bottles of beer to the living area. Elle was already seated, with one leg tucked up under the other. He handed her one of the bottles, sat down across from her, and opened the second one.

"You can never go wrong with a night at BB King's place in Memphis," she said as she twisted off the bottle cap. "How about that Will Tucker? Who knew a skinny white kid could play the blues like that?"

"Elle, you know why I'm here, right?" he asked.

She put her left elbow on the arm of her chair.

"You love the blues?" she said with a half-smile on her face. "No, wait. You *like* the blues, you *love* torch songs."

"That I do. But good music is just a sidebar on this trip."

Elle set her beer on the coffee table. She folded her hands and started rubbing her left thumb over her right. He'd seen her do it before, when a conversation changed lanes and became uncomfortable.

"Most of the world can hardly stand to be around people like us, Elle. We remind them what an ugly place this can be. And we're just as bad when it comes to them. From our perspective, they're do-gooders. They haven't been in our gutter, and so everything out of their mouths sounds sugar coated. It really isn't, you know. Some really are standing in the light with an out-stretched hand."

Cal watched as Elle started changing right in front of him. She leaned forward in her chair and looked him full in the face.

"Yeah, Cal, but a lot of them are waiting for you to grab hold just so they can let go when you start to feel the warmth."

"Key words, Elle. 'A lot of them,' not all of them. I'll even name one of the latter for you."

"Save your breath. I don't need *anyone* to get me into *their light*. If I should decide that's where I want to be, I'll get there by myself."

Cal set his beer on the table. She'd shut down one avenue, so he headed for another.

"When I first met you, the only thing that mattered about the

291

men in your life was that their names and faces changed every week or two."

Elle put her bottle of beer to her lips and drained half of it.

"Slowly, their numbers diminished as you started to take control of your life. There were months that went by when a cheap motel room didn't figure in the picture. You even stopped your disappearing act. So, what, or should I say who, has made you run twice in one week?"

"Don't go there, Cal."

"You're scared to death of him, aren't you? You can't believe he just might be for real."

"Let's just say, I have my doubts, and be done with it."

"Elle—," he began, but she cut him off.

"I'm not the 'lost lamb in the woods' from that Linda Ronstadt song you play all the time. I don't need to be 'shepherded' around by Rick Hadley," she spat out.

Cal shook his head.

"Don't think of a shepherd as someone trying to keep you in line. Remember, that frame of reference bit, Elle? Consider the shepherd in this play. He's like a guide, helping you get back on the right path. Chelle acts like one all the time. You don't have a problem when she hauls your butt back on track. Why do you object at the thought of Hadley doing it?"

"Who are you to be giving me advice about relationships, Cal?" She went on the attack. "There's no significant other in your life."

"If Rick Hadley was knocking on my door, there would be."

Cal waited as Elle finished her beer, went to the small fridge and brought out another. She looked at the bottle in her hand and then at her friend.

"Cal, you know about sexual predators—how they will do or say anything to gain your trust, and then use that trust against you. Hell, Cal, I know how they operate, I was one. What's his motive? What does he want with me?"

Cal rubbed his hand over his mouth before he answered.

"He's in love with you, Elle."

"How can he be? I'm a mess."

"Ask him. I'll lay money down, he can tell you."

Elle looked down at the floor and then did an about face. She took in a deep breath.

"I'm going to bed. I'll see you in the morning." She took two steps toward the bedroom, then stopped. Without turning around, she spoke to her friend one more time. "Chelle and Greg are on his side. John's on his side. Even you, Cal. Why is everyone on *his* side?"

"That's an easy one, Elle. Because *he's* on your side."

Elle woke to the smell of freshly brewed coffee. She headed to the bathroom for her morning ritual. When she emerged, she was startled to see Cal leaning on the wall by the door with one foot crossed over the other. He had a big grin on his face as he held out a cup of coffee.

"Damn, Cal! You scared the bejeebers out of me," she said as she took the cup out of his hand. "You sure do clean up nice—standing there looking like Michael Fassbender in a GQ ad and all."

"What can I say?" he said, feigning innocence.

"You can say you're buying breakfast."

"Okay, I can do that. I'll just drink my coffee and listen to some music while you get dressed," he said.

"Nelson Riddle and his Orchestra featuring Linda Ronstadt?" she asked.

"Can you think of a better way to start the day?"

After breakfast in the hotel restaurant, they returned to the suite. Cal opened the drapes and looked at the huge pyramid across the way.

"Okay, I get it. They saved the Memphis Pyramid. But why did they have to put a huge logo on the side?" he asked, referring to the Springfield-based Bass Pro Shops neon sign on the structure.

"I'm thinking it's a belt buckle kind of thing," Elle answered with a smile.

"You better not say that in Springfield. You'll get exiled."

"Hey, the Nelsons and Wyatts are heavy hitters, too."

They both laughed as they sat down.

"Elle, I'm going to head back home in a bit," he told her. "Lance could only fill in for me for a couple of days. Where are you headed next?"

"Nashville's Honky-Tonk Highway. Beer, pool, and good music from ten o'clock in the morning till three A.M. the next day."

"Sounds like fun."

Cal paused and looked at a newspaper he'd left on the coffee table earlier.

"Go ahead, Cal, say what's on your mind." He picked up the paper and handed it to her. "Page three. Inside column," he said.

It was a Springfield newspaper dated four days ago. She turned to the third page and saw the headline, "Additional charges filed in assault case." She read on:

> Charles Fraim of Springfield was charged yesterday with violating Missouri's hate crime statute in an alleged attack on a woman in July of this year. Working on an anonymous tip, the Greene County District Attorney's office uncovered evidence they believe shows Fraim to be part of the male supremacy online community known as the *manosphere*. Some members refer to themselves as *incels*—involuntary celibates.
>
> According to The Southern Poverty Law Center, women on these sites are referred to as *femoids,* derived from combining the words female and humanoid. A tenet set forth by such male supremacy groups allows that women are obligated to provide sex to men. Some social news and discussion websites have banned such communities, due to postings advocating violence against women, including rape.
>
> Fraim was charged with aggravated assault and the attempted rape of a Marshfield woman on July 14, 2018 at his residence in eastern Springfield. A trial date has yet to be set.

Elle looked at Cal.

"Are you the anonymous source?" she asked.

"No."

There was only one other person she could think of.

"Rick?"

"He's been working on it for a while. All I did was confirm some of his suspicions." He watched as she started to fume. "And, no he hasn't been investigating *you*."

"Then how did he get a name?"
"You talk in your sleep, Elle."

32

Elle was about to begin a second game of pool in a Nashville tavern when a new band took the stage. After the first notes were played, both Elle and her opponent stopped to listen.

"Now, that's one righteous harmonica," said her competitor.

Elle placed her stick on the table and walked through a brick archway to the main room as a familiar face took the mic. She didn't spend time trying to place it, because at the moment, it was the music that was important.

"Now this is the way it should be done," she thought as the singer sang about a honky-tonk with only a few rules. The biggest being that having fun was "mandatory"—"We don't take kindly to serious." After the song ended, the lead guitarist said, "Ladies and gentlemen, please thank Christian Kane for sitting in with us tonight." Kane left the stage. He walked by Elle and another woman on his way out of the bar.

"Christian Kane," Elle said, remembering where she'd seen his face before. "TV's *Leverage* and *The Librarians*."

"Yeah, the music is always good in here, but, occasionally, we get lucky and get the real thing," said the woman.

Elle returned to the pool room and found someone had taken her place. The man she'd been playing with looked at her and shrugged his shoulders. She found a seat in the main room, ordered a beer and enjoyed the music.

Elle rolled out of bed a little before 7:00 A.M. She showered, packed her bag, and checked out of the hotel. As she ate a breakfast sandwich in a fast-food parking lot, she planned the next leg of her trip. Since she wanted to make sure she'd be staying in her favorite hotel in New Orleans' French Quarter, she went ahead and booked a room online.

At Lawrenceburg, she pulled up Christian Kane on satellite radio and settled in for the rest of the drive. Kane didn't disappoint—that is until she was almost to the Alabama line when three lines into a slow song, she wished she'd never heard his name.

"Go on and find what you been missing, and when that highway's tired of listening, you'll see I'm not that easy to forget."

A horn blared as she almost side-swiped a car in the next lane.

Elle pulled off the road.

"So go on . . . put a million miles between us, but you'll still feel me like I'm right there at your side."

Elle closed her eyes, and still holding the steering wheel, leaned her head on her hands. She knew there was only one way to be rid of Rick Hadley. She got back on the road and took the next exit.

John Hutsell and Rick Hadley were in John's office when John received a call from his Aunt Jean. Standing at the filing cabinet, he hit the speaker in order to have both hands free.

"She's not going to New Orleans."

"Aunt Jean, New Orleans was only a guess. I'm sure she's fine," said John.

"No, something's wrong. I just know it. She *was* headed south. She even booked a room in New Orleans for tonight. She stopped at a convenience store in Ardmore, Tennessee, and gassed up in Chattanooga. She's now heading east, John. If she'd planned on going to Chattanooga to begin with she would've taken a different route out of Nashville, and she wouldn't have booked a room in New Orleans."

Rick Hadley rose quickly to his feet. He got John's attention and mouthed, "Find out what time she was in Chattanooga."

John gave him a puzzled look but did as asked.

"What time did she gas up?"

"Twelve-twenty."

John looked at the wall clock. It wasn't even noon.

Rick mouthed, "Eastern time." He then twirled his finger in a circle signaling John to wrap up the call.

"Okay, I'll look into it," he said.

As soon as John disconnected the call, Rick was making one of his own.

"Greg, meet me at the airport as soon as possible."

What the hell is going on?" John asked.

"I know where she's going."

"So what? I thought you were all about letting her do her thing."

"She doesn't know everything that's in play." On his way out the door he said, "I'll call as soon as I can."

33

Elle drove up a small hill and curved right with the road.

"In five hundred feet, your destination will be your right," said her android assistant.

A car facing the wrong direction was parked just past the driveway she'd planned to enter. Elle drove on, since it appeared the home's occupant would soon be having company. The driver had taken a few steps toward the house when he saw Elle, then turned and walked back. He opened the hood of his car. As she drove by, he hid his face from view. She rounded a left curve and peered over her shoulder. He wasn't looking under the hood. He was watching her. She followed the road around another right curve before pulling into an empty drive. Elle got out and walked to where she could observe the car's driver. She positioned herself behind a hedge and watched as the man slowly put down the hood of his vehicle in such a way that the clank of metal on metal was diminished as much as possible. He looked in all directions before resuming his original path.

Elle returned to her Cadillac, pulled her elongated jacket from the back seat and slipped it on. She retrieved Sila's gun and holster from the glovebox and strapped both in place. Back in the driver's seat, she made her way past the 'disabled' car and pulled in the drive of her original destination.

Elle walked to the front door and pushed the doorbell. She heard it ring. When there was no answer, she knocked several times. The home's owner partially opened the door and said, "I'm sorry, this is not a good time. Could you come back later? Thank you."

Elle was not deterred. "Mrs. Hadley, we've never met. My name is Elle Wyatt, and I'm a friend of Rick's."

"Rick isn't here. He lives in Missouri now."

A voice came from behind the door. "Sylvia, by all means, invite Rick's friend in."

There was fear in Sylvia Hadley's eyes as she slowly pulled the door toward her, allowing enough room for Elle to enter.

Elle quickly took in the front room.

Ignoring Mrs. Hadley's visitor, she made her way to the mantle over the fireplace.

With her back to the man she asked, "Is that Rick's senior picture?"

Mrs. Hadley quickly followed. "Yes."

"When was it taken?"

"Rick graduated in 2001," said the man. "So probably the fall of 2000."

"Yes, that's right," said Sylvia Hadley as she positioned herself where she could see Elle's face and that of her visitor at the same time. Elle's body was hiding Mrs. Hadley's right hand from the man's view. She held it at her waist with the bottom three fingers curved in, her thumb pointing up and index finger extended. Elle understood the implication.

"Sylvia, move where I can see you, and Miss Wyatt, don't you move at all."

Sylvia Hadley moved left.

"That's better," he said. "You know Sylvia, none of this would have happened if it hadn't been for you?"

Mrs. Hadley didn't respond.

"My mother should've had the part. You should have stepped down."

"I tried to," said Mrs. Hadley.

"I don't believe you," he replied. "Besides you added to the problem by making Richard include me in things he did with his friends. What's worse? Being excluded all together or being excluded when you're part of a group?"

"It's never going to be over, is it?" Sylvia asked.

"Not as long as there's a Hadley breathing. The original idea was to put you in a situation in which you wouldn't want to continue living. And the best way to have done that was to have taken Richard from you. The whole town knows you favor him over everyone else. And I almost did it, too. But it turned out better this way. Think how he's going to blame himself for your death? What a 'tortured soul' he'll become," he said with a smile.

"Do you really hate him that much?" asked Mrs. Hadley.

"That much and more."

Elle turned, and in one fluid motion, shoved Sylvia Hadley to the floor with her left hand, pulled the gun free of its holster with her right, and shot Everett Ryan Highly in the heart.

34

Rick walked into his parent's home with purpose and authority. He quickly took in the scene in the living room. The work being done by the lab techs on the bloody carpet did not interest the investigator in him. There was only one thing, one person he was concerned about. He made his way to the kitchen. His eyes moved around the room and stopped as soon as he saw her. She was sitting at the bar. Elle was staring at the floor with her arms wrapped around her waist. She was wearing a Shannon County Sheriff's jacket.

Both his parents watched him maneuver around other people in the room. He acknowledged no one, not even them. He stopped in front of her. His first thought was to hold her but he wasn't sure what her reaction would be, so he stood until she looked up at him. Her eyes showed surprise upon seeing him.

"Rick . . . how did you get—?"

"Let's get you out of here before we talk," he said. She stood and leaned into him like she had only a few days before. He put his arms around her and placed his chin on the top of her head.

"Whose jacket are you wearing?" he asked.

"I don't know. They took my shirt and jacket. There's blood on them. Someone handed me this jacket. Rick . . .."

"Shhh. Don't say anything. Just walk with me."

He led her to a corner of the kitchen.

"Give me the jacket and put this on," he said as he unbuttoned his shirt and pulled its shirttail out of his jeans. "I don't want them using the jacket as an excuse to contact you later."

He helped her into his shirt.

Rick surveyed the room. His father was standing next to his mother. He looked at his dad and gave a slight nod toward the door leading from the kitchen to the mudroom and the garage beyond. Rick's dad moved his head in the affirmative. Wearing only a white T-shirt, he guided Elle toward the door and tossed the jacket on the counter as they passed. It was at that moment District Attorney J. Evan Litle made his appearance. Litle stood in the doorway, blocking their path.

"Where do you think you're going, Hadley?" he challenged, spittle spewing from his mouth. "I'm not done questioning her."

To Rick, spraying spit had become Litle's trademark.

"You can question Ms. Wyatt again later," Rick said as he pushed his way through. Litle tried to stand his ground, but being eight inches shorter than Rick, he didn't have much to work with. Litle looked around for a deputy to help him keep Hadley from taking Elle off the premises. He finally caught the attention of Deputy Larry Timbrook and signaled for assistance.

"You're not taking her out of here," Litle said, his back straighter with Timbrook standing beside him.

"Then arrest us."

Timbrook shrugged at Litle. Rick was right. Litle had to either arrest them or let them pass.

"Don't worry, J. Evan, we're not leaving town," Rick informed the district attorney. "Ms. Wyatt will be with me. Now move out of our way."

Litle stepped aside.

"Where will you be?" he yelled at Rick's back, trying to save face.

"The Shannon County Sheriff has my number," he said. "Get it from him."

Chris Hadley was waiting for them in the church parking lot next to the Hadley family home. He opened the door to the rear seat of his GMC Yukon. Elle met his eyes as she and Rick climbed in. Chris closed the door, walked around to the opposite side of the vehicle, and got in the driver's seat.

"Did you have any trouble?" Chris asked as he looked at his brother in the rear-view mirror.

"J. Evan tried to detain Elle, but with no recourse other than arrest her, he had to let her leave."

"Good," Chris said as he started the vehicle and put it in drive. "The investigation has been transferred to Hays County by the way. J. Evan won't even be involved—a fact I'm sure will infuriate him."

"Elle, meet my brother, Chris," Rick said. "Chris, this is Elle Wyatt."

"Ms. Wyatt," Chris said.

Elle nodded at his reflection in the mirror

"Chris is an attorney and has offered to be your counsel if you'd like," Rick told her as his brother pulled out of the parking lot and turned left toward the center of town. "You don't have to make up your mind right now, but he'll see that your rights are protected during questioning, until you decide who you want to represent you if the case should arise."

"Thank you, Chris," she said.

"Ms. Wyatt, your car and everything in it has been impounded. I'll explain more when we get to my office. My secretary, Alex Cline, will acquire any clothing and personal care items you will need for the next few days. What about medications?"

"There are a few. I'll contact my doctor and have him call prescriptions into a local pharmacy."

"Rick, as for accommodations," Chris said, "Alex is in the process of reserving Taylor's cottage on Little River for you and Ms. Wyatt. I hope arrangements will be finalized by the time you rent a car. If not, the den at my office is available for as long as you need it. Mom and Dad will be staying with me."

"Thanks, Chris."

The younger Hadley stopped in front of the car rental agency's entrance. "Come to the office as soon as you're done here. You can get the keys to the cottage, and we'll formulate a game plan."

Rick and Elle disembarked. Rick tapped the side of his brother's door signaling they were clear of the vehicle and Chris could safely drive away.

Neither Rick nor Elle spoke on the short drive from the rental agency to Chris' law office. Rick pulled the rented Range Rover into a parking space and turned off the ignition. He swiveled in his seat so he was facing Elle.

"Hi, Rick," she said. "What's new?"

"Quite a bit," he answered, resting his left elbow on top of the steering wheel.

"Yeah. I really stepped in it this time."

"Elle, you—."

"What happens now?" she interrupted.

"There will be an inquiry. Frank Jessup, sheriff of Hays County, will conduct the investigation, since my mom's involved. He's good, and he's fair."

"But you're involved, too, right?" she asked. "Because of me."

"Indirectly."

Once again, silence fell between them. She looked down, thinking of Cal's insistence that Rick Hadley's grip on her hand was genuine, and that she was almost out of the black hole she'd fallen into twenty-two years ago. The problem was the black hole just wouldn't give her up. Its hold was too strong. Instead of letting her go, it was pulling him in.

"Elle—," he tried again before she cut him off a second time.

"Why?" she asked.

Elle paused, slowly turned her head and looked at a puzzled Rick.

"Why do you continue?"

He held her eyes.

"Because I love the smell after it rains."

Elle turned away. She waited a few moments before opening the Rover's door.

"You've got to let me go," she said and jumped out.

· 35 ·

Alex Cline hadn't arrived with clothing and supplies so after showering, Elle had no recourse but to don Rick's shirt again. She looked at herself in the dresser mirror. She closed her eyes and brought the collar up to her face so she could breathe in the scent of him.

"You don't need my shirt, Elle. I'm right here."

She opened her eyes and saw him standing behind her. He moved in closer, put his arms around her and buried his face in the space between her neck and shoulder. Elle took his hands and shoved away from him. She spun around, gripped the bottom of his shirt and pulled so hard the buttons went flying. She threw it at him.

"I don't need you or your damn shirt."

He raised his hands in surrender. Naked, Elle pushed Rick hard to her left in an effort to get around him, and lost her balance. He reached out to catch her and bumped into a free-standing lamp. It crashed to the floor as they fell against the wall.

Elle heard footsteps and turned so her back was facing the door. Her arms and hands were flat against the wall.

Chris burst through the door. "Is everything all right?"

"Get him out of here," she whispered.

"Everything's fine." Rick replied, his hands up beside hers, shielding her nude body. "I knocked over the lamp. My fault entirely," he said over his shoulder.

Chris took in the whole scene, noticing the tone of his brother's voice as well as his shirt lying buttonless on the floor.

"I'll be out in a few minutes, Chris. Just shut the door behind you."

Once they were alone, Rick pulled his hands back.

"You don't have to fight the idea of 'us' any longer. I'll do what you've asked. When this is over, Elle, I'll walk away."

He turned and left the room.

Elle closed her eyes and pressed herself further into the wall.

"It's not what it looked like in there," he tried to explain to his brother.

"None of my business," said Chris.

His mother looked at him.

"Gentlemen, it's time for us to go," she told her husband and youngest son.

Mike and Chris Hadley stood and headed for the door. Rick's dad held the door open until he realized his wife wasn't behind him.

"I'd like a few minutes with Rick. I'll be out shortly."

Once they were alone his mom asked, "How's she holding up?"

"In all honesty, I don't think she cares one way or the other what happens to her."

"Does she know you're in love with her?"

Rick looked at his mother. "Let's put it this way . . . she doesn't want me to be."

"Well that tells you something right there. If she's pushing you away at a time like this, there's one thing she does care about, and that one thing is you."

Sylvia Hadley watched her son as he put his hands in his pockets and averted his eyes. She knew he wasn't convinced. He needed to hear the full story.

"Do you know why she pulled the trigger?"

Rick looked back at his mom.

"She was standing next to me as Everett held a gun on us. He was smiling, so confident he controlled the situation."

Rick knelt down by his mom's chair.

"He said killing me would make you a 'tortured soul.' I asked him if he really hated you that much. 'That much and more' was his answer. And that's when she shoved me to the floor and her right hand moved to her hip. She turned around and without a word, shot him. He got off a round but it went wild. She walked over, looked at him on the floor and said, 'You won't hurt him or anyone he cares about—ever.'"

Rick's mom ran her fingers through his hair like she'd done when he was a boy.

"There were two shots and in regard to the law, it really doesn't matter who fired first. *He* was the intruder and *he* did threaten us with a loaded weapon," Sylvia said. "Rick, her voice was cold and hard. That told me everything I needed to know in terms of her feelings for you. Don't you see, where she was concerned, shooting him wasn't as much about self-defense as it was about protecting you?"

Rick looked away.

"She won't let me in, Mom. She's told me she wants me out of her life."

"And what do you want?"

"It doesn't matter what I want. I can't make her see what she doesn't want to see."

"Maybe someone else can."

Rick's eyes went wide. "Mom, I don't know . . .."

"It'll be fine."

Sylvia Hadley used the table to push herself up and picked up the shopping bags Alex had dropped off. "I'll take these in to her, visit a little, and then be on my way."

Rick watched his mom walk through the living area to the master bedroom and lightly rap her knuckles on the door.

"Elle, is it okay if I come in? I've got the things Alex brought for you."

"Yes, Mrs. Hadley," Elle answered

Elle was covered in a sheet, sitting up in bed with her legs crossed when Sylvia entered the room and placed the bags on a desk next to the door. She watched as Rick's mom made her way across the room, picking up her son's shirt and a few buttons along the way. Sylvia draped the shirt on the back of a chair before she sat on the bed.

"So, which way is it? You don't belong in his world, or he doesn't belong in yours?" Elle's face registered surprise. "My son and I have few secrets from each other."

Elle looked directly into Sylvia Hadley's eyes. "I'm not right for your son. I can't give him what he needs."

"Well, it seems to me you came here looking for answers concerning my son, and now you've come to a conclusion without getting them. I'm a firm believer in making informed decisions, so here are the facts.

"Fact one. He's in love with you. And telling him to take a hike won't make him stop loving you."

Sylvia opened her hand and began fiddling with the buttons in her palm.

"Fact two. He is genuine. That's what you wanted to know, isn't it? Let me tell you a story. In 1996, while his dad was stationed in the Middle East, Rick came home and found me lying on the bathroom floor covered only by a towel. He'd seen a family 'friend' driving away moments before, and he put two and two together."

She looked up at Elle.

"No thirteen-year-old boy should ever come home to find that his mother has been raped. Rick's the one who held us together until the army flew his dad home. And he's kept stepping up to the plate ever since."

Elle's eyes followed Mrs. Hadley as she rose from the bed, leaned over and laid the buttons on the night stand in full view. The older woman walked to the door, turned and caught the younger woman's eyes.

"Fact three. He's not the one that sees you as damaged, Elle. You are."

She placed her hand on the door knob.

"Rick will be in the next room if you need anything. Good night."

Sylvia Hadley walked out the door, leaving it ajar.

Rick saw the light from the master bathroom come on through the partially opened bedroom door. He checked his cell. It was 3:10 A.M. He gave her a few minutes, then walked to the door and lightly knocked.

"You need anything, Elle?"

"No," she said. He turned to walk back to the living area when she called out to him. "Rick . . . what's it like?"

He pushed the door aside so he could see into the room. She reached up and turned the bedside lamp on to its lowest setting. She brought her arm down, placed her elbow on the bed and laid her head in her palm. Rick walked to the chair and sat down. He leaned back and put his hands on the arms of the chair.

"What's 'what' like?"

"Making love."

Rick paused before answering.

"Well . . . what's the best way to explain it," he began as he collected his thoughts. "Sex is a physical act. It's biological. It feels good, it's gratifying, but in a lot of ways, it's selfish."

He hesitated, as he searched for the right words.

"Making love on the other hand transcends the physical and involves every part of you. Your mind, your body, your heart, your soul. And because you are sharing yourself with another person in all those ways, you feel vulnerable."

Rick leaned forward and placed his elbows on his upper knees.

"To truly make love to someone, you have to let down all your defenses. You have to allow someone to touch you in ways you never thought possible. Making love is the giving of yourself totally to another person. And if you can do that *freely*, the vulnerability goes away. It disappears, because you are giving your love, and true love is never selfish.

"It may be a cliché, but it's true. When you're making love with someone, you become one with that person. The result is indescribable. To fully comprehend what making love to, and with, someone is like, you have to experience it."

Rick watched as Elle's eyes moved from his. They were both silent for several moments before she looked at him again.

"Show me," she said.

He looked at her, not sure what she meant.

"Make love to me, Rick."

He searched her face, especially her eyes, before he responded.

"Are you sure this is what you want, Elle?"

"Yes," she replied. "I'm sure."

She sat up as he walked over to the bed. The sheet fell from her arms revealing her naked body. He sat down next to her, took her hand in his and pulled her gently to him. He moved her hair and kissed her ear. He then kissed her cheek and looked at her.

Rick put his lips on hers and kissed her deeply, passionately. He took her hand and placed it so she could feel him. Together they removed his clothing, and he lay down next to her. They explored each other, until he moved, so his body was on top of hers.

"Elle, don't close your eyes. Look at me," he said.

Following his cues, she allowed him to orchestrate the rest of their love-making. His gaze never faltered, as he watched her reaction to his every move, until her entire body began to convulse, and he finally allowed himself to release.

It was several moments before her whole body stopped

trembling. Her eyes were wide, not fully understanding what had taken place.

"Rick," she asked tentatively. "What just happened?"

"You went full body, Elle."

He started to move.

"Please, Rick," she said. "Don't leave."

"I'm not going anywhere."

"That's not what I meant. Stay inside me."

He kissed her and cradled her head in his shoulder.

They were still joined together, when she asked, "Can you make it happen again?"

"*We* can make it happen again."

Elle used her body to caress him. She could feel his body's response, and soon they were moving in unison once more. The morning sun was coming through the window, when they finally fell asleep.

·36·

Sylvia Hadley showed up at eight-thirty with groceries and clothing from Rick's brother's closet.

"I know the sleeves are too short," she said, handing him a shirt. "But the stores aren't open yet, and finding one in town with the length you need is going to be a challenge. You may end up with mallard green or iron gray instead of classic white or cobalt blue."

Rick smiled and took the items.

There was a knock at the door.

"How's my timing?" asked Chris as he walked into the cottage.

"Not quite as good as you'd like," said his mother. "You can peel the potatoes."

Alex Cline arrived as the table was being cleared after breakfast. She carried an expansion file for her boss. 'Good mornings' were being exchanged when Rick's phone rang. He checked the screen.

"Elle, it's Jean."

She nodded, an indication she would take the call. Rick handed his cell to Elle and she disappeared into the bedroom.

Chris walked his secretary to her car as his mother and brother observed from the kitchen window while they did the dishes.

"Does he still think we're clueless?" he asked.

They watched between the trees as Chris leaned against Alex's car, put his hands on her hips and pulled her close.

"He'll tell us when he's ready," she answered. "Alex has enrolled in law school for the spring semester. He's helping her financially. She protested but he told her he was having none of it. He said he was already practicing for the interviews that would follow, after she was confirmed as the first black female Supreme Court justice. Your brother told her he wanted to be able to say he 'knew her when.'"

"Sounds like him."

"Glad to see things are better this morning," she said, changing the subject from one son to the other.

"She crossed a big hurdle last night in terms of trust." Rick

312

paused.

"You and I both know how hard that is," his mother said.

"She's got some we can't even imagine, Mom. You and I were betrayed as adults. She was betrayed as a child."

Elle knocked on the wood encasing the entryway.

"How'd it go?" he asked of her conversation with Jean.

She handed him his phone. "Fine. She's anxious for me to get home."

Chris appeared and asked Elle if she was ready for their meeting as lawyer and client. She nodded, and they made their way to the dining room. An hour later, Rick and Elle, in one vehicle, followed his mother and brother in another, to the Hays' County Sheriff's Office.

Rick pulled the Range Rover into a parking space. Elle started to open the door when he said, "Hold on."

He backed out and drove across the street. He called Chris.

"Do you see what I see?"

"I do now," said Chris. "I'll make a call and get back with you."

"What is it?" asked Elle.

"The silver Toyota Corolla in front of the sheriff's office belongs to Elise Highley, Everett's mom."

Rick's phone sounded.

"She's leaving now. Give it ten minutes, and we'll head in."

Rick and Elle watched as a small woman with graying hair walked out of the Hays County Sheriff Department front door. Her left hand was covering her mouth. She was supported by a man on her right and a woman on her left.

"Is that her?" asked Elle.

"Yes."

Who are the people with her?"

"Her pastor and his wife."

The two women got in the back of the Corolla. The pastor took the driver's seat. When they were out of sight, Rick drove across the street.

"How did it go?" Rick asked after he and Elle were back in the

Range Rover.

"Much the way Chris expected. The biggest issue is 'intent' of carrying concealed—gun and switchblade. So, most questions focused around my reason for being in Tennessee and my relationship with your family. It helped that your mother and I had previously 'talked' on the phone and the conversation was 'cordial'."

Rick gave a puzzled look.

"The night you moved into the loft, and she was on speaker phone."

"Oh, sheets that 'breathe'. Nice way to work it, Elle."

"Rick, was Highley the family issue that brought you home two weeks ago?"

"Yes. We knew he'd been paroled early, but we, along with a Missouri Department of Corrections psychiatrist, lobbied against transferring his probation from Missouri to Tennessee on the basis that Elise would serve as an enabler. Back in February, she'd advocated Everett was innocent due to a mental disorder that prevented him from understanding his actions were unlawful. We lost, as he had a means of support and a place to live in Shannon County—his crafts business and family's home studio."

Rick pulled into a shopping center several miles down the road.

"C'mon," he said. "I need some clothes that fit, and you could use a back-up phone until yours is returned."

Rick finished talking to John Hutsell and went looking for Elle. He found her sitting on a chaise lounge on the covered deck watching it rain. Her arms encircled her legs at her chest. He listened as drops pelted the overhang. There was a flash of lightning, followed by the roll of thunder. She drew her legs up tighter. Leaving her with her solitude, Rick walked away and went to the kitchen to begin dinner.

He was staring out the kitchen window, drinking a cup of coffee, when Elle entered and said, "Something smells good."

"Mock chicken pot pie—all done in a saucepan except for the 'previously' frozen biscuits."

With leftovers stored and the day's dishes in the dishwasher,

Rick and Elle moved to the living room. The last few rays of sunlight were streaming through the glass door leading to the deck. Rick took her hand, and they walked over together.

"It's stopped raining," he said. He slid the door open and took a deep breath. Rick put his arm around Elle's waist and felt her shiver. "You cold?" he asked.

"A little."

"Fireplace, comforter or both?"

"No need to go to the trouble of building a fire," she said. "We didn't get much sleep last night and I'm pretty tired. What I really would like is to sit on the couch and listen to music before going to bed."

Rick picked up the Smart TV remote and gave it to Elle. He pulled a quilt from the back of the sofa, sat down, and draped it across their laps. She handed the remote to him and said, "You decide."

Rick chose a seventies folk radio station. The voice of James Taylor came through the speakers, as Elle leaned her head against Rick's chest and closed her eyes.

She was asleep in the dimly lit room, when Rick received a text.

"Sorry, lost the car."

Rick heard the bark of dogs from a neighboring cottage. He jostled her.

"Elle, wake up," he whispered.

She opened her eyes, and he put his finger to her lips.

"Be quiet—we don't have much time."

She sat up straight.

"You have to trust me. Where's the phone we bought today?"

She pulled it out of her jean pocket.

"Come with me."

Rick picked up the sofa's cushions and hurried her into the bedroom.

"We are about to have a visitor," he warned.

He turned on the light in the bathroom, then pulled the door, so there was barely enough light for them to see each other.

Rick placed the cushions under the bed's comforter and told her to dial his number. When his phone rang, he opened the line and propped it, speaker up, on the pillows. He pulled his 9mm from his ankle holster and handed it to Elle.

"Take this and go to the pantry. Pretend to carry on a conversation with me like we are both in bed. I won't be answering so you have to do all the talking. Do you understand?"

Elle nodded yes. The dogs barked again.

"No matter what you hear, do not come out of that pantry until I tell you to. Now go!" he whispered.

With Jim Croce's voice providing cover, Elle did as directed.

Rick positioned himself in the closet, leaving the door ajar. It was a few minutes before he heard Elle's voice through his phone's speaker. She talked in a slow and even voice.

"I'm telling you, Rick, in the world of superheroes, no way would you be Iron Man. Captain America, all the way. Now, my cousin John, I can see him as Tony Stark, but not you. I know what you're going to say, 'I've got the scientific brain of a Tony Stark.' But consider this little tidbit. Steve Rogers is taller than Stark—yeah only by an inch, but an inch is an inch. Then there's the military connection. Captain——."

Elle heard a series of gunshots. She strained to hear more but music from the living room drowned out all lesser sounds.

Rick counted five shots and then nothing. He knew there could be more, but wagered the intruder was checking to see if the fired rounds had found their mark before pulling the trigger again.

He slammed the closet door forward into the room. It clipped the elbow of the person in front of him, squashing the ulnar nerve against bone and causing weakness in several of the intruder's fingers. The gun dropped to the floor. Rick grabbed the attacker's right arm and twisted it behind the person's back, then kicked the weapon into the hallway. He elbowed the bathroom door open for more light. He shoved the intruder forward, tore the cord from a lamp, tied the attacker's hands and shoved the person in the chair.

"It's over," he said.

Rick backed up to the bed, reached around, picked up his phone and told Elle all was clear. She rushed to the bedroom, turned on the ceiling light and saw the petite woman from earlier that day. She was bound and occupying the chair Rick had the previous night. With one eyebrow higher than the other, Elise Highley gave Elle a sardonic smile. Elle's attention transferred to Rick as he began talking into his phone.

"Yes, Dad" he said. "She's here and restrained. Elle and I are safe and unharmed. Elle will meet you at the door." He looked at his gun and held out his hand. Elle placed the weapon in his palm before heading to the front door. She heard the sirens on the way.

Sheriff Frank Jessup arrived at the Taylor Cottage and took Elise Highley into custody. The next morning, Sunday, September thirtieth, she asked for a Bible. Six hours later Jessup placed copies of pictures, found behind a cabinet toe-kick in Highley's home, in front of her. He tossed a bag containing the key to the Taylor cottage on top of the photos. She looked at them and told her lawyer to make the best deal possible and she would confess—but she would do so only to Shannon County Sheriff Mike Hadley.

Several lawyers and law enforcement officials were watching through a two-way mirror when Elise Highley began her confession.

"Sylvia took everything from me, starting with the lead in *Camelot*. She was standing beside me when we overheard Mrs. Nehl tell Mr. Townsend I had the better voice. He said I wasn't pretty enough. Sylvia knew I deserved the part, but she didn't step down."

"Is that it? This all started because you didn't get the lead in a high school play?"

"There's more. Sylvia batted her eyes and soon you broke up with 'Gwen' Shackleford and started dating 'Guinevere' instead."

"If you were concerned about Gwen, then why the pictures?" he asked referring to doctored photos showing her face in the place of Sylvia Hadley's on the table.

"I was the true Guinevere. I should have been your leading lady. It's me you should've fallen in love with. It should have been you and me crowned King and Queen at the prom. I should've been the one walking down the aisle with you four years later. And I should've given you your first born."

She leaned forward before continuing.

"Beautiful people like Sylvia Reale get everything in this world. And in the end, she and those like her, have to pay."

"So you turned your husband and son into killers out of hate and jealousy," said Mike Hadley. She didn't answer. He continued, "They were nothing more than pawns to you."

"I *am* a great actress," she said, explaining her success at manipulation. "Far better than Sylvia." She smiled. "All these years no one had a clue."

"Well, your career has just come to an end."

He stood up and leaned against the wall adjacent to the two-way mirror.

"The night she learned about the casting decision, Sylvia told her father she wanted to bow out—that you were the one for the part. Her father said no. A few weeks into rehearsals, Townsend told her she needed extra coaching—in his office. He said she wasn't convincing in the love scenes. I noticed what was happening and started hanging around. He wouldn't get by with that today, but back then . . .."

Highley remained stoic.

"Concerning Gwen Shackleford. She and I were no longer together that last semester. She'd graduated in December and started college in January, remember? She let me know in February that college 'men' were preferable to high school 'boys'."

"As for Townsend, he went on to teach at The University, where, if you will recall, he was brought up on sexual harassment charges. He killed himself before a hearing could take place."

At the mention of Les Townsend's death, Elise Highley's eyes locked with Mike Hadley's and she smiled. The implication did not go unnoticed.

"He was your first, wasn't he?" Hadley guessed. "The accusing student's name was never revealed. It was you."

"He went by his own hand."

"Did Townsend get Halloween cards, too?"

"No. The Day of the Dead angle was Kenneth's idea."

Mike Hadley walked to the door, stopped, and turned around. "You know, it seems appropriate that in the end, it was our son, Sylvia's and mine—*our* first born—who brought you down."

· 38 ·

Tuesday afternoon Rick Hadley drove Elle Wyatt to the Hays County Sheriff's Department to collect her belongings. He waited in the reception area while Chris accompanied Elle to an interior room.

When Chris opened the door to the lobby, Elle saw Rick, his hands in his pockets, standing in front of an attractive woman. Even though his eyes were averted, the woman continued to have a conversation with him. Elle recognized Meredith Embrey, and picked up her pace. Chris made several quick moves, and stepped in front of her.

"Let him handle it," he said.

Elle stopped, and steeled herself. Embrey's mouth was still moving, when Rick turned and walked away. As Chris and Elle moved forward, Chris slightly shook his head.

"You're unlike anyone he's ever dated before," he told her. "You must be the one."

Rick saw them approach, and met them before they reached the door.

"Elle's got her keys. Her car is in the back lot," Chris said to his brother. "I've got a few more things to take care of, so I guess this is goodbye."

The two brothers bear-hugged. When Rick and Elle reached the door, she stopped and stepped aside.

"Did you forget something?" he asked.

Elle nodded at the door. He opened it, and followed her through. Outside he said, "You've never done that before."

"What?"

"Let me open the door when you're leading the way."

"It's something you like to do, right?"

"Yes, ma'am, it is." He smiled.

"Just don't go expecting it all the time."

At the car rental agency in Eagle Ridge, Rick and Elle transferred their belongings from the Range Rover to her car. He went inside, and dropped off the key. She was standing inside the open door of her Cadillac when he returned. Rick moved in close and put his arms around her waist.

"'Come on, baby, let's get out of this town'," he said.

"'I've got a full tank of gas with the top rolled down'," she followed with the second line from a song on the playlist she'd given him.

"'And, baby, you can sleep while I drive.'"

The first night back in Springfield, Elle stayed with Rick in his apartment. He accompanied her to Pat and Jean's the next day and watched as Jean took the first step and leaned in to hug Elle. What no one anticipated was that Elle's arms would come up to do the same.

Former clients of Elise Highley's maid service changed the locks on their doors and businesses shortly after her arrest. Highley began her life sentence in Tennessee's women's prison in Nashville without much fanfare. The consensus was that, within six months, she would manage to create her own 'congregation' within its walls.

Rick and Elle walked into his loft on the afternoon of October twenty-fourth. He deposited his keys in the catch-all by the door, walked over to a bar stool, and indicated she take a seat beside him.

"There was an arrest made in Tulsa County today," he said.

Elle stiffened.

"Jamie Rabern was arrested for criminal impersonation."

Elle waited for him to continue.

"Rabern pretended to be Kaela, and met numerous times with the couple who eventually adopted Kaela's baby. Rabern has now come forward and is cooperating with authorities. The family has been informed of duplicity on the parts of both Marcum and Rabern."

He took her hands.

"Elle, I would suggest that Kaela try to work out an open-adoption arrangement with the family. I've seen Kaela's baby. She's happy, and living with loving parents."

"Where?"

"Arkansas."

Elle thought for a moment. "That's where you were in August."

He nodded. Having learned his history a month earlier, she now understood why he'd held her the way he had on the dance floor the day he'd returned to Springfield.

"What made Rabern come forward?" she asked.

"She had a change of heart."

Elle suspected the man who had instigated the 'change of heart' was sitting next to her.

"What about Marcum?"

"No one has seen or heard from Lonnie Marcum since February twenty-second."

Those in Springfield got used to seeing Rick and Elle together again. Only this time their assumptions were correct—they were an item. What they didn't know was behind the scene, there was no talk of a future. They were exclusive, but both still had issues that needed to be resolved.

Rick had his phone on speaker Thanksgiving evening, so Elle could be a part of the family conversation when Chris said that Rick and Elle could participate in family movie night if they streamed *Avengers: Age of Ultron* at the same the Hadleys did so in Eagle Ridge.

"Can you believe Elle thinks I'm more a Captain America than an Iron Man?" Rick asked his family.

"I've told you before Rick, you're such a Boy Scout," explained Elle.

There was a pause, then Rick's mom asked, "You going to tell her Rick, or am I?"

Rick looked at Elle and said sheepishly, "Eagle Scout, actually."

On the evening of December fifth, Elle walked into Rick's place after helping Chelle with wedding plans.

"She's at least decided on colors. Sea Mist and Apricot."

She deposited her bag on the bar and started toward the sofa. She was halfway there, when he stood, and waved a CD in the air.

"Cal stopped by the office today and left this for you. He said you've pretty much kept it to yourself, but the first track is your favorite song."

Rick slid the disc into his media player. The sound of an unmistakable flute flowed through the room. Elle dipped her chin and shook her head. It was the song she and Cal had disagreed over while in Memphis.

"May I have this dance, ma'am?" he asked.

Elle raised her head and smiled. She held her left hand poised to place on his right shoulder. Her right hand went out for him to encircle with his left. Rick took a step toward her, put his arm around her waist, and drew her body close. With his left leg inside her right, they spun together as one.

Elle held it together, until Ronstadt sang, "Tell me . . . where is the shepherd for t-h-i-s l-o-s-t l-a-m-b?" She couldn't stifle the laugh any longer.

"I can see where that line would crack you up," he said.

Elle lay her cheek against his chest, closed her eyes and enjoyed the music and Ronstadt's strong voice, "I'm a little lamb who's lost in the wood . . . I know I could always be good . . .."

They danced until the song ended.

"Mmm, Hadley?"

"Yeah, Wyatt."

"I don't know about that one line."

"The one about being good? Yeah, I've got my doubts on that one, too."

He put his hands on her waist and fell to the sofa bringing her with him.

EPILOGUE

The Friday before Christmas, all except Rick were gathered in John's office at Gambit Investigations.

"Hammer's six-five, about 210 and he can give the 'look,'" said Elle. "Yeah, I gotta go with Armie Hammer."

"Who's Armie Hammer?" asked Rick, as he entered the room.

"Elle's suggestion to be the new Jack Reacher," replied John.

"Author Lee Child is asking for suggestions on who should play Jack Reacher in a new cable TV series," Chelle said. "You're six-four, Rick. What do you think—see yourself as Reacher?"

"He'll have to bulk up," Greg commented with a smile.

"Nah, won't work." John said. "Rick's too pretty."

"Oh, we can ugly him up," Elle said.

"And with that, Rick Hadley has left the building," said a smiling Rick as he turned and exited the room. After the laughter died down, he peeked around the corner. "You coming, Buttercup?" he asked Elle.

"Right behind you," she answered.

"Never thought I'd see the day a man would get by with addressing Elle Wyatt as 'Buttercup'," said Chelle.

She looked out John's window and watched as Rick spun Elle by the waist so her back was leaning on the side of his truck. Chelle stepped aside so the others could take in the scene. Rick slid his fingers between Elle's and brought both her arms up above her head then slowly lowered them until his elbows were at his waist. He looked at her for several seconds, and then leaned in and kissed her.

"Never thought I'd see that, either," she said. "John, it was a good day when you brought that man to town."

Elle was leaning on the kitchen bar with her back toward Rick, her hands on her cell, when he received a text.

"What now?" he thought as he tapped the message icon.

"Did you smile when you saw my name pop up on your phone

just now?" read the text.

She looked over her shoulder at him. Rick grinned and shook his head. He made his way to the kitchen and, standing in front of her, typed, "What am I going to do with you, Wyatt?"

Elle looked over at the pool table Rick had purchased a few days ago.

"No . . . not my new pool table. It's perfectly balanced." He winced. "Do you know how long it takes to get a pool table perfectly balanced?"

Elle gave a Groucho Marx wiggle of her eyebrows.

Rick smiled. "Oh, what the hell," he said.

"Rick Hadley, did you just cuss?"

Rick looked down and typed, "Y-O-L-O."

"Y-O-L-O?"

"You only live once."

ACKNOWLEDGEMENTS

Special thanks to the following for their expertise, encouragement, suggestions and support in the writing of *Whispers*.

Sharolynne Barth, your hand is throughout *Whispers*. Whenever I was stuck for the perfect word or idea, your quick mind and wit came to the rescue. We often talk about how dangerous we are when we get together––ah, but it is a glorious danger.

Becky Stephenson, when my memory failed, yours was there to get me up and going again. You know the major players, those who made cameo appearances, and the ones I only dreamed about.

Wayne Walden, my dad, for the Clayton Roberts character and helping me find the perfect place to hide a body in Mark Twain National Forest.

Christian Kane and Brand X Management, for granting permission for Mr. Kane's 'appearance' on Nashville's Honkytonk Highway.

Douglas Perret Starr PhD, for editing.
Bruce Patrick
Kyle Davis
Billy Fields
Bryan Sanders
Charlie Blake
Christopher A. Edwards, MD
Conzy Mitchell-Burns
Dylan Faulconer
Elizabeth Rodriquez
Ginger Killingsworth Cashio
Heather Heinrichs
Hieke Fisher
Jonathan Starr
Julie Walden Scott
Kayla Campbell Hillhouse
Kathy Mock Boykin
Lauren Donica
Lindsay Scott
Marcy Ibrahim
Marshall Buffington

Monica Jarvis
Patty Edens Fielding
Zoe Ann Miles

Current and former associates and managers of JCPenney Store 1188 in Springfield, Mo, for great character names: Alexandra Cline, Blair Marken (Simpson), Ed Smith, Heather Stanley, Jesse James Golden, Jimmy Matthews, Jonathan Starr, Kaela McGuire (Stafford), Kathryn Bryce Bartlett, Kathy Ann Huff (James), Lauren Tomboc, Lewis Smith (Cantrell), Logan Hale, Lori Bryant (Chandler), Myles Stafford, Ra-Chelle Johnson (Chelle Thomas), Ryan Highley (Everett, The Anniversary Killer), Sarah Bennett, Sharon Moore (Nelson).

Songs of *Whispers*
Part One

Elton John, Whispers
https://www.youtube.com/watch?v=oiyV_zM1CCU
The Beatles, All You Need is Love
https://www.youtube.com/watch?v=_7xMfIp-irg
John Lennon, Give Peace a Chance
https://www.youtube.com/watch?v=Q_8-4kioxO0
Little Willie John, My Love Is
https://www.youtube.com/watch?v=ur48VqryK9c
Ricky Nelson, It's Up to You
https://www.youtube.com/watch?v=lQ0oMl34MAo
The Eagles, One of These Nights
https://www.youtube.com/watch?v=ESc2Tq2HzhQ
Ronnie McDowell, Older Women
https://www.youtube.com/watch?v=mg0Wb7YvhU8
Aerosmith, Dude (Looks Like a Lady)
https://www.youtube.com/watch?v=Qs97ZmUeUa4

Part Two
Dixie Chicks, Not Ready to Make Nice
https://www.youtube.com/watch?v=YTj1CbcnuoA
Walela, Cherokee Morning Song
https://www.youtube.com/watch?v=fxdAqv5SnCg
Billy Currington, Must Be Doin' Somethin' Right
https://www.youtube.com/watch?v=mkUifSvubRg
Eric Clapton, After Midnight
https://www.youtube.com/watch?v=UkWccgl-9vs
Nick Waterhouse, I Can Only Give You Everything
https://www.youtube.com/watch?v=aazFoWCIE0M
Jackson Browne, Running on Empty
https://www.youtube.com/watch?v=5WhDTS2AeLw
Robert Goulet, If Ever I Would Leave You (Camelot)
https://www.youtube.com/watch?v=VwfYHVJHMOA
Gail Davies, You're a Hard Dog (To Keep Under the Porch)
https://www.youtube.com/watch?v=QcFOTqkUUbo
Rhonda Vincent/Keith Urban, The Water is Wide
https://www.youtube.com/watch?v=wqcXpWQ7NcA
Lee Roy Parnell, When a Woman Loves a Man
https://www.youtube.com/watch?v=_hUzXXK61Uk
Jesse Pearson, Ann-Margret, Bobby Rydell, A Lot of Livin' to Do
(Bye Bye Birdie)
https://www.youtube.com/watch?v=rS38PiZ2-RA
Randy Rogers Band, Buy Myself a Chance
https://www.youtube.com/watch?v=voStsQfPLbg

Michael Bublé, You Don't Know Me
https://www.youtube.com/watch?v=yoROqjb0A6M
Pam Tillis, We've Tried Everything Else
https://www.youtube.com/watch?v=giYEB4gKuQc
Bobby Darin, More
https://www.youtube.com/watch?v=Gt1IVGmGgM0
Richard Harris, How to Handle a Woman (Camelot)
https://www.youtube.com/watch?v=_nBYEl6uD94
Manhattan Transfer, The Thrill is Gone
https://www.youtube.com/watch?v=aLORIe3GgQ4
Dinah Washington, Romance in the Dark
https://www.youtube.com/watch?v=N8UBT4etYdM
Vern Gosdin, Set 'Em Up Joe
https://www.youtube.com/watch?v=kLTitnGJSjY
George Strait, Unwound
https://www.youtube.com/watch?v=WaSbkQB87M8
Brooks and Dunn, A Man This Lonely
https://www.youtube.com/watch?v=w4yXpDEJSpo
Dixie Chicks, There's Your Trouble
https://www.youtube.com/watch?v=-ATEMp-P1OI
Pam Tillis, Let That Pony Run
https://www.youtube.com/watch?v=-EfEK9DJUpw
Mary Chapin Carpenter, Shut Up and Kiss Me
https://www.youtube.com/watch?v=Qpu9RTE3Ec8
Brooks and Dunn, I Am That Man
https://www.youtube.com/watch?v=2OYGGPDdX3Y
Bruno Mars, That's What I Like
https://www.youtube.com/watch?v=JucvYrdSIcM
Shelby Lynne, I'll Hold Your Head
https://www.youtube.com/watch?v=JhPUODBioAM
Lucinda Williams, The Night's Too Long
https://www.youtube.com/watch?v=hL2NgJ4DE08
Shelby Lynne, I Want to Go Back
https://www.youtube.com/watch?v=zoijWt5ifIs
Radney Foster, Again
https://www.youtube.com/watch?v=Nog79Lu3pBI
Radney Foster, What Are We Doing Here Tonight
https://www.youtube.com/watch?v=nDX8Qssy6Gg
Trisha Yearwood, Nothin' 'Bout Memphis
https://www.youtube.com/watch?v=tRcYpsYARdw
Linda Ronstadt, Someone to Watch Over Me
https://www.youtube.com/watch?v=gjUXG-Fz8pc
Christian Kane, House Rules
https://www.youtube.com/watch?v=6Z1NPihh6oA
Christian Kane, Thinking of You
https://www.youtube.com/watch?v=Wlc_PlLd0bE

Trisha Yearwood, You Can Sleep While I Drive
https://www.youtube.com/watch?v=zLWtkB0s1qE

Films of *Whispers*

They Shoot Horses, Don't They? (1969)
The Birds (1963)
Psycho (1960)
Titanic (1997)
The Bride of Frankenstein (1935)
Big Trouble in Little China (1986)
Lone Star (1996)
Eight Men Out (1988)
Misery (1990)
Basic Instinct (1992)
Camelot (1967)
Snow White (1937)
Young Frankenstein (1974)
Some Like It Hot (1959)
Bye Bye Birdie (1963)
Casablanca (1942)
The Avengers (2012)
The Strange Love of Martha Ivers (1946)
Dead Reckoning (1947)
Avengers: Age of Ultron (2015)

Television Shows of *Whispers*
Snake Salvation
Svengoolie
Homicide Hunter
Dexter
I Love Lucy
Bosch
X-Files
Doctor Who
Torchwood
Supernatural
Magnum, P.I.
Miss Fisher's Murder Mysteries
The Voice
Leverage
The Librarians